The Book of Ten Nights
and a Night

Books by John Barth

The Floating Opera

The End of the Road

The Sot-Weed Factor

Giles Goat-Boy

Lost in the Funhouse:
Fiction for Print, Tape, Live Voice

Chimera

Letters

Sabbatical: A Romance

The Friday Book:
Essays and Other Nonfiction

The Tidewater Tales: A Novel

The Last Voyage of Somebody the Sailor

Once Upon a Time: A Floating Opera

Further Fridays: Essays, Lectures,
and Other Nonfiction, 1984–1994

On with the Story

Coming Soon!!!

The Book of Ten Nights and a Night:
Eleven Stories

THE BOOK OF

Ten Nights

and a Night

E L E V E N S T O R I E S

❖ ❖ ❖ ❖ ❖ ❖ ❖ ❖ ❖ ❖ ❖

JOHN BARTH

Atlantic Books
London

For Shelly,
sine qua non

First published in the United States in 2004 by Houghton Mifflin,
Houghton Mifflin Company, 215 Park Avenue South, New York, New York 10003

First published in Great Britain in 2005 by Atlantic Books,
an imprint of Grove Atlantic Ltd.

Earlier versions of the stories here framed first appeared in the following
publications: "Help!" (designed by Rudolph De Harak) in *Esquire*, September 1969;
"Landscape: The Eastern Shore" in *The Kenyon Review*, Winter 1960; "The Ring"
in *Press*, December 1996; "Dead Cat, Floating Boy" in *The Yale Review*, April 1998;
"A Detective and a Turtle" in *Conjunctions* 37, October 2001; "The Rest of Your
Life" in *Tri-Quarterly* 107/108, Winter/Spring/Summer 2000; "The Big Shrink" in
TriQuarterly, Winter 1997/98; "Extension" in *Writers Harvest 3*, Delacorte, 1998;
"And Then There's the One" in *Conjunctions*, May 1998; "9999" in *Granta*, Autumn
1998; "Click" in *The Atlantic Monthly*, December 1997.

9 8 7 6 5 4 3 2 1

A CIP catalogue record for this book is available from the British Library

ISBN 1 84354 406 7

Book design by Melissa Lotfy

Printed in Great Britain by CPD Wales, Ebbw vale

Atlantic Books
An imprint of Grove Atlantic Ltd
Ormond House
26–27 Boswell Street
London WC1N 3JZ

CONTENTS

The Book of Ten Nights and a Night

INVOCATION: "WYSIWYG"

❖

There was meant to have been a book
called *Ten Nights and a Night,* which, had it gotten itself written before TEOTWAW(A)KI 9/11/2001—The End Of The
World As We (Americans) Knew It—might have opened with a
sportive extended invocation to the Storyteller's Muse, more or
less like this:

*Tell, O Muse of Story, the hundred-percent-made-up tale of a
modern-day Odysseus's interlude with the brackish tidewater marsh-
nymph here called WYSIWYG—*

"Wissywig?"

Spelled W-Y-S-I-W-Y-G. Explanation to follow, if called
for. *How, in an advanced but still-healthy decade of his sleeping and
waking, breathing air and pumping blood, eating/drinking/pissing/
shitting, learning and teaching, dressing and undressing—*

"Shall we cut to that part?"

Not yet. *Talking and listening, reading and writing, making
love and sentences—*

"First part of that last part!"

All in Miz Muse's good time. *He found himself lost—*

"Found himself lost?"

Paradoxically speaking. *Not shipwrecked like the original Odysseus for seven years on fair Calypso's isle and obliged to service that*

nymph nightly, with the promise of immortality and eternal youth if he'd stay put for keeps—

"He'd have a problem with that?"

—when what he really wanted was to get his aging mortal ass back home to his ditto ditto wife.

"Lucky wife. Unlucky nymph."

Nor was our chap lost like Dante, in the Dark Wood of a midlife crisis from which only a detour through Hell to Heaven could get him back on track. Too old, this one, for midlife crises.

"Not that they're the only kind."

Granted. *Neither would he presume to compare his position to Scheherazade's, who humped King Shahryar through a thousand nights and a night and told him her tales under threat of death if she pleased him not, her aim being to save not only herself and "the virgin daughters of Islam" from the guy's murderous mysogyny, but the King too, and his kingdom. . . .*

"Men, I swear."

Yes, well. But, as I was saying, *No: The situation of this Senior Talester—* Have we mentioned our strandee's trade? So let's maybe call him *Graybard. . . .*

"Got it. His situation, you were saying?"

—was meant to be an Extended Congress, shall we say, with the above-invoked muse, or with some serviceable surrogate therefor—

"Serviceable surrogate? And what manner of quote *congress* did the gentleman have in mind, may one ask?"

Patience, please. *Their uppercase Congress* (and accompanying dialogue) *to extend over eleven nights and serve as battery-charging interludes between his reviewing with her . . . post-Congressly? . . .*

"Now we're talking!"

Merely talking, mind.

"On to the interlude!"

Soon's we're done with this hypothetical invocation: . . . *his retelling her, et cetera, eleven several stories: the previously published but hitherto uncollected fruits of her long collaboration both with their Original Author—whom never mind—and with their Present Teller: most of said stories perpetrated over the decade past* (i.e., the closing decade of the Terrible Twentieth), *but a couple of them dating back considerably farther; most of them pure fiction, but a couple more or less non-; most of them Autumnal, shall we say, in theme and tone, addressing such jolly topics as the approach of old age, declining capabilities, and death—but a couple not. And several having to do, for better or worse, with* (hang on to your hats, folks) . . . *the Telling of Stories!*

"O very joy."

Well. *Graybard-the-Talester's purpose—this odd couple's or trio's purpose—in so doing would have been twofold: first, to put these originally unrelated tales into a narrative frame, connecting their dots to make a whole somewhat larger (and perhaps a bit friskier) than the mere sum of its parts, as in such exemplary instances as* The Book of a Thousand Nights and a Night; *also Boccaccio's* Decameron, *Marguerite of Navarre's* Heptameron, *Giovanni Battista Basile's* Pentameron, *and other such* -amerons . . .

"In a word, a Hendecameron?"

Why, thankee there, Wys: *Hendecameron, yes! And second, by their Present Teller's thus clearing the narrative decks, so to speak, to recharge and reorient their Original Author's imagination. Whom never mind.*

"She's on the edge of her chair. If Present Teller happens to feel a bit frisky?"

Patience, s.v.p.: The guy's preoccupied with, among other things, this meant-to-have-been Invocation. *In other words, between or among themselves to discover where they-all might go next by determining where they are now by reviewing where they've been lately, storywise and otherwise.* Sound familiar?

"She's on the edge of her bed, this Wissywhatever."

-WYG: explanation to follow, inexorably. *Thus their initial intention: Original Author's (whom never mind), old Graybard-the-Teller's, and their muse-in-common's*—muse's-in-common?—*who serviceth the first of those through the second, and vice versa.*

"Kink-*y!* Shall they get on with it, then? Extended Congress and such?"

Surely they would have so gotten, well ere now, *had not shit hit the world-in-general's fan, and the US of A's in particular, on that certain September morn, killing thousands of innocents and, just possibly, American Innocence itself. And by the way so distracting Talester Graybard and present company—*

"Speak for himself. Present Company can still concentrate, believe it or not, when she puts her mind to it, and other relevant parts."

He stands corrected.

"Then let him *lie* corrected—beside her, and they'll get on with Getting It On while old Never-Mind-*Him* shakes his mostly Autumnal head and the world goes kerflooey."

There's the problem, Wys: one of the problems, anyhow. If we think of capital-A Author as being the mere narrative hardware, so to speak (which is why we can forget about him), and Yours-Truly-quote-Graybard as embodying Narrative Imagination—the Art-of-Fiction software, if you will, for *rendering* Author's story-ideas—

"I will if you will. Whenever you're ready?"

—then *lying* might be said to be their collective vocation, right? *Lying with her,* we could even say, she serving after all as muse and accessory before, during, and after the fact of their fictions—although those wordplays are bound to be lost in translation.

"First a Serviceable Surrogate, now an Accessory! Such gallantries!"

She knows what we mean. And that they're meant as compliments.

"Mm-hm. How about quote *brackish tidewater marsh-nymph,* some pages back? Another compliment?"

Of course. As Reader will have noticed, she's both fresh and salty. . . .

"Compliments accepted, then, she supposes. She reminds all hands, however, that there are other kinds of play than wordplay."

Perpended—and now back to our hypothetical and subsequently shot-down Extended Invocation, if I may? *Their quandary* (Graybard's and Wysiwyg's) *is that for him to re-render now, in these so radically altered circumstances, Author's eleven mostly*

Autumnal and impossibly innocent *stories, strikes him as bizarre, to put it mildly indeed—as if Nine Eleven O One hadn't changed the neighborhood (including connotations of the number* eleven*), if not forever, at least for what remains of Teller's lifetime. And yet not to go on with the stories, so to speak, would be in effect to give the mass-murderous fanatics what they're after: a world in which what they've done already and might do next dominates our every thought and deed.*

"Hell with *that.*"

Hell *is* that. And *Thus,* I say, *his situation and their quandary: GB-the-Teller's task*—shall we call him GeeBee?

"Ick."

Forget it, then: *Teller's not-unfamiliar task*, if I may recapitulate, *had formerly been the more or less routine one of assisting Author by reviewing, in a maybe-sportive narrative frame dreamed up for that purpose, those eleven not-so-sportive waypoints from their Stories Thus Far, and, thus oriented, to proceed. After Black Tuesday, however, it's how to tell those or any such tales in a world so transformed overnight by terror that they seem, at best, irrelevant.*

End of aborted invocation.

"Okay. May I talk now?
I mean this brackish Wissywiggy accessory-surrogate, whose name you've yet to explain to her and whose utterances to date have been mainly mere teasing interjections?"

Be Graybard's guest—since, truth to tell, it's he who's hers.

"You got that right, pal, and here's how she sees it: First off, while we're forgetting about Whatsisname the Original Author or Mere Narrative Hardware, let's forget about old Odysseus too, who at his final raft-wrecked landfall before reaching home simply reviews for the locals everything that's happened to him in the ten years since he and his now-dead shipmates set sail from Troy's Ground Zero, and whose four-chapter recounting of those tribulations is understandably short on lightness, not to mention humor."

Point taken: Farewell, Odysseus, or however it goes in Greek.

"Ἔρρωσο! as we say on Mount Helicon."

Epharisto.

"And let's set aside Mister Middle-Aged Dante, whose excursion through Hell, Purgatory, and Heaven can scarcely be called light storytelling, and whose predicament, like O's, is his own, not his society's. And who, by the way, never returns to that narrative frame of the Dark Wood that he *found himself lost* in, to wrap it up after his culminating vision of the Big Gee—as if Homer were to end the *Odyssey* when its hero winds up that review of his Story Thus Far, and leave the whole second half of the epic unsung!"

Addio, Dante. What a memory you have.

"Yes, well: I was *there*, more or less, right? I am, after all, the Serviceable Surrogate."

More than serviceable!

"Yet yet to be serviced. Setting aside, I say, that pair, let's consider your pals Scheherazade and Boccaccio. *Her* stories are mainly gee-whizzers: light in tone, heavy on special effects like magic rings and genies in bottles, often erotic and sometimes scatological, meant purely to entertain and keep her audience wanting encores—"

Or else.

"Exactly: The girl's in bed with the Guinness World Record serial killer: a thousand innocent virgins deflowered and murdered in as many nights since he offed his unfaithful wife, and Scher's next in line if she doesn't get his rocks off and leave him wanting more. Talk about Performance Anxiety: If she'd been a man, she could never have gotten it up! Talk about Publish or Perish! Yet for *ninety-one times* our piddling eleven nights she delivers the goods both sexually and narratively; bears the monster three children and then marries him when he finally lifts the curse—despite there being never a hint anywhere that she *loves* the bastard! She's just Doing What the Situation Calls For: telling marvelous stories with the ax virtually at her neck and the kingdom on the brink of collapse. . . ."

Amen. And we believe we know what you're going to say about the *Decameron*, but please say it anyhow.

"Great Plague of 1348 devastates city of Florence! People

dropping like flies from the Black Death that'll kill one out of every three Europeans over the next dozen years! Corpses piling up in the streets; law and order down the drain, if they'd *had* any drains—and in the face of this horror, what do Boccaccio's three young lords and seven young ladies do? Why, they retreat with their lucky servants to their country estates (*of which each of us owns several*, one of the ladies points out), and they organize their own little play-world, with its rotating king- or queen-for-a-day and its chivalrous rules for ordering their pleasures, and they virtuously stroll and dine and sing and dance and tease and flirt, and then in the hottest part of the afternoon, after siesta-time, they amuse themselves with witty and/or racy *stories:* one tale per person per day for ten not-quite-consecutive days (Fridays and Saturdays off) while the world dies unnoticed off-screen. And at the end of that period—congratulating themselves on having maintained their collective virtue despite the collapse of their society and the naughtiness of their tales, but apprehensive that prolonging their idyll will either lead them into capital-V Vice or tarnish their reputations back in the city (an odd scruple indeed, under the circumstances)—they return to the church of Santa Maria Novella in Florence, where they'd just happened to meet two weeks earlier, and there they bid one another *arrivederci* and go back to their town houses and on with their lives and business."

With nary a word, as I remember, about the devastation they're returning to.

"Nary a word—but we'll get to that later. The point to be made now is, dot dot dot?"

Point made: Catastrophe, if not quite apocalypse, has them by the throat, but they spin their yarns nevertheless.

"Not nevertheless, Geeb: *therefore*. And not apocalypse-tales, we note, but How Abu Hasan Farted, and How Friar Rinaldo Lies with His Godchild's Mother and Her Husband Finds Him with Her and They Make Him Believe That the Friar Is Charming Away the Child's Worms? Stuff like that."

So what we'd like to believe . . . ?

"Is that to tell *irrelevant* stories in grim circumstances is not only permissible, but sometimes therapeutic. That their very irrelevance to the frame-situation may be what matters, whether the frame's grim and the tales are frisky or vice versa. As somebody's grandma-from-Minsk used to say about *shtetl* humor back in the time of the pogroms, *If we didn't laugh, we'd hang ourselves.*"

Oy: Observation perpended. On with the Mostly Autumnal, Mostly Recent, Mostly Fictive stories, then?

"Well: There remains the matter of a certain adverb back in that trial-balloon invocation: *Present Teller reviews eleven tales with Muse, post-* . . . How did it go? Not *post-nuptially.* Not *post-partumly.* Not *postmodernly.* . . ."

Post-invocationally, maybe. Ms. Wysiwyg had a grandma from Minsk?

"Maybe. And maybe other kids besides young quote *Wys* shared her good luck in the Grandma way—if, in Wyssie's case anyhow, not much good luck otherwise. A loving grandma from Minsk: If only!"

Now her colleague's on the edge of *his* chair. On with *her* story?

"Maybe somewhere down the line. First—assuming consent of all parties concerned?—they get that adverb out of the way. Then, post-adverbially, they start over again from Square One, explaining that queer name of hers and who and where she is and what's going on here besides adverbing. *Then* Graybard Teller tells Forget-About-the-Author's dozen-minus-one stories, if that's how the game goes, between or after which maybe we'll in a manner of speaking squeeze in hers? Never mind Homer and Dante and Boccaccio: Let our models be your pal Scheherazade (minus the nightly menace from her bedmate) and the Sanskrit *Ocean of Story*, as told by the god Shiva to his playmate Parvati: the longest story ever told, spun out by the Lord of Creation and Destruction as a thankyou-ma'am for big-time bedplay while the goddess sits on her lover's lap. In both cases, comrade, it's Ess-Ee-Ex before Story-telling; otherwise this game's over before it starts."

Yes, well: Now that "Graybard" has been safely distinguished from Never-Mind-Whom as Software from Hardware, and both of those from Inspiration, which is Ms. Muse's department, her wish, we guess, is *ipso facto* Imagination's command. On one major condition? And with one minor adjustment?

"Like, say, Imagination's left hand *here*, while his right carries on . . . exactly . . . *so?*"

Her pleasure's his, in the nature of the case and their respective job-descriptions. *And although their situation remained still Pre- rather than Post-Congressional, and the world-at-large's was unimproved, and "GB's" Major Condition and Minor Adjustment remained unstipulated, much less met or made, and even Ms. WYSIWYG's alias du soir had yet to be glossed for the patient reader—not to mention where they-all are and how they got there— old Graybard-the-Teller at this point fetched forth, for his muse-friend's possible delectation . . .*

"Yes!"

HELP

a stereophonic narrative for authorial voice.

R = Right channel of disc or tape recording, separately recorded.
C = Central voice, either recorded equidistant between stereo microphones, in synchrony with and superimposed on R and L, or live interlocutory between R and L.
L = Left channel, separately recorded in synchrony with R.

R Help!

C Help!   help!   HELP   HELP!   Help help!   Help *help*   HELP!   Hel   **HELP!**

(et cetera at random pitches, volumes, frequencies, timbres, and inflections for 30 sec.)   LP!

L HELP! **HELP!**

R **HELP!** (exclamatorily) | 8-second pause | (unison shouts) HIP-hip **HELP!** | **HELP!** 2-second pause | **HELP!** 2-second pause | **HELP!** 3-second pause

R 11-second pause

C **HELP.** (declaratively) | 5-second pause | HIP-hip **HELP!** 1-second pause | HIP-hip **HELP!** 1-second pause | **HELP!** 2-second pause | **HELP!** 3-second pause

C 14-second pause

L **HELP?** (interrogatively) | 12-second pause | **HELP!** 1-second pause | **HELP!** 2-second pause | HIP-hip **HELP!** 1-second pause | **HELP!** HIP-hip **HELP!** 1-second pause | **HELP!** 3-second pause

L 7-second pause

R Help. . . .help. . . .help . . .help. .help. helphelphelphelp! *(peremptorily: gradual accelerando from very slow to very fast, 15 seconds)* | 3-second pause

C Help?   Help help?   HELP?   Helphelphelp?. . Assistance? *(last time)* *(interrogatively: random intervals, 15 seconds)* | 3-second pause

L Help help help help help help help help . . . . HELP! *(crescendo from whisper to shout, about twice/second, 15 seconds)* | 3-second pause

(read as if from list, about one per second)

Assistance Aidance Boot Providence Ministration Favor Shot in the arm Mercy Encouragement

Fosterage Charity Guidance Sustenance Nourishment Manna Provision Alleviation Easement

Redress Reinforcement Pardon Shrift Abettance Succor Cast Subvention Ministry Boost

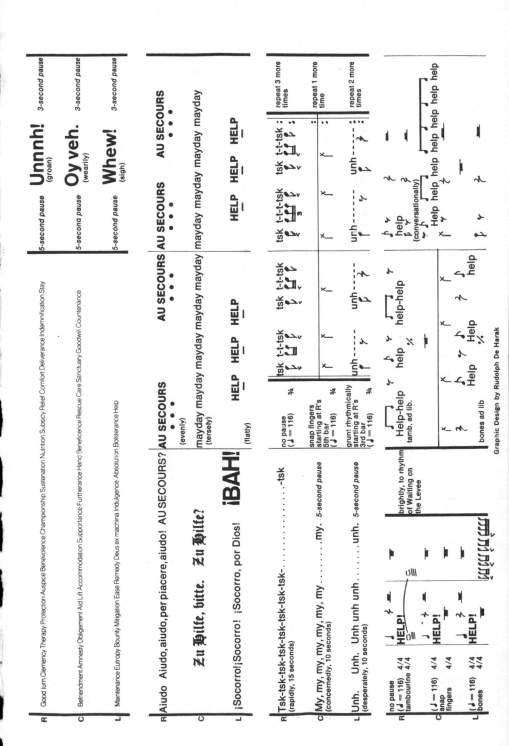

Graphic Design by Rudolph De Harak

brightly, to rhythm of Johann Fischer Augsburgiensis, Tafelmusik, Ouverture: 2nd & 3rd movements. Vivace (♩ = 192)

R: Help-help help help help-help (etc. ad lib.)

C: (booming interlocutory voice)

L: Help Help (etc. ad lib.)

3-second pause & end tamb.

Et ceteral end finger snap

3-second pause & end bones

3/4 Dear God (groan) · Help! H-E-L-P · (resignedly) · Help! H-E-L-P-H-E- · H-E-L-P-H-E- · elp!

3/4 · (sigh) · (resignedly) · help help help help help helphelp,diddly · Help! H-E-L-P

Help! H-E-L-P · help help help helphelpDiddly -elp! · -elp! · E-L-P help! Helphelp! · elp!

H-E-L-P-H-E- · H-E-L-P-H-E- · H-E-L-P-H-E- · H-E-L-P-H-E- · elp!

R: Help help! · H-E-L-P-H-E- · L-P help! Help helphelp! Help · Helphelp,help · -elphelp,help

C: help help! · H-E-L-P · helphelp help · H-E-L-P-H-E- · Helphelp! Diddly

L: H-E-L-P help! · H-E-L-P-H-E- · elp help! · H-E-L-P-H-E- · elphelp Diddly · -elp! H-E-L-P · helphelp,diddly

---

R: help! Help · Help · Help · Help · help · help help help · help help help

C: help help help · Help help · help! · help! · help! · help help help help · help help help

L: -elp! H-E-L-P · help! H-E-L-P · help! Helphelp · help! Helphelp · Help, H-E-L-P · HELP! · Help help

---

Grave (♩ = 102)

R: help help help · help! · Help · ritard.----- help! · H-E-L-P · Help! Help

2/2

C: help help help · help help help · help help help help · ritard.----- help! · help help help help · H-E-L-P

2/2

L: Help help help! · Help help help! · Help,help,help,helphelp!Help · ritard.----- Help,help,help,helphelp!Help · H-E-L-P · 2/2 help, helphelp, help

R	help! *Helphelp!* Help.	help help help!	Help help! Help	help! E-L-P-H-E-L-P	help! H - E-L-P
C	help! Help help!	**H-E-L-P!**	**H-E-L-P!**	**H-E-L-P**	help! Help help!
L	**H-E-L-P!**	Help, *helphelp*, help	help! Help	help!	H - E-L-P-H- E-L- P

R	help! Help, **H-E** -L-P help help help!	(sustained crash-ing sounds, 5 seconds)	(add sirens & penetrators, 5 seconds)	(1 small crash & tinkle)	5-second pause
C	**H-E-L-P** help-E-elp!	Help-E-elp help help!	(thuds, grunts, ouches, oofs, other urgent noises, 10 seconds)	(1 short & 1 long blast of police whistle)	10-second pause
L	help! E-L-P help! Help	help! *Helphelp* Help	(sustained splashing & gurgling, 5 seconds)	(add alarm bells & buzzers, 5 seconds)	10-second pause	(1 small splash & gurgle)

R	6-second pause	10-second pause	10-second pause	10-second pause
C	**He-e-e-elp!** (croak, 3 seconds) 3-second pause	(... faintly, sound of horses & bugles, growing louder as if approaching from R, building to a tremendous crescendo as it reaches C, sustained for several seconds at C, then moving toward L and growing ever fainter and fainter until it recedes entirely into silence at L...)	**HELP.** (matter-of-factly)	10-second pause
L	6-second pause		10-second pause	10-second pause

First
Night

"Whoa, there! Hold on!"

My pleasure. By which we mean, of course, Graybard's-the-Present-Teller-of-These-Tales.

"But not mine, as promised. Not Wyssywhatsit's?"

WYSI*WYG*'s. Problem?

"*Three* problems, at least. First off, when you said your guy was quote *fetching something forth for her possible delectation*, his waterbedmate not unreasonably assumed, dot dot dot—you know? I mean, *look* at her!"

Who could not? Savoring every aspect and detail of what Narrative Imagination sees in (begging his colleague's pardon) the perhaps counterproductively too-bright lights of Inspiration's remarkable boudoir. Maybe hit the dimmer-switch a bit? Mood lighting, et cet.?

"Not yet: She *wants* him to see it all, because *What you see*, as the saying goes, *is what you get*. Hey! . . . ?"

There it is: *WYSIWYG*, as the computer-types used to say back in the far-off Nineteen Eighties, when PCs were first actually able to show text on the monitor with the same fonts and line-breaks as the hard-copy printout. What you saw is what you'd get: WYSIWYG.

"I get it: Quite appropriate. Even painfully so."

For her getting it, a Graybard kiss, right here. For its being maybe a tad painful in ways as yet unknown to him and *a fortiori* to our Reader, another . . . here?

"There. And when he's finished—I mean, when *she's* finished . . .

"*There. Thankee kindly, sir,*
and now to Problem One: Wyssie's not unreasonable expectation, back at that Trial Invocation's end, *re* what was about to be fetched forth by her visiting colleague-not-yet-in-arms?"

Yes. Well.

"She thought they'd agreed: Love before Language! Ardor before Art! He's got a problem with that?"

Certainly not in principle. In homely, high-mileage fact, however, Hers Truly could use a bit of, shall we say, *Help?* Night One of their reconnection and Extended Congress may be young; her present company isn't. Thus that forewarned-of Minor Adjustment: his fetching forth, in lieu of et cetera, Story Number One, believe it or not, of the aforespecified eleven: a little *jeu d'esprit* from the rambunctious High Nineteen Sixties, meant to illustrate not so much that art may be a cry for help as that Distress, like any other emotion, circumstance, or what have you, may be grist for Ms. Muse's mill. Shall they grind on?

"Presently. Perhaps? One hopes."

The above was Problem One, he believes she said? Of three, he believes she said?

"*Three at least*
is what she said, but three'll do—and we haven't even gotten to that Major Condition somebody spoke of awhile back. Problem Two is that by any reasonable definition, this Minor Adjustment by him fetched forth wasn't a capital-S Story."

Not a story?

"Granted, it had a Beginning, a Middle, and an Ending— but so does any sentence, any day, any life, without their therefore being Stories, as Wys and Graybard both well know. The thing even built through sequential escalations to a sort of climax and resolution, or at least a petering out, if one may so put it. But then so does any wave breaking on a beach, any off-the-shelf symphony or fireworks display—or, so one hears, the capital-A Act of capital-L Love, when all goes well. Does that make them stories? Not in Fiction Writing 101: Check your pardon-the-expression Software."

What can one say?

"Oh, well: that mere *jeux d'esprit* don't count—except as *jeux d'esprit,* bless them. That if there're to be eleven several stories in this Hendecameron of ours, then somebody still owes us, among other things, Story Number One. That, on the other hand, as *jeux d'esprit* go in the shadow of Black Tuesday, that one was certainly apropos. And finally, that our current, several-decades-older caller for *Help!* will forthwith accept and administer unto himself a certain software-upgrade potion from his Brackish Tidewater Marsh-Nymph Here Called WYSI-WYG. . . ."

Presumably helpful upgrade tentatively accepted—on the same Major Condition sooner or later to be laid down. Take it now?

"Not yet: There's that Problem Three to deal with, for one thing—following which I propose a change of agenda after all, from Shiva's-and-Parvati's or Scheherazade's-and-Shahryar's to Graybard's-and-Wysiwyg's."

Which is? But wait: first, your Problem Three and my Major Condition.

"Problem Three's already solved, come to think of it. What it was was, you started off saying *There was meant to have been* a book called et cetera, which *if it had been written before* et cetera *might have opened* with such-and-such an invocation. Right?"

Right, alas. *Sportive,* I believe it was: *Foreplayful,* let's say. Those were the days. . . .

"All which implies that—shit having hit fan and World As We'd Known It having effectively ended on Nine Eleven 0 One—said book cannot now so open?"

Correct, alas: 'Twould be impertinent. Bizarre. Obscene, almost: idle quasi-erotic fantasizing in the very smoke of Ground Zero!

"But in fact said book *did* so open; *has* so opened, Nine Eleven or not! That's what looked from here to be Problem Three, until it occurred to the muse thus sportively invoked to declare it a non-problem."

Oh?

"Their story's started: Graybard's and Wysiwyg's, Wysiwyg's and Graybard's. Muse here declareth this to be Night One of their eleven—which night she is further inspired to imagine as Black Tuesday's itself."

No.

"Yes. In spite of terror, in the face of who knows what, on with the stories! On with their Hendecameron!"

Brave talk, Wys, but tall order.

"So bid old GeeBee-the-Narrative-Software stand tall—as presently he shall, with his assistant's already proffered and conditionally accepted but yet-to-be-administered musely upgrade."

Yes, well: His Major Condition, however, is that not for one nanosecond shall Reader conflate Present Reteller of these tales with their Original Author—

"Conflate Software with Hardware? Not for a microsecond, nanosecond, picosecond. . . . What comes after pico?"

Femto? O.A. and mate being a happily long-wed pair who treasure their quite comfortable, quite conventional, pleasantly busy, agreeably unadventurous, decently private, and blessedly unstoryworthy life together—

"So forget about *them* already!"

Precisely. Whereas Graybard-the-Present-Teller, in his professional capacity as Narrative Imagination, is by definition virtually free of restraint and inhibition, at liberty to project himself into any age, gender, ethnicity, circumstance, and situation whereinto Ms. Muse may inspire him in *her* capacity as supplier not only of said Inspiration, but of Material for Author to transform into stories via the about-to-be-upgraded Graybard Software application. Condition accepted?

"Goes without saying: Software may become Firmware, but

Teller remains Teller and Author Author, whom never mind.
Shall we, then?"
    By any and all means. You mentioned a change of M.O.?
    "Indeed, for Inspiration's elixir needs time to make its vir-
tues felt. Let us therefore reverse our order of business: Up-
grade-time now—maybe taken with a glass of the house white,
a really quite drinkable marsh-country pinot gris. . . ."
    Potion taken. Pinot gris indeed commendable.
    "And needs no breathing-time, unlike potion, pinot noir,
and world in general. Let the pair therefore Sip and Tell: Both
sip; Present Teller tells Original Author's Story Number One;
Brackish Marsh-Nymph listens—quietly, but by no means passively—after which, at long last, et cetera! Said story and those
that follow it on nights ahead to be strictly *irrelevant*, in the
sense of having nothing directly to do whatever with today's disaster."
    Today's? Ah, so: their little Let's Pretend; their (in my judg-
ment) highly questionable make-believe.
    "Not make-believe, Geeb: *as if,* the better to make our
point. Promise promised?"
    No problem there: O.A. originally authored this one even
longer ago than *Help!* Granted, Relevance may laugh at Chronology like love at locksmiths, but we'll take that chance.
    "And another sip of Upgrade. Then on with First Night:
Story Number One! Entitled?"

LANDSCAPE: THE EASTERN SHORE

❖

IN THE TEMPERATE LATITUDES of Captain Claude Morgan's culture—the parallel of Athens and Maryland's Eastern Shore—it is winter. The solstice, in truth, is not yet upon us, but so unequal is the Sun's daily skirmish with the dark that though he blinds our eyes as usual (so that, looking away, we see his lingering image where he is not), he warms no more than our clothing and the clapboards of our houses: The chill of the night behind us and of the longer night to come never leaves our bones and hearts and inner rooms, where not long since it came only now and then in dreams. So late does he take the field that the skipjacks and bugeyes dredge oysters from the Chesapeake by starlight every morning; and so early leave it that bright Orion will have risen from the ocean, will have thrown an arm and leg over the marshy flats of Maryland, before ever the women get supper. In what other season might the old man sit thus in a ladderback chair by the window of his bedroom and watch Andromeda on an empty stomach?

His house, which he has given to his married daughter, is in East Dorset, near the creek. He put it up before his own marriage, two storeys of crab-fat-yellow clapboards; picked over the lumberyard for clear true pine and drove his nails with love. But now the ridgepole sags; the weight of the chimney has begun to push the entire structure down to the sand. Should you walk the several streets of Dorset, as he did until lately on fine afternoons, or drive through the muskrat-marshes of the county, you might infer from various houses the entire process: On this lot the ground has been cleared but no cellar dug, for the area is six inches above the level of the sea; down the road, brick foundation piers are up and strung with joists, and studs and braces are toenailed home—the lumber is fresh from the yard and something green, so that every nail wears a ring of moisture around its head. Across town the chimney is up and the sheathing tongued and grooved; down-county, near one of the crabhouses, the siding is on and the top-flooring laid—painters and plasterers are already at their work. Then, if you pick the right houses, you may know their common fate: the shrubbery grows where the soil permits; the yellow-brown paint weathers in nor'easters, is replaced, and weathers again; the maples in the yard mature, overgrow, rot inside, lose branches, and hold themselves erect by little save their cambiums, until at length a hurricane topples them, unsymmetrical from long-lost limbs and hollow and gone inside; concrete sidewalks dapple like old saltines, and the children read an atlas in the splotches; they hump and split from the roots or ice or soft beds under them, and the children on rollerskates memorize and name the bumps—Leap's Bump, Moore's Bump, the Puddle-Crack; the even lawn of fescue grows dark green and plantained, retreats for its own protection into separate clumps and hillocks with gray dirt between and the ancient white stools of many dogs. Next the earth itself, weary, begins to relax where its load is heaviest, and the house comes down to meet it: Door sills sag, and doors must be shaved, for they hang askew, and shaved again if they are to be closed at all; windows no longer move easily in their sashes; gaps wider than the tongues run down between certain floorboards, and a child's marble on the floor will of itself roll uncertainly to a place and stop. As the load shifts, the plaster goes with it and is filigreed by cracks, or the wallpaper wrinkles into appalachian chains. The earth moves aside once more beneath the chimney, and from a distance you observe that the ridgepole now describes no proud straight line, but an obtuse angle against the sky. By this time the houses, cheap to begin with, may have depreciated past any waterman's means to repair; they are lived in until the sag makes housekeeping unfeasible, and this takes a long time, for the people in Dorset are not generally young, and move reluctantly. Grappled and besieged by gravity like an oyster by a starfish, the houses settle as much as a foot before being abandoned, and then (as if occupancy had sustained them in the war to preserve their form), *mirabile dictu*, how the end is hastened! Windowpanes go overnight, as if by magic. Bricks fall from the chimney like teeth from an old man's head, and shingles like his hair, in every wind. The clapboards weather for the last time and spring free, as if only the countless layers of paint had held them fast. The roof buckles and caves under its own weight. Presently the house sinks to rest upon the ground, so slowly that one scarcely notices until it is down. Bright green weeds—ailanthus, Saint John's wort, false dragonhead—grow up through the boards; green frogs and blue dragonflies sun themselves on the corpse.

The day long, of late, Captain Claude's mind has been a heavy, barely perceptible droning, such as men in their twenties may experience for an hour after sleeping too far into the morning: a continuous thick sound that makes clear thought impossible. Sometimes going out-of-doors has improved it, sometimes not, but he seldom goes out anymore at all. He seldom needs to, for the creek there by his yard, though it separates East Dorset, in a way, from the rest of the world, is the harbor of his mind, as for years it was the harbor of his dredge-boat: From it his memory daily casts her mooring, warps riverward, reaches down the bay, and runs free to the oceans of the earth and all their compass.

Sitting in his straight chair he can feel the whole town at once about him. He knows in the morning the sundry cars and trucks, the sound of the oyster-boats leaving the creek, of the bridge-bell, the fire siren, and the shipyard whistle. The fall of light upon the catalpa tree outside his window gives him the time of day. At night he hears the town quiet, the wind soughing off the river and clicking through the Chinese cigars of the tree, the water slapping at the creek bulkheads and sucking at the freeboards of the boats.

He can feel all his house at once, around and beneath him. So familiar is the structure that looking at the plaster wall he thinks he sees through to the lath and thence to the studs and draught-plates. Just beneath him, in the kitchen, he knows his daughter is stirring a certain agate saucepan. Moreover, from an earlier, rhythmic sound he knows that she has been shelling beans against the usual late arrival of her husband, a red-eyed bull of a waterman. Butter beans. On the mantel in the parlor, under a glass bell, is a clock that he has lived with for years—a wedding gift to him from his bride and again from him to his daughter: the "problem clock," his wife christened it, from the choice given her by the watchmaker, either to keep the glass bell sealed and enjoy but not use the fine machine, or to remove the bell daily for winding the spring, at the risk of letting in the salt moisture of the county. She chose to wind it, and perhaps in consequence its chimes have never really sounded, but he can feel the twist of its four-balled pendulum. All day he hears the electric refrigerator whir and click, the kitchen faucets open and shut, various doors swing on their hinges and latch into their jambs, various persons enter and depart. Like a blind man he knows the sounds and all the persons by their sounds. At night he hears his daughter and her husband in their bed, and the small sounds of the house itself: the same boards popping in the cold night air or the fourth and seventh risers creaking in the staircase, and occasionally a new sound, the pop of a different board, marking yet another step in the house's progress to the ground.

This old man can hear himself—the slow pulse of his blood in his neck, in his temples, behind his eyes, in the ends of his thumbs, in his groin, and in his ankles as he crosses his legs. When he moves he feels the bones slide against each other in their joints, where the cartilage is calcareous and gone. He hears the systole of his heart, eight decades old, which first commenced its labors in the year of the Franco-Prussian War.

He hears the droning in his head. So familiar is his body that when he looks at his hand or at his face in the glass, it seems to him that he can see through the old skin to the bones themselves; that under the thin mask of his face, so well known to him that he really cannot see it, he beholds the naked skull.

"Daddy?" His daughter's voice, toneless in middle age, sends up a preliminary summons to dinner.

Outside the old man's body, beyond the walls of his house, the people of Dorset are doing in the first dark what he can sense them doing, and did himself when he was younger and had reasons; things he still recalls so clearly having done, some of them decades past, that even now it seems he is resting from just doing them. He clearly feels his life, stretched out behind him but tied so securely to the present moment that he can sense it all about, as though everyone in Dorset at that instant, doing those things, were living *en bloc* the successive instants of his history; as though his past were so close at his heels—the earliest feelings of wharfboards under his feet and the blue glare of the river in his eyes, the freezing dredge-ropes in his man's hand, the coal-stove smell of his bridal chamber, the green feel of first grass on his old wife's grave—that should he trouble to turn his head he must see it all rushing to overtake him. He has no need to turn. He feels it go back to the commencement as surely as he feels the whole length of his legs extending over the chair-edge and down to the varnished floor.

"Daddy?"

Andromeda is now above his window, and he has been looking for the first stars of Perseus climbing after: Almost at the instant of his daughter's second call, splendid Algol, the Demon Star, heaves into view at its highest magnitude, and how the golden years pour in on him! From his father he first learned what stars to steer by; in his ears their Moorish names had been a music. What long spring nights they'd seen him toss to it, afire with seed and aspiration! On his wedding night hadn't they twinkled as he introduced them, one by one, to his bride—a receiving-line that took till dawn to pass! Hadn't he shown them to his little girl, and wept for pleasure at her garbling of their names!

And now the firmament swims in his salt tears, cold and joyless as the memory of old sins, curses hurled at all creation, grass gone clumpy on a mound, the weariness attendant on a surfeit of experience. When he left this chair of late to walk without needing to look along streets as familiar as the bloodcourses of his body, he walked only to reach his chair again, so it seems to him; he reached it hardly conscious that he had left, and for some days now he has not gone out at all. The walks are as useless, knowing as he does all that he will see and seeing as he does now only what he knows, as would be looking down each inch of his leg to see how far and in what manner it extends, when he can feel it. They are as useless as are the motions required to put his daughter's food into his stomach. He has no need to move about: Those butter beans are fuel for an old and vacant house.

"*Dad-dy!* Come on to supper! He's here!"

The gibbous moon, far down in the bay, strikes under the broad catalpa leaves and makes the tree glow ever so faintly. All his life he has followed the water, as they say, and it has led him here. In recent nights as he has stared at the wheeling heavens it has seemed to him that he might almost hear a sound. Outside his body, outside his house, beyond the town and the endless oceans—if the small droning were not in his head he would hear the stars go over the sky. That would be something! If only at the last one might hear them sing, sing in their courses!

Has he spoken aloud? No matter: His tears are dry. Algol, silent, returns his stare. It will not soon occur to him to make the effort to move his joint-bones, one against the other, to carry himself downstairs so that he might stoke butter beans into his stomach in order to lift himself back into this room and place his body upon this chair, where it rests at present from living years that stretch behind him like a taut dredge-rope.

The house pops. A new board, under his chair; a second-floor joist. He will need no longer undress this body and place it on the bed to watch the constellations scrape across the town, so tiring himself to hear them that he must rest all day when he has re-dressed his body in the morning.

"He's coming up, you hear?"

His leg has gone to sleep. He dreams of small frogs, translucent as new grass, waiting in the dirt around the brick piers of the house. Metal-blue dragonflies hesitate in the air and flit from stem to stem. No need to stir his leg. So long as his body remains still, he will know clearly where his foot was when last he felt it. And that, so near the solstice, will quite do.

Second
Night

"That's it?"
one imagines "the brackish tidewater marsh-nymph here called
WYSIWYG" wondering, in her saltyfresh way, toward the close
of Night One of her and her accomplice Graybard's Hendecameron: "Tuesday, 9/11/01," at her insistence, and a less than
satisfying "night" after all for both parties, it must regretfully
be acknowledged. For although this pair are allegedly collabo-
rators of long standing, their current *modus operandi* is, as has
been established, new; likewise Ms. Muse's current embodiment as "WYSIWYG," yet to be accounted for, and their current
trysting-place, yet to be specified; and the specter of Black
Tuesday, 2001, not surprisingly proved, to put it gently, anaphrodisiac.* In the wake of that world-altering disaster, for
them or anyone to rehearse "irrelevant" stories is not indefen-
sible; Reader has heard their rationale for so doing, and may
accept it or not. But for such retelling to serve as foreplay for

---

* Number of innocent victims still unknown at that time; initially estimated at 6,000
to 10,000 at the World Trade Center alone, later scaled down to just under 2,700 at
Ground Zero, another 100+ at the Pentagon, and 200+ passengers and crew on the
four hijacked airliners: nearly 3,000 dead or missing at latest count, not including the
19 suicidal terrorists themselves.

what certainly appears to be post-narrative erotic frisking, possibly extramarital to boot, strikes at least some of us as a touch much—although one grants that the same rationale might be invoked on behalf of sex as such: life in the shadow of death; a bit of joy or anyhow pleasurable diversion in the teeth of terror; a brief relief from fruitless obsession with catastrophe. An unattached bachelor talester and ditto muse might be another story; but what if this "Graybard" fellow is by some extension a happily wed monogamist like his tale's Original Author?

In any case, what happened was that the muse-nymph's software-upgrade potion kicked in more or less midway through the narrative of that evidently expiring old Chesapeake waterman, and whether for chemical or dramaturgical reasons or both, by the time Captain Claude arrived at his terminal epiphany that effect showed signs of winding down along with the tale. Ms. Wysiwyg (let's drop the caps), having attended the recounting "silently but not passively" as promised, desired nothing more than to launch at once into comradely discussion of it—nothing, that is, except to get on with their already-delayed battery-recharging "congress" before that elixir wore off altogether. They therefore came together per program, though more cordially than passionately, on her curious bed in her curious mid-marsh work-play-bedroom, yet to be described: she preoccupied with her musely reflections upon the tale, he distracted by her distraction and by lingering reservations about what was taking place. In what ought then to have been the cozy afterglow, when *he* might have drifted into uneasy sleep, *she* found herself restless with both erotic unfulfillment and pent-up commentary—along with a clutch of new questions about and suggestions for, if not necessarily problems with, their situation: matters that had occurred to her during their not-particularly-extended First Night Congress in this new chapter of their connection. But she contented herself with declaring, in effect, that while it might be right and proper in that *Landscape* story for the old skipper to content himself with the mere memory of physical life and to declare (in what were apparently meant to be his last words) that "that, so near the solstice, will quite do," she would have her waterbedmate remember that they themselves had yet to attain the autumnal equinox, and that a repeat of this First Night flopperoo would not "quite do" at all. No particular complaint about the *story*, he should understand, which, taken together with *Help!*, sufficiently announced the themes of Distress and Autumnality, with a brackish tidemarsh setting thrown in for good measure—perhaps an early foreshadow of her saltyfresh self? But their M.O. was in clear need of readjustment.

Again?

"Q.E.D.! Just another little change in our order of business, okay? No need to review it now; let's cop us some Z's before Night One becomes Night Two."

Easily advised—and for the nymph, at least, to all appearances easily managed despite her restlessness of just a few paragraphs past. Although for her colleague's accommodation she had considerably dimmed the room-lights at his recitation's close, she never turned them fully off (so she had informed him) except when bright moonlight took their place. Now, by the last-quarter moon's faint shine through her glass ceiling and the night-light glow of the room itself, he saw and heard her doze off promptly at his side, her face turned himward, her breathing somnolent, her nimble body prone, altogether relaxed, and even in the dimness entirely visible crown to sole through those transparent bedsheets. Across her shapely back, the dark green "straps" of her whimsically painted-on bikini bra; across the top of her buttocks and into their cleft, the similarly painted-on thong bikini bottom.

Yes, well.

For Graybard, on the other hand, now that his immediately post-Congressional drowsiness had passed, sleep in such unaccustomed and questionable circumstances was another story, which—if only because where *he* came from it was mid-morning, as shall sooner or later be explained, not late evening as in hers—with a frown and a sigh he reviewed for himself (and thus conveniently here reviews for Reader) where in the bloody world he was, and by what extraordinary route he found himself there:

Call it a dream,
if you will, although "dream sequences" in stories and screenplays make some of us fidget. In any case, it went like this: On a certain late-summer weekday morning early in the twenty-first century, the Narrative Hardware of these tales was sitting per usual at his worktable in his workroom in his-and-his-spouse's tidewater domicile, scratching out notes toward his Next Thing while his helpmeet busied herself in her own workroom or with family matters elsewhere. "Found himself lost" is how that aborted Invocation paradoxically put it; Reader should understand, however, that there was nothing novel or troubling in this state of affairs, par for his and many another scribbler's course between extended projects: He mentions it here merely in order to get on with his story. Without physically leaving his chair, he dispatched his idling, restless fancy or Narrative Software on a stroll through the familiar "rooms" of what might be dubbed their Imaginarium, recalling the protean muse who could be said to have inspired this one and that, or in figurative collaboration with whom (via his strolling scout, whom he here dubbed "Graybard") this or that of his pen's offspring had been engendered—all the while attentive, as his reconnoitering fancy strolled, for hints, clues, suggestions of encore.

It was upon that scout's returning to headquarters empty-handed, so to speak, from this "house"-tour that—as happens now and then in dreams—he found himself . . . not lost, but *astray,* let's say, in an altogether foreign precinct of that so-familiar habitation. Where ought to have been the workaday Scriptorium from which he had set out was instead what appeared at first startled glance and proved upon amazed inspection to be an all-glass bed-sitting-workroom: Not only its walls

were glass (through which the prospect, instead of creekfront
lawn and shade trees, was a vista of wetland cordgrass, spartina,
and winding marsh-waters), but also the partition between the
room and its attached bath, and even the floor and ceiling.
Through the former he remarked that tidemarsh extended
right under the room, which was built on what looked, improbably, to be glass pilings. Through the latter he observed that
while the day out there seemed as summery as the one he'd
left behind (warm humid air moved off the marsh through
opened sliding glass doors giving onto a glass deck with glass
railings), it was, unaccountably, far past its forenoon: Indeed,
a red-orange sun was just setting behind a distant stand of
loblolly pines. The room itself, however, was bright, and replete with further marvels: transparent "blinds" and draperies
on the windows, see-through pictures on the glass walls, transparent area rugs on the glass floor; tables, chairs, computer
hutch, and all other furnishings made of clear Plexiglas or some
such; transparent queen-size waterbed made up with transparent "linens," Lucite lamps with transparent "shades" and even
unfrosted bulbs; an iMac computer in clear plastic case, as were
the television, telephone, mini-fridge, and other appliances—
including a see-through digital bedside clock that flashed, un-
nervingly, *9:11 9:11 9:11*. Cups, plates, and flatware he saw
through the transparent cabinets to be all clear glass or acrylic;
glass bookshelves held what looked to be unfamiliar editions of
familiar titles, printed on—what, clear vinyl pages?—and similarly bound; through the glass partition he saw not only a glass-
enclosed shower stall but a clear glass toilet, seat, and lid, glass
washbasin, fixtures, and plumbing, even transparent towels and
washcloths on their clear glass rods, and a mirror that not only
reflected but could be seen through! This fetish for transparency extended to incidentals as well: knickknacks of crystal and
sometimes tinted but never opaque glass; see-through anatom-
ical dolls, male and female, their internal organs also tinted but
not opaque; clear food and drink containers in pantry cabinets
and fridge.

As the inadvertent interloper registered these wonders with some mix of fascination, amusement, curiosity, and head-shaking dismay, late afternoon turned into crystal-clear and summer-warm evening. Since the room's light remained constant as if automatically regulated, "Graybard" stepped out onto the glass deck (equipped with a glass ladder, he now noticed, leading down to a cove, creeklet, or marsh-gut, its water far from glass-clear but evidently deep enough for swimming, as he could hear vigorous splashing down there somewhere) to contemplate this unsettling shift of hour and venue and to see whether someone was actually paddling about in what "back home" would be by now jellyfish-infested Chesapeake tidewater. Over the deck railing, he noticed, was draped one of those patterned-but-transparent towels he'd noticed in the bath, and beside it a woman's dark green two-piece swimsuit and a likewise mainly transparent overgarment of some sort. . . .

Hello?

"Come on in, friend," a woman's voice called warmly from the now-dark space below. "The water's fine."

Although he couldn't place it, that voice sounded half familiar. He peered over the rail, at first saw nobody, then located the splashing underneath the deck and could just make out, through its transparent planks in the glow of the room behind him, what appeared to be a shapely female figure paddling about down there in a seaweed-colored bikini like the one beside his hands on the rail.

I guess not, thanks, he called back—though the water certainly looks inviting. Then added, lightly, If I'd known I was coming I'd've brought a swimsuit!

Who could she be? And where in the world . . . ?

Splash splash—and sparkle of phosphorescing algae, *Noctilucae*, at her every movement. "Don't be shy. It's almost dark, and I'm not wearing one either. I *hate* wearing clothes in the water!"

Really? Then why was she . . . Yes, well, he said: likewise, as it happens. But I'll sit this one out.

At the base of the ladder now, "Make yourself comfortable, then, and I'll come sit it out with you."

Do we know each other?

A word of advice, Reader,
from a professional dreamer-up of characters and situations: If ever, in what you take to be Real Life, you "find yourself lost" in one of these Call-It-a-Dream scenarios, *blow the whistle on it promptly,* or else risk losing your return ticket. Gregor Samsa's mistake, e.g., when in Franz Kafka's famous story he "wakes" to find himself transformed into a man-size bug, is to explore and *consider* his metamorphosis instead of kicking and yelling in the tale's second sentence. Next thing we know, he's assenting to his condition: "It was no dream." Granted, if the "dream" happens to be delicious (or at least inviting, intriguing, and not immediately threatening), and/or if you feel "in charge" enough to exit it at any point you choose, your whistle-blowing may be less than reflexive. But there, precisely, lies the danger—as witness Let's-Call-Him-Graybard's behavior thus far already in this improbable scene, even before our improbable marsh-maiden climbs the improbable glass ladder onto the improbable glass deck of her ditto habitation, gives her (probably) dark brown cropped curls a shake and her bemused visitor a conspiratorial smile, and sets about toweling herself dry with that improbably transparent terry-cloth towel aforenoted. Why did he not haul ass out of there two pages ago, sound the alarm, backtrack posthaste to wherever his figurative wanderings led him astray, and thence home to *terra cognita* instead of yielding to his fascination, registering and reconnoitering those multiple transparencies—*initiating dialogue,* even, with the dream-creature, and now permitting himself the voyeuristic male titillation of realizing, as he watched her towel-work in the ever-brighter light from her living-quarters, that this trim, quite attractive, intelligent-faced stranger, while less young than he'd at first supposed, was in fact buck-naked, her nipples, pubic bush, and posterior cleft in plain view as she rubbed dry

what he could see now to be a painted-on bikini? *You like?* her smile and unselfconscious movements as much as asked while, dried now to her satisfaction, she spread the towel over one of two transparent deck chairs, slipped that actual swimsuit on over the virtual one, and donned over that the transparent wrap—upon which was printed, sure enough, the bra cups and nether triangle of a dark green bikini! But did he even then bolt the scene, dash for the nearest entrance in search of exit? He did not: only returned her mischievous smile with his puzzled own and asked, not *Where the hell am I?* and *How did I get here?* and *Who on earth are you?* and *What's going on?*, but (again) Do you and I know each other from somewhere? Thereby assenting at least provisionally to what has the earmarks, if one may so put it, of puerile male erotic fantasy. He can't help noticing now, for example—not that he's striving to *avoid* noticing—that the woman's aureoles and pubes remain darkly visible through all those layers. Her "real" swimsuit too, then, and its printed likeness on her beach-wrap, must be see-through!

"Do we *know* each other?" Standing perkily before him, hands on her hips, she rolled her probably dark brown eyes. "What a question! I should feel insulted, but never mind." Fetching up her towel then, "Make yourself at home, Geeb; *mi palapa es su palapa*, et cet.? I need to go potty, and then we'll get down to what we're here for." And over her shoulder, as he helplessly admired her retreating buttocks, "Meanwhile, anything you see that looks appetizing, help yourself to."

Yes, well. And to himself, *Geeb?*

It has perhaps been established that as dusk turned to dark out on the marshscape, the strange studio grew brighter, as if some rheostat were cued automatically to compensate for ambient light. The white and blush wines in the glass fridge (no reds), like the clear stemware in the glass cabinets, were even more conspicuously displayed now than when Errant Imagination first wandered in—as were the bathroom, its fixtures, and its current occupant, going unabashedly about the business of urinating, flushing, and—*voilà!*—washing herself after in a clear glass bidet that hadn't caught his eye before but then cascaded in: the first and second WTC towers hit again and again, in the repeated videos, by planeloads of surely terrified innocent passengers and flight crews; the unassimilable spectacle of the towers' collapse straight down upon their thousands of blameless tenants and hundreds of heroic would-be rescuers; the near-bull's-eyed Pentagon; the goodbye cellphone calls from about-to-die passengers struggling with their hijackers over nearby Pennsylvania; the mounting evidence that Osama bin Laden's Islamic terrorists had scored again, outdoing by several orders of magnitude all their previous strikes. The couple went numbly through the motions of that day's remainder: prepared and ate without appetite their lunch and dinner, touched base by telephone and e-mail with professional associates in Manhattan and with family all about the republic, did a few perfunctory housekeeping chores, lit a 24-hour *Yahrzeit* candle in memoriam to the innocent dead—and returned and returned to the horrific real-life story in murky progress, wondering with the rest of America when, where, and in what form the next blow might fall. A rogue nuclear bomb in Philadelphia, Chicago, or Los Angeles? Sarin nerve-gas in the D.C. Metro, such as other terrorists had used in Tokyo? The Father of Waters, the Mississippi, parricided with some unstoppable germ? And no doubt the booming but already troubled national economy—not to mention their own immediately upcoming travel-and-other plans—collapsing like what the media were already calling Ground Zero. . . .

Sleeping pills for all hands that night, after even more than usually appreciative embraces. Next A.M., further grim numbers and pictures from New York and Washington; cobbled-up bravado from the nation's dubiously elected President; no good news except the absence so far of additional catastrophes. So many lives snuffed or shattered! And after breakfast and the morning newspaper, what could they do but, *faute de mieux*, try to carry on with their routine work? Stars and Stripes half-staffed on their waterfront pole, then each to his/her home office, where in her near-stunned state she soon abandoned her attempt at normalcy, while her thicker-hided mate . . .

most certainly did now, he reasoning that inasmuch as privacy was clearly not among the woman's priorities, there was no cause to avert his eyes on her behalf from those ablutions. Indeed, when she hauled up her bikini bottom, rearranged her wrap, and, patting her hair into place, rejoined him where he stood bemused in mid-studio, he felt free to ask, No shower after your swim?

She shook her head. "I like the feel and smell of creekwater on me. Don't you? Have a sniff." She drew his face into her hair, which did indeed have a pleasantly brackish fragrance — and, he noted, a few precociously silvered strands among the glossy nutmeg brown. Taking his hand then in hers and drawing him toward that ample (and now interiorly lighted!) waterbed, "To work?"

Waitwaitwaitwait. He stopped still, shut his eyes, withdrew his hand, put it to his brow, and gave his head a wake-up shake — but found himself still lost in that bright dreamchamber, its amused habitant still beckoning him bedward, even shedding nonchalantly now the sheer shift that she had so shortly before slipped into and dropping it onto the transparent-carpeted glass floor. Her eyebrows questioned.

So okay,
he declared aloud to himself: We have here the archetypical Familiar Stranger. Some novel embodiment of the Muse, one bets; just the person old quote *Geeb* was looking for, metaphorically speaking, but never till now encountered in the flesh, excuse the metaphor. . . .

"Metaphor shmetaphor," said she, and peeled off the seagreen bra, stepped out of the ditto pants, and stood in mocking challenge at her bed-edge, feet apart and hands hipped again, naked but for the body paint here and there. "Better get busy; it'll be daylight before we know it."

In fact that clear-cased digital clock on the floor beside her waterbed still flashed *9:11 9:11 9:11* — in the evening, obviously, although her visitor's analogue wristwatch displayed the same hour of the routine work-morning he'd wandered out of

Oh, plugged ears per usual, filled pen, and tried further notes toward some framing-situation or -story for his project-in-mind: a situation deriving from—might as well say *inspired by*—"Graybard's" peculiar experience of the day before. WYSIWYG. Ten nights and a night. Dot dot dot.

Impossible to concentrate in those circumstances: people doubtless still dying at Ground Zero with his every vainly scribbled word. After an hour or so he packed it in, capped pen, popped plugs, went to refill coffee mug. Found himself—and his scattered but still active Imagination—the house's only occupants; mate most likely outside gardening in hope of distraction. Mug topped off with breakfast-brewed mocha java, he made their way back through the intervening rooms and, continuing through his Scriptorium to the adjacent bathroom, for some reason imagined seeing on its farther side (more precisely, imagined that "Graybard Software" fellow suddenly seeing there) not the house's daylit main bedroom, but a certain marsh-nymph's night-lit glassy lair. Moreover, the cubicle in which his projected fancy stood was now as-if-magically transformed into her transparent-fixtured bath, and perched smiling yonder on her waterbed-edge—beside which that clock now flashed *9:11 9:12 9:11 9:12*—was that studio's still-green-bikini'd occupant, as unsurprised at "Graybard's" reappearance as if two dozen seconds instead of as many hours had elapsed since their initial tête-à-tête.

"You were saying?"
she teased. And he—setting aside both his dispatcher's mug and, in those unprivate circumstances, the urge that had fetched its current user toiletward—presently found himself declaring to her, in effect, The fact of the matter is, ma'am, *there was meant to have been a book called* Ten Nights and a Night, *which if it had gotten itself written before 9/11/01*, et cetera, per Invocation. After which, and the ensuing dialogue afore-transcribed, "Graybard" fetched forth for "WYSIWYG's" possible delectation that stereophonic item entitled *Help!*, and there followed (1) their First Program Adjustment (po-

tion>recitation>Connection), (2) the nymph's proffered Software-Upgrade Elixir, accepted on her guest's One Major Condition, (3) the Present Teller(not to be conflated with Original
Author)'s rehearsal of that old waterman's *Landscape* tale, and
(4) nymph-and-narrator's Metaphorical (and thus still at least
technically innocent, as well as less than impressive) Congress
and subsequent Second Program Adjustment—to wit, as she
now in her turn declared to him: (1) Potion henceforth first
(she had already poured a fizzy Portuguese rosé into a pair of
goblets on a nearby end table), followed not by Narration yet,
but by (2) comradely Conversation about the story past and/or
the one to come, along with any other matters that they might
incline, so to speak, to touch upon, as it were. Said conversation
to be at any point happily set aside (as storytelling should *not*
be) for (3) a proper whizbang-though-mind-you-Metaphorical
conjunction at last of Inspiration and Imagination. Which workout should serve in turn to inspire, in their post-Congressional
lassitude, (4) the tale *du soir.*

"It worked for Scheherazade," she reminded her guest, "and
it'll work for us. Because Inspiration's the name of the game,
right? It's who and what I freaking *am!* Or at least its Serviceable Surrogate?"

The interloper sighed. Smiled, but shook his head. Yes, well.
But I have a thousand and one questions, Wys. . . .

"So ask one or two—*after* we sip, okay?"

Okay. And sit and sip they did, Inspiration on her bed-edge,
Imagination on a Plexiglas chair before her, their wine this
"evening" gently sparkling and its flavor unaffected by whatever additive it contained.

"Questions."

Mm. Like who are you *really*, and where the hell *are* we?
But never mind those, I guess: You're the physical embodiment
of every yarn-spinner's indispensable collaborator, materialized
here in a marsh-country version of Mount Parnassus—

"So far, so good."

—and functioning under the nickname Wysiwyg—

"Not *her* idea." She reclined now on her left side, propped her head on her hand, and sipped her wine, simultaneously leaving both little and much to Imagination's imagination.

—said alias laid on her by Yours Truly for reasons obvious enough, although the behavior and accoutrements that inspired it have yet to be laid bare either to him or to the postulated Gentle Reader.

"Keep talking, friend, while Gentle R and I make note of your verbs. *Laid on. Laid bare . . .*"

Small wonder, Wys!

"Not to worry: It won't stay that way. But the explanation of what prompted your nickname for me can wait for some night down the line. Meanwhile, the other verb you used back there was *inspired*, as I recall, and something tells me that Inspiration is beginning to take hold."

Could be. But some uppercase Reservations linger yet, Wys, even granting my Major Condition afore–laid down—

With a smile, "*Laid down . . .*"

Afore*stipulated*, *-specified*, whatever. M/M Original Author are nowise open-marriage types, as we both know, and I'm the guy's Roving Imagination. . . .

Unfazed, "We *do* both know, Geeb, and in my capacity as your-and-his Roving Muse, I here dismiss for good and all those malingering reservations, since all parties understand we're talking *metaphors*. Like putting some Lead in the old Pencil? Metaphors are free; we settled that on Night One." Raising her glass, "Even this wine is metaphorical: When did you and I ever drink on the job?"

Her guest nodded: No disputing that. But it doesn't *taste* metaphorical, Wys: It tastes like a perfectly literal Portuguese rosé. And as I may have mentioned, you certainly don't *look* metaphorical!

"Sure sign of an inspired metaphor. And speaking of Inspiration . . ." She set her glass aside, turned her darkbright eyes himward.

So, he declared:
Thousands dead at Ground Zero alone, some maybe even still

painfully dying at this narrative moment; the nation in shock, the economy reeling, air travel disintegrating, Afghanistan about to be devastated yet again, all hands clueless about what dreadful thing'll happen next and whether life in the US of A will ever return to normal in our lifetime—and you and I are supposed to enjoy guilt-free Metaphorical Congress between telling irrelevant Autumnal stories?

Smiling gravely up at him: "You've got it, friend. Now come and get it. Maybe a couple of asterisks'll help? Bit of a spacebreak? Allow me. . . ."

* *

And somewhile later, her post-Congressional voice subdued and husky, "By *irrelevant,* of course," she said, "we mean irrelevant to Black Tuesday's terrorism, American unilateralism, Islamic fundamentalism versus post-Enlightenment Western rationalism, the fallout from economic globalization, and like that?"

Mm.

"We *don't* mean irrelevant to the human experience of life, language, and storytelling."

Mm-mm.

"In fact, since you were feeling some twinges awhile back about Metaphorical Intimate Congress between bard and muse, maybe while you're still somewhat inspired you can spin us a story relevant to *that.*"

Mm?

"About, um, Innocent Guilt, shall we say?" Up on one elbow again and drumming fingertips on his chest: "Innocent *Marital* Guilt, even?"

Mm . . .

All business now, "Listen up, Geeb: You've now downloaded your guy's two items-from-way-back-when, right?"

Mm-hm. The rest, for better or worse, are all reasonably recent, early-Autumnal stuff.

"And you mentioned that a couple of those are not exactly made-up stories?"

Mm: Stories they are (unlike old *Help!*), but not hundred-percent fiction like *Landscape* and you and me. Enhanced Fact, I guess? Creative Nonfiction? There're just two in that category—both, as it happens, tinged with TIMG: Totally Innocent Marital Guilt.

"So let's knock those off tonight and tomorrow and then get on with stories not only Reasonably Recent and Irrelevant to the national crisis but fabricated out of the all-but-whole cloth. Yes?"

Mmm . . .

Climbing over him and out of bed, "You get your narrative act together while I go wash off the Sweat of Inspiration, and then your no-longer-brackish marsh-nymph is yours for the telling." Over her retreating shoulder, "Don't say *Mm* again, okay?"

. . . Okay.

And upon her presently rejoining him—and his refinding, in time, his narrative voice—Talester Graybard duly came up with a Second Night story. Inspired by his collaborator's charming hydrophilia and by their serial mid-morning sunsets thus far, this first of his two not-altogether-fictive narratives was entitled

THE RING

❖

OFF DISCOVERY POINT, appropriately—a quiet condo-spread in West Bay, Grand Cayman Island, where the American couple were celebrating a happily high-numbered wedding anniversary—as they snorkeled out from the beach one languid afternoon in six to twelve feet of crystalline water over a field of stubbled coral, Narrator's eye was caught by a metallic glint down among the gaudy squirrelfish, wrasses, sergeant majors. He dived, the fish scattered, and he retrieved from the wrack a bright gold ring. A man's wedding band, it looked to be, lost no doubt by some swimming vacationer like himself from one of the many resorts along Seven Mile Beach. Back at the surface he raised his mask, confirmed the discovery, and signaled his mate to come see it: a simple, square-edged ring, like a bushing from some golden machine. No engraving or other decoration; no inscription on the inside (such as the coded pledges on their own wedding bands) except the 14K mark.

Treading water, we tsked at the unlucky husband's loss (from professional habit, Narrator was already conjuring scenarios and various narrative points of view). We would post a FOUND note on the receptionist's notice-board, we agreed, when we came ashore; meanwhile, as we had just swum out a considerable distance toward a fish-rich clutch of coral formations that we'd discovered earlier in the visit, we decided to carry on with our snorkeling. Where to stow the little sea-treasure? Since the taking of coral specimens was illegal in those waters, we carried no trophy-bag. Small empty shells we sometimes snugged for safekeeping into the crotch of our pocketless swimsuits, but it would have felt odd, let's say, to deposit another man's wedding ring with either Narrator's own genital equipment or his wife's. The most convenient carrying-place, obviously, was the ring finger of his right hand—which, as it happened, the gold band fit perfectly.

"I thee re-wed," Wife vowed as Husband slipped it on. Still lightly treading water, the couple kissed, then repositioned their masks and went on with their exploration. At no time in the next hour, as we leisurely paddled, dived, and pointed out for joint admiration the splendid formations and brilliant fish, was Narrator unconscious of his new jewelry item—the way I normally am of my wristwatch, say, which I seldom remove except to clear airport security checkpoints, or of my own (deeply patterned) wedding band, which after twenty-plus years was gratifyingly all but unremovable. The "new" one was as constant a sensation as a loose tooth: mildly obtrusive, yet mildly interesting, too; agreeably disconcerting. I found myself rotating it with adjacent fingers as I floated, and "testing" its fit with the other hand. It slipped over the knuckle easily but not freely; just enough resistance there to prevent, under normal circumstances, its second loss.

Scenario: Some divers maintain that barracuda can mistake the glint of a ring or a stainless-steel watch for a small fish; they therefore remove such jewelry and wear black-cased watches to avoid a misguided bite. Perhaps the sight of one such predator, not uncommon near coral heads, prompted a snorkeling husband to slip his ring off belatedly for safety's sake (M/M Narrator have never bothered to, although they've often swum among barracuda), and in the process of transferring it from ring finger to wherever, or of trying to swim with one closed fist . . . et cetera.

Back ashore, we warmed ourselves in the poolside Jacuzzi, where, to begin getting the news out, Narrator displayed and explained his find to some fellow hot-tubbing condo-renters. "Maybe it wasn't lost," a swarthy chap from Ontario wryly suggested; "maybe some pissed-off husband threw it away with a curse." Much amused, his Quebecois wife added, "Or maybe some celebrating divorcé threw it with a hurrah."

We four then cordially disagreed whether, in either spirit, one could throw a wedding band so far out from the beach. Narrator thought not. "He would have to set down his champagne glass first," the Canadienne supposed. Reverting to his own scenario, "He already threw that at his wife," her husband corrected her, "to get even for her dumping *her* champagne on his head." "Which he no doubt deserved," Narrator's wife joined in. All hands agreed, however, that the only real test of the matter would be for me to fling the ring itself back into West Bay—assuming that a contented husband's throwing arm could match that of a disaffected one or a celebratory ex.

"Use mine," the Ontarian offered, and extended his hairy hand, presumably in jest. His wife laughed enthusiastically.

Et cetera. Spa'd, sundried, relotioned, we apprised the Caymanian receptionist of our find—"Ah, such a pee-tee!" she commiserated with its imagined loser—and posted a notice with the necessary info and our apartment number. *May be reclaimed by accurate description.* "Why not just leave it here?" my wife suggested. Because, I supposed, my professional curiosity would be less gratified by a secondhand, amateur account of the claimant and his "story" than by a vis-à-vis. And then there was that aforementioned low-grade fascination: For whatever reasons, I rather enjoyed the unfamiliar feel of the thing on my "free" ring finger.

As we changed into tennis outfits for a late-afternoon workout once the courts were shaded, "Remember that young bridegroom in Jamaica?" my wife asked. On a similar vacation there some anniversaries past, a hefty, pinkfaced pair of Kansan newlyweds on the resort's snorkel-boat had told us of the groom's having lost, just minutes earlier, his brand-new wedding ring while we all were exploring the reef on this first morning of their married life; of his frantic dive for and lucky retrieval of it as it sank through a school of bar jacks, any one of which might have gobbled it; and of the couple's being now so shaken by their near loss (the water depth there was fully five fathoms, and the sea floor a tangle of broken coral) that they would neither re-enter the water with their rings on nor leave them behind on the boat. "Come on," one of us had teased, "take 'em off. It'll be exciting, like being lovers again." "For us," the cherubic young groom had gallantly replied, "it's still exciting to have them *on*"; and his literally blushing bride, wetly embracing him, added, "Even more so now." We were pleased to imagine that they could scarcely wait to get off the boat and scamper back to their hotel room, plumply to go to it.

For us, likewise, we had assured them, it still was, even after a score-and-more anniversaries.

"Is that really so?" the now teary-eyed girl had asked Narrator's wife directly. "Cross your heart?"

Through our tennis game I was particularly aware of the ring's pressure against my racquet-grip, which pinched the band against my finger. Even so, I chose not to remove it. Our set done, while Narrator fetched our gear back to the condo, his partner stopped by Reception to see whether our notice had had any response. The second-shift receptionist, she presently reported—an elderly British woman whom from earlier business we had judged more or less daft—had excitedly informed her that "the American widow-lady in B-Six" had lost her diamond-studded wedding ring two days before (in the facility's parking lot, the now doubly bereft widow believed) and in her great distress was persuaded, as was the receptionist, that "ours" must somehow be hers.

"Despite the circumstance," my wife said through our glass shower door, "that ours is a plain gold band found underwater a hundred yards offshore."

And male besides, I added. I was showering first in order to fix drinks and hors d'oeuvres while *she* showered, before our nightly dinner-expedition into town.

"All rings are female," she declared. "Anyhow, that dip of a receptionist is absolutely convinced we've found B-Six's ring,

and the poor woman herself is in such a state that I'd better pop
over and show her the bad news. Where'd you put it?"
   A bit sheepishly, I handed it out to her.
   "In the shower, yet. What *is* it with you and this ring?"
   Beats me: a story, maybe.
   As she did what she called her fool's-errand-of-mercy and I
toweled myself dry and prepared rum drinks and finger food
for the sunset ritual on our lanai, Narrator wondered whether
what he now felt so distinctly on his right ring finger was the
Absence of Presence or the Presence of Absence. In either case,
it reminded him of the sharply ambivalent feeling on his other
hand decades earlier, when he had removed for the final time
the symbol of his twenty-year first marriage. *That* ring he had
been reluctant enough to dispose of (unlike the Canadians' hypothetical disaffected husband) that it had spent the next dozen
years, at least, at the bottom of his cufflink-and-collar-stay box:
a box so seldom opened since those items went out of fashion
that he could not now recall whether in fact the thing was still
there. He couldn't imagine either sentimentally still keeping it
on the one hand, so to speak (he had, after all, grown children
as prized souvenirs of that life-chapter), or callously tossing it
on the other, any more than he could dishonor history by tossing his share of the family photo albums from that period—
which, however, he found it discomfiting to review more than
rarely.
   Over cocktails, "my ring" back in place, my wife described
the Nice Jewish Lady in B-Six's tearful acceptance of the facts.
"You want vis-à-vis," she told me, "you should've seen her
turning that ring in her fingers, as if it were her dead husband's.
They rented down here forever and then finally bought B-Six
two years ago and bingo: ruptured aneurysm. They're from
Boston. Life, I swear."
   Likewise. And maybe it *is* her husband's, in a manner of
speaking: resurfaced at their old hideaway.
   "*She* sure wanted to believe something like that. I told her to
keep the thing, if that would help. . . ."
   Narrator's reaction was being watched. He did, in fact, feel

an irrational twinge of alarm, but of course said at once, Of course.

"But her husband's ring was heavily carved," my wife went on, "like hers, she said, but without the diamonds. So she held out her hand to show me, and of course broke down because her ring wasn't there."

Ah.

"Plus, get this: They bought those rings right after V-J Day, 1945, guess where?"

Put thus, the question's only possible answer was "Shreve's": Shreve, Crump & Low, the old Boston establishment where we had bought our own wedding rings a quarter-century later — and now nearly a quarter-century since.

Well. We toasted that coincidence and watched for the elusive Green Flash as the sun's upper limb sank into the Caribbean.

"Did you see it?"

Maybe.

"I didn't."

En route to and from dinner, and now and then during it, the couple found themselves invoking notable rings from myth, legend, literature, and cultural history: signets and scarabs, proposal and betrothal rings, memorial and "decade" rings, "posy" rings and class rings; Plato's Gygean ring of invisibility, a thought-experiment for testing true virtue; jealous Hans Carvel's fabliau dream-ring for guaranteeing his wife's fidelity as long as he wore it; Browning's *The Ring and the Book*, appropriately cyclical in form; Tolkien's *Lord of the Rings* and the several magical rings in *The Thousand and One Nights*; also tree rings, key rings, earrings, nose and nipple rings, annular eclipses, ring nebulae.

"Jesus's foreskin," Wife volunteered, sometimes thought of as the wedding ring for Brides of Christ.

The space shuttle *Challenger*'s fatal O-ring, Husband riposted.

"Ring around the rosy," said by some folklorists to echo the dreadful "all fall down" of London's Great Plague of 1665.

The labia ring worn by the hapless heroine of Pauline Réage's *Histoire d'O.*

"Labi*um* ring, no? Or did they stick it through both?"

Et cetera.

With tempered incredulity, "You're wearing it to *bed?*" she asked when that time came.

Unless it truly bothered her, Narrator guessed so, yes.

"Oh, wow. A kinky new chapter in our story?"

We'd see.

Now, then, Reader: From considerable experience, this ring-tale-bearer can readily diagnose his problem with the narrative in hand. A *story*, typically, comprises both a "ground situation" and a "dramatic vehicle." *Ground Situation:* Almost without their realizing it, two people have (a) fallen in love; (b) fallen out of love; (c) what have you, as long as it carries some overt or latent dramatic voltage. *Vehicle:* And then one day, (a) the woman receives the first of a series of anonymous, teasingly prurient phone calls; (b) the couple are abducted by extraterrestrials in a UFO; (c) what have you, as long as it turns the screws on the Ground Situation. As a rule, one without the other will not make a story: No matter how wretched or exalted, a GS without a DV is no more than a state of affairs; no matter how exciting or "dramatic," a DV without a GS is no more than a happenstance.

What one had there in Grand Cayman, clearly, was an instance of that second case: an arresting, even portentous Dramatic Vehicle sans any Ground Situation to give it meaning. Narrator's fortuitous discovery and retrieval of a golden ring—at and from "the bottom of the sea," moreover, to be deep-dived for from the surface upon which the finder had been floating—is fraught with potential significance, the more for its having happened to a previously married man on or near a wedding anniversary just a bit higher-numbered than the last attained by his earlier marriage. It needs no professional to imagine any number of Ground Situations out of which that vehicle might drive a story. Imagine, e.g. [GS], that that ruddy

Kansan bride aforementioned had only with difficulty persuaded her rufous beau to leave off playing the field and "take
the plunge" with her in Jamaica; that then on their first literal
post-nuptial plunge—just when, perhaps, the gravity of his new
condition is coming home to him—the symbol of their vows
slips as lightly from the bridegroom's grasp as the groom himself (so his bride has worried) will slip from hers at the first extramarital temptation. Tears, doubts, consternated re-avowals,
sorely blemished honeymoon and uncertain maiden year of
marriage, at the close whereof (and the opening of this specimen story) they return ambivalently to their wedding-place as
if hoping for some sign there. Soaking their misgivings in the
resort's Jacuzzi, they are joined by a middle-aged couple just in
from snorkeling, the man of whom [DV] displays his freshly
ringed right hand to them and explains [et cetera]. Or imagine
[GS] that those latter snorkelers themselves, gratified as they
are that their union has now successfully outlasted any previous
connection in their life-stories, are nonetheless experiencing
certain marital stresses, perhaps unrealized or unfocused until
[DV] one day off Discovery Point, appropriately, the fellow's
eye is caught by a metallic glint down among [et cetera]. Imagine, even (although one winces at such self-reflexivity), an aging storyteller who [GS] for the first time in his long career
goes to his muse's cupboard and discovers it altogether bare!
He to whom inspiration has ever come as reliably as urination
or tumescence finds to his quiet but growing dismay no lead
in his narrative pencil, shall we say, and, half fearful of that
association, follows his muse's example by going on vacation—
to Discovery Point, say, in West Bay, Grand Cayman Island,
where, after some days of trying unsuccessfully *not* to try in
vain to come up with a good story-idea, he snorkels out from
the beach with his beloved spouse of twenty-plus years in six to
twelve feet of crystalline water over a field of stubbled coral and
[DV] by merest chance [et cetera].

Et cetera. But none of those scenarios applies. The Kansans
were who they were and not otherwise; ditto your present Narrator, his lively mate, and their marriage-bond, duly tempered

by time and trials and the stronger for that tempering. Ditto too Yours Truly, this (this-time-true) talemaker, now and then temporarily stymied or by his muse misled, but never seriously "blocked." That being the case (Narrator natters on, looking round about him in Discovery Point to discover a pointed Ground Situation while turning on his right ring finger that fourteen-karat Dramatic Vehicle, anyhow its symbol), might it not be said that what obtains here in this recounting is in fact just the opposite of what obtained there in Grand Cayman— i.e., that the circumstance of having a DV without a GS is itself a GS, awaiting its DV?

Indeed it might so be said; Narrator said as much to his notebook and was tempted to say so too to his life-partner, but forbore: Irritant enough to her that in the absence of response to our FOUND notice I continued to wear the interloping ring day and night through our vacation, while swimming, sleeping, shopping, shaving, showering, making love and lunch and notebook notes, reading on beach and lanai, playing tennis— until, with the often unsubtle symbolism of nonfictive life, in that last-mentioned activity it began to chafe the hand-grip of my racquet and raise a blister on my finger as well. For that hour each early morning and late afternoon, therefore, I took to removing it (not without some difficulty now, as that blister/ callus thickened the finger-joint) before playing—and replacing it promptly after.

"The curse-bearing ring of the Nibelungs," Wife added to their ongoing catalogue: forged from Rheingold and guarded submarinely by dread Fafnir.

Also Wagner's opera cycle based on that cycliform myth.

"*Anelli della morte*," she remembered from somewhere: the poison-rings fashionable among Renaissance Italian gentry for suicide and/or murder.

One divines a growing though still-tempered impatience with Narrator's little fixation; one could readily imagine a story in which Wife becomes not only increasingly impatient but downright jealous, or in which Husband finds himself deliberately provoking her irritation, perhaps to his own fascinated dismay, until the new ring actually bids to threaten the old, so to speak. But in fact nothing of that sort was anywhere near the case, and as many of her catalogue-contributions as his were emotively neutral.

"Ringling's three-ringers."

Vienna's Ringstrasse. Remember it?

"Mushroom fairy-rings. The brass rings on merry-go-rounds."

Ringworms?

"Bathtub and collar rings?"

Telephone and doorbell rings, then.

"The postman always twice."

Tintinnabulation in general and Narrator's own mild tinnitus in particular: the "crickets in his head" that make it difficult for him on occasion to distinguish external from internal cricketry but do not, as a rule, prevent him from hearing when his friend has heard enough. Had that Kansan/Jamaican snorkeling bridegroom (I therefore reflected to my notebook but not to my bride) *not* caught his slipped ring in time, the noble metal would never have corroded down there on the Carib floor. In time, however, assorted coral polyps would have encrusted it the way salt crystals fantastically encrust those twigs cached deep belowground by salt miners for that purpose: Stendhal's famous image for enduring love. Better that the marriage outlast the ring, Narrator hopes he would have thought to console the newlyweds in that case, than the ring the marriage.

Had he really disposed of his from his first? Had he really not? If he had, by whatever means (Narrator knows a woman who flushed hers down the toilet on divorce-suit-filing day), where was it now, and encrusted with what?

"Smoke rings. Piston rings."

Pissed-on rings.

"What?"

I once heard old Robert Frost remark, near the end of his life, that for as long as he could remember he had observed that the oaks in his New England woodlands were the last to shed their autumn leaves—indeed, that here and there a brown oakleaf-cluster would hang on right through the winter; and that that latter sight had never failed to suggest to him the last shreds of a storm-blown sail; and that in that image he recognized there to be not only a poem but, specifically, a *Robert Frost* poem—but he had never worked out what that poem was. In like wise, Narrator imagined this ring-thing ringing on in his imagination, tinnitus of the muse, to the grave and who knows whereafter, should its notebooked image prove as high-karat as the metal. Come to think of it, though (I then came to think), my case was the opposite of Frost's: Narrator could imagine any number of possible Yours-Truly stories based on this *anneau trouvé* (it only now occurs to him, writing *anneau*, that the *annus* of "anniversary" is itself a ring-root: the circle of the year, just as *anus* is the [etc.]), but some benign daimon like Socrates's warned him not to write them.

A proper ring-story, he satisfied himself with noting instead, *should quietly circle back upon itself, like the Rheingold to its river-bottom rest-Platz at the Nibelung-cycle's close.*

"The volcanic Ring of Fire in the South Pacific."

Dope rings. Boxing rings. Life-rings. Teething rings.

"Rings into which one throws one's hat."

Rings run around the competition. Was that the Green Flash?

"Green Flash, definitely."

That fine anniversary-vacation ended, as what does not. *Faute de mieux*, in the closing hours of it I left the ring on our condo kitchen counter as a fourteen-karat tip for the Caymanian chambermaid. The happy couple flew home to their non-holiday lives and preoccupations—in Narrator's case, the resumption of whatever bona fide story-in-progress he had set aside for their celebratory recess. Although it was doubtless time and past time to get rid of the thing (if he had fetched it home and left it lying about, he might be fretting yet over what to *do* with it, storywise and otherwise), he rather wishes now that he had recycled it, if not into the Caribbean, then into some aptly symbol-fraught outflowing river—Wagner's Rhine, Twain's

Mississippi; better yet into the tidewater creek that flows and ebbs just a ring's-throw from where he here closes this account. In the *very* long run, to be sure, the thing will recycle itself, atom by atom, to there and everywhere—ashes to ashes, dust dust, in the universal recirculation—although in a run that long there'll be (as Gertrude Stein said of Oakland) "no *there* there."

Where is it now? one meanwhile wonders, knuckling one's ring-free right ring finger pensively with its neighbors. Narrator had hoped that this account of it might close some circle, discharge him of the symbol as he discharged himself of its referent. But in his notes and imagination it glitters yet: unresolved, unexplained, unaccounted for; like the element itself neither corroding nor (except for these vain musings) encrusting; as brightly agleam yet finally explanation-proof as life itself, as love.

Third Night

Referring to Narrator Graybard's Ring-*story of the "night" just past,*
"Well, now," observed the Brackish Et Cetera (perched this time cross-legged on her deck rail, above the water she had evidently not long since emerged from), "*that* was to the point."

You mean the Innocent Guilt bit?

"Who cares about that? I mean the story about a non-story that *becomes* a Story after all by acknowledging that it isn't one. Not unlike our meant-to-have-been Hendecameron, you know?"

Mm.

"Kinky! Plus I'm partial to anything with *swimming* in it."

So one guessed.

Reader him/herself might be interested to know that this pair are commencing Night Three ("Thursday, 9/13/01," Yankee style) of their project-more-or-less-in-progress after all; that they are once again tête-à-tête in Wysiwyg's peculiar glass domain—mid-morning in the still-stunned time zone of Islamic terrorism's latest grisly spectacular and headquarters of the wounded nation's scramble for military response, but after dark already in marsh-nymphland, whereinto Graybard has this time neither strayed nor stumbled, but proceeded directly, now that he has the hang of it, to get on with their figurative collaboration. Reader will have noted further that the muse-nymph does not, after all, go soapless day after day, as may have seemed the case between Nights One and Two. While she insists on a dip in "her" tidewater before getting down to business, so that during Conversation and Intimate Metaphorical Congress her skin and hair will be "marsh-mellow" (her colleague's pun, whereat she winces), as of their latest Program Adjustment she withdraws to her glass-enclosed shower stall after their asterisked Connection and then rejoins her guest for the tale *du soir.*

Thus did she, even as recounted, back on Night Two, affording her inspiree the appealing though steam-fogged spectacle, through the intervening glass partitions, of her lathering up and scrubbing off not only "the sweat of inspiration" but what remained of that singular painted-on green swimsuit, then toweling herself dry before returning *au naturel* to hear the tale of those sundry fictive and nonfictive rings. At the close whereof, its Teller found himself back in the late-morning study that its Author had never left, and the pair carried on as one with *their* work, first drafting an account of Night Two, then making speculative notes on what a Third Night might have in store, then calling it a day, musewise, and permitting Author to join patient Mate for the routine chores and errands of an ordinary middle-class-American late-summer working weekday—but with their flag still half-staffed and their memorial candle, remarkably, still burning, as was Ground Zero in lower Manhattan.

Did he share with her (Reader may wonder) this questionable new conceit of Narrative Imagination's serial encounters with a frisky manifestation of the Muse? Or permit himself instead a bit of Innocent Marital Guilt at not so doing? None of Reader's business, really, okay? That enhanced-fact *Ring*-tale and the *Dead Cat* one presently to follow it notwithstanding, we're talking *fiction* here now, for the purposes whereof suffice it to say that their routine domestic pleasures—a swim between groundskeeping labors, frozen margaritas on the screened porch at afternoon's end, the daily satisfaction of preparing and eating together on that same porch their evening meal, the post-prandial exercise-walk around their neighborhood, the evening's reading and other diversions as the *Yahrzeit* candle guttered out—were both sharpened and made strange by the dreadful tidings from Manhattan, Washington, and the rural Pennsylvanian plane-crash site apparently meant to have been either the Capitol or the White House. How enjoy, on the fine next morning, making love and breakfast while such grimness beclouds their newspaper's every page? How stretch their customary after-breakfast stretchies, bid each other light see-you-laters, and withdraw to their separate office-workrooms, when for all they know Osama's terrorists or some like-minded others might strike before lunchtime—if not with hijacked airliners, then with some even more dreadful nuclear or biochemical device or simply an array of homemade truck bombs, like the infamous Timothy McVeigh's in Oklahoma City a few years back? On the other hand, how *not* proceed with such innocent, pleasurable, *irrelevant* routine, savoring it all the more for its very irrelevance? As in pages past one has heard it argued, if perhaps not conclusively demonstrated, vis-à-vis storytelling . . .

As for pages present and in progress: There she perches, Wysiwyg, on that flat-topped glass deck rail, her hair still adrip from her swim while the nymph herself patiently awaits crown-to-sole description—so patiently, indeed, that she bids her imminent describer to sip first his presumably doctored wine (and to hand her the other glass, please, of those two fumé blancs on yonder deck table). Here's looking at you, Muse of Description and Narration, et cetera!

Whose dripping hair, to begin with, will turn out to be this time not her curlybrown mop *per se*, but a close approximation thereof—Wyssie's wig?—worn over the also-dripping Real Thing (it had *looked* a bit larger than life). What it dripped upon, in front, was a skin-tight photomask of her fair face, which at first glance *had* struck her describer as a tad unreal: its contrast with her actual flashdark eyes, white teeth, pink tongue, and unpainted lips seen through their respective cutouts. Thence it dripped on down upon a similarly skin-tight leotard or Span-dex wet-suit imprinted with the image of . . . you guessed it, Reader: Caucasian Female Nude, faithfully detailing in every particular the nymph's naked self and completed with appro-priately manicured latex gloves and pedicured slippers. And what (Graybard, for one, is wondering already) might she be wearing under all that?

But

"Well, now," observed the *Brackish Et Cetera as aforequoted,* referring to his not-altogether-fictive story of the previous "night." Per program, they sipped and Conversed: about that ring-tale, to be sure—its theme and setting, its cast of charac-ters and narrative construction—but also and mainly about her current get-up; likewise the night before's and (Graybard Imagination already in high gear) how many and what sort of further variations one might dream up on the theme of What One Sees being What One Gets.

"Oh, *that,*" peeling off with evident relief the wet wig and facemask and depositing them with her soon-emptied wine-glass on the nearest table: "Well, we've eight nights yet to go after this one. . . ."

On the last of which, if the world's still here, one finally sees and *ipso facto* gets The Real Thing?

One would see when that time arrived, she supposed. *"Mean-while"*—standing now directly before him, who had seated him-self in one of the clear plastic deck chairs facing the fragrant low-tide marsh—"bottoms up, okay?"

Not okay, s.v.p. Although by definition and job description ever at her service, he declared to her, he was by disposition and established habit a Sipper, not a Chugalugger; otherwise he would have satisfied by this time his considerable curiosity *re* what she was or was not wearing under that remarkable outer layer.

His in-no-hurriness seemed to please her: Deftly unzip-ping that imaged wet-suit's (hidden) zipper and slithering out of it like some agile amphibian shedding its skin, "Take your time," she said, and seated herself not on the waterbed yet but in a deck chair alongside his—after displaying to him at point-blank range that tonight's Layer Two was no swimsuit like the night before's, but bra and underpants as meticulously photo-printed as Layer One: aureoles and nipples on the former, pubic bush and vulva on the latter.

Shaking his head, So let me guess, he said, and sipped: Skin-colored body paint, pubic wig, and nip-colored pasties under that? And under *them*, at last, the subject of all those serial representations?

"Yours to discover, Geebso. Whenever you're ready?"

Which presently he would become,
but not before exploring with her in a preliminary way, between winesips, some aspects of her predilection for . . . *full disclosure*, he had been going to say, but the business wasn't that simple or straightforward. Granted that he knew nothing, yet, about who she might "really" be beyond her current role, was there not something problematical all the same about her obsession with transparency? Not psychologically problematical, mind; nothing to do with her motives: He meant *logically* problematical.

Her smile was unsurprised. "E.g.?"

Oh, like her clothing herself with transparencies? Not even transparencies, quite, but replications? Projections of what lies beneath?

"*Waits* beneath." Stretching her lissome limbs. "But take your time."

She is, for example, by her own acknowledgment impatient with clothing, and yet she covers herself with teasing expressions of that impatience. . . .

"Not for long, she hopes."

Is frustrated even by *skin*, he has gathered—as witness her preference, in the wall-art way, for x-rays, MRI films, and plates from Gray's *Anatomy* over more conventional renditions of the human figure. But which would be more "authentic," a naturally skinless apple, if such can be imagined, or one whose "peel" extends to its core? In his own view, both are not only unnatural, but (excuse him) unap*peal*ing: The latter is like that man of whom some humorist remarked, "Deep down, he's superficial." The former is a story that begins with its climax, or a joke with its punchline; it's a man who wears not only his heart on his sleeve, but all his other internal organs as well. Speaking of which . . .

"Could we postpone speaking of that Which till Night Four?" Clearly bothered now by the course of their discourse, she pushed herself up from her chair, suggested they do External Organs instead, and slipped out of her extraordinary undies, beneath which were no next layers of high-fidelity replication after all ("Enough's enough," she'll claim later, "sometimes"), but—Reader understands what we mean—*her:* anyhow the epidermal layer thereof. Who or which, indicating his now-nearly-empty glass, bade "Bottoms up for real now, sport, okay?" And proceeded forthwith waterbedward (where that clock flashed *9:11 9:13 9:11 9:13*) to await, bottoms up indeed, his joining her.

* * *

Shower. Story.

"You understand," she said after her post-Congressional showerbath, "it's not *you* I was upset by back there. . . ."

Back there?

"Not *there.* Back there in our Conversation."

Ah.

"It was your getting . . . too close to the bone, let's say. No wisecracks."

On with your story, Wys. Please.

"Maybe—though it's time we went on with yours." She was not, she would have him understand, arguing Back There that a joke should lead off with its punchline or a story with its climax and dénouement. She was, after all, the fucking *Muse* of Story, right?

Aptly put.

She quite appreciated that some things by their nature re-

The book of ten nights and a night :
eleven stories / John Barth.

<u>Date Due</u>   **6 Jan 2020**

To renew your items:

Go online to librariesireland iii com
Phone us at (01) 222 8488

Opening Hours Mon & Wed 10am to 5pm
Tue & Thu 1pm to 8pm
Fri & Sat 10am to 1pm & 1 45pm to 5pm

veal themselves only over time: stories, music, even painting and sculpture (although only the first of those was truly her department). Likewise one's understanding of oneself and others, of experiences and places and situations. While it was true that she inclined to up-front disclosure—like the classical invocation to the muse, which (as he might remember) lets us know from Square One that wily Odysseus will get home after ten years of war and ten more of wandering, et cet.—she granted that such disclosure does not preclude deeper and enhanced understanding over time. Speaking into his left shoulder, "All it precludes is Homer's springing on us in Book Twelve or Twenty-two that Odysseus *doesn't* go back to Penelope after all, but opts instead for eternal youth and virility in the sack with Calypso."

No surprises allowed, then? Not even pleasant ones?

She considered this. "Surprises, maybe, but no tricks. Fuller Disclosure, but no Prior Deception. And the fuller disclosure shouldn't *contradict* the invocation or initial impression or whatever, but confirm and enhance it."

So: No wolves in sheep's clothing or vice versa, but a sheep in sheep's clothing is okay? Or must it be either wool right through or else mutton from the inside out, like those apples we mentioned before? No: *Bone*, come to think of it, it'd have to be. A sheep made of sheep-bone!

"You're needling me."

And you're inspiring *me*, per job description. Wouldn't even a sheep made of sheep-bone be a deceptive cover-up of the essential marrow?

She sighed, rolled onto her back. "As a matter of fact, I happen to *love* bone-marrow. Lamb shanks! Osso buco!"

Aha: Something we've learned about Miz Wys that we didn't know before. Enhanced understanding!

"Superficial penetration, excuse the expression. But think not of the marrow, Geeb; sufficient unto this night is our Conversation therein. Tell us that other not-entirely-fictive story now, okay? I've shown you mine, more or less; now you show me yours, or Whomever's."

Done, more or less—always bearing in mind that Less can be More. It's another riff on both our Totally Innocent Et Cetera theme and on images (like last night's *Ring*) whose narrative exploitation neither exhausts nor exorcises them. My guy calls it

DEAD CAT, FLOATING BOY

✣

IF NARRATOR WEREN'T an already happily married man, it might have been what screenwriters call a Cute Meet: end of a spring afternoon in Baltimore; rush-hour traffic exiting the city on the arterial that ran past the couple's house; Wife off on family business while Husband scratches out yet another sentence or two before Happy Hour; doorbell-chime interruption of—perhaps by?—the muse. He caps his pen ungrudgingly (longish workday, story stuck), and from the pitch of the bell decides en route downstairs from his worktable that the ringer is at the seldom-used street-facing door. Ignoring its peephole out of trusting habit, he duly undoes that portal's city bolts and chains, et voilà: a tall, slender, uncommonly handsome early-thirtyish woman in white sweatshirt, black leotard, and considerable distress. Dark hair drawn back in short ponytail; New Age–looking headband of some sort; fine high cheekbones (was anyone ever described as having *low* cheekbones?); tears welling in her I-forget-what-color eyes behind wire-rimmed specs.

Can one help her?

She doesn't know. Does one own a black-and-white cat?

Afraid not.

Maybe one of one's neighbors does?

Could be . . . ?

The car just in front of hers, she explains, just struck just such a cat just up the street and just kept right on going. She stopped and tried to help; fears the poor thing's hurt really badly; wondered if it belongs to one of these houses; decided she'd try to get help even though she's illegally parked and backing up traffic and running late for her yoga class out in Towson. Nobody home next door, so here she is. Excuse her sniffles (she removes her glasses and dabs her eyes with a sweat-shirt-sleeve); she just recently lost her own cat to just such a hit-and-runner.

Let's have a look.

The arterial is indeed clogged, its two outbound lanes squeezing into one to pass her hazard-blinking gray Honda hatchback. Impatient commuters honk as she leads Narrator across the front lawn toward a white bundle on the curbside of the Episcopal church, two doors up. Oh be quiet! she calls in their general direction: *You're* not dying!

To her shapely back I observe, Not at the same rate, any-how, and she gives me an over-the-shoulder smile. I'm twice her age. So what? And anyhow, so what?

I wrapped the poor thing in a towel, she says as we reach it; it's all I could think to do. Her voice is a hormoned contralto, stirring even in distress. I know you're not supposed to move them, but I couldn't just leave him in the street, you know?

Let's have a look. As if he's a veterinarian paramedic instead of a stalled storyteller, Narrator hunkers with her over the vic-tim and peels back the towel. Big black-bodied, white-nosed/-bibbed/-forepawed tom, sleek of coat, well-fed, unsquished— indeed unmarked, on the upside anyhow, although there's a spot of blood on the towel under his terminally snarled mouth. Doornail dead.

What do you think? she asks tautly. Our faces are a foot apart. Fine estrogenic Mediterranean-looking skin over those aforenoted cheekbones.

Kaput, I'm afraid. I point to the bloodstain. Internal bleed-ing?

She makes a tight-throat sound, strokes the glossy fur. One

of the bottlenecked commuters is actually pounding the outside of his car door through its open window. *Stop* that! she all
but hisses himward. Like a television doctor, Narrator draws
her towel back over the deceased. Then stands. Neither a pet-
lover nor a pet-hater, he finds himself unmoved by the anonymous animal's demise except in the most general tsk-tsk way.
He rather admires Ms. Leotard's more emotional response:
She's still hunkered, reluctant to accept the tomcat's death,
while *he* coldheartedly though warmbloodedly appraises her
excellent neck and shoulders, lithe-muscled legs and compact
butt, imagining them-all in the lotus position, for example.
Back when his children were children, there were important
cats and dogs—but that was decades ago, in another life.

Now she stands, too. The backed-up traffic extends by this
time all the way to the stoplight down the block. Narrator
imagines a TV news camera shooting the scene artsily from
pavement level: dead cat on curb, framed by car bumpers;
mourners standing tall, heads bent, the woman's outfit nicely
echoing the deceased's; church spire in background, pointing
to Cat Heaven.

May she use my phone to call the animal disposal people?

I find momentarily piquant the thought of her in my house,
using my telephone—and then loyally reprove myself: It's *our*
house, *our* telephone, our monogamously happy life. Better get
on to your yoga class, I advise her, before the cops impound
your car. I'll pop the poor guy into a garbage bag and put him
out with my trash.

She gives me a full-faced look of lovely concern. Won't he
get yucky? When's your pickup date?

Not to worry; I'll take care of it. I even retrieve her blood-
spotted towel. Here you go, now.

She smiles, takes the towel, touches my forearm lightly with
her other long-fingered hand, looks wonderfully into my eyes
with her, oh, forget-me-not-colored ones, and thanks me *so*
much.

Not a problem. Have a good life.

So wide and moist a smile. You too!

By when I return with a plastic garbage bag, the gray Honda is gone, and traffic on the arterial has resumed its normal rush-hour flow. The limp cat-corpse, hoisted by the tail for headfirst bagging, is surprisingly heavy. Uncertain of city regulations in the matter, I incorporate the bundle into a larger bag half full of leaves and weeds and put the whole into a tightly lidded trash can at the alley-end of our driveway, trusting that it won't stink noticeably by pickup time, two days hence. Over wine and hors d'oeuvres a short while later on our backyard porch, Narrator narrates to his homecome mate a slightly edited version of the little incident. Cute Meet, we agree, and toast our own of so long past.

One hopes and trusts that she *has* had, is having still as one writes this, a good life, that emotionally and physically endowed human female. The first of three sequels to our encounter is a note from her in the mail shortly thereafter—on garbage-collection day, in fact, when the remains of our path-crossing occasion passed without incident into the municipal trash-stream. Addressed to *Good Samaritan* (with the same presence of mind that had concerned her regarding "our" cat's potential yuckiness, Ms. Leotard had either made mental note of Narrator's street address or—intriguing thought—returned to the scene post-yogaly to register it, perhaps to verify as well that I had done my promised job), it read only *Thank you, kind sir;* and, parenthesized under illegible initials, *(the cat lady).* No name or return address; I liked that. *End of story,* it declared in effect, as if she had sensed . . . and, like me, had dismissed . . .

The stuck story that this non-adventure relieved me from was meant to have been inspired by a season-old item in the daily newspaper of the southwest Florida city where M/M Narrator had spent the winter prior to this dead-cat Baltimore spring. In mangrove marshes well up the Gulf Coast from our rented condominium, a fat and severely autistic ten-year-old boy had somehow "drifted away" from his parents and siblings at a swimming hole, the article reported, into the vast circumambient swamp. Over several following days and nights, while helicopters, air boats, swamp buggies, and foot-slogging rescuers searched in vain, he had floated through the warm, labyrinthine waterways: naked (he seems to have shucked his shorts somewhere along the way), oblivious to snakes and alligators and mosquitoes, buoyed up and insulated from hypothermia by his obesity, entertained by the sight of those overflying machines. Evidently he quenched his thirst as necessary from the freshmarsh water he floated in; no one knows whether and what he ate. On the fourth day he was spotted by a sportfisherman and retrieved—unalarmed and evidently unharmed except for incidental scratches and a bit of sunburn—a full fourteen miles from the swimming hole. His parents had no idea, they declared, how he had managed to drift away unremarked, to a distance beyond ready refinding. They had alerted the authorities, they declared, as soon as they noticed his absence. He wanted to go back, they declared he declared upon his untraumatized restoration themto, to see the helicopters.

Taylor Touchstone, the boy's name was—cross my heart—and in the weeks following that newspaper account, the image of him adrift among the mangroves like a bloated infant Moses among the cattails became a touchstone indeed to Narrator's imagination: a *floating* touchstone, like the lad himself. As now in the matter of The Dead Cat, I made notebook entries on The Floating Boy, whose serene misadventure spoke to me in a way I recognized. In addition to Moses (set adrift to escape Pharaoh's massacre of the Hebrew firstborn, then found and retrieved by his would-be killer's maiden daughter) I noted other mythic heroes floated off or otherwise rescued in early childhood from vengeful or fearful authority: baby Perseus snugged in his sea-chest, baby Oedipus plucked from hillside exposure, the Yavapai-Apache Prophet's baby daughter floated off in her cottonwood canoe—the list is long. More generally, I noted other voyagers from domesticity into dreamish irreality and back—Odysseus, Sindbad (the list is even longer)—and floaters into radical metamorphosis: sperm and ovum, fetuses in the Amniotic Sea—all of us, come to that, floating through our life-stories like unread messages in bottles or galaxies in the void, and into dream-country every mortal night. *Ukiyo-e,* I made note of: the ephemeral "floating world" of Japanese painting—and, by association, those as-if-magical Japanese Crackerjack-favors of Narrator's pre–World War II boyhood: tightly folded little paper somethings that one dropped into a glass of water and waited for the slow exfoliation of into intricate flowers or brightly colored castles.

Just so (I noted), like seeds at sea, do art's gametes float in the fancies of those whose calling it is to fertilize and deliver them. Some sprout/bloom/fruit with the celerity of time-lapse nature films; others eddy like that messaged bottle tossed experimentally into the Pacific by (Japanese) students in August 1985 and found ten years later on a beach north of Honolulu, the Togane High School Earth Science Club members who launched it having long since graduated and set out upon their own life-voyages. And some, to be sure, remain forever flotsam, embryos no longer gestating in the muse's womb but pickled in the formaldehyde of fruitless notes.

So was it with this suspended floating-touchstone tale, displaced now by the dead-cat interlude with its mild but not insignificant erotic aura (if the doorbell-ringer had been male or unattractive, Narrator trusts he would have performed the same neighborly service, but his imagination would have been unengaged). "The cat came back," went a song from my small-town childhood, echoed in my children's childhood by Dr. Seuss's *The Cat in the Hat Comes Back.* Likewise the above-told cat-encounter:

> *. . . the very next day,*
> *The cat came back like he'd never been away.*

Indeed, the species' homing abilities are so acute that they can be notoriously difficult to ditch; thus (together with their knack for literally landing on their feet) the folk-proposition that they have "nine lives." In an afore-alluded-to earlier life-chapter of Narrator's own, when he was about that comely cat-woman's age, his then spouse and he prepared to make their maiden expedition to Europe on the occasion of his first sab-

ters of importance. She was all for having him SPCA'd, to be by them "put to sleep" when and if his adoption-period expired; I held out for turning him loose a sufficient distance from home, in the farm and forest lands round about the state university where I then taught. That would only condemn him to a slow and painful death instead of a quick and painless one, she argued, and cited the Humane Society's support of her position. I didn't deny that possibility—although wily Tuck had demonstrated his hunting skills on enough fieldmice and songbirds, even while well-fed at home, for me to doubt that starvation was a likelihood in his case. My position was simply that in *his* position, if offered those unpleasant alternatives, I would unhesitatingly opt to take my chances in the wild.

What if you disappear him and we lie to the children and then he finds his way back and we have to disappear him again?

Second time we'll tell them the truth. But I'll disappear him good.

Do as you please. But you know what they say about cats.

I did, but, in this instance anyhow, did—not as I pleased, for it was no pleasure, but as I truly thought best: packed the chap into our up-for-sale station wagon one late-October afternoon while the kids were in school; drove him a dozen miles over the Allegheny ridges, through forests of oak and hemlock, mountain laurel and rhododendron; chose a roadside spot where woods bordered corn and alfalfa fields, to give the guy some options (farmhouse and outbuildings just up the lane); grubstaked him with a paper bowl of 9 Lives cat food and another of milk in the dry ditch just off that lightly traveled road; sincerely wished him the best of luck . . . and drove away, returning home by a fairly extensive loop rather than directly. One winces at the memory of that evening's charade of gradually mounting concern, and the next day's and the next (*Where's old Tuck? Still hasn't come home?*); of the children's calling and combing the neighborhood, and one's mate's low-volume after-their-bedtime reproaches (*I keep seeing him* out there *somewhere, meowing for us.*) (*You'd rather see him chloroformed and tossed into the vet's incinerator?*) (*Yes! Yes.*); and of one's multiple burden of guilt,

batical from university teaching. They would pick up a wagen Microbus in Le Havre at autumn's end, camp th therein down to the Mediterranean with their three children, winter somewhere cheap in the south of Spain, tour from campground to campground through western rope in the spring. They arranged to take the kids out of i fourth, and second grades for a semester, rent out their h house in the countryside near the university, and sell their ing car. One problem remained: the family pets. The fish the tropical-fish tank, they explained to the children, would l "returned to the store"—and perhaps some were, although memory haunts Narrator yet of being discovered by his ten-year-old daughter in the act of flushing several down the toilet ("*Da-a-d!*").

The cat was another matter. Survivor of a frisky pair of litter-mates named Nip and Tuck, the latter was a handsome three- or four-year-old, dear to all of us since his kittenhood. Except that his coat was smoky gray instead of black, his markings resembled those of that Baltimore casualty: tidy white bib, nose-blaze, and forepaw-tops. Taking him with us by crowded camperbus through a dozen foreign countries was out of the question, likewise imposing him on friend or neighbor for half a year; and boarding him with a vet for so long a period was beyond our straitened means. Anyhow, "Tucker Jim," as the children called him, was used to roaming freely the rural neighborhood and nearby woods; we couldn't imagine kenneling him for months on end even if we could have afforded to. His similarly free-ranging sister had one day simply disappeared, perhaps struck by a car on her country rambles, perhaps shot for sport by a farm kid or a bored deer hunter (the venue here is the Alleghenies of central Pennsylvania, where schools are closed for the opening day of deer season and prudent parents keep children and pets grounded till the fever abates). The then Narrator and his then partner concurred that sometime in this pre-departure season dear Tuck must likewise officially disappear; as to the covert means, however, they disagreed, as alas they had found themselves lately doing on more and more mat-

shared concern for the animal's welfare and the children's sor-
row, and complex apprehension that Tuck might find his way
home after all.

He didn't. Three dozen autumns later, Narrator still stands
by his course of action in *l'affaire* Tuck and, less firmly, the pa-
rental cover-up. (Would it have been better overall to tell children aged ten, nine, and seven that their parents were in effect
dumping a virtual family-member in order to make the trip?
They would have pleaded with us to spare him and stay home;
we would have been obliged either to override their tearful
protests or to present them with a fairly brutal *fait accompli*.)
Other much-loved cats and dogs and tropical fish followed our
return; other cars, other houses and universities in other states
as those children floated, sometimes bumpily, into and through
their adolescence, and their parents ever more rockily through
the terminal stages of their once-happy union—which ended as
the offspring one by one sprang off to college.

Such things happen.

Did I ever tell them, it occurs to Narrator to wonder now
in these dead-cat notes, what really happened to Tucker Jim?
They're older these days than their parents were in those, and
presumably could handle the Truth. Am I, perhaps, telling
them for the first time here? (How would *you* have handled it,
mes enfants? Those of you especially who've had pets and children and marital vicissitudes of your own?) One wonders, for
that matter, what really *did* happen to the good gray puss: that
prolonged and wretched death foretold by one's ex, the abun-
dantly blessed next life-chapter enjoyed by *her* ex, or something between? Look here, Tuck boy: You still float through
my memory thirty-six years later, now and then. Of how many
cats can that be said?

(*Big deal*, I imagine him meowing: *You* ditched *me, man. Literally.*) (*But hey, it was either that or . . .*) (*Yeah, right: Lucky Tuck.*)

Where are you now, fellow? Where are those freshfaced
children smiling gamely from family photos of *Europe 1962/
63?* The snows and roses of yesteryear, *ubi sunt?* Where, for
that matter, this shorter while later, is that leotarded lass en

route to yogaland, who in a different story might have been a Cute Meet indeed? Where now is the cat-corpse by Narrator bagged and dumped on her lissome behalf; where the briefly stymied talester who dumped it; where that house in that city, and the life-routines involved therewith? One *knows* where, to be sure, in a general way (See So-and-So's *101 Uses for a Dead Cat*, recommends the still-prowling sardonic ghost of Tucker Jim)—but where are they all *exactly*, as one puts this question?

That, too, in some instances at least, deponent can report, and in one case will: We being both of us newly retired from teaching and its attendant life-rhythms—which in our case had for many years involved busily straddling the Chesapeake between our modest "teaching house" in town and a likewise modest weekend/summer retreat on Maryland's Eastern Shore—during a second trial Floridian winter Down There with the other Snowbird pensioners, my wife and I judged our urban base to be no longer earning its keep and arranged its sale to another, younger schoolteaching couple. During that same winter, as it happened, we were recalled north from sunny Geezerville on the unhappy errand of assisting the transfer of an aged parent, Alzheimer's-cursed, into a New Jersey nursing home for the closing chapter of her life-story. We stopped over in Baltimore, to begin preparing the Teaching House for springtime occupancy by its new owners. The two businesses each melancholied the other, sharply reminding us of our own new life-stage and ongoing drift down Time's non-tidal river. And in course of inspecting the house's exterior and grounds—refastening a storm-loosened shutter, picking car-tossed litter from the streetside shrubs—I came upon the second sequel to that dead cat non-adventure: on our front lawn, down near the seldom-used sidewalk of that traffic arterial, just a few dozen car-lengths from its predecessor . . . *another dead cat*, this one so flattened by traffic before being somehow shifted from street to lawn (perhaps by snowplows), and so weathered and decomposed in our absence, that without examining the corpse more closely than I cared to I couldn't judge its sex or even quite its fur-color. Indeed, so virtually merged was it with the winter lawn, it seemed more the imprint or *basso-rilievo* of a cat than the former animal itself.

A calling card, it amused Narrator to imagine, from Ms. Lotus Position, as—who knows?—perhaps the first had been: the 102nd Use, her kinky way of striking up a potential new relationship, starting a new story. *Still there, Mr. Good Samaritan? Still interested?*

No and yes, ma'am'selle: Your Samaritan doesn't live here anymore, practically speaking, but (disinterestedly) interested he remains—not in your shapely self, thanks, but in this all-but-shapeless souvenir, so desiccated past disgust that I let it rest in peace where it lay, reasonably confident that by spring lawn-mowing time it would be recycled altogether.

As in fact it proved to be, except in the recirculating tide of my imagination, where it remained a floating touchstone. Two months later, over late-March wine and cheese at our last cocktail-time in the Teaching House before the movers came to shift us from the city for keeps, Maybe it was old Tuck, Narrator proposed to his wife: It took him thirty-six years, but the cat came back. Tracked me all the way from that life to this one, he did, from Pennsylvania to upstate New York and Massachusetts and then back here to Maryland, and just as he was dragging his weary old bones down the last city block to this house, the Cat Lady nailed him with her cat-gray Honda.

Cute M-E-A-T, replied my patient partner, and we touched wineglasses in a sober toast to Time: It spared him the disappointment of finding you not home.

Tuck would've waited me out, I declared, or tracked me to Florida or the Eastern Shore. What're thirty-six years, after all? It took *me* that long to get from where I was then to where I am now.

Mm-hm. And where is that, exactly?

Good question, beloved sharer of one's life-story and reader of these lines, to whom Narrator responds as to himself: Why, where that is exactly is at the floating point of this pen as it writes *at the floating point of this pen;* it's at the track of your eye as your eye tracks the words *the words* in this final sequel to or reprise of that now-disincarnate cat, in its decomposition composed at last.

(*Sez you*, comes back the ghost of Tucker Jim. For even as there are touchstone images that the narrative use of far from exhausts; that when we believed we had done themwith not only continue to float or prowl upon their uncomprehended way but return, return to tease or spook us, so there are stories, Reader—this themamong—that hopefully substitute the sonority of closure for the thing itself; that may *sound* done but are not; that, like an open parenthesis, without properly ending at least for the cross-fingered present stop.

Fourth
Night

"Friday, September 14, 2001" in Hendecameronland:
morning showers on the Chesapeake and cooler than the days
just prior, but with promise of clearing skies by midday.
Ground Zero still ablaze; National Moment of Silence declared
for noon to mourn Black Tuesday's victims—maybe "only" four
or five thousand after all, instead of six or seven? Narrator uncertain—as Author filled his pen, plugged his ears for a few
hours against Reality, and dispatched Graybard Imagination
off to its daily dalliance with the Muse of Story—whether the
entire nation was to observe that solemn moment as one (at
12 noon Eastern Daylight Time, 11 Central, 10 Mountain,
9 Pacific, 7 Hawaiian, or whatever it's called out there) or suc-
cessively at each time zone's noon. As he saw it, the virtue of si-
multaneity would be its implication of national unity, its trade-
off an East Coast–centricity that must weaken the High Noon
Effect progressively zone by zone across the Union. If it be
argued in the former's favor—but who's arguing?—that the
disaster venues were themselves East Coast and included the
nation's capital, it could be counter-argued—but who's coun-
ter-arguing?—that those targets were struck not at noontime
(EDT), but *seriatim* through the morning hours: at 8:46, 9:03,
et cetera. . . .
     In any case, their house flag having flown half-staff since

9/11, its owners have decided over breakfast (and after tele-phonic consultation with functionaries at their local post office, fire department, and county courthouse) to raise it high after that midday memorial moment, and then at (local) sundown to lower and stow it. Full-staff likewise over the weekend, they reckon, after which they'll maybe leave the pole bare for some days before resuming their custom of flying a different, merely decorative banner each day from their supply. Be it established that this pair are pleased to be American and regard them-selves as normally patriotic; neither, however, goes in for ex-tended national flag-waving, so often exploited by whatever ruling party to suppress dissent. Both inclining, moreover, to the Liberal persuasion and *ipso facto* to distrust of their nation's current right-wing administration, they worry that a country-wide orgy of patriotic display will obscure and serve that ad-ministration's pre-9/11 agenda, just when its prospects had looked happily dim in the divided Congress. No Kyoto Proto-cols against global warming for us Yanks, thanks! No Anti–Ballistic Missile or Anti-Landmine treaties or International Criminal Court for us, either; maybe no more *Roe v. Wade* abor-tion-rights too, while they're at it, and forget about stricter gun-control legislation and protection of our national parks against corporate predation. Instead, zillions for the futile and counter-productive "Star Wars" missile-defense program and for gar-gantuan military buildups; even more tax breaks for the very wealthy; huge budget deficits where there had been healthy surpluses, and never mind national health care, Social Security, the environment, and separation of church and state!

Et cetera: your Knee-Jerk Bleeding-Heart Liberal's off-the-shelf nightmare.

But what has any of that to do with the muses, and with the conceit of a high-mileage Narrative Imagination's "nightly" A.M. get-togethers with one of their number, allegedly the Muse of Story, a.k.a. Wysiwyg? And where was she anyhow, Ms. Wys, this meteorologically pleasant Friday forenoon eve, EDT? Not in her see-through domicile, Graybard observed, nor on its ditto deck—where however were, in token of her recent presence, two glasses of some white wine (a Sancerre, perhaps, by the sharp sip of it, and still chilled), flanked by a brace of clear wax candles, newly lighted by the look of them, in tall Lucite holders. Uncertain which glass was "his," but he being right-handed and they side by side equidistantly himfrom, he sipped from the rightmore themof. Although the sun had set, the sky over the westward tidemarsh still pinkly incandesced. He listened for splashing in the dark water below; heard none; moved ladderward to have a look, but paused en route to put two and two together, so to speak: twin tall candles lit at sundown on a Friday; Somebody-or-Other's affectionate passing mention of a maybe-grandma from Minsk. . . .

Okay, he got it: *Shabbos*-time—or *Shabbat*, whichever. While he knew that the Jewish Sabbath day, like all others on Judaism's calendar, begins at sunset on the day "before" and ends at sunset on the day proper, thereby straddling two solar-calendric dates, he bemused himself with wondering (a) whether once the Sabbath candles were lighted, "today" (i.e., "Friday, 9/14/02") effectively ended and "tomorrow" began; and (b) more vertiginously, whether a hendecameronic "Fourth Night" commencing at "sundown" on what was literally a Friday mid-morning should be said to be happening Today, Tomorrow, or Yesterday?

"*Shabbos* is Ashkenazi," her voice called up from the ladder-base. "*Shabbat*'s Sephardic."

Right, right. So she reads minds, too?

"We Story-Muses read everything." She nimbled up onto the deck—no see-throughs or painted-ons this time, just her shapely, dripping, dainty-furred embodiment—and without bothering to towel dry, picked up the other glass and raised it in greeting. "Sephardic's the official lingo these days, but folks who grew up hearing Ashkenazi still incline to *Shabbos* and *bas mitzvah* and like that. Hi?"

Hi indeed. Did I take the right glass, or was the left glass the right glass?

Flick of dripping hair. "Doesn't matter; it's all Metaphorical anyhow."

He considered this, and her. Alertly pensive, she watched him considering as they sipped the no-doubt-figurative Sancerre.

"You knew this *Shabbos/Shabbat* stuff anyhow. You said your guy and his missus lit a *Yahrzeit* candle on Nine Eleven."

Okay. But we *didn't* know our Miss Wys was raised Ashkenazi. Now we do.

"Your Miss Wys wasn't raised much of anything. She's just an effing metaphor?" Still adrip—but the evening was warm—she plumped herself into a transparent director's chair, sipped again, frowned, twirled her glass-stem between thumb and forefinger, and regarded the dusk that had been shell pink but was now deep rose.

Yet she does candles on Friday nights. . . .

"Forget it. And please stop looking at me like that?"

Not easily managed, Wys. To himself he wondered—wondering too whether she was reading his mind even as he wondered—*What'll it be on Fifth Night? Skinless?* But "So we're done now with the Oldies?" she wanted to know: "And the Non-Ficties too, right? From here on out it's all Reasonably Recent Hundred-Proof Fiction?"

And capital-S Stories to boot, Graybard affirmed, if I'm not mistaken. Reviewing the inventory in those terms, he then remarked between wine-sips that whereas that old bit called *Help!*, back at Invocation-time, had been truly a fiction but not truly a story, Third Night's *Ring* and Fourth's *Dead Cat* had been truly stories but not truly fictions, they being more-true-than-not Reasonably Recent productions both. The intervening item (First Night's *Landscape*) had been truly both Fiction and Story, but by no means Reasonably Recent. Muse willing, the remaining items would all be all three—cross his heart and excuse the *goyishe* expression. Seven to go, is it?

She shrugged her still-wet shoulders. Sipped.

Just trying variations, one might say. Not unlike one's muse?

"Okay." Contemplating her wineglass. "But we have another problem."

What problem? And hey, you're not chilly?

Looking out at the last of the last light: "Not literally." At him then, her left hand twiddling a short lock of her hair: "The problem is that back in that Invocation you said that this Graybard character was on the lookout for a narrative frame for his boss's eleven stories, of which however the lead-off item by your own acknowledgment turned out to be a non-starter. Which leaves ten presumably bona fide stories to be told at the rate of one per night . . . for eleven nights?" For the first time this "evening" she smiled in his direction, a quizzical *Gotcha?*

You thought I hadn't done the numbers? Four told already, seven left to tell, and we've eight nights yet to go, counting this one. . . .

"So unless we want to get in the ring, so to speak, with Signor Boccaccio and call our thing *Decameron Two—*"

No, thanks.

"—or go to the mat with Scheherazade and stretch at least one story over more than one night—"

Sounds more fun than duking it out with Boccaccio. But my guy's stories are all one-nighters.

"Then we'd better drink up." Near-empty glass re-raised: "To Inspiration?"

Plus Imagination.

Clink and drink. What we'd better do, Graybard ventured then, is get our storytelling heads together.

"Heads too? Ready when you are."

So how about Here's to crossing narrative bridges when we come to them?

"You're on. Good *Shabbos*, Geeb."

Good *Shabbos*, Wys. Good *Shabbos* all.

* * * *

After which four-asterisked Interlude, as her clock flashed 9:11 9:14
9:11 9:14—
his muse fresh-showered now and for a change primly nightied
for story-time—Graybard spun out "for her possible delectation" an altogether fictive pairing quite as unlikely as Third
Night's nonfictive dead cat + floating boy. To wit, yet another
story-about-storytelling (and about Talester + Muse), this one
entitled

A DETECTIVE AND A TURTLE

❖

"*PROMISED . . . BUT NEVER . . . SEEN!*" the voice sang out as
from a soundtrack: "*A detective . . . and a turtle!*"

To Charles P. Mason, sleeping protagonist of this story, the
words made sense at the time as a comment on the action in
progress, and the singer's amused, ironically sprightly tone was
appropriate: Dreamer and female companion were in automotive transit from some Point A toward some Point B, and, sure
enough, neither the promised detective nor the expected turtle
was in evidence. When a moment later our man awoke, however—in bed beside his still-snoozing wife in their satisfactory
house at first light on a rainychill March morning in the Appalachian hills of Northern-Neck Virginia—the sense-lending
context evaporated: where the couple had been going and why;
what relevance a "promised" detective and turtle, of all unlikely
duos, had to the situation, whatever that situation was; and
what their no-show portended for the travelers. Who those
travelers *were*, even, Charles couldn't say for sure—Connie and
himself, he presumed, but the woman in that dream-vehicle
had been an unvisualized though palpable and familiar presence—any more than he could recall whether the "soundtrack"
voice had been male or female, solo or chorus, instrumentally
accompanied or *a cappella*. Only the words, cryptic now, distinctly survived his waking, along with their melody: the rising,

fanfarelike first phrase—*Táda tadáda* tá!—and the playfully lilt-ing, rising-then-falling second—*Tadadát-tá da da táda.*

Don't ask Charlie, Reader; he just works here, anyhow tries to, between dreams and waking obligations. Our man is by vocation a storyteller: a dreamer-up and writer-down of con-fected characters, situations, scenes, and actions; one whose specialty, worse luck for him—as quaint a calling nowadays as shoeing horses or fletching arrows—is the all-but-profit-free genre of the Short Story. Ah that he were a novelist in-stead, C.P.M. sometimes can't resist wishing: not mainly, but at least *occasionally* a novelist, preferably of the commercial-blockbusting variety. As a medium of art and entertainment, your Novel still manages some audience share in the age of cable TV and the Internet; not what it was this time last cen-tury, but still much with us. Look at your bustling bookchains, between their calendars and their cappuccini; at your lending libraries, between their videocassette and CD racks and their banked computer terminals. Look at folks on beaches, pool decks, cruise ships, airliners and their associated passenger lounges, where cell phones, earphones, and the not-*quite*-al-mighty Screen compete with, but have yet to supplant alto-gether, the novelistic Page. Lovers of *short stories*, on the other hand—whose ranks a hundred years ago happily included just about everyone who could read at all—have become as small and special a minority as lovers of verse: literary support groups, really, akin to those for the clinically addicted and the terminally ill.

Understand, our chap isn't complaining; he's just acknowl-edging the situation, reporting the news—which in the nature of the case isn't likely to *be* news to whoever's reading these words, and so enough of that. Nobody forced Chuck Mason into this "business," as he wryly calls it: this vocation so far from being a profession (as it genuinely was for many a talester in the years B.T., Before the Tube) that he's been obliged life-long to ply a gainful trade in pursuit of his gainless calling. The late poet/novelist Robert Graves remarked of his commercially successful novel-writing that he was like a man who breeds and sells dogs in order to keep a cat. C. P. Mason, in order to keep his short-tale tabby purring—in order, i.e., to contribute his share to the family economy and still free up enough time to conceive, gestate, and deliver his unmerchandisable little darlings at the rate of three or four per annum into a world almost entirely ignorant of and indifferent to their existence, let alone their welfare—pays the rent mainly by . . . *teaching.*

Yup: teaching. *School*teaching. Drilling the language's grammar and elementary composition into prospective teachers of same at what used to be called a teachers college before such places elevated themselves to branch campuses of the state university system. English for Teachers 101, in short, and the occasional Intro to Literature course: four overloaded sections per semester, decade after decade until quite recently, while Connie worked her butt off as Librarian Et Cetera in a not-bad area private school (always plenty of Et Ceteras in private-school job descriptions) so that their son and daughter could attend the place gratis, the public schools in their neck of the woods being alas less than impressive.

So? Nothing to sniff at in any of that, you considerately protest: certainly not in librarianing, and not in downscale branch-campus Learn-Your-Native-Language-teaching, either. *Somebody* has to do it, and Charles Mason has done it conscientiously, uncynically (despite his tone when speaking of it), and pretty effectively, if less than wholeheartedly, for his entire adult life. With only a State U master's degree himself, he entertained no academic ambitions beyond reasonable job security, a fair salary plus fringe benefits till the kids were on their own, and the liberal holidays and long summer break of the academic calendar in which to pursue his real calling. Wallace Stevens sold insurance; T. S. Eliot worked in a bank; Charles P. Mason, like more poets and short-story writers than not in the USA these days, schoolteaches for a living. Which doesn't mean that he likes to natter on about it, is all we're saying, as we've done here.

So went their decades, zip-zip-zip, of life's short story: in the Masons' case, the twentieth century's latter half, during which, so it seems to them, American decades lost their former flavor. Before their time you had your World War Nineteen Teens, your jazz-age Roaring Twenties, and your swing-band Depression-era Thirties; *in* their time, your World-War-again Nineteen Forties, your crewcut and tailfinned postwar Fifties, your sideburned and bellbottomed druggy Sixties, which rock-and-rolled on for the dozen-plus years from JFK's assassination until the Arab oil embargo and America's retreat from Southeast Asia. After that—from C&C's perspective anyhow, although they'd grant that their children, not to mention any Russian, South African, or Iranian, say, might see things quite otherwise—the decades lose adjectival character. Okay, there's the "me decade" Eighties. But the Seventies? The Nineties?

Comes then Y2K, and while neither The World As We've Known It nor this story-of-a-story ends with the millennium, the Masons find themselves officially senior citizens. Connie takes early retirement from the Blue Ridge Day School and volunteers three days a week at the local branch of the county library—to "keep her hand in," she declares, without getting in her Blue Ridge replacement's hair. Her husband scales down from full- to half- and then to quarter-time professoring: one course per semester wherever his old department finds itself temporarily shorthanded by leaves of absence or higher-than-expected enrollments. He compares himself to those "utility men" on factory assembly lines who learn the operations of ten or a dozen regular assemblers in order to relieve them serially for their coffee breaks, fill in for absentees, and train replacements. Inasmuch as his job has always been not only to teach language-mechanics, composition, and a bit o' lit, but to teach student teachers how to *teach* those subjects—in short, teaching Teaching, and even, to his more "advanced" students, teaching the *teaching* of Teaching—we oughtn't to be surprised if at least now and then a C. P. Mason short story has to do with Stories and their Telling. Much as he prefers to keep Mason the breadwinning pedagogue separate from Mason the narrative wordsmith, those are ineluctably two aspects of the same fellow, and the muses are notorious for taking their procedures as well as their material where they find them, concerning themselves only with the transubstantiation of those P's and M's into art.

Exciting, no? While ethnic hatreds lacerate much of earth's burgeoning human population; while poverty, disease, and malignant governments afflict millions more; while those of us fortunate enough to be spared such miseries busily overconsume our planet's natural resources, despoil the environment, and confront sundry crises of our own at every stage of our so-brief-no-matter-how-long lives, Charles P. Mason scribblescribblescribbles! And while some others blessed with his gifts of language and narrative imagination manage to illuminate in just a few pages some aspect of human experience and to render that illumination memorably into life-enhancing art, our Chuck spins yarns about . . . yarnspinning!

Yes. Now and then, anyhow, and among other subjects. Because, damn it— No, not *because:* He doesn't do it *because* of what I'm about to say, but if questioned on the matter he would most likely assent to the proposition that telling stories is as characteristically human a thing as we humans do, and is thus itself at least as fit a story-subject as another. How goes it, friend? How was your weekend, your childhood, your parents' divorce, your first life-changing love affair, most painful disenchantment, biggest mistake, dying day? And what does it tell us about you that you tell us *those* particular stories about yourself and others—that, moreover, you tell them the way you tell them—rather than telling some other stories some other way? Nay, more: Though neither philosopher nor cognitive scientist himself, Charles P. Mason would, if asked, almost certainly agree with those "neurophilosophers" who hold that consciousness itself has evolved to be essentially a scenario machine; that in order to make sense of and to navigate through the onstreaming flood of signals deluging all our senses, our brains posit the useful fiction of a Self that attends, selects from, organizes, considers, speculates, and acts upon that data—an "I" who invents and edits itself as it goes along, in effect telling stories to itself and to others about who it is. Indeed, an I whose antecedent *is*, finally, nothing other than those on-going, ever-evolving stories, their center of narrative gravity.

Okay? Anyhow, that's what "I" can imagine part-time pro-fessor Mason nodding Yes to if obliged to affirm some rationale for his spending precious autumnal hours writing stories about writing stories, and for his imagining that even a handful of his species-mates might trouble to read them. *That*, however (he'd want quickly to add), has to do at least as much with the quality of the telling as with the matter of the tale, with the How as much as with the What, to the extent that those are separable — and here we join the chap at his "business." Short-story-mak-ing may be less than a profession, but our Charles is nonethe-less a pro: He knows a C. P. Mason story idea when he sees one; just as important, he knows how to make a C. P. Mason story out of that idea. He inclines to the snowflake analogy: Just as nature requires for flake-making, along with sufficient mois-ture and proper temperatures, a speck of atmospheric dust for ice crystals to coalesce upon and grow their intricate hexagonal lattices, so your storymaker needs some *given*—a newspaper item, a mote of gossip or conversation, witnessed behavior or personal experience, even a dream—from which to grow the narrative artifact. And like the dust-grain in the fallen flake, the real-life datum may be all but imperceptible after narrative imagination has wrought it into finished fiction.

"Even a dream," did we hear somebody musing? *Yea, verily*, nods frowning Charles—at his old worktable in his old work-room now, breakfast and morning stretchies done and his wife off on business of her own—*even a dream*. And he sets to work.

Detective. Turtle. Promised. Never seen. His frown manifests not only authorial seriousness (along with bemused puzzle-ment at that odd-coupled brace of nouns and cryptic pair of participles), but the frowner's reluctance to address the subject of Dreams—a reluctance that I quite understand and share. Since the heyday of Freud and Jung, much has been learned by neuropsychologists about the *processes* of dreaming: REM-sleep and the rest. Dream *content*, on the other hand (aside from the obvious general relevance of post-traumatic night-mares), is scarcely regarded these days in scientific circles as significant or interpretable, although beyond those circles one needn't look far to find dream-books, psychic dream-readers, and the age-old like. In no story by C. P. Mason will you find a "dream sequence"—at least not one meant to be taken by the reader as Significant or Portentous—and he is impatient with such sequences in other folks' fiction. Even such famous plot-turning dreams as Raskolnikov's and Svidrigailov's in Dostoyevsky's *Crime and Punishment*, or Gustav Aschenbach's in Thomas Mann's *Death in Venice*, make Charles squirm; appropriate though they doubtless are to the psychology of their respective dreamers and their historical periods, he can accept them only as he accepts the witches in *Macbeth*, the ghost in *Hamlet*, or the interaction of gods and mortals in Homer and Virgil.

That said, he grants of course that our dreams continue to fascinate us, at least mildly, when we recall them at all. So *weird* they can be sometimes! So amusing, distressing, or merely puzzling. And he would regard it as quite legitimate for a C. P. Mason character to manifest such fascination; even for that fascination (as distinct from the dream's "meaning") to drive or turn the story's action. Indeed, now that the subject has his full attention he'll go so far as to allow that even the dream's meaning—i.e., what the dreamer or some fellow character takes it to mean—might legitimately motivate the action, if it's clearly implicit that the author him/herself isn't demanding our assent to the character's interpretation. For no doubt people's real-life behavior is occasionally influenced by their dreams, or by the reported dreams of their spouses, lovers, comrades.

Take for instance a dream Charles dreamed just a few nights prior to the one currently under his muse's consideration: He and Connie were finishing an early-morning bicycle ride on the boardwalk of some seaside resort. Dismounting to rest, they're asked by a pleasant-appearing middle-aged fellow where he might rent a bicycle himself for half an hour or so. Impulsively (and quite uncharacteristically) Charles insists that the stranger borrow *his* bicycle, gratis, and return it at this same spot in half an hour. But then he and Connie are on some residential back street; she needs his help in applying an unguent to her itching rectum (!), but he can't for the life of him puzzle out the unfamiliar instructions on the more-or-less-familiar unguent applicator. He then remembers that in time past a few eggs whipped in a blender have served the purpose just as well (!), but when he makes to prepare that poultice (on a residential sidewalk?) he finds the blender-vessel alarmingly encrusted with *dead ants* (!). Fortunately, a hose is running in a nearby yard; he's able to rinse off the thick layer of insect-corpses and beat the eggs (where's the electrical outlet?), thinking to himself that Con would have a fit if she knew the thing hadn't been scrubbed with hot soapy water. But she *won't* know, and in all this distraction he has lost track of time: The agreed-upon half-hour has long passed; he'll never get his good bike back, which of course he should never have loaned to a total stranger. All the same, he'd better hurry to the boardwalk and hope against hope—but it's dark now; lights are coming on in the houses; he's not even sure which way the boardwalk is, and anyhow he's suddenly wearing nothing but Jockey briefs and undershirt. In one of the illuminated houses he sees several well-dressed women about to sit down to dinner; on their side-board is the blender with the beaten-egg poultice in it! How explain all this to waiting Connie, and where is she now anyhow? At this point the dreamer woke, only mildly and momentarily anxious, but tsking at the nutsiness of dreams. Go to it, Freudians! C. P. Mason won't take seriously either the dream or your reading of it, but he won't deny that a less skeptical character might, and consequentially so.

An unusual dream, in short, like any other unusual impingement upon or turn of events in the protagonist's life-situation, may become the vehicle of dramatic action, the dust mote that precipitates a story. Precipitates it out of what? I've used the term "life-situation"; Charles himself, like some other teachers of literature, prefers to call it the Ground Situation (mentally capitalizing because both term and concept sound Germanic to

him): a state of affairs pre-existent to the story's present action and possessed of some dramatic *potential,* a voltage of which the characters themselves may be scarcely aware; a situation ripe (excuse his shifting metaphor; the guy is concentrating just now, not editing) for precipitation. Given such a . . . *Grundlage?*
. . . the protagonist's dreaming of, for example, a promised-but-never-seen detective and turtle (!)—more exactly, his subsequent waking puzzled fascination with that dream—could conceivably trigger a story. Otherwise, it's as dramaturgically inconsequential as would be his seeing a goldfinch flit across the road, or hearing a distant siren, or farting after a heavy meal (any one of which, to be sure, in just the right circumstances . . .).

So, then: What's the Ground Situation here? The as-yet-unnamed because as-yet-unimagined Protagonist's, we mean, of this yet-to-be-dreamed-up C. P. Mason short story? Since its author *has* no Protagonist on the payroll yet, and inasmuch as that chirpy dream was in fact his own, not some made-up Character's, he now directs his muse's attention experimentally to his own "life-situation," to see what in it might be said to have the makings of a proper *Grundlage,* ready for storyflake-making. Semi-retired sixty-plus East Coast American White Anglo-Saxon (lapsed-)Protestant branch-campus English prof and modestly successful practitioner of regrettably now-marginal art form (his output sooner or later finds a home in some small lit-mag or other and very occasionally in what remains of the American large-circulation-magazine market, and has been collected into two volumes by two different "small presses") has been more than contentedly married for some forty years to coeval and co-ethnic now-retired librarian. One half-assed reciprocal infidelity in their long-distant past, so entirely healed over that if anything chances to remind them of that reckless episode (as this life-summary may do) they merely roll their eyes at their then selves. Two grown children: daughter Carla, thirty-seven, a prospering estate-and-trust lawyer down in Richmond, divorced, childless, and evidently content to remain so; son Mark, thirty-three, a rising associate professor of marine biology at San Diego State, married, father of three-year-old only-grandchild Juanita (Mark's wife's Hispanic), whose grandparents wish she lived three thousand miles closer. Both elder Masons enjoy prevailingly good health, as do their offspring; their six decades have thus far spared them serious disease, serious accident, untimely death of loved ones, fire and flood and suchlike natural disasters, war and criminal depredation and suchlike man-made ones. Their quite comfortable suburban house is "free and clear"; their pensions, savings, modest investments, and insurance coverages are adequate to their needs; their country is (as of this writing) strong, prosperous, and at peace. Even Carla's divorce was amicable, as such things go: Her public-defender and civil-rights-activist husband discovered or decided that he was gay, or more gay than not, and that was that; the pair remain on cordial terms.

Indeed, so equable and agon-free has been the senior Masons' life thus far that it lacks the makings of a story. The only thing Charles sees in it, now that he's looking, that might amount to a voltaged Ground Situation is their good fortune itself: their recognition (his, anyhow; he has spared Connie this morbid *aperçu*) that the law of averages hangs over them like Damocles's sword. No one escapes death, and next to none are spared prior affliction: Sooner or later—and at their present age it can't be *much* later—disease, disability, and dying will overtake one of them, leaving the other searingly bereft and burdened until likewise overtaken. In some humors Charles can't help grimly envying a couple from their neighborhood, happily married retired professionals like themselves, who in the summer of 1996 were en route to revisit Paris aboard TWA Flight 800 when their 747 exploded over the Atlantic, killing all hands more or less instantly. The only improvements on that scenario that Charles can imagine (when he's in this mood) would be to make their quietus ten healthy years farther down the road instead of three or four, and in circumstances such that they not only "never knew what hit them" but never even knew they'd been hit.

In that case, though, he acknowledges, there'd still be no

Story—not that that matters to our author vis-à-vis himself and Connie, but it obviously won't do for *our* story, Charles's story, the C. P. Mason story-not-yet-in-progress. The "And then one day" that typically introduces the Dramatic Vehicle to generate a story from the Ground Situation cannot likely be "And then one day he died" (although one can point to some odd, beyond-the-grave narrative exceptions). Whereas it might very well be something like "And then one day he woke from an amusingly obscure dream of a detective and a turtle, *promised but never seen*"—if there were a proper Ground Situation. He can imagine, e.g., a character not unlike himself determinedly, even obsessively, analyzing that so-brief nonsense dream (along with his uncharacteristically sustained fascination with it) and in the process . . . what? Alienating his family, friends, and colleagues, perhaps, who are initially amused, then off-put, and finally concerned that old Chuck has gone bonkers? Or actually *going* bonkers, perhaps, to the extent of becoming convinced that the voice in the dream was God's, addressing him personally (Charles remembers J. L. Borges's observation, in *The Secret Miracle*, that according to Rabbi Maimonides "the words of a dream, when they are clear and distinct and one cannot see who spoke them, are holy") and in effect directing him to search out the promised but thus far unfound Detective and Turtle? Which would amount, would it not, to his becoming an unlicensed though divinely appointed detective of sorts himself, pursuing—like Achilles, was it, in Somebody-or-Other's famous paradox?—a turtle. Perhaps the Turtle of Truth? The Turtle of Story? But wait: Achilles's quarry was a tortoise, not a turtle; does Charles remember the zoological distinction?

He thinks so (turtle : water :: tortoise : land), but clicks the terms up anyhow in his online dictionary, wondering as he does, *Is this how Chekhov went about his art? Has any storyteller from Homer to Hemingway, Poe to Pasternak, attempted to fabricate a narrative something out of so nearly nothing?* Not likely (though not impossibly, either), and no matter. Our talester is none of those: He's Charles the Mason, surveying the materials at hand with a professional eye and a skilled artisan's imagination, to see whether there might be in them not an *Iliad* or a *Dr. Zhivago* but a C. P. Mason short story. If there be no *weather* in it, say (as there's been next to none so far in this), or pungent sense of place, eloquent details, memorable characters, grand passions, and high drama, then *tant pis:* It'll at least be architecturally complete, with a proper story's incremental raising of stakes, climactic even if quiet "turn," and consequential dénouement.

Or else it won't be, in which case it won't get told.

His mention of Edgar Allan Poe—*somebody's* mention of that nineteenth-century East Coast American WASP inventor of the analytical detective story—prompts the reflection that most folks' experience of detectives is happily limited to printed fiction, films, and television dramas. Charles himself has, to the best of his knowledge, never laid eyes on a real-life detective, although in addition to police detectives even a quite small city's telephone directory will list one or two private investigative agencies—employed chiefly by disgruntled spouses and their lawyers, Charles imagines, to get the goods on errant mates in connection with divorce suits. Thus actual detectives *have* in fact been, in that sense and by Charles P. Mason, "never seen"—appropriately enough, he supposes, given the undercover aura of their business. But none was ever "promised," either, and so there goes that.

And turtles? (His dictionary modifies Charles's rough distinction by defining *tortoise* as "any of various terrestrial turtles.") Turtles are another story, he would acknowledge with a small smile: live and altogether visible baby turtles in Carla's and Mark's childhood terraria; box turtles on rural roads and occasionally in suburban yards, including the Masons' own; the odd snapper spotted in pond or creek; even large sea turtles admired in city aquaria or while snorkeling warm-water reefs off vacation resorts. Seen too on public-television nature shows and featured prominently—their terrestrial subset, anyhow— in folktale and fable: Aesop's Hare and Tortoise; Zeno's aforementioned paradox (he now remembers) of Achilles and the tortoise; the four turtles in Hindu cosmology upon whose chelonian carapaces stands the great elephant who in turn supports the earth (those last, he grants, like Poe's M. Dupin and Doyle's Sherlock Holmes, are "seeable" by the mind's eye only). Charles remarks further that turtles tend to withdraw from "sight" into their shells when approached or otherwise alarmed, as (with some stretching) the sense of a dream might be said to do upon investigation. . . . But "promised"? Quite possibly he and Connie had "promised" one or both of the kids those pet turtles before acquiring same; if so, however, the promise had most certainly been kept, the turtle-tykes delivered to the Mason-tykes and by all hands appreciatively "seen." So there goes *that.*

In short, while your typical character-in-the-street will likely have had more direct dealings with turtles than with detectives, neither can properly be said to be *never* seen, only seldom seen "live." And surely (with the minor sort of exception above-noted) neither was *promised:* Promised by whom? To whom? For what?

Which leaves? Setting aside the dream-singer's D & T, Charles can think of any number of things Promised but Never (or Not Yet) Seen, from U.S. congressional action on a political-campaign-finance reform bill to the Christian Messiah's Second Coming and the Jewish Messiah's First. The Masons' own revisit to Paris/London/Rome, which they've been promising themselves for the past ten years but can't seem to get around to, what with Connie's involvement in her volunteer work and Charles's in his scribblescribblescribbling. The over-committed housepainter who swore he'd get their exterior wood-work done before summer but more often than not doesn't even get around to answering their telephoned Where-are-yous. Peace on earth. The significance and/or relevance of the dream-song upon which short-story-writer C. P. Mason has now expended more than half a morning's professional attention and accumulated pages of notes without coming noticeably closer either to understanding it or to making fictive use of it—two quite separable matters, whereof the former is not always prerequisite to the latter.

So? So (he walks to the kitchen, pausing en route at the

downstairs lavatory to pee; refills his thermal coffee-mug; returns to his workroom; considers briefly whether to set this silly business aside and leaf through his notebook for some more promising bit toward which to direct his muse's energies. But there is none, he's fairly certain; inspiration doesn't come to him as readily or frequently as in decades past; anyhow, the detective/turtle bit, if only *faute de mieux*, won't let go [he recalls—and makes written note of, to keep his pen moving—the folk-belief that when a turtle bites, it will hold on until either thunder or nightfall, he forgets which], and he's really rather persuaded now—perhaps also *faute de mieux*, but who cares?— that *there's a C. P. Mason story hiding here somewhere*): Aging protagonist's only Ground Situation is that he *has* no apparent Ground Situation, other than his relatively misery-free life-history thus far versus the law of averages; *and then one day*—by dawn's early light, actually—he awakes from an untroubling but distinct and perplexing dream of . . .

Car radio, it suddenly occurs to him. There is less music in the Masons' house than in time past, when they routinely played their jazz or Caribbean LPs (and later their audiocassettes, followed by their compact discs) through cocktails and dinner prep, then quiet classical while they ate, and sometimes rock or disco to dance to when they felt frisky at evening's end. More and more in recent years they've found the sound bothersome; have progressively reduced the volume toward inaudibility, and often as not nowadays prefer to dine without background music. It is when traveling by car that they most often now punch up the local classical, jazz, or pop stations; and in that dream, Protagonist and Mate were "in transit"; and it is of course recorded music that most commonly presents us with invisible vocalists. So maybe the detective-and-turtle voice wasn't God's, but merely some pop singer's on the easy-listening station?

Nah: It was more *ubiquitous* than that; more "out there" than the sound of their aging Toyota's front-and-rear loudspeakers—and thus more interesting, at least potentially. Anyhow (Charles reminds himself), the stuff of dreams needs no such homely accounting for, although the impulse to rationalize the intriguingly mysterious he would grant to be human and honorable. There may well be, at least theoretically, some neurological or even psychological explanation of why C. P. Mason's dreaming brain came up this morning with an unlocatable voice singing of a reneged-upon detective and turtle rather than with, say, a recklessly loaned bicycle and an ant-encrusted blender for the curbside preparation of rectal poultices. But at such explanations the Muse of Story shrugs her Parnassian shoulders—unless, valid or not, they prompt some dramaturgically significant action on the protagonist's part.

Such as? Oh, well . . . such as his near-overwhelmment, at this point in this narrative, by a hot mix of unsortable emotions at the sudden vivid recollection (prompted by that nutsy rectal-poultice business above) of his adulterous anal intercourse thirty-plus years ago with an adult female former student of his at the teachers college: one DeeDee Francis, a grown-up Sixties Flower Child, exotic in that academic venue, to whose hippie husband her vagina was inviolably pledged but not her other orifices, which she offered with Hubby's blessing in their psychedelically painted Chevy wagon to such of her admirers as were also her admirees, and she had really really grooved on Charles's Introduction to the Teaching of Poetry course the year before. Dear down-to-earth, high-as-a-kite DeeDee, with her "sidelong pickerel smile" (as poet Theodore Roethke phrased it in the course's text), smiled fetchingly overshoulder in mid-buttfuck; where was she now, and doing what with whom? No matter: That early, uncharacteristic infidelity (and Connie's tearfully furious retaliation therefor with one of Charles's departmental colleagues upon his confessing it to her; such were the High Nineteen Sixties, Reader, even in the boondocks of Academe) had most certainly been a pain in their marital backside, poulticed only by the passing of many a semester. And it could quite imaginably become so again if, say, a reawakened interest in or nostalgia for it came to reflect, perhaps even to *cause*, some growing, till-now-unrecognized dissatisfaction with his mate, his marriage, his life. . . .

Nonsense! our man protests (too strongly?). How could he even hypothesize such a thing? he asks himself (like a wily psychoanalyst?).

Et cetera: *There's* a Ground Situation for you!

But not for C. P. Mason, who declines even to consider what "dramaturgically significant action" he (he means his protagonist-character) might take in consequence of this dream-cued recollection/revelation. With relief he offers himself and us an alternative Such As, altogether safer though less voltaged: Small-time academic and middlingly successful practitioner of fading literary genre, now in the twilight of his career and of its, has become accustomed to and patient with occasional recalcitrance on his muse's part, as with other exactions of relentless aging. *But then one day,* seasoned professional that he is — after throwing several mornings' worth of good imaginative money after bad in his effort to discover the C. P. Mason short story that he feels strongly to be "hypertexted" behind the imagery of a certain C. P. Mason dream-fragment — he confronts not only the growing likelihood that there's no story there after all (Who cares, finally, about that?), but the vertiginous possibility that the cupboard is bare, the well gone dry for keeps. For would the C. P. Mason of even five years ago, not to say twenty or thirty years ago, have spent a whole week's work-time poking and puttering at the memory of a silly dream if his notebooks burgeoned, as once upon a time they did, with other story-seeds awaiting his consideration and cultivation? Anton Chekhov is said to have remarked, no doubt ironically, that if a story took him longer than an afternoon to write, it probably wasn't worth his time. No Chekhov, Charles has never cared how long a C. P. Mason story remains in the works, as long as it's working. In better days, however (which is to say, right up to page one of this story), he would have reshelved so unforthcoming a "bit" as this detective-and-turtle dream to germinate while he developed some other, less resistant item from his backlog.

Such as? There's the rub: There *is* no backlog of notebook entries awaiting his authorial attention; nor has there been, for longer than it's comfortable for Charles to remember. That's why, when he awoke this morning with that dumdum dreamsong still reverberating in his head, he fetched it expectantly from bed through breakfast-with-Connie to his workroom, to see what might be made of it.

Nothing. Nada. Niente. Nichts. Nichivo. He has that notebook open now, just checking: the original brown looseleaf pocket notebook in which since apprenticehood he has accumulated trial offerings to his muse. Its most recent entry is the opening sentence of this story. The one before it—scratched through after its deployment, like all the entries before *it*—is dated a semester earlier: the touchstone of his most recently completed C. P. Masonry, long since out of the shop and making its slow rounds of likely periodicals. The two stories preceding that one had likewise been worked up from prior-year inspirations, now duly crossed out: three withdrawals from an account into which he has made no new deposits since, its balance zero. . . .

Until now. Impulsively—perhaps only for the gratification of seeing two uncanceled entries instead of one—below the detective-and-turtle nonsense he copies that phrase from Roethke's *Elegy for Jane*, his student killed in a fall from her horse: *a sidelong pickerel smile*. The poet's grief is pure ("I, with no rights in this matter," the poem concludes: "Neither father nor lover"); Charles's memory of *his* long-ago (ex-)student's similar smile is not, although from so distant a remove and in so autumnal a humor as his current one, it has its own innocence. The movement of his pen on paper is, as always, agreeable. It occurs to him, regarding the two notebook entries thus juxtaposed, to imagine that smile—DeeDee Francis's over-the-shoulder, go-to-it-big-boy smile in the back of that old station wagon—as his muse's. His protracted search for usable significance in that dream—his detective-work upon it, one might say—has proceeded slowly and deliberately (and thus far futilely): at tortoise-speed, one might say. And yet, quite like DeeDee's *in flagrante delicto*, Ms. Muse's sidelong pickerel smile has at once encouraged him to go to it, reassured him that what they are about is pleasurable, anyhow not unpleasant, for her as well as for him, and suggested tantalizingly that she's on to something—something amusing to herself—that he is not. In DeeDee's case (so he learned after the subsequent debacle), that Something had been or had at least included the datum that yet another of her admired admirers, Charles's then-colleague Fred Sullivan, had confided to her in that same vehicular venue his hankering to do with Connie Mason what he was just then doing with her. As subsequently, Q.E.D., the fellow did—for such were the lusty-among-other-things High Sixties.

And Mademoiselle Muse? What piquant infobit might *she* be savoring as they two go to it? Perhaps that, hump her as he might, she has conceived her last by him, whether that last be this misbegotten detective-and-turtle story or, more likely (for whoever made babies *this* way?), the comparatively bona fide item composed just before it, finished months ago and now in the mails with its self-addressed stamped return envelope. Perhaps, on the contrary, that Charles's current fallow season is no more than a rather-longer-than-usual downtime, to be followed by fruitful intercourse again before his inevitable *finis*. Or perhaps that that *finis* is very much closer than he supposes; that it will come—via ruptured aneurysm or out-of-the-blue fatal accident or who knows how—within the hour of his putting the closing period to what after all (so I choose to imagine her mercifully or mischievously granting, in honor of their long and not-unproductive connection) will turn out to be a by-hook-or-by-crook C. P. Mason short story, obscurely promised and finally, if obliquely, seen: one having to do, more or less and by golly, with a detective and a turtle.

Fifth
Night

Meanwhile, back at the ranch—
in this case, the modest rural Eisenhower-era "ranch house"
where all but the earliest of these several stories was Originally
Authored—their common perpetrator finished first-drafting
"Fourth Night," with its quadruply asterisked Interlude leading to that detective-and-turtle tale, and called it a morning.
Capped pen. Unplugged ears. Shut down computer after
checking e-mail. And once again shook his authorial head at
the luxurious *irrelevance* of such yarning: Caribbean getaways
and winter retreats! Lost and found wedding rings (he kissed
his treasured own) and images neither exhausted nor exor-
cised by their narrative employment! Ground Situations, Dramatic Vehicles, and stymied minor-league storytellers like that
Charles P. Mason fellow! All these while one's outraged nation
imperiously mounts a massive military campaign against an
elusive, ubiquitous enemy's encavements in a destitute country
already made miserable by religious zealots, feuding local war-
lords, and contending foreign powers; when on any day or
night of this projected Hendecameron the Al Qaeda terrorists
might strike again, worse than before. . . .

Yes, yes, he knows: Boccaccio, Scheherazade, and company;
the relevance of Irrelevance. But as he and his mate went about
their afternoon routines (as did the neighbors mowing lawns

and tending mid-September gardens, the commercial and
amateur crabbers working the nearby creek, the sailors and
kayakers and sport-fisherfolk out on the river and bay beyond),
and then made and enjoyed their Friday-evening meal, and
then did an hour's pleasure-reading and miscellaneous correspondence, and then wound up their own Fourth-Night-since-
Black-Tuesday with TV newscasts of their like-him-or-not
President doing his presumable best to manage the crisis, and
then retired to however-many-asterisked an Eleven-Thou-
sandth-Plus Night of their own, he could not but . . . well . . .
shake his Original Authorial head at what its Narrative Imagination and that imagination's unorthodox Muse were up to.

However, or perhaps therefore,
on the following morning—Saturday, September 15—he felt
impelled deskward, as was not his weekend custom unless some
weekday had been pre-empted from sentence-making: Even
Boccaccio's plague-fleeing young Florentines, one remembers,
took their weekends off from storytelling. Perhaps he feared
(anyhow allowed the possibility) that unless he kept "Graybard"
and "Wysiwyg" at their quasi-erotic narrative enterprise, that
enterprise might be swamped, drowned out, overwhelmed by
circumambient, anaphrodisiac Reality?

Whatever the case, as *was* his workaday custom he began
by refilling his fountain pen and reviewing The Story Thus Far
of these stories thus far, in particular that most recent, "Fourth
Night" installment of its narrative frame, emending and editing as he went along, right up through the authorial head-shaking just recounted. Aided by that momentum, he launched into
the section subtitled *However, or perhaps therefore,* and when—
at, shall we say, 9:11 A.M. or thereabouts?—he found himself
writing the words *He dispatched his emissary Graybard from
Scriptorium to Imaginarium,* he dispatched his emissary Graybard from Scriptorium to Imaginarium, where, not at all surprisingly, the room-lights glowed as the twilight faded, and the
clear-cased bedside digital clock flashed alternately *9:11 9:15
9:11 9:15.*

"So you're getting nudgy about our project," Ms. Wys informed that emissary before he her. All business this "evening," his collaborator was awaiting him not on her deck, much less in the creek below, but seated in the now-bright bed/sitting room, wearing faded cutoff jeans, blue shortsleeve sweatshirt, and worn leather deck moccasins. Clipboard on lap. Ballpoint pen in one hand, wineglass in other. No sign of her having swum except still-damp-looking nutmeggish hair.

Maybe.

"Me too. Probably not for the same reasons." Ballpointing at second filled wineglass beside bottle of Napa Valley sauvignon blanc on low table between chairs: "Drink up, and let's hear it."

Yes. Well. Sip. Smiling and nodding herward: Nice.

"Something non-kinky for a change. Glad you approve." Still holding pen, wineglass, and now clipboard as well, she spread her arms to display her simple outfit. "No surprises underneath, either: just plain old cotton undies."

Actually, he was embarrassed to say, he meant the wine, although her get-up—get-down, whatever—was nice too, he supposed. Refreshing.

"*Crisp structure and complex finish, with accents of blackberry and pear,* as the wine freaks say? How come they never ever mention *grapes?* So what's your problem?"

Not mine, actually: *his.* It's our playing Scheherazade and Boccaccio while a War of Civilizations might be brewing. . . .

For the first time that evening, she smiled at him. "All the more reason to get to it! Sip up, Geeb; we've got work to do."

Mm. And what might *your* problem be, Wys-o'-my-heart?

Frowning: "O'-your-heart?"

Just a friendly expression.

Has it been mentioned, Reader, that our nymph's bright eyes are a lustrous walnut brown? They are that, and she considered her visitor intently themwith for a moment before consulting her clipboard and quoting, from Fourth Night's detective-and-turtle tale, "*The Muse of Story shrugs her Parnassian shoulders*—at the Relevance issue, for one thing. We've *dealt* with that already. Tell your guy to forget it."

Consider him told. And shapely shoulders they are, Wys, even sweatshirted.

"*Inspiring*, maybe?"

Remains to be seen.

"So sip and see."

He sipped. What *is* Miz Muse's problem, then? Our storytelling?

Shake of head: Not for her to complain about *that*, it being she who allegedly inspires these tellings. No: What was beginning to pall on her, frankly, was neither the capital-I Irrelevance of these tales nor the caliber of their telling, but some of the material—with respect whereto she found herself moved to propose a Third Ultimatum before tonight's Narrative Empowerment kicked in.

There've been two already?

"No more Oldies," she reminded him; "no more Not-Quite-Ficties."

So what's it this time? He sipped. No more Sidelong Pickerel Smiles?

"SPSes can stay." Indeed, she here treated him to one that would have recharged even "Charles P. Mason's" narrative batteries. "Ultimatum Three is no more asterisks unless you promise no more Stories About Storytellers, okay? Especially stuck ones! No more yakking about Ground Situations and Dramatic Vehicles! *Autumnality* I can deal with—I've maybe got a thing about older guys? More-or-Less-Totally-Innocent-Marital-Guilt riffs we'll take case by case. But if you and I are going to go on with this Hendecameronic closet-clearing, there'll be no more Narrative Impotence, agreed? Enough limp-dickery already!"

Graybard's responding smile was neither sidelong nor, he'd bet, pickerelish of aspect, but front-on. He tabled his wineglass, took the liberty of tabling hers as well, and would have led *her* this time forthwith to five-starred Metaphoric Congress on her shimmering waterbed, had she not instead drawn the pair of them directly from transparent chairs to ditto carpet. Thereupon, at her pleased insistence, their Fifth Night communion was effected *a tergo:* Muse on all fours and Imagination astern, like C. P. Mason and his hippie former student in that psychedelic Chevrolet as aforenarrated—the better, in this present case, for the principals to transact their pleasurable business fully clothed, he merely unzipping before and she, *mirabile dictu,* behind (special zipper in crotch of shorts despite her promise of No Surprises, and "plain old cotton undies" slit parenthetically for his convenience). . . .

* * * * *

"All to the end,"
she declared, smiling sidelong-pickerelly back at him from amid those asterisks, "of one's *getting* . . . as nearly as can be *managed* . . . what one *sees. Unh!* Ain't . . . inspi*ration . . . fun?"*

Ah. Ah. Wysiwyg!

Whereafter, in her unpredictable way, she showered without bothering to undress. Wrapped her dripping self in a hooded white terry robe, stretched out not quite facedown upon her lighted bed, and with another (eyes-closed) S. P. Smile, bade him pay for their joint pleasure with the bedtime story *du soir.*

"Entitled?"

THE REST OF YOUR LIFE

❖

"SOUNDS LIKE THE BEGINNING OF A STORY" was George Fischer's busy wife's opinion, and her husband quite agreed, although just *what* story remained to be seen.

What had happened, he'd told her over breakfast, was that the calendar function on their home-office computer appeared to have died. When George called up the word processor's stationery format, for example, the date automatically supplied under his "business" letterhead read *August 27, 1956*. Likewise on their other letterhead formats, their e-mail transmissions and receptions—anything on which the machine routinely noted month, day, and year. George had first remarked the error while catching up on personal and business correspondence the evening before this breakfast-time report (the date of which, by weak coincidence, happened to be *July 27, 1996*, just one month short of the fortieth anniversary of that letterhead date). Wondering mildly how many items he might have dispatched under that odd, out-of-date heading—for as Julia would now and then remind him, he had become less detail-attentive and generally more forgetful than he once was—he made the correction both on the correspondence in hand and on the computer's clock/calendar control . . . and then forgot to mention the matter when his wife came home from her Friday-night aerobics group. Up at first light next morning, as usual in recent years, he let the "working girl" sleep on (her weekend pleasure) while he fetched in the newspaper, scanned its headlines over coffee—OLYMPIC BOMB INVESTIGATION CONTINUES, TWA 800 CRASH CAUSE STILL UNKNOWN—set out their daily vitamins and other pills and the fixings of the breakfast that they would presently make together, then holed up in his office to check for e-mail and do a bit of deskwork until she was up and about. Again, he noticed, the date came up August 27, 1956. He corrected it and experimentally restarted the machine.

August 27, 1956. "Must be a dead battery," he opined over their Saturday-morning omelet.

Looking up from the paper's Business section: "Desktop computers have batteries?"

Some sort of little battery, George believed he remembered, to keep the clock going when the thing's shut down. Maybe to keep certain memory-functions intact between start-ups, although he hadn't noticed any other problems thus far. Not his line; he would check the user's manual.

"How come it doesn't default— Is that the right word?"

"Default, yes." Words *were* his line.

"How come it doesn't default to the last date you set it to, or come up with a different wrong date each time? Why always August Whatever, Nineteen Whenever?"

"Twenty-seven, Fifty-six. Good question, but not one that I could answer."

Encouragingly: "Sounds like the beginning of a story."

Yes, well. They finished breakfast, did their daily calisthenics together (hers more vigorous than his, as she was ever the family jock), refilled their coffee mugs, and addressed their separate Saturday chores and amusements: for Julia, first her round-robin tennis group, then fresh-veggie shopping at the village farmers' market, then housework and gardening, interspersed with laps in their backyard pool; for George, a bit of bookkeeping at the desk and then odd jobs about the house and grounds, maybe a bit of afternoon crabbing in the tidal cove that fronts their property. Then dinner *à deux* and their usual evening routine: a bit of reading, a bit of television, maybe an e-mail to one of their off-sprung offspring, maybe even a few recorder-piano duets, although the couple make music together these days less frequently than they used to. Then to bed, seldom later than half past ten.

Then the Sunday. Then a new week.

They had done all right, these two; rather well, actually. Classmates and college sweethearts at the state university, they'd married on their joint commencement day—shortly after World War II, when we Americans wed younger than nowadays—and promptly thereafter did their bit for the postwar Baby Boom, turning out three healthy youngsters in five years. George had majored in journalism, Julia in education, and although she'd graduated summa cum laude while he had simply graduated, after the manner of the time she had set her professional credentials mostly aside to do the Mommy track while Daddy earned their living. He had duly done that, too: first at a little New England weekly, where he'd learned what college hadn't taught him about newspapering; then at an upstate New York daily; then at a major midwestern daily, where on the strength of a Nieman Fellowship year at Harvard (the young American journalist's next-best thing to a Pulitzer Prize) he had switched from the Metro desk to Features; then at the Sunday magazine of Our Nation's Capital's leading rag—from which, as of his sixty-fifth birthday this time last year, he'd retired as associate editor to try his hand at freelancing. Over those busy decades, as their nestlings fledged and one by one took wing, Julia had moved from subbing in their sundry schools to part-time academic counseling—whatever could be shifted with George's "career moves" and expanded with the kids' independence—thence to supervisoring in the county school system, and most recently, since the couple's move from city to country, to full-timing as Director of Information Services at a small local college. No journalist or educator expects to get rich, especially with three college tuitions to pay; but the Fischers had husbanded (and wifed) their resources, invested their savings prudently along with modest inheritances from their late parents, and watched those investments grow through the prosperous American decades that raised the Dow Jones from about 600 to nearly 6,000. Anon they had sold their suburban-D.C. house at a substantial profit and retired—half of them, anyhow—to five handsomely wooded acres on the high banks of a cove off the Potomac's Virginia shore, complete with swimming pool, goose-hunting blind, guest wing for the kids and grandkids, His and Hers in the two-car garage, and a brace of motorboats at the pier: one little, for crabbing and such, the other not so little, for serious angling with old buddies from the *Post*. Enough pension, dividend, and Social Security income to keep the show going even without what George scored for the occasional column or magazine piece, not to mention Julia's quite-good salary. Her own woman at last, as she liked to tease, *she* meant to keep on full-timing until they threw her out: the Grandma Moses of information service directors.

What's more, this prevailing good fortune, not entirely a matter of luck, applied to their physical and marital health as well. Both had survived their share of setbacks and even the rare knockdown, but in their mid-sixties they were still mentally, physically, and maritally intact, their midlife crises safely behind them and late-life ones yet to come, parents in the grave and grown-up children scattered about the republic with kids and midlife crises of their own. On balance, a much-blessed life indeed.

And by no means over! Quite apart from the famously increasing longevity of us First-Worlders, George and Julia had their parents' genes going for them, which had carried that foursome in not-bad health right up to bye-bye time in their late eighties and early nineties. Barring accident, the couple had an odds-on chance of twenty-plus years ahead—longer than their teenage grandkids had walked the earth.

"Time enough to make a few more career moves of my own," Julia teased whenever her husband spoke of this.

August 27, 1956. George recorrected the date, went on with his work, with the weekend, with their life; took the Macintosh in on Monday for rebatterying or whatever and made shift meanwhile with Julia's new laptop and his trusty old Hermes manual typewriter—stored in their attic ever since personal computers came online—until the patient was cured and discharged. The problem was, in fact, a dead logic-board battery, the serviceperson presently informed him, and then tech-talked over George's head for a bit about CMOS and BIOS circuitry. The chap couldn't explain, however, why the date-function defaulted consistently to August 27, 1956, rather than to the date of the machine's assembly, say (no earlier than 1993), or of the manufacture of its logic board. Did electronic data-processors in any form, not to mention PCs and Macintoshes, even exist on August 27, 1956?

Truth to tell, George Fischer doesn't have all that much to do at his desk these days, and so "making shift" was no big deal. Indeed, while both Julia and Mac were out of the house he turned his fascination with that presumably arbitrary but spookily insistent date into a bit of a project. Veteran journalists do not incline to superstition; a healthy skepticism, to put it mildly, goes with the territory. But why August? Why the 27th? Why 1956? Was something trying to tell him something?

Out of professional habit he checked the nearest references to hand, especially the historical-events chronology in his much-thumbed *World Almanac*. In 1956, it reminded him, we were halfway through what the almanac called "The American Decade." Dwight Eisenhower was about to be landslided into his second presidential term; Nikita Khrushchev was de-Stalinizing the USSR; Israel, Britain, and France were about to snatch back the Suez Canal from Egypt, which had nationalized it when we-all declined to finance President Nasser's Aswan Dam; the Soviet-U.S. space race was up and running, but *Sputnik* hadn't yet galvanized the competition; our Korean

War was finished, our Vietnamese involvement scarcely begun
... et cetera.

What couldn't he have done back in his old office, with
the *Post*'s mighty databases and info-sniffing software! But to
what end? Since the computer-repair facility was associated
with "Julia's college," he contented himself with a side trip to
the campus library when he drove in to retrieve the machine.
A modest facility ("But we're working on it," his wife liked to
declare), its microfilm stacks didn't include back numbers
of George's former employer; it did file the *New York Times*,
however, and from the reel *Jul. 21, 1956–Dec. 5, 1956* he
photocopied the front page for Monday, August 27. SOVIET
NUCLEAR TEST IN ASIA REPORTED BY WHITE HOUSE was the
lead story, subheaded *U.S. Contrasts Moscow's Secrecy with Ad-
vance Washington Warnings*. Among the other front-page news:
BRITISH CHARGE MAKARIOS DIRECTED REBELS IN CYPRUS,
and EISENHOWER STAY IN WEST EXTENDED (the President
was golfing in Pebble Beach, California, from where the nuclear-test story had also been filed). The lead photo was of the
newly nominated Democratic presidential and vice presidential candidates, Adlai E. Stevenson and Estes Kefauver, leaving
church together with members of their families on the previous
day; the story below, however, was headlined TV SURVEY OF
CONVENTIONS FINDS VIEWING OFF SHARPLY, and reported
that neither the Republican nor the Democratic national conventions, recently concluded, had attracted as many viewers on
any one evening as had Elvis Presley and Ed Sullivan.

So: It had been a Monday, that day forty Augusts past (its
upcoming anniversary, George had already determined, would
be a Tuesday). He showed the page to Julia over lunch, for
which the Fischers sometimes met when he had errands near
her campus.

"Still Eight Twenty-seven Fifty-sixing, are you?" She pretended concern at his "fixation," but scanned the photocopy
with mild interest, sighing at the shot of Stevenson (whose lost
cause they had ardently supported in the second presidential
election of their voting life) and predicting that *this* year's

upcoming political conventions, so carefully orchestrated for television, would lose far more viewers to the comedian Jerry Seinfeld than that year's had to Elvis Presley. And she pointed out to him—how hadn't he noticed it himself?—that the Soviet nuclear-test story had been filed "Special to the New York Times" by a sometime professional acquaintance of theirs, currently a public-television celebrity and syndicated columnist, but back then already making his name as a young White House reporter for the *Baltimore Sun*.

"While I," George reminded Julia, "was still clawing my way up from the *Boondock Weekly Banner* to the *Rochester Democrat and Chronicle*. Don't rub it in."

"Who's rubbing?" She ordered the shrimp salad and checked her watch. "It was an okay paper already, and you made it a better one. Which reminds me . . ." And she changed the subject to the college's plan to install fiber-optic computer cables in every dormitory room during the upcoming academic year, in order to give the students faster access to the Internet. Her scheduled one o'clock meeting with a potential corporate sponsor of that improvement cut their lunch-date short; George wished her luck and watched her exit in her spiffy tailored suit while he (in his casual khakis, sportshirt, and old-fart walking shoes) finished his sandwich and took care of the check.

Yes indeedy, he mused to himself, homeward bound then: the dear old "Democrap and Chronic Ill," as they-all used to call it when things screwed up at the city desk. Heroic snow-belt winters; summers clouded by the "Great Lakes effect," though much milder in August than the subtropical summertime Chesapeake, and blessedly hurricane-free. The inexhaustible energy of an ambitious twenty-six-year-old, chasing down story-leads at all hours, learning the ins and outs of their newly adopted city as perhaps only a Metro reporter can, yet at the same time helping Julia with their three preschoolers, maintaining and even remodeling their low-budget first house, and still finding time over and above for entertaining friends, for going to parties and concerts (a welcome change from Boon-dockville)—time for everything, back when there was never enough time for anything! Whereas nowadays it sometimes seemed to George that with ample leisure for everything, less and less got done; July's routine chores barely finished before August's were upon him!

Once Mac was back in place (and correctly reading, when George booted him up, *August 6, 1996*), he did a bit more homework with the aid of some timeline software that he used occasionally when researching magazine pieces. By 1956, it reminded him, the world newly had or was on the cusp of hav-ing nuclear power plants, portable electric saws, Scrabble, elec-tric typewriters and toothbrushes and clothes dryers, oral polio vaccine, aerosol spray cans, home air conditioners, aluminum foil, lightweight bicycles with shiftable gears and caliper brakes, wash-and-wear fabrics, credit cards, garbage disposers, epoxy glue, Frisbees, milk cartons, pantyhose, ballpoint pens, FM radio, and stereophonic sound systems. Still waiting in the wings were antiperspirants, automobile air conditioning and cruise control, aluminum cans, birth control pills, bumper stickers, pocket calculators, decaf coffee, microwave ovens, felt-tip pens, photocopiers, home-delivery pizza, transistor radios, home computers (as George had suspected), contact lenses, disposable diapers, running shoes, Teflon, scuba gear, skateboards, wraparound sunglasses, audiocassettes (not to mention VCRs), touch-tone telephones (not to mention cord-lesses, cellulars, and answering machines), color and cable tele-vision, Valium, Velcro, battery-powered wristwatches, digital anythings, and waterbeds.

"Disposable diapers," Julia sighed that evening when her husband spieled through this inventory. "Where were they when we needed them?"

"Fifty-six was the year Grace Kelly married Prince Rainier the Third," he told her, "and Ringling Brothers folded their last canvas circus tent, and the *Andrea Doria* went down, and

Chevrolet introduced fuel-injected engines. Harry Belafonte. The aforementioned Elvis. *I Love Lucy*. . . ."

"I *did* love Lucy," his wife remembered. The early evening was airless, sultry; indeed, the whole week had been unnaturally calm, scarcely a ripple out on their cove, and this at the peak of the Atlantic hurricane season, with Arturo, Bertha, Carlos, and Danielle already safely past, and who knew whom to come. Back in '56, if George remembered correctly, the tropical storms all bore Anglo female names; he'd have to check.

They were sipping fresh-peach frozen daiquiris out on their pier while comparing His and Her day, their summer custom before preparing dinner. As Julia was now the nine-to-fiver, George routinely made the cocktails and barbecued the entrée as often as possible, although it was still she who planned the menus and directed most of the preparation. She'd had a frustrating afternoon; hadn't hit it off with that potential co-sponsor of the college's fiber-optic upgrade, an old-boy type whose patronizing manner had strained her professional diplomacy to the limit. Excuse her, she now warned, if the male-chauvinist bastard had left her short of patience.

"Enough about Nineteen Fifty-six, then," George suggested.

"No, go on. Obsessional or not, it soothes me."

"Steak eighty-eight cents a pound, milk twenty-four cents a quart, bread eighteen cents a loaf. Average cost of a new car seventeen hundred bucks—remember our jim-dandy Oldsmobile wagon?"

"A Fifty-five bought new in Fifty-six, when the dealer was stuck with it." The Fischers' first new car, it had been: two-tone, green and ivory. "Or was it a Fifty-six bought late in the model year?"

"A bargain, whichever. Median price of a new house—get this—eleven thousand seven hundred. I think we paid ten-five for Maison Faute de Mieux."

"Dear Maison Faute de Mieux." Pet name for their first-ever house, afore–referred to. "But what was the median U.S. income back then?"

"Just under two thousand per capita per annum. My fifty-six hundred from the *D and C* was princely for a new hand."

Julia winced her eyes shut in mid-sip. "Headache?" her mate wondered.

"Unfortunate choice of abbreviations." It had been in '56 or '57, she reminded him (as he had unwittingly just reminded her), that she'd found herself pregnant for the fourth time, accidentally in this instance, and they had decided not only to terminate the pregnancy by dilation and curettage—D & C, in ob-gyn lingo, and a code-term too for abortion in those pre–*Roe v. Wade* days—but to forestall further such accidents by vasectomy. "Shall we change the subject?"

Agreed—for a cluster of long- and well-buried memories was thereby evoked, of a less nostalgic character than their first house and new car. Duly shifting subjects, "What's that floating white thing?" George asked her, and pointed toward a something-or-other drifting themward on the ebbing tide.

"Don't see it." With her drink-free hand Julia shaded her eyes from the lowering sun. "Okay, I see it. Paper plate?"

It was an object indeed the diameter of a paper or plastic dinner plate, though several times thicker, floating edge-up and nine-tenths submerged in the flat calm creek. On its present leisurely course it would pass either just before or just under the cross-T where they sat, a not unwelcome diversion. Their sport-fishing boat, *Byline*, was tied up alongside; George stepped aboard, fetched back a crabber's dip-net, and retrieved the visitor when it drifted within reach.

"Well, now."

It was, of all unlikely flotsam, a *clock:* a plain white plastic wall clock, battery-powered (didn't have those back in '56). Perhaps blown off some up-creek neighbor's boathouse? But there'd been no wind. Maybe negligently Frisbee'd into the cove after rain got to it? Anyhow quite drowned now, the space between its face and its plastic "crystal" half filled with tidewater (hence its slight remaining buoyancy), and stopped, *mirabile dictu*, at almost exactly 3:45, so that when George held it twelve o'clock high, the outstretched hands marked its internal waterline like a miniature horizon.

"Time and tide, right?" Then, before he'd even thought of the other obvious connection, Julia said, "Now we're in for it: not only August Twenty-seventh, but *three forty-five* on August Twenty-seventh. A.M. or P.M., I wonder."

They tsked and chuckled. During their coveside residency a number of souvenirs had washed up on their reedy shoreline along with the usual litter of plastic bags and discarded drink containers from the creek beyond—wildfowl decoys, life vests, fishermen's hats, crab-trap floats—but none so curious or portentous. In a novel or a movie, George supposed to Julia, the couple would begin to wonder whether some plot was thickening, whether something was trying to tell them something, and whether 3:45 A.M. or P.M. meant Eastern Daylight Time in 1956 or 1996.

"At three forty-five A.M., Eight Twenty-seven *Ninety*-six," Julia declared, "your loving wife intends to be sound asleep. You can tell her the news over breakfast." And she wondered aloud, as they moved in from the pier to start dinner, what they had each been up to at 3:45 in the afternoon of August 27 forty years ago in Rochester, New York.

Another memory-buzz, and it was well that the couple were single-filing, for George felt his face burn. Would it not have been that very summer, if not necessarily that month . . . but yes, right around the time of "their" abortion. . . .

Without mentioning it to Julia, he resolved to check out discreetly, if he could, a certain little matter that he hadn't had occasion to remember for years, perhaps even for decades. His intention had been to drop the dripping clock *trouvé* into their trash bin, but as he passed through the garage en route to setting up the patio barbecue oven (didn't have those in '56, at least not with charcoal-lighting fluid and liquid propane igniters), he decided to hang it instead on a nearby tool-hook, to remind him to notice whether anything significant would happen to happen at the indicated hour three weeks hence.

Not that he would likely need reminding. Unsuperstitious as George Fischer was and idle as was his interest in that approaching "anniversary," he was more curious than ever now about what—in his and Julia's joint timeline, if not in America's and the world's—it might be the fortieth anniversary of. He was half tempted to ask the *Democrat and Chronicle*'s morgue-keepers to fax him a copy of the paper's Metro-section front page for August 27, 1956, to see what had been going on in town that day (but the reported news would be of the day before; perhaps he ought to check headlines for the 28th) and whether he himself had bylined any Rochester stories while his more successful friend was filing White House specials to the *Times*. But he resisted the temptation. Frame-by-framing through Julia's college's microfilm files had reminded him how each day's newspaper is indeed like a frame in time's ongoing movie. We retrospective viewers know, as the "actors" themselves did not, how at least some of those stories will end: that Stevenson and Kefauver will be overwhelmed in November by Eisenhower and Nixon; that the U.S.-Soviet arms race will effectively end with the collapse of the USSR in 1989. Of others we may remember the "beginning" but not the "end," or vice versa; of others yet (e.g., in George's case, Britain's troubles with Archbishop Makarios in Cyprus) neither the prologue nor the sequel. But who was to say that what would turn out to be the *really* significant event of any given day—even internationally, not to mention locally—would be front-page news? Next week's or month's lead story often begins as today's page-six squib or goes unreported altogether at the time: Einstein's formulation of relativity theory, the top-secret first successful test of a thermonuclear bomb. And unlike the President's golf games, what ordinary person's most life-affecting events—birth, marriage, career successes and failures, child-conceptions, infidelities and other betrayals, divorce, major accident, illness, death—make the headlines, or in most instances even the inside pages? George reminded himself, moreover, that such "frames" as hours, day-dates, year-numbers—all such convenient divisions of time—are mainly our human inventions, more or less relative to our personal or cultural-historical point of view: What would "August 27, 1956" mean to an Aztec or a classical Greek? Oblivious to time zones and calendars, though not to astronomical rhythms, the world rolls on; our life-processes likewise, oblivious to chronological age though not to aging.

8/27/56. No need to consult the *D & C:* Prompted by some old résumés and other items in his home-office files, George's ever-slipperier memory began to clarify the personal picture. In the late spring of that year, he and Julia and their three preschoolers had moved to their first real city—in their new Olds wagon, it now came back to him, bought earlier in Boondockville on the strength of his Rochester job offer, and so it had been a leftover '55 after all. After checking neighborhoods and public-school districts and balancing the city's higher real-estate prices against their freshly elevated budgetary ceiling, they had bought "Maison Faute de Mieux," its to-the-hilt mortgage to be amortized by the laughably distant year 1986. And on July 1 George had begun his first comparatively big-time newspaper job, for which he'd been hired on the strength of a really rather impressive portfolio from what he's calling the *Boondock Weekly Banner.* No *annus mirabilis,* maybe, 1956, but a considerable corner-turn in his/their life: formal education and professional apprenticeship finished; family established and now appropriately housed; children safely through babyhood and about to commence their own schooling; the Fischers' six-year marriage well past the honeymoon stage but not yet seriously strained; and George's first major success scored in what would turn out to be a quite creditable career (for if he could point to some, like that *Times*/PBS fellow, who had done better, he could point to ever so many more who'd done less well) in a field that by and large served the public interest, not just the family's personal welfare. Reviewed thus, in the story of both their married life and George's professional life the summer of '56 could be said to have marked the end of the Beginning and the beginning of the Middle.

Over that evening's cocktail-on-the-pier, "You left something out," Julia said, and George's face reflushed, for he had indeed skirted a thing or two that his day's digging had exhumed. But what she meant, to his relief, was that it had been that same summer—when George Jr. was five, Anne-Marie four, and Jeannette turning three—that their mother had felt free at last to begin her own "career," however tentatively and part-time, by working for "pay" (i.e., reduced kiddie-tuition) in their daughters' nursery school.

"Right you are. Sorry about that."

"It may seem nothing to you, George, but to me it mattered."

"Properly so."

She looked out across the cove, where the sun was lowering on another steamy August day. "I've often envied Anne-Marie and Jeannette their *assumption* that their careers are as important as their husbands'."

"I'm sure you have." By ear, George couldn't tell whether "their husbands" ended with an apostrophe. The fact was, though, that if their elder daughter and her spouse, both academics, had managed some measure of professional parity in their university, their younger daughter's legal career had proved more important to her than marriage and motherhood; she'd left her CPA husband in Boston with custody of their ten-year-old to take a promotion in her firm's Seattle office. Even Julia's feelings were mixed about that, although the marriage had been shaky from the start.

More brightly, "Oh, I forgot to tell you," she said then: "I asked this computer friend of mine at work about that default-date business? And he said that normally the default would be to the date when some gizmo called the BIOS chip was manufactured, which couldn't be before Nineteen Eighty.

BIOS means Basic Input-Output System? But this guy's a PC aficionado who sniffs at Macintoshes. Anyhow, he's putting out a query on the Net, so stay tuned."

George was still getting used to some of his wife's recent speech habits: those California-style rising inflections and flip idioms like "stay tuned" that she picked up from her younger office-mates and that to him sounded out of character for people his and Julia's age. But he suppressed his little irritation, told her sincerely that he appreciated her thoughtfulness, and withdrew to set up the charcoal grill before the subject could return to Things Left Out.

On 8/27/56, yet another bit of software informed him next day, the Dow Jones Industrial Average had been 522, and *Billboard* magazine's #1 pop recording in the USA had been Dean Martin singing *Memories Are Made of This*. Whatever other desk-projects George had in the works—and his "retirement," mind, had been only from daily go-to-the-office journalism, not from the profession altogether—were stalled by distraction as the Big Date's anniversary drew nearer. In "the breakaway republic of Chechnya," as the media called it, a smoldering stalemate continued between rebel forces and the Russian military, whose leaders themselves were at odds over strategy. In Bosnia a sour truce still held as election-time approached. Julia found another possibly interested corporate co-sponsor for her college's fiber-optic upgrade. The queerly calm weather hung over tidewater Virginia as if Nature were holding her breath. There would be a full moon, George's desk calendar declared, on the night after 8/27/96; perhaps they would celebrate the passage of his recent lunacy. On Sunday, 8/18, trolling for bluefish aboard *Byline* with pals from the *Post*, he snagged his left thumb on a fish hook; no big deal, although the bandage hampered his computer keyboarding. His "little obsession" had become a standing levity since Julia (without first consulting him) shared it as a tease with their friends and children. George Jr., who worked for the National Security Agency at Fort Meade, pretended to have inside info ("We call it the X-File, Dad") that extraterrestrials were scheduled to take over the earth on

8/27/96. Picking up on her brother's tease, his academic sister e-mailed from Michigan that the first UFOs had secretly landed on 8/27/56; their ongoing experiments on our family—in particular on its alpha male—would be completed on the fortieth anniversary (as measured in earth-years) of that first landing. ("We'll miss you, Dad.")

"So guess what," Julia announced on Friday, August 23. "I had lunch again today with Sam Bryer—my computer friend? And he found out from some hacker on the Net that all Macintoshes default to Eight Twenty-seven Fifty-six when their logic boards die because that's Whatsisname's birthday—the founder of Apple Computers? A zillionaire in his thirties! Sam says everything about Macintoshes has to be cutesy-wootsy."

"Aha, and my thanks to . . . Sam, is it?" To himself he thought, Lunch again today with the guy? and tried to remember when he had last lunched with a woman colleague. The bittersweet memories then suddenly surged: a certain oak-paneled restaurant in downtown Rochester, far enough from the office for privacy but close enough for clandestine lovers to get back to their desks more or less on time; a certain motel, inexpensive but not sleazy, on the Lake Ontario side of town; the erotic imagination and enviable recovery-speed of a healthy twenty-six-year-old on late-summer afternoons when he was supposed to be out checking the latest from Eastman Kodak or the university. It occurred to George to wonder whether it might have happened to be exactly at 3:45 P.M. EDT on August 27, 1956, that a certain premature and unprotected ejaculation had introduced a certain rogue spermatozoon to a certain extramural ovum: *"Our imperious desires,"* dear brave Marianne had once ruefully quoted Robert Louis Stevenson, *"and their staggering consequences."*

For the sake of the children, as they say—but for other good reasons, too—Mr. and Mrs. had chosen not to divorce when the matter surfaced; and except for one half-hysterical (but consequential) instance, Julia had not retaliated in kind. The Nieman Fellowship year in Cambridge, not long after, had welcomely removed them from the Scene of the Crime as well as testifying to George's professional rededication; its prestige enabled their move to St. Louis (the *Post-Dispatch*), thence to D.C., excuse the initials—and here, forty years later, they were: still comrades, those old wounds long since scarred over and, yes, healed.

"Tell your pal Sam," George told his wife, "that Eight Twenty-seven is Lyndon Johnson's and Mother Teresa's birthday, too, though not their upcoming fortieth, needless to say. Virgos all. Birthstone peridot. What's peridot?"

Julia, however, was communing with herself. "My pal Sam," she said deprecatingly, but smiled and sipped.

Who knows what "really" happened when the Big Day came? The explanation of George Fischer's computer's default-date, while mildly amusing, was irrelevant to the momentous though still vague significance that it had assumed for him, and in no way diminished his interest in its anniversary. By then his fish-hook wound, too, was largely healed. He and Julia made wake-up love that morning—she had been more ardent of late than usual, and than her distracted husband. He cleared breakfast while she dolled up for work and then, still in his pajamas and slippers, lingered over second coffee and the Tuesday paper before going to his desk. Another sultry forecast, 30 percent chance of late-afternoon thundershowers. Second day of Democratic national convention in Chicago; Hillary Rodham Clinton to address delegates tonight. Cause of TWA 800 crash still undetermined; Hurricane Edouard approaching Caribbean. He decided to try doing an article for the *Post*'s Sunday magazine—maybe even for the *New York Times* Sunday magazine—about his curious preoccupation, which by then had generated a small mountain of notes despite George's professional sense that he still lacked a proper handle on it, and that those of his associated musings that weren't indelicately personal were too . . . philosophical, let's say, for a newspaper-magazine piece. As mentioned already, the Really Important happenings, on whatever level, aren't necessarily those that get reported in the press: the undetected first metal-fatigue crack in some crucial component of a jetliner's airframe; the casual mutation of one of your liver cells from normal to cancerous; the Go signal to a terrorist conspiracy, coded innocuously in love-seekers' lingo among the Personals. But George's maunderings extended from *What's the significance of this date?* through *What's the significance of the whole concept of date, even of time?* to *What's the significance of Significance, the meaning of Meaning?*

Never mind those. He quite expected 8/27/96 to be just another day, in the course of which we Americans (so said some new software sent by the Fischers' Seattle-lawyer daughter) would per usual eat forty-seven million hot dogs, swallow fifty-two million aspirin tablets, use six-point-eight billion gallons of water to flush our collective toilets, and give birth to ten thousand new Americans. But George was not blind to such traditional aspects of Forty Years as, say, the period of the Israelites' wandering in the desert, or the typical span of a professional career—so that if, as aforesuggested, 8/27/56 had been for his the end of the Beginning and beginning of the Middle, then 8/27/96 might feasibly mark the end of the Middle and thus the beginning of the End. He was even aware that just as his "little obsession" therewith had assumed a life of its own, independent of the trifle that had prompted it, so his half-serious but inordinate search for Portent might conceivably generate its own fulfillment—might prompt Julia, for example, this late in their story, to settle a long-dormant score by making, as she herself had teased, "a few career moves" of her own; or might merely nudge her obsessed spouse gently around some bend, distancing him from her, their family and friends and former colleagues, so that in retrospect (trying and failing, say, to make a marketable essay out of it or anything else thenceforward) he would see that August 27 had indeed been the beginning of the end because he himself had made it so.

Just another day: the first for many, for many the last, for many more a crucial or at least consequential turning point, but for most of us none of the above, at least apparently. George ate an apple for lunch; phoned Julia's office to check out *her* Day

Thus Far and got her voice-mail message instead: a poised, assured, very-much-her-own-woman's voice. As was his summertime post-lunch habit, he then ran a banner up their waterfront pole from the assortment in their "flag locker," choosing for the occasion a long and somewhat tattered red-and-yellow streamer that in the Navy's flag code signifies Zero; it had been a birthday gift some years past from George Jr., who jokingly complained that his dad read too much significance into things and therefore gave him something that literally meant Nothing. After an exercise-swim he set out a half-dozen crab traps along the lip of the cove-channel and patrolled them idly for a couple of hours from *Sound Bite*, the Fischers' noisy little outboard runabout—inevitably wondering, at 3:45, whether his wife and Sam Whatsisname, Sam Bryer, might actually be et cetera. At that idea he found myself simultaneously sniffling and chuckling aloud with . . . oh, Transcendent Acceptance, he supposed.

Not enough crabs to bother with; they seemed to be scarcer every year.

At about 4:30—as George was considering whether canteloupe daiquiris or champagne would make the better toast to Beginning-of-the-End Day when Julia got home—the forecast thunderstorm rolled down the tidal Potomac, dumping an inch of rain in half an hour, knocking out local power for twenty minutes, and buffeting the cove with fifty-knot gusts, as measured on the wind gauge in the Fischer family room. Busy closing windows, George absent-mindedly neglected to fetch in the Zero flag before the storm hit; as he watched nature's sound-and-light show from the house's leeward porch, he saw the weathered red and yellow panels one by one let go at their seams in the bigger gusts and disappear behind curtains of rain. By five the tempest had rolled on out over the Chesapeake, the wind had moderated to ten and fifteen, and the westward sky was rebrightening. Dock bench and pool-deck chairs would be too soaked for Happy Hour sitting; they would use the screened porch. George reset all the house clocks and hauled down the last shredded panel of his son's gift-flag, thinking he might mount it on a garage or basement wall behind that waterlogged clock as a wry memorial to the occasion: his next-to-last rite of passage, whatever.

Normally Julia got home from work by half past five; that day George was well into the six o'clock news on television—Russians resume pullout from Grozny; Syria ready to resume talks with Israel; big hometown welcome expected for First Lady's convention appearance—when the garage door rumbled up and his wife's Volvo rolled in. Often "high" from her day at the office, she arrived this time positively radiant, forgetting (George noted as he went to greet her) to reclose the garage door as usual from inside her car. Tugging her briefcase off the passenger seat with one hand while removing her sunglasses with the other, "Any champagne in the fridge?" she called. She kneed the car door shut—George pressed the garage-door wall button—gave him an exaggerated kiss hello, and exhilarated past him into the kitchen. Plopped down her briefcase; peeled out of her suit-jacket; yanked the fridge open; then stopped to grin Georgeward, spreading her arms victoriously.

"Congratulate me! I *nailed* the guy! Fiber optics, here we come!"

Well, he did congratulate her—wholeheartedly, or very nearly so. Popped the bubbly; toasted her corporate co-sponsoral coup; let her crow happily through half a glass before he mentioned what he'd thought she would be celebrating, perhaps prematurely: the unremarkable close of what had proved after all to be just another day. When he did finally bring that matter up, it was via the heavyhanded portent of the thunderstorm and George Jr.'s flag.

"So here's to Nothing," Julia cheered, and although she topped up both glasses and bade them relink, her mind was obviously still on her successful courtship of that potential college-benefactor. Presently she excused herself to change out of office clothes and take a swim before hors d'oeuvres and the rest of the champagne. George wasn't even to *think* of starting the charcoal for the veal grillades and marinated eggplant wedges; she was flying too high to fuss with dinner yet.

"So *I'll* fuss," her husband volunteered, but contented himself with merely readying the grill for cooking. Their pool was well screened from the neighbors, and the Fischers skinnydipped on occasion, though not as a rule—since who knew when a delivery- or service-person might drive up, or the lawnmowing crew. But presently out she frisked jaybird-naked, did George's triumphant mate, and like a playful pink porpoise dived with a whoop into the pool's deep end.

"Come on in!" she all but ordered him after a bit. "Drop your drawers and take the plunge!" Not to spoil her fun, George did, but couldn't follow through when, to his surprise, she made to crown her triumph with a spot of submarine sex.

On 8/27/96 the Dow Jones closed up 17, at 5,711. The Fischers ate late; watched the First Lady's convention speech on television (Julia raising her fist from time to time in a gesture of solidarity); decided not to wait up for the ensuing keynote address. Instead, nightcap in hand, they stepped outside to admire the moon over their cove—still officially one night shy of full, but looking already as ripe as a moon can look.

"So," said George: "That's that."

"What's what?" She clearly had no idea what he was referring to.

"Old Eight Twenty-seven Et Cetera."

"Oh, right." She inhaled, exhaled, and with mock gravity, said, "You know what they say, George: *Today is the first day of the rest of your life.*"

How right she was.

Sixth
Night

So okay,
mused Graybard Imagination—to himself, Itself, whateverself:
Here one has the fine mild morning of Sunday, September 16,
2001; things still frantic up in Manhattan, where fires burn
yet at Ground Zero's mass grave and Wall Streeters worry, as
do many of the rest of us, what'll happen when the stock market reopens tomorrow after its longest closure since the crash
of 1929. Busybusy likewise over in Our Nation's Capital, where
the Pentagon de-rubbles its blasted fifth side, buries its 184
dead, and prepares to Strike Back at the Evil Whomever, while
many another federal office full-throttles through the weekend. Across the bay in Tidewaterland, however, except for
the flags and patriotic decals sprouting from rural mailboxes,
small-town shop windows, and automobiles (mostly SUVs, vans,
and pickup trucks, by GB's count), life proceeds much as always
on a sunny Sunday morn: The Christian-religious prep for
church and midday dinner; the non-Christian and/or secular
pursue whatever weekend activities, not *oblivious* to the alarm-
ing and unpredictable new international situation, but largely
unaffected by it in any direct way so far.

Thus, e.g., M/M Narrative Hardware of these tales, that
couple being altogether of the secular persuasion, for better or
worse, but conditioned by past decades of Monday-through-

Friday work to take weekends off, by and large. Amen then, shruggeth Graybard: If after five straight days of Hendecam-eroning the bloke wants a "Sixth Night" break (especially having scribbled away the Saturday A.M. recording "Wysiwyg's" kinky latest inspiration), let him spend this fair Sunday on odd jobs and family errands, bicycling *à deux* about the neighborhood, catching up on snail- and e-mail, and leafing through the hefty *Times* (CONGRESSMEN CALL FOR BROADER FBI/CIA SPY POWERS IN WAKE OF 9/11, etc.). As for himself, however—in his capacity as Narrative Imagination Embodied, the Software from whom issue such formulations as *As for himself, however—* having declined, along with their unorthodox and likewise secular muse, to take the Jewish Sabbath off from their joint work, he saw no reason to make a holiday of the Christian. In the nature of their case and per their separate job descriptions, he's free to wander undispatched while his weekday Dispatcher swims exercise laps, washes the family car, reads the newspaper, maybe even dozes off in a lawn chair shaded by a large mimosa. At the morning's voltaged ninth-hour-plus, therefore, he makes the now-routine excursion from (unoccupied) Scriptorium to Imaginarium, to see what if any new twists or surprises Ms. Inspiration may have up her sleeve, shall we say, this time around. Little as he knows about that female entity—who she "really" is, if that question even makes sense, and what might account for her extraordinary accoutrements, habits, and habitation in this latest and most physical of her manifestations—he knows himself to be grateful indeed for her invaluable assistance over the decades and appreciative of her curious new embodiment, unprecedented in their longstanding partnership.

Good in the metaphorical bed, too, she is, as he hopes he may, with her assistance, be being also. Whatever the merits of their collective narrative offspring, the inspiration themof has been refreshment indeed. Even those serial ultimata of hers— no more Oldies, no more Not-Quite-Ficties, no more Stories About Storytelling, especially about Narrative Impotency or the specter thereof—he has found more stimulating than in-

hibitory, like that (metaphorical) potion wherewith she claims
to spike his (metaphorical) wine before their (metaphorical and
incrementally asterisked) "nightly" Congress.

So: Abracadabra, Once upon a time, whatever,
and per usual it was Rosy-Fingered Dusk out over her marshscape, and her bedside digital flashed *9:11 9:16 9:11 9:16*, by
which time of evening on which date in this 39th degree of
north latitude it ought to have been entirely dark already—as
indeed it became even as he reflected this reflection. And all
was as ever brightly lit and more or less transparent *chez* Wysiwyg, and there on a cellophane "napkin" was his wineglass
(anyhow *a* wineglass; where was the usual second?), filled and
waiting beside a lighted clear-oil candle-lamp out on the deck
table; and okay, Herself nowhere in sight, but that had been the
case initially on First and Fourth Nights too, as he recalled. No
doubt the sprite was pleasurably marinating in her marsh.

Yo, Wys? he called down from the deck rail, at the ladder-
top.

No reply. No splash-sounds, either, or flash of fair wet skin
asparkle with agitated *noctilucae*.

Wysiwyg?

Well, now. No way he could've missed seeing her indoors—
au toilette, say—given her apartment's see-through partitions,
floor, and ceiling. Either she was bathing farther off in the
marsh-creek tonight than usual, or else she hadn't arrived yet
(from where?), or else she had, without notice, simply up and
left—just at the midpoint, it now occurred to him, of their
projected eleven-night stand. Consternated by that possibility,
he fetched up the single wineglass; sniffed and sipped, experimentally: a simple jug chablis, he'd guess, quite all right, and
still chilled, therefore poured not long since. . . .

Well, he'd wait a bit and just see. The woman might of
course have other business than attending to his inspiration;
perhaps even (twinge of jealousy here) other imaginations
than his to inspire in her singular and delightsome fashion.
Although the muses as such are as old as Greek mythology,

their embodiments are typically represented in full female flower: Maybe the wench was having her period? Even so, they could've rendezvoused, at least, could they not've? At least, in workmate fashion, sipped and chatted? And (*vide* Fifth Night's kinkish come-together) where Inspiration hooks up with Imagination, there's more than one way to skin the old cat.

Wys?

No reply beyond the irritated squawk of a great blue heron lifting off or landing out there somewhere. Had that Fourth Night detective-and-turtle tale about the absence of inspiration perhaps inspired Inspiration's absence, despite his agreeing to lay off that subject thenceforward? Come to think of it — and remembering "Narrator's" maunderings back in Night Two's wedding-ring story — was what he felt now the absence of her presence or the presence of her absence?

Too French a question for the likes of Graybard. Perhaps this was her (not especially inspired) solution to their eleven-night/ten-story problem afore-remarked: Just skip one? Not likely. Nor could he seriously imagine her simply abandoning him and their project without notice, little as he knew of who she "really" was and how she and her unusual domicile came to be here. One of her seventeenth-century forebears had already inspired Giovanni Battista Basile's *Pentameron* (a.k.a. *Lo Cunto de li Cunti*), replete with Cinderella, Snow White, Rapunzel, and other notable *cunti;* the corpus didn't need another five-day talefest. More likely tonight's scenario was some sort of trial; if among its objectives was to make him miss her presence (quite apart from her assistance) and feel her absence, then it quite succeeded. That absence was everywhere present: in the so-familiar low-tide marsh-tang, combined as on her naked self with the perfume of mallows abloom amongst the reeds; in her yesternight's wet duds (shortsleeve sweatshirt, cutoff jeans, and cotton underpants — ordinary-looking but oddly tailored, those latter two, in certain respects) still lying where tossed after she'd showered in them between Fifth Night's Inspiration and his Recitation of *The Rest of Your Life*. . . .

✦ ✦ ✦

Wysiwyg?

Glass in hand, he wandered through her spaces. Was half tempted to ransack the place for clues to her, but forbore: What one saw, without prurient prying, was what one would get. Contemplating "their" waterbed, he stopped and sipped. If the wine was per usual potioned, was she suggesting Metaphorical Masturbation? No thanks, *chère* Wys: All storymaking, viewed unsympathetically, might be called that. Let's you and me stay with the *ménage intime* of Muse/Tale/Teller/Told—and where the fug are ye, luv?

Only as his glass neared empty did he register that on "his" pillow, like a goodie left by a turndown-service chambermaid, was another transparent beverage-napkin, whereon rested a believe-it-or-not transparent Chinese fortune cookie, its paper-slip message visible though not readable inside. With sigh and headshake (in case she was somehow somewhere watching, scanning this very parenthesis over his shoulder) he set aside the wineglass, broke the tidbit open—a plastic shell after all, not an edible see-through pastry—straightened the slip, and read: *4: NO MORE DISMAYING (AND HALF-NOSTALGIC) SUDDEN RECOLLECTIONS OF REPRESSED-MEMORY INFIDELITIES, WHETHER UNILATERAL OR RECIPROCAL, FROM PROTAGONIST'S EARLIER LIFE-CHAPTERS OR INCARNATIONS.*

Can't the woman even say *please*? he complained to himself—and at once apologized, the facts being (a) that "the woman" was as delightsome and helpful (if enigmatic) a collaborator as he could, literally, imagine; (b) that this fourth "ultimatum" of hers was scarcely unwarranted, his two recentest tales having turned in fact on just that category of recollection: Enough already! And finally, (c) that it was not for her to say please, when the giving of narrative pleasure was his very *raison d'être*. How right she was!

Stand by me, then (please), O frisky unpredictable spirit,
he implored her bed, her room, her deck, her night-marsh. I feel your stimulant taking hold: a very Viagra of the Imagination. If, like my First Night Invocation, it somehow summons

your physical presence, I'll welcome you with an eager and grateful six-asterisk embrace. If, on the contrary, what I get of you at this midpoint of our Hendecameron is only what I've seen of you tonight thus far, then so be it. Now I lay me down to please my muse, if she so inspire me, with a tale that, in observance of her serial strictures, is not an Oldie, not Non-Fictive, not About Storytelling, and devoid of Dismaying Sudden Recollections of Et Cetera. Should said tale please our Wysiwyg, where- and whoever she may be, that will be Sixth Night pleasure enough for its Present Teller.

Having delivered himself of this soliloquy, he deposited Ultimatum #4 in the empty wineglass and unhurriedly shucked his clothing (the male counterpart of hers from the night before), tossed them among and atop hers, and took his narratorial ease on the glowing waterbed, stretching himself out neither on His side thereof nor on Hers, but straight down the middle. As if cued by his open-ended resolve, all the room-lights dimmed as one and then went out entirely. The simple symbolism pleased him, as had that of his and her clothing in damp bedside congress: In the imminence of their muse, even seasoned practitioners of any art are finally naked and in the dark, waiting (with honed attention) to see what will happen next. The novelty, too, of this evening's progress thus far he found not unarousing; likewise this lights-out evidence that Ms. Wys *was*, somehow, on the premises. Her chablis-flavored elixir coursed through him. Expecting at any sentence to hear her bare footpads cross the room and then to feel her strictly metaphorical but nonetheless delicious conjunction himwith, to the circumambient darkness he declared aloud: *Certain present evidence to the contrary notwithstanding, tonight's story is entitled*

THE BIG SHRINK

❖

THE PARTY WAS OVER, really, but a few of us lingered out on Fred and Marsha Mackall's ample pool deck to enjoy the subtropical air, the planetarium sky, and a last sip before heading homeward. Half a dozen or more at first, we lingerers were; then just our hosts and Roberta and I, sitting in deep patio chairs or on the low wall before the Mackalls' great sloping lawn.

"The other thing I wanted to get said," Fred Mackall went on presently, "—that Marsha's story and those stars up there reminded me of?—is that the universe isn't expanding anymore, the way it used to."

We let that proposition hang for a couple of beats in the cricket-rich tidewater night. Then my Bertie, with just the right mix of this and that, set down her decaf, kicked off her sandals, said brightly "Oh?," and propped her feet on a low deck table.

"If you're starting that . . . ," Marsha Mackall warned her husband—*amiably but not unseriously*, I guess I'd say.

Fred twiddled his brandy glass in the patio-torchlight. The catering crew, assisted by the Mackalls' caretaker-couple, were unobtrusively cleaning up. In a tone calibrated to match his wife's, "It's what's on my mind to say," Fred said.

"*I'm* ready," Bert volunteered, who generally was. "Hey: There went a meteorite."

I corrected her. Mildly. Good-humoredly.

Sleek Marsha Mackall pushed up out of her Adirondack chair. "Tell you what," to her husband: "I'll go help the help while you do the universe."

From his wall-seat, "You do that," Fred seconded—*levelly but not disagreeably*, I guess I'd say. And she did.

"Did you see it?" my wife asked me.

"Didn't need to, actually. Meteor*ite*'s what hits the earth. Right, Fred?"

"You didn't *need* to?" *Quizzical but with an edge*, Bert's tone, and I thought, Uh-oh. "How do we know it *didn't* hit the earth?" she asked me further, or perhaps asked both of us.

"For a while there," Fred said on, "the universe expanded, all right, just as we were taught in school—your Big Bang and all? The whole show expanded in space up there for quite a little while, actually, everything getting bigger and bigger."

"Well . . ." I could tell what my wife was thinking: Not expansion *in* space, Fred-O, but expansion *of* space; space itself expanding, et cetera. Bert might get meteors and meteorites ass-backward, but she knew more stuff than I did, and we shared all our interests, she and I; discussed everything under the sun with each other. What she said, however, was "Try eight to twelve billion years, okay?"

Fred Mackall turned his perfectly grayed, aging-preppie head her way, then shook it slowly and spoke as if to the flickering highlights in his glass: "Fifty, fifty-five, I'd say. Sixty tops. Then things sort of stalled for the next five or so, and after that the *volume* of space held steady, but your galaxies and stars and such actually began to *shrink*, at an ever-increasing clip, and they're shrinking still."

In the Amused Nondirective mode, one of us responded, "Mm-*hm*."

Down-glancing my way, "The effect," Fred said, "is that your astronomers still get pretty much the same measurements—your Red Shift and such?—but they haven't yet appreciated that it's for the opposite reason: because everything's *contracting*, themselves included; everything but the overall universe itself. Not condensing, mind; *shrinking*."

We didn't laugh, as we would've just between ourselves. *The rich man's joke is always funny*, goes the proverb, and the rich host's anecdote is always respectfully attended. By an order of magnitude, the Mackalls were the wealthiest people we knew: light-years out of our class, but hospitable to us academic peasants. They were Old Money (Marsha's, mainly, we understood), with the Old Money liberal's sense of noblesse oblige. Fred had once upon a time been briefly our ambassador to someplace—a Kennedy appointee, I believe, or maybe Lyndon Johnson's. Latterly, he and Marsha had taken a benevolent interest in our little college, not far from their Camelot Farm: stables, kennels, Black Angus cattle, pool and tennis court, gorgeous cruising sailboat in their private cove, the requisite eighteenth-century manor house tastefully restored, overlooking the bay, and more acreage by half than our entire campus.

Cockamamie, I could almost hear Bert saying to herself. But apart from her professional interest in the Mackalls, which I'll get to presently, she took what she called an anthropological interest in them—ambassadors indeed, to the likes of us, from another world—and with Fred especially she had established a kind of teasing/challenging conversational relation that she imagined he enjoyed. I myself couldn't tell sometimes whether the fellow was being serious or ironic; but then, I had that trouble occasionally with Bertie, too, a full fifteen years into our marriage. In any case, although they made a diplomatic show of interest (perhaps often genuine) in their guests, both Mackalls had the philanthropist's expectation of being paid deferential attention.

My turn. "So your theory's different from the Big Crunch, right? The idea that after the universe has expanded to a certain point, it'll all collapse back to Square One?" No polymath even compared to Bert, I was an academic cobbler who stuck to his trade (remedial English and freshman composition), but I did try to stay reasonably abreast of things.

"Oh, definitely different," Fred said. He perched his brandy glass beside him on the wall-top and tapped his half-splayed fingertips together . . . *as if in impatient prayer*, I guess I'd say. "In the Big Shrink, everything stays put but gets smaller and smaller, and so your space between things appears to increase. *Does* increase, actually."

"Now hold on just a cottonpicking minute," my Roberta teasingly challenged, ". . . ."

"There's no holding on," Fred said. Smoothly. "And no stopping it or even slowing it down. In fact, the shrink-rate increases with proximity to the observer—just the reverse of your Big Bang?—but since the measurements come out about the same, it's not generally noticed." He smiled upon his fingertip-tapping hands, his say said.

Neither of us knew quite how to reply to that; *I* didn't, anyhow, and Bert seemed to do a five-count before she cleared her throat *mock-ostentatiously* and asked, "So where d'you get your fifty billion years, Fred, when your cosmologists all say eight to twelve billion?"

She was teasing him with those *your*s, I was pretty sure. Bertie'd do that: feed your little idiosyncrasies back at you, and not everybody took to it kindly. Now instead of tapping his fingertips five on five, Fred Mackall kept them touching while he expanded and contracted the fingers themselves—not *splayed and unsplayed* them, but *pulsed* them, I guess I'd say; pulsed them leisurely—leisurelily?

I give up.

No I don't. Fred Mackall pulsed his spread-fingered, fingertip-touching hands leisurely like . . . some sort of sea creature, say, and said, "I didn't say billion." *Smiling, though not necessarily with amusement.*

There.

"Did I say billion?"

Without at all meaning to, I presume, the Mackalls had gotten Bert and me in trouble once before in one of these post-party-nightcap situations. Just a year or so prior to the scene above, it was: first time they and we had met socially. Bertie had recently landed her new position in the college's Development office, where part of her job-description was to "coordinate" the friendly interest of potential benefactors like the Mackalls. In her opinion and her boss's, she turned out to be a natural at it; in mine, too, although I was less convinced than Bert that her jokey-challenging manner was universally appreciated. In any case, now that our kids weren't babies anymore and we had to start thinking Tuitions down the road, I was pleased that she had this new job to throw herself into with her usual industry. The Mackalls, we agreed, were doing at least as much of the "coordinating" as Bert's office was; the April buffet-dinner at Camelot Farm that year was their idea—for our young new president and his wife along with several trustees of the college and their spouses (Development was hoping that Fred would agree to join the Board); also Roberta's boss, Bill Hartman, and his missus, who happened to be a friend and part-time colleague of mine; and—bottom of the totem pole—Bert and me: Assistant to the Director of Development ("Not *Assistant Director* yet," Bert liked to tease her boss when she gave her full title) and the lowercase director of the college's freshman English program, although I suspect that I was there less as Faculty Input than as my wife's Significant Other. The evening went easily enough: We were a small college in a small town with a clutch of well-to-do retirees from neighboring cities and a few super-gentry like the Mackalls; the prevailing local tone was relaxed-democratic. Toward the close of festivities, as most of the guests were making to leave, Marsha Mackall said, "Anybody for another brandy and decaf out under the stars?," and although President and Ms. Harris begged off along with the trustees, Roberta said right away, "Count us in." Bill Hartman—whether pleased at his protégée's quick uptake or concerned to monitor the conversation—glanced at his wife and said, "Sounds good," and so we were six: same venue as this later one, but a fresher, brighter night.

Don't ask me how our conversation turned to Inherent Psychological Differences Between Women and Men, a minefield at any time of day but surely even more so at the end of a well-wined evening. Marsha Mackall—as tanned in April as the rest of us might be by August—was the one pursuing it, apropos of whatever. The form it soon took was her disagreeing with Becky Hartman and my Roberta (good liberal feminists both) that there were no "hard-wired" psychological differences between the sexes; that all such "stereotypical gender-based tendencies" as male aggressiveness versus female conciliatoriness, male logical-analytical thinking versus female intuition and feeling, the male hankering for multiple sex-partners versus the female inclination to exclusive commitment—that all of these were the effect of cultural conditioning (and therefore malleable, in their optimistic opinion) rather than programmed by evolution into our respective chromosomes and therefore more resistant to amelioration, if amelioration is what one believed was called for.

"Some of them are like that, maybe," elegant Marsha had allowed—meaning that some of the abovementioned "tendencies" were perhaps a matter more of Nurture than of Nature. "But when it comes to polygamy versus monogamy, or promiscuity versus fidelity—"

"Objection," put in Fred Mackall, raising a forefinger.

"Sustained," Bill Hartman ruled, *mock-judicially:* "Counsel is using judgmental language."

"Counsel stands corrected," Marsha conceded. "I don't mean it judgmentally—yet. And we're talking happy marriages here, okay? Happy, faithful, monogamous marriages like all of ours, right?"

"Hear hear," Bill Hartman said at once.

"All of *mine* have been like that," Fred Mackall teased, and lifted his glass as if in toast.

I followed suit.

"All I'm saying," Marsha Mackall said, "is that sexual fidelity comes less naturally to you poor fellows than it does to us, and that while some of that might be a matter of cultural reinforcement and such, what's being reinforced is a plain old biological difference between men and women. Okay?"

"*Vive la différence*," Fred said—not very appositely, in my judgment.

"Men are just naturally designed to broadcast their seed to the four winds," Marsha concluded. "But pregnancy and maternity make women more vulnerable, so we tend to be choosier and then more faithful, quote unquote—and we evolved this way for zillions of years before things like marriage and romantic love and conjugal fidelity were ever invented."

"Before they were *valorized*," handsome Becky Hartman said, "is how the jargon goes now," and Marsha Mackall nodded: "Valorized."

"Amen," Fred said.

I hated conversations like this, whether sportive or serious. In my view, which I wasn't interested enough to offer, women and men are at least as importantly different from other members of their own sex as they are from each other categorically; I myself felt more of a kind in more different ways with Roberta than with either Bill Hartman or Fred Mackall, for example— and, truth to tell, maybe more of a piece *temperamentally* in some respects with Becky Hartman (we had successfully team-taught a course or two in past semesters) than with my wife, even. What's more, it didn't seem nearly so obvious to me as it evidently did to them that a culturally acquired trait is *ipso facto* more manageable than a genetically transmitted one, where the two can even be distinguished. Et cetera. But intelligent people do seem drawn to such subjects—women, in my experience, more than men. This much I made the mistake of volunteering, by way of a Bertie-like teasing challenge to the three ladies—and then, of course, I was in for it. Becky Hartman now took the (female conciliatory) tack of agreeing with our hostess that, whatever the cause, men were indeed categorically more inclined than women to sexual infidelity—"seriality, polygamy, promiscuity, call it what you will—though mind you," patting her husband's knee, "I'm not saying they *pursue* the inclination, necessarily—"

"Heaven forfend," Bill Hartman said, *mock-solemnly.*

"—only that the inclination is definitely there, more often and more strongly than it is with women."

"Now we're talking," Marsha Mackall said, satisfied.

"I deny it," firmly declared my Roberta. "I don't believe Sam's any more sexually interested in other women than I am in other men."

"Uh-oh," Fred Mackall warned, or anyhow uttered in some vague sort of warning spirit.

"We're not saying that he goes around panting after the co-eds," Marsha made clear.

"Much less that he *drops his pantings,* huh?" Fred said, and ducked his handsome head. Bill Hartman politely groaned; Bertie hissed. "Sorry there," Fred said.

"Right," said Becky Hartman, agreeing with Marsha. Directly to her, then—I mean to Becky, as I had only just met the Mackalls—I said, "What *do* you mean, then, Beck?," and, in a way that I remembered with pleasure from our team-taught classes, she pursed her lips and narrowed her bright brown eyes in a show of pensiveness before replying, in this instance with a hypothetical scenario: "Suppose there were absolutely no guilt or other negative consequences attached to adultery. No element of betrayal, no hurt feelings—let's even drop the word *adultery,* since it has those associations."

"Right." Marsha Mackall took over: "Suppose society were such that it was considered perfectly okay for a married man to go to bed with another woman any time they both felt like it."

"Neither admirable nor blameworthy," Becky Hartman specified, in my direction; "just perfectly okay with all parties, absolutely without repercussions, any time they felt like doing it."

"Then would you?" Marsha asked me—with a smile, but not jokingly. "Or not?"

Lifting his right hand as if on oath, "I plead the Fifth Amendment on that one," Fred Mackall said at once, although it wasn't him they were asking, yet.

"Like*wise,*" Bill Hartman agreed, with a locker-room sort of

chuckle. But it was me the two women happened to be pressing, and I had the habit, even in social situations, of taking
seriously-put questions seriously and replying as honestly as I
could. Occupational hazard, maybe, of teaching college fresh-
men in the liberal arts.

So, "Blessed as I am in my marriage and happy as a clam
with monogamous fidelity, I guess I might," I acknowledged,
"in some sort of *experimental spirit*, I imagine, if there were no
such fallout as guilt or social disapproval or hurt feelings or
anything of that sort, so that it wouldn't even be thought of
as 'adultery' or 'infidelity.' " I used my fingers for quotation
marks. "Which is unimaginable, of course, so forget it."

"But if things *were* that way," Marsha Mackall triumphantly
bore in, "then you would. Right?"

I reconsidered. Shrugged. "I guess I have to admit I might."

Bert said to me then, "I'm astonished," and although her
tone was amusedly *mock*-astonished, I saw her face drain. "I am
totally astonished."

"Uh-oh," Bill Hartman said, quite as Fred Mackall had
earlier.

"No, no," my wife made clear to all: "No blame or anger or
anything like that—"

"*No hurt feelings*," Fred teased, "*no guilt, no repercussions.*"

"I just couldn't be more surprised if you'd said you're bisexual," Bert said to me, "or had a thing for sheep."

"Sheep," Fred said, "baah," and most of us duly chuckled.

"It's an impossible hypothetical scenario," I protested to
Bert, and without blaming Marsha Mackall directly (we had
just met the couple, after all, and they were our hosts, and Development was courting them), I declared to all hands, "I feel
like I've been suckered!"

"My friend," Fred Mackall said, "you *have* been suckered."

"No, I swear," Bert tried to make clear: "I'm not upset. I'm
just totally, totally surprised."

Becky Hartman did her lips-and-eyes thing but said nothing. Notching up his characteristic joviality, "Time to pack
it in, I think," her husband declared. Perfect-hostess Marsha

made a few let's-change-the-subject pleasantries, perhaps with Roberta in particular, and we did then presently bid our several good nights.

In the car, I apologized. "No need to," Bertie insisted, and as we drove homeward down the dark country roads under the brilliant stars, she reaffirmed that she didn't *blame* me in any way; that she felt as did I that all this essentially-male/essentially-female business was so much baloney—that had been precisely her and Becky Hartman's *point*, remember?—but that for all those years she had thought our connection to be something really really special. . . .

"It *is* special!" I rebegan, more calmly: "That was a dumbass hypothetical scenario, hon, and I made the dumb-ass mistake of taking it seriously instead of doing a *faux-galant* cop-out like Fred Mackall and Bill Hartman."

"Maybe they weren't being fake-gallant," Bertie said from her side of the car. Her voice was distant; I could tell that her head was turned away. "Maybe what they said was *true*-gallant, but expressed ironically under the social circumstances."

My face tingled: She had me there, as not infrequently she did. "So," I said—mock-bitterly but also true-bitterly, et cetera, and in fact with some dismay: "The honeymoon is over."

"No, no, no," my wife insisted. "I was just surprised, is all."

"And disappointed." I felt miserable: annoyed at Marsha Mackall, at Becky and Bert, at myself. Bum-rapped. But mainly miserable.

"Yes, well."

Sixteen months later—smiling, though not necessarily with amusement, and pulsing his spread-fingered, fingertips-touching hands leisurely like some sort of sea creature—Fred Mackall said, "I didn't say fifty *billion*. Everything's shrinking, see, but since it's us who're shrinking fastest of all, other things seem larger and farther away." He picked up his empty glass, set it down again. "That's why Marsh and I don't get to Europe much anymore, you know? We used to pop over to London and Paris as if they were Washington and Philadelphia, but even though the planes fly faster and faster, everything's too far away these days. And this *house* . . ." He turned his perfectly grayed head toward where the caterers were finishing up. "We rattle around in it now, where before we were forever adding on and buying up acreage left and right. There're parts of this property that I don't set foot on anymore from one season to the next."

"I get it," Bertie said, *cheerily*, as if a joke had been on us. "So even though the farm and the house are shrinking too . . ." She let him take it from there.

"They're all farther and farther apart from each other, not to mention from town. D'you know how long it's been since I trekked down to our dock to check the boat? And look how far away the house is now, compared to when we-all came out for a nightcap!"

"You know what, Fred Mackall?" Bertie said, *mock-confidentially*. "You're right. Sam and I will never get home."

"Oh, well, now," Fred said, chuckling my way as if across a great divide: "You two are still in the Expanding mode, I'd guess, or at most in the capital-P Pause. . . ."

One patio torch guttered out; several others were burning their last. Fred Mackall spoke on—about "your stars and such" again, I believe, although I could scarcely hear his words now, and about how his Big Shrink theory applied to time as well as to space, so that what astronomers took to be billions of years was actually no more than a cosmic eyeblink. "My" Bertie's tone was still the cheery straight-man's, mildly teasing/challenging to draw him out, but essentially in respectful accord.

I say "tone" because *her* words, too, were barely audible to me now across the expanse of pool deck, theoretically smaller than it had been when Fred Mackall began his spiel, but in effect so vast now that I didn't even try to call across it to my wife. I'd have needed hand signals, so it seemed to me: semaphores such as beach-lifeguards use to communicate from perch to perch. We still had what you'd call a good marriage, Bert and I: We were still each other's closest friend and confidant, still unanimous with the children, or almost so. But it wasn't what it had been. We made love less often, for example; less passionately, too, lately, by and large. Par for the course, some might say, as time shrinks and the years zip by; but our connection truly *had* been special, just as Bert maintained. The queen-size bed on which she and I had slept and such for fifteen satisfying years had come to seem king-size; although per Fred Mackall's theory it was doubtless down to a double by now and on its way toward single, its occupants were still further reduced, and thus farther apart.

I happened to recall from some freshman textbook a journal entry of Franz Kafka's, I believe it was, about his grandfather: how the old fellow came to marvel that anyone had the temerity to set out even for the neighboring village and expect ever to arrive there, not to mention returning. I remembered how my own mother, in her last age, found going upstairs in her own house too formidable an undertaking, like a polar expedition. Once upon a time I might have contributed those anecdotes to this nightcap conversation: a bit of Faculty Input. By now, however, I couldn't even hear Fred Mackall's and Roberta's voices, much less have called across to them. Even if I could have—by bullhorn, cell phone, whatever—I doubt I'd have found the right words: They, too, were retreating from me, would soon be out of my diminishing reach altogether, as would even my self itself.

The star-jammed sky was terrifying: moment by moment emptier-seeming as all its contents reciprocally shrank. We would never imaginably pull ourselves out of the Mackalls' Adirondack chairs, Bert and I, and make our way off their pool deck, enormous now as an Asian steppe; far less off their interminable estate, through the light-years-long drive home, the ever-widening, in effect now all but infinite, space between us.

Seventh
Night

"* * * * * *,"

is how Graybard had hoped his absent muse-friend might somehow respond at his Sixth Night tale's tail end—she having declined to give him pause, so to speak, by manifesting herself
in mid-narration as he'd imagined she just might. In his experienced though not impartial judgment, *The Big Shrink* not only
observed her several No-Nos but was moreover an okay story.
When it shrank to its dénouement, however, he found himself as Wysless as at its opening words—and no longer in the
woman's oddly lightless precinct, but back willy-nilly in day-
bright Reality.

Was "the party over, really," then, as those opening
words had declared? For here it was Monday morning already,
9/17/01: another fine mild still one where one writes this, while
a world away the newly forged alliance of just-barely-elected
U.S. President and unelected Pakistani CEO issues a joint ultimatum to Afghanistan's Islamic-fundamentalist Taliban rulers:
Give us Osama bin Laden, dead or alive, or you and your al-
ready-blasted country ain't seen nothin' yet. Wall Street open
again for stock-trading after four-day closure: Would the sky
fall? Was the party over, really?

Not quite, one knows now but did not then. By day's end the
Dow Jones Industrials would lose 7 percent of their value—far

less than feared—and would thereafter regain, relose, and re-regain, hanging just above or below 10,000 for several more months, during which the Taliban would be forcibly deposed and largely destroyed along with the luckless nation it had so sternly governed, but Osama & Co. would slip away to regroup elsewhere and plan their next atrocity against the infidel West. Hundreds of the innocent and guilty, by whatever standard, would perish in Afghanistan, Israel, Palestine; reactionary political parties would gain strength in Europe, along with anti-immigrant, anti-American, and anti-Israeli opinion.

Shall we go on?

Not in this grim vein, it was decided in the Scriptorium by 9:11 that morning. On with this half-told Hendecameron, then, so altogether irrelevant to the above? Let's just see. *Hie ye hence six minutes hence, Graybard ambassador,* and find out what's what, party's-overwise: where we-all stand in the Missing Asterisks Department.

Hie he did at the appointed time, with appropriately mixed feelings and certain advice from his dispatcher: hied himself by the routine route Imaginariumward; found that sanctum still as uncharacteristically pitch-dark as when he'd left it, or it him, involuntarily, at last night's story's close, its only light that infernally blinking bedside clock, stuck still at *9:11 9:16 9:11 9:16*, as if time had stopped when her lights went out. No less surprisingly, at that instant he felt himself as jaybird-naked again as after his solitary yesternight divestment. What was going on? Or, rather, *not* going on?

Then . . .
"* * * * * *!" his suddenly-there collaborator greeted him in effect and without words: room-lights up, the nimble nymph naked as himself, adrip from her dip as usual, and upon him with such wordless fervor that sans elixir or any other potion than their pure (if only because Metaphoric) passion, they made good their six-asterisk deficit and lay happily spent through the after-oscillations of her waterbed, beside which the clock now duly flashed *9:11 9:17* et cetera.

GB: Well, now, ma'am: Wow.

W: Likewise, sir: Good show.

And good *no*-show, he could not resist replying; for yesternight's presence of her absence, or whatever, while not a little troubling and yet to be explained, had had its own perversely inspiring effect. As maybe she had observed?

"Maybe. Anyhow, your mixing your dry clothes with my wetties was a turn-on. Reminded me of us?"

Gotcha. Touching her nearer bare shoulder: Missed you, Wys. Missed seeing; missed getting what one saw, et cet.

"Yes, well." She sighed and stretched. Sat up. "I see you got it, then. The point?" But enough of that, her now-businesslike manner seemed to say: He'll please excuse her while she fetches the *vin du soir*, and then it's on with Seventh Night, and *L'Shanah Tovah.*

Hey, you're right: Tonight's Rosh Hashanah! Happy Fifty-seven Sixty-whatever!

"Two." They clinked the glasses she returned with—an upstate New York Manischewitz muscatel, oversweet but appropriate to the holiday, one supposed, and toasted their Hendecameron's Sabbath, so to speak, coming on the heels first of the Jewish and then of the Christian, and coincident with the turn of the Hebrew calendar. It was to mark that Sabbath's eve, she now declared, and the midpoint of their project, that she had taken her Sixth Night sabbatical; also to herald or anyhow propose certain changes in their M.O.

Again? It's been nothing *but* changes, Wys: never the same twice!

They were sitting now cheek to cheek, as it were, on her bed-edge, sun down and lights up as usual. No complaint, understand, he added, and sipped the too-sweet stuff. Keeps a guy on his toes, we guess. So what's new?

Lips pursed at her glass-rim, "A rebeginning of sorts?" she supposed. "No stunts, costumes, or gimmicks, at least for the next few nights?"

Shucks: I'd come to look forward to those. Then, remembering his dispatcher's advice, But whatever you say, of course. I really wondered last night whether our party was over. . . .

"I *wanted* you to wonder. But it's just the funny hats and pussy-paint and such that we'll do without for a while. As for the rest, our Hendecameron is hereby granted a night-by-night extension, so drink up; we'll work our way back to drier stuff in the nights ahead."

The nights ahead,
he echoed, with happy anticipation qualified only by that "night-by-night" proviso, and did as bidden. Whither wilt thou, Muse o' mine, lead on.

She duly did: led him out onto the deck and over to the ladder, and informed him that they would now initiate the second semester of their joint project with a joint immersion, after which he might towel himself dry or not as he saw fit, but she would remain tidewatered, and on with their stories. "All set?"

He peered overside. Mighty black down there.

"The better to see the light." Pertly she swung herself half around, flashed himward those V.S.O.P. eyes of hers, and started down-ladder. "Follow me?"

My pleasure. And pleasure it was, to be totally immersed in that saltyfresh warm element with naked ditto Inspiration. Had he imagined her creeklet or marsh-pond shallow? It was over his head! She wrapped bare arms and legs around him, pressed mouth to his and drew him under, then back up for air, then under and up and under and up until, breathless both, they clung to the ladder and each other. There the tide-pond itself became their waterbed, whereupon and wherein they achieved Metaphorically what on the literal level (as Reader her/himself may have learned from disappointing experience) does not come naturally to *Homo sapiens:* seven-asterisk submarine sex.

* * * * * * *

After which, back on deck,
—she still wet but he dried off now, per each's pleasure—"You

understand, I trust," his pleased muse trusted, "that these asterisks aren't *ratings*, like stars or forks in the *Guide Michelin.*"

So you say. But there you sit, Wys (at ease and adrip in her
deck chair, her fine wet thighs insouciantly open to the light air
off the marsh), and wow.

Ignoring his admiration, "They don't mean that each new
story or Metaphorical Make-Out is better than the one before. . . ."

So you say.

"So I say: They're just Due Approval plus Incremental Tabulation."

Come again?

"Maybe tomorrow." She gave him a look. "No need for Seventh Night to be better than Sixth, is what I mean, or Eighth
than Seventh, either storywise or otherwise. Once the bar's in
place, which it's been since Night One, we don't raise it night
by night."

Except by Incremental Ultimation.

"Yes, well." Sidelong pickerel smile: "Those."

Four so far, by my count: No more Oldies! No more Non-
Ficties! No more Stuck Storytellers! . . . What was the last one?

"No more Sudden Recollections of Repressed-Memory
Adulteries in Long-Past Incarnations."

Ah, so: I'd forgotten.

"To which four she now adds a fifth, notwithstanding her
approval of that *Big Shrink* story: No more riffs on the Innocent Marital Guilt Theme, s.v.p., even the Totally Innocent
kind. Enough already."

Enough IMG, your grateful servicer wonders aloud, or
enough ultimata?

As she knew he knew, she let him know, it was the former
that she was up to here with. As for the latter, there might be
yet one more down the line, but not for some nights yet—after
which, no more No-Nos. "Meanwhile, extension granted. On
with the stories?"

Maybe.

Genuinely surprised: *"Maybe? What's this maybe?* To the Muse of Inspiration he says maybe?"

Maybe. No more this, that, and the other, per your serial proscriptions. But I can't promise no more Autumnality. . . .

Dismissive flick of hand. "Oh, *that.* No problem, Geebsie, at least for a while." That smile. Those eyes. "As I may have mentioned, I have a thing about older guys? Don't ask."

He duly didn't, although (as Reader may now notice) the plurality of her noun did not escape his notice. But

Speaking of Extension,
he contented himself with responding, that just happens to be tonight's tale's title:

EXTENSION

❖

TWO QUICK DECADES LATER, in the assisted-living facility, I hear him telling the story this way, perhaps to himself:

"The little project seemed on the face of it desirable, feasible, even *natural*. We would enlarge and re-equip my home office (Myrna found hers adequate as it was), together with our bedroom and the bath between. Contiguous to that main bedroom and the long screened porch we would add a solarium/spa/exercise room to help us stay fit in our approaching retirement: all this in an integrated, architecturally pleasing extension to our modest rural hideaway overlooking the bay and, by extension, the Atlantic and thence all other oceans. In one's elder years, Myrna liked to joke, it's important to remain in touch with the world.

"Granted, this proposed extension was more ambitious than a number of our earlier, trial-run improvements to what we had bought, some dozen years before, as a weekend retreat and vacation house. An unremarkable but adequate and nicely situated single-story cottage, it was replete with picture windows, fake shutters, brick-veneer siding, stock asphalt roof-shingles, bare-bones landscaping. The place was meant to supplement our equally modest, okay-for-its-purposes house in the city across the bay, convenient to our main offices. Over the years of our part-time residency we had white-painted the bricks, replaced the Thermopane picture windows with divided-pane bays, redecked the pier, added a freshwater pool to complement the brackish bay, relandscaped the lot, remodeled the kitchen and the guest accommodations, upgraded the heating, air-conditioning, and water systems, installed skylights, overhead paddle-fans, and privacy fencing, and replaced the roof, as well as making less extensive improvements to our town house—older, but better built and less in need of upgrading.

"Our His-and-Her counseling careers (investment and marriage, respectively) had gone well, as had our lives in general; we were comfortably-off, upper-middle-class Americans. I myself happened to be of just the right age to have missed all the wars of our horrific century—not here for the First World War, too young for the Second, student-deferred from Korea, too old for Vietnam—and to have prospered in the post-WWII economy; nothing worse had thus far befallen the pair of us than the dissolution of our respective first marriages (pains more than assuaged by our successful second, with its live-in counselor), the loss of aged parents, the occasional illness, injury, or child-rearing crisis, and other such less-than-mortal shocks. If this house-extension project was more considerable than its forerunners, it was less so than numerous other of our major life-moves: the engenderment of children, the several changes of job- and living-venues that are par for the American professional course, the divorces and remarriage aforementioned, the purchase and furnishing of those two houses and their predecessors.

"Not only did our economic position and life-situation make the proposed extension appear unremarkable (up and down the bayshore one saw much more ambitious projects in progress); it was itself just another extension both of our personal joint history and of our American generation's—indeed, of our American Century's. Over the hundred-odd years since our respective grandparents had immigrated, each crop of their descendants (until our own Baby-Boom children, anyhow) had on average grown taller, more prosperous, and longer-lived than its forebears. Like most of our middle-class compatriots, we ourselves had grown not just bodily from infancy through childhood to maturity but likewise (and thus far lifelong) in our physical, mental, and other capacities—our skills and responsibilities, our professional status, authority, and earning power— and, along with those (as the stock market levitated and the American divorce rate climbed with it), in the number, size, and quality of our material possessions and accommodations. From spartan student lodgings, Myrna and I had 'moved up,' separately and together, through entry-level urban apartments and secondhand automobiles to our first new cars and minimal home-ownerships; from one child to two, one car to two (one marriage to two, I'm tempted to add), one house to two plus a small boat, *two* small boats, two less-small boats plus more-expensive cars and houses plus more frequent and less frugal vacation trips plus that swimming pool and paid-off mortgages and country-club memberships and ever-growing equity accounts and 'starter' trust funds for the grandchildren and those several initiatory remodelings and property improvements aforementioned—all leading almost logically, one might say, to this latest, really not extraordinary extension-in-the-works.

"Did we *need* it? Well: Does one 'need' a larger cabin-cruiser, a better-made automobile, a more extensive (and expensive) vacation? We *wanted* it; we *could use* it; we had, in our opinion, *earned* it. It would be yet another 'improvement,' another . . . *extension*, in a word, of our life-estate as well as of our (number two) house—an extension the more desirable for its being, not impossibly, our last such. We were, as afore-remarked, approaching the traditional American retirement age, and although we enjoyed our professions and had by no means decided to quit them entirely, it had in fact been some years already since we'd last *increased* our separate counseling responsibilities. Indeed, we had not only leveled off on that particular front but cut back a bit (in my case especially, as I was the elder of us and less in need of an outside office): fewer and less extended business trips, shorter working hours, longer and more frequent vacations, fewer days per week and month and year in the city place, and more in the country. Did we need the extension? With our children out of the nest and raising nestlings of their own in distant cities, we didn't really 'need' the residential square-footage that we occupied already, enough to house half a dozen ghetto or Third World families. But we were neither of those, and particularly given this recent gradual shift of our domestic gravity-center from city to country, the proposed extension seemed, as aforedeclared, both desirable and feasible. It was not, after all, another or newer or bigger-and-better *house*, as might have been the case ten years before. It was simply . . . an extension.

"And so we made preliminary measurements and sketches; with some misgivings, we re-engaged the architect who had done our trial-run projects; we studied and annotated and conferred upon and revised her more extensive drawings and specifications. Over the following year-and-then-some, as we went about our businesses and pleasures, we bethought ourselves and more than once revised the design, even the whole project. I say 'with some misgivings' because those earlier remodelings had by no means been hassle-free. When were such things ever? There were the usual (perhaps rather more than the usual) unforeseen problems, cost overruns, delays, compromises. With the results we were, on the whole, quite pleased, though perhaps mainly relieved to have the several little ordeals behind us and still unhappy with certain features of the jobs—those if-we-were-doing-it-again things that we continued to believe a better architect would have anticipated, or a more knowledgeable builder warned us of. And so rather than bolstering our confidence in those professionals and in ourselves, the trial runs had proved ambivalent trials indeed. To shift designers now, however, would have been to turn this more considerable project into another trial run, when as far as we could see (and had by now come rather to hope), nothing in the 'extension' way lay beyond it. *Life is not a dress rehearsal,* declares the bumper sticker; *Better the devil you know than the devil you don't,* advises the proverb. All the same, we felt less prepared for the

Main Event than we had expected to feel when its time came. Thus our misgivings.

"But the calendar was running. As seasons passed, we found ourselves more and more merely maintaining the town house while chafing at the limitations of what, after all, we had never intended as our primary residence. And so we came to put ever more time, energy, and money into planning that capital-E Extension, as we now thought of it. On corkboards in our home offices we pinned volumetric drawings of the remodeled country-seat-cum-extension, to encourage and inspire us in odd moments. Perhaps because those drawings were thus always before us, we further altered several major features of the design, as well as countless details. Every one of those alterations, needless to say, added slightly or substantially to the architect's fees, already so much higher than we had anticipated that we half-seriously wondered whether her 'trial-run' bills had been bait to hook us with. Like lawyers and some other sorts of counselors (myself and Myrna not excluded), hourly-rate designers thrive on complications and changes of plan; while we hemmed and hawed and revised and unrevised, her meter profitably ran. We had expected to have our extension built, decorated, furnished, landscaped, and ready for occupancy by retirement-time, but when at last we declared the blueprints final (no doubt partly from fatigue, although every one of our many modifications and nearly every one of hers had been an improvement) and put the project out for bids, the several contractors' estimates came in so startlingly above even our architect's guesstimations that—frustrated, chagrined, and weary of the whole business—we put the project on hold for a year in order to recollect ourselves, recounsel, reconsider. We shifted furniture to make more efficient use of our present space, ran in extra fax and computer-modem lines, did some much-needed temporary landscaping of the area that the Extension had been meant to cover, and promised ourselves not to think further about the thing for a full twelve months. Although the drawings remained in place on our corkboards, other matters distracted us: passing illnesses, pleasure travel upon those interconnected oceans and the continents they separate, problems large and small in the extended family, further drawdown of our professional activities, financial planning for our retirement—in all, a welcome return to normalcy.

"The turning point, I see now, was not our yearlong moratorium, but our discovery—when in an eyeblink that year passed and we duly fetched out for reinspection the sheaf of blueprints and specifications labeled EXTENSION—that we had come to feel we didn't really 'need' (you understand my meaning) quite so *much* extra space—although if we could have had it simply by snapping our fingers and paying the bills, we would have done so unhesitatingly. Why not scale the project down a bit, we asked ourselves—perhaps rather a lot? Halve the size of A, for example, while going forward with B as originally planned but dropping C entirely? The idea seemed feasible enough to warrant our reopening, no more eagerly than before, the connection with our architect; she cheerfully redrafted our scaled-down plan (to which we ourselves had devoted days, in hope of scaling down her fees as well) and billed us therefor. Ironically, however, we found our enthusism comparably reduced. Now that the country place had become in effect our main residence, the prospect of camping in half of it for several months while the other half was being noisily and messily extended seemed more disagreeable than ever, especially given a scaled-down payoff at the end. Moreover, in the period of our moratorium we had installed a hot tub on the barbecue patio beside the porch, a somewhat crowded but on the whole acceptable substitute for the room deleted from our scaled-down plan. And that 'temporary' landscaping had settled in and begun to grow handsomely; and we had begun seriously to consider selling the little city house when our professional phase-out was complete—all the more reason to enlarge the country place, we supposed, yet all the more daunting a prospect to do so, as the town house itself by this time needed substantial sprucing up if it was going to sell in what had lately become a buyers' market.

"And so we dallied, counseled our respective (and reduced) clienteles, did other things—and noticed, for the first time, really, that doing them took longer than it had used to. Autumn upon us before summer's chores were done; how had we ever managed them when both of us were working full-time, not to mention when we were raising children too? A day came when—in the process of shifting further items from our 'main house,' now for sale, to our 'weekend house,' now unequivocally our headquarters—we took down from our corkboards those aging volumetric sketches (which anyhow depicted the original, larger Extension, not its scaled-down later versions) and filed them away with the so-costly blueprints, spec sheets, light-fixture catalogues, builders' proposals, and related correspondence. We told each other that when the convulsions of selling the town house and reordering our life were behind us, we might very well come back to the project. To ourselves, however, we acknowledged (at least one of us did) that we almost surely would *not* come back to it; that our time for ambitious extensions had passed.

"Indeed (we came to see but not necessarily to say), the contrary had quietly become the case: For us, the theme of the season and no doubt of all seasons to come was not Extension, but Contraction. Just as we no longer needed two houses, so we no longer really needed two cars, far less a virtual flotilla of assorted watercraft. Why we continued to maintain separate home offices, even, except as personal retreats, had become a reasonable question, now that neither of us was really 'working.' One house (unextended), one car, one boat (small) would surely do: With our children scattered to the four winds and their parents grayhaired, who water-skied any longer behind our aging outboard runabout? When had we or any guest last used our much-weathered old canoe? Soon enough we would scarcely 'need' even our dear old flagship, so laborious for us to maintain and so expensive to hire the maintenance of; soon enough we would doubtless come to wish that our single, too-large house were a carefree condominium somewhere, so that we'd have more time to spend with our far-flung offspring and to explore further the world's interconnections while we were still able—except that traveling had lately become as much a chore as an adventure, and our relations with those offspring, while certainly affectionate, were inevitably attenuated by distance and by their own divorces/remarriages. Even visiting nearer-by family and friends, not to mention entertaining them at home, we found yearly more burdensome.

"They say that the universe itself is extending, extending; seems to me the case could be made that for some time now it's been holding still at best, while we ourselves have begun to shrink. Time was when the pair of us each worked a job and a half, raised kids and pets and vegetables and flowers, cooked and sewed and housecleaned, maintained scrupulously our properties and sundry possessions, even did much of our own carpentry and house-painting and electrical repairs—and somehow still had time and energy left over for hobbies, sports, community activities, hospitality, good works. Lately it's enough to keep ourselves respectably dressed, groomed, fed. . . .

"Who would have imagined that so trifling a matter as taking down a drawing from a corkboard could discover the Abyss? That in the mere canceling of a proposed house-extension one would feel brushed by the Dark Angel's wingfeathertips? Yet here we sit at our lorn bay window, Myrna and I, like ticketed passengers in an airport lounge, looking dully about us at the scene we're about to leave; waiting for the boarding call, for the ultimate contraction."

Eighth
Night

Before she could demand it
in the form of yet a sixth ultimatum or narrative constraint on his remaining stories, *No more Recycled Shrinkage*, Graybard promised his unpredictable muse when the pair reconvened *chez* Wysiwyg at 9:18 (P.M., by *her* clock) the next day.

"Good."

—except insofar as the theme of Autumnality may touch upon assorted losses, as is not unlikely.

Assent nodded: Autumnality (she reminded him once again) she had no quarrel with; but the preceding night's Extension-piece had felt to her more like early winter. "*Brrr!* Enough Shrinkage already! Enough Contraction!"

Agreed—except insofar as et cetera.

"So, then: To our Hendecameron's eighth eleventh?"

Also to us, most valued and comely comrade.

His compliment appeared to please and ease her. They clinked glasses and sipped a presumably elixired white Rioja: a welcome return to crisp and dry libation after Seventh Night's too-sweet muscatel. Time was, Reader may recall, when after their inspirational asterisks and Graybard's consequent story-telling, Muse and Talester might doze off, separately or to-gether, in her illuminated space: See, e.g., Night One, as re-viewed on Night Two. Every "night" since, however, end of story has meant end of get-together, its teller transported back to headquarters in the latter forenoon of that same day, to stand by until dispatched again on the morrow.* Not confusing, really, once one got the hang of it, and while one might expect such time-shifts to do odd things to our chap's circadian rhythms—some sort of narrative jet-lag?—he seems to have accommodated to "waking up" in the late morning of a day whose "evening" he has enjoyed already.

Just thought we'd get that straight.

So what's our lass wearing, if anything, on this eighth of their tête-à-têtes, and what's she up to on this one-week anniversary of catastrophic Tuesday, 9/11/01? Nothing kinky on either count, just as she'd given notice the night before (indeed, on the former count, nothing whatever). In the charnel house of Ground Zero, subterranean fires still burned; acrid smoke and dust still fouled the lower Manhattan air. As observing Jews marked the turn of the Hebrew year (5,762 years since the world's creation according to whom?, Graybard means to ask his partner to remind him), Muslim anti-Semites promulgated the outrageous charge that the 9/11 atrocity was one more Jewish Conspiracy, a plot to besmirch Islam, adducing as "evidence" the totally unsupported claim that four thousand Jewish employees in the World Trade Center had stayed home from work that morning! While altogether secular herself,† it is to protest that monstrous slander, as well as to honor the still-uncounted thousands of dead, that Ms. Wysiwyg has declared tonight's patio candles to be both memorial to last Tuesday's victims and observant of Rosh Hashanah's end—an occasion not normally marked by candles, if Graybard remembers correctly, and the holiday observed for a single day only by Reform Jews (two days by Conservative and Orthodox), but never mind.

In that same grave spirit, the woman's handsome nudity to-

---

* See, e.g., Night Two, as reviewed in the preamble to Night Three.

† In her current manifestation, anyhow. One readily acknowledges the historical importance of religion as a source of, though by no means a prerequisite to, artistic inspiration.

night had a different aspect from Night Seven's, not to mention from her kinky get-ups on Nights One through Three: Much as on Night Four, she wore her nakedness, so to speak, with the air not of a come-on but merely of a Here I Am; and their brief joint after-the-wine tidewater immersion—a regular feature of her latest M.O. revision, Graybard gathered—seemed more a Rite of Autumn than one of Spring: less a sportive romp than a ceremonial ablution. All the same, by when they were back on deck he felt the onset of Inspiration, enough so that immediately following their appropriately starred Intimate Metaphorical Congress—

* * * * * * * **

—he was moved to declare to his water-beaded waterbedmate *And then there's the one called*

---

* Reader will kindly bear in mind that these incrementing asterisks are mere tabulations.

AND THEN THERE'S THE ONE

❖

...ABOUT ADAM JOHNSON BAUER, retired American, who, like many of his now age (late middle) and class (middle middle), had married in the mid-twentieth-century postwar euphoria, before such concerns as runaway population growth and environmental degradation had set in, and with his then mate begat children three, all of whom survived to adulthood and, as of the time of this telling, a healthy early-middle age.

Of that thriving trio, however (this is what's on their dad's mind just now, at the abovementioned century's end), only two married—nothing amiss there—and of those two, only one, the middle child and elder daughter, bore children: Ad's teenage granddaughter and grandson, living currently with their mother and virtual stepfather half a continent from their grandfather and stepgrandmother. In short, those five robust, well-educated, reasonably prosperous Americans—the three Baby-Boomer Bauers and their two original spouses—were bequeathing to the new millennium only a single pair of descendants: a reproductive rate of 40 percent, compared to Ad's and his (first) wife's 150 percent.

Bear with this arithmetic, Reader, of which there'll be yet more anon. Our Adam is a newly pensioned-off community-college teacher who, lacking both doctorate and scholarly publication, will not aggrandize himself with the title "Professor" (although that was in fact his rank at Hampton County Com Col and is the basis of his annuities), but who has a still-lively general curiosity, a head for figures, and more time on his hands these days than he's been used to. He now discovers that that foregoing progenitive analysis, if applied to his extended family, yields a similar result. Ad himself is one of three siblings, born in the Great Depression and wed (all three of them) in the 1950s. That sextet promptly bore seven children: Adam's aforementioned three, his sister's three, and his younger brother's one, an overall reproductive rate of 117 percent. But those seven and their six spouses—thirteen Boomerites in all—have seen fit to generate only half a dozen offspring: a 54 percent attrition. Ad's Radio Shack calculator next reports that this same reproductive decline marks even more the family of his somewhat younger current wife, the former Betsy Gardner, and the children of her and her siblings' initial marriages, for the most part still issue-free.

Good news for Planet Earth, our man supposes, if the whole human race, and not just its "advanced," post-industrial nations, followed the Bauer/Gardner example: less resource depletion, less pollution of the biosphere, more room for the whales and the wombats and whatever—but that's not what's on his mind. Nor is the circumstance that his pair of only grandkids bear their father's surname, as do his nieces and nephews and their dwindling spawn, in consequence whereof the Bauer name-line, if not its DNA, must expire with Ad himself not many years hence. In that department he has no qualms either of religion (Who'll say Kaddish for me?) or of personal vanity (No Adam Bauer, Jr., or III or IV? *Tant pis*). What has prompted these calculations and reflections is a remark that Granddaughter Donna blithely made last week toward the end of her annual late-August visit with Grandpa Ad and Grandma Bets: that she intends never under any circumstances to have babies ever. Had it been Grandson Mark who'd so declared, Ad might simply have smiled: What fourteen-year-old boy, with the world to conquer or at least his peers to impress, fancies himself a paterfamilias? But to hear a sunny, attractive, well-

adjusted, and responsible seventeen-year-old girl so unequivocally reject motherhood . . .

And what prompted dear Donna's remark? Through nearly
every one of her seventeen summers she has shuttled happily
among her three sets of grandparents, spending a week or two
with each: her dad's folks in San Diego, her mom's mom in Milwaukee, and her mom's dad and stepmom—Adam and Betsy—
in their modest Cape May summer cottage. In the beginning
she came with her parents and, later, her baby brother. From
about age ten, as her parents' marriage deteriorated, she and
young Mark flew out from Denver with their mother only;
since about age twelve—because she and her brother get along
ever less well, and her now-divorced mother has been scram-
bling to make both a living and a new life—she and Mark have
come out unaccompanied and separately, using the airlines'
minor-child escort service. All this hither-and-yonning (the
complicated logistics of which remind Ad of the virtually insol-
uble Traveling Salesman problem in mathematics) has been
financed by the several grandparents, at first because the young
family was "just starting out" and couldn't afford the air fares,
then because they were divorcing and couldn't, then because
they were divorced and couldn't. By and large the visits have
been a treat for all concerned; possibly they still are for Ad's ex-
wife and the parents of his ex-son-in-law. As he and Betsy
have aged, however, and young Donna has evolved from bubbly pre-teen through high-spirited early-teen to supercool and
therefore bored latter-teen, the interludes have become, though
outwardly no less cheery, a touch more strained all around.
The girl would so obviously rather be trolling the Denver
shopping malls with her false-fingernailed and triple-earringed
contemporaries than beaching out in funky South Jersey with
the old folks, their swimsuited high-mileage bodies no doubt
distasteful to her. Ad and Bets in turn, after the first get-reac-
quainted day or two, find it annually more wearing to set aside
their usual preoccupations for most of a fortnight and "relate"
almost without respite (as everyday parents and children never
do) across the two-generation gap. They foresee already that

the problem will be even more acute with young Mark as his testosterone kicks in and the teenage American mall-and-media culture claims him. All hands still officially, indeed actually, love one another, but they would unanimously now prefer more frequent, less extended, and less exclusive interactions—such as were the rule back when a family's generations lived closer together—to these protracted annual one-on-ones. Distance, airfare, and available calendar time, however, rule out more than a single visit each way per annum, and so . . .

Homeward bound from the Atlantic City airport, whereto they delivered the girl at visit's end for her commuter flight to Philadelphia and thence on to Milwaukee via Chicago, "It was the way she said it," Betsy reflected, and Ad agreed: "So unhesitating. So *definite*." They agree too that despite their reciprocal affection, the youngster must have been prevailingly as glazed over by the visit as were they, as surfeited with bridging the age gap, as ready to get back to her more usual and congenial pleasures once she was done with the *next* grandparent. They'll be saddened but not at all surprised, they concur—perhaps even, guiltily, a bit relieved—if next August Donna finds some diplomatic reason not to make the grandparental circuit, or else abbreviates her Cape May stay to a long weekend, should they see fit to underwrite such teenage jet-setting.

"Kids grow up," Ad says, and sighs—not simply at that fact of life.

The question before us, however, is what prompted young Donna's declaration of non-reproductive intent. On the final evening of her visit, as the trio lingered over dessert on the cottage's duneside deck (lightheartedly sighing that they'll not be crossing paths again till Christmastime in Denver), their granddaughter asked, apropos of something or other, whether Betsy's parents had brothers and sisters; she couldn't recall ever hearing Grandma Bets mention aunts and uncles. Unlike young Mark, whose curiosity seems seldom to range beyond skateboard stunts and video games, Donna takes a genuine interest in other people's lives and interconnections, as evidenced by her remembering details of them from visit to visit better than Ad himself does. It must be, therefore, that for some stepgrandmotherly reason Betsy hadn't spoken of her parents' several siblings, at least not in recent Donna-visits; perhaps she felt that a non-lineal descendant wouldn't really be interested. In any case, as she duly supplied the basic info on her aunts Jan, Milly, and Eunice and her uncles Fred, Howard, and George, it occurred to Ad to fetch from the house the Gardner Family Tree, which that same (maiden-)Aunt Jan Gardner—mentally intact but physically infirm and confined these days to an extended-care facility in Delaware—happened to have drawn up earlier that same season and distributed through the clan.

"Oh, she's not interested in *that*," Bets protested when he brought the chart out. But Donna brightly counter-protested that she was, too, interested—and not impossibly she was, although her social skills are well enough developed, unlike her brother's, to bring off a polite show of interest even if she felt none. Ad therefore reviewed with her the diagram of his wife's descent from two generations of New Jersey Gardners, themselves descended from a nineteenth-century immigrant Liverpudlian whose own ancestry was unknown to Aunt Jan and company. Leaving who knows what or whom behind him, young Lewis Gardner in 1884 had crossed from Southampton to Boston, there to marry one Martha Ewell Stone and sire seven children, of whom five survived and one moved to Trenton, New Jersey, to sire Betsy's dad and his several sibs. Her genealogical lesson done, Donna left off twiddling the topmost of her left-lobe earrings, stretched her carefully tanned arms fetchingly over her head, and said, "One thing I know for sure: no kids for me."

Surprised—and in Ad's case, dismayed—her grandparents scoffed, questioned, teased: A healthy, intelligent, popular, good-looking, and good-humored girl like her uninterested in marriage and motherhood? "Not that those two always have to go together," Bets reminded all hands.

"Oh, I'll probably get married once or twice," Donna cheerily allowed. "But babies? Forget it."

Ad might have pressed further for her reasons, but his wife at this point observed that she herself at Donna's age had felt paradoxically vice versa: uninterested in marriage, but eager to have children, if only to counter-exemplify her own parents' botched job, as she saw it. Donna picked up on that subject, perhaps to deflect attention from herself, and their table talk presently shifted to other things.

As he later kissed the girl's forehead good night, "You'll have children," Ad murmured. "Jim-dandy ones, too."

His granddaughter chuckled in his hug. "Don't hold your breath, Grandpa."

Well, he hasn't held his breath. But while his respiration has proceeded at its average unconscious rate—one inhale/exhale cycle every five or so seconds, Ad once calculated, or two dozen dozen such cycles per day, or a couple thousand over the week since Donna's visit and the Bauers' return to "normalcy," or nearly seven million since his first, sixty-five years ago (which comes, he reckoned by the way, to only one-point-one breaths for each European Jew murdered in the Holocaust)—he has found he can't get the girl's upbeat negativity in this matter off his mind. To have pressed her further the next morning for explanation would have been tactless, and while Bets's position is that grandparents have a time-honored right to such tactlessness, Ad found himself reluctant to pry. Could be the fallout from Donna's parents' messy divorce, he and Bets agree, not to mention her grandparents' divorces; could be the geographical scattering of her extended family; could be the seize-the-day media culture of end-of-the-century Americans—narcissistic and ahistorical, changing addresses every four or five years and rarely dwelling where their parents dwelt, let alone their grandparents. Could be all of the above plus the increasing parity of the sexes, Bets reminds him, and the growing reluctance of many young women to hamper their career moves with maternity.

"In short," his wife intones, mock-seriously, "it's your effing decline of your effing Family Values."

And in fact, Ad has just about decided, it effing *is*. He himself lived from birth through high school in the white clapboard house in the smallish Pennsylvania town where his parents spent their entire life and his paternal grandparents their American adulthood, the two families literal next-door neighbors. Before Helmut Bauer's emigration from rural Germany, his stock had doubtless peasanted the same neck of the Sachsen woods from time out of mind—so Ad must infer from the family surname, inasmuch as his immigrant grandpa's actual ancestry, like Betsy's Great-Grandpa Lewis Gardner's, is off their respective genealogical charts. That's how it was back then with the mass of ordinary folk, Ad reckons—small farmers, tradespeople, shopkeepers—until America siphoned off the burgeoning European population. Ad's mother (née Margaret Johnson) had faithfully tended the respective families' grave-plots in the county cemetery, where the American generations of Bauers and assorted Johnsons were laid to rest: the men and their spouses; the women who died unmarried, still bearing the family name, or, wed and widowed, came home to finish out their life; the bachelor casualties of two world wars; the stillborn or otherwise non-surviving children. But neither Ad nor his siblings, all of whom "went off to college" and seldom thereafter returned to their hometown except for family gatherings, took much interest in those gravesites, especially after the older generation died off. Ad almost never bothers to "pay his respects" to his predecessors, as people do in most other cultures and some perhaps still in ours (he is invariably surprised, passing a cemetery, to see a considerable number of beflowered graves). A non-believer, he has no plans to join those buried Bauers either physically or spiritually upon his own demise. About the disposition of his remains he is shrug-shouldered; has agreed with Betsy, who shares his attitude, that their dead bodies would best be incinerated and recycled into their sideyard compost pile for the eventual benefit of their roses, irises, chrysanthemums (the former Miss Gardner is in fact an ardent gardener). Never mind tending *their* graves; they'll be quite satisfied if their house's next owners keep up the landscaping—

and those next owners, they take for granted, will not be Ad's or Bets's children or any other member of his or her family. Although their main house and beach cottage are a major part of the estate generously apportioned to their several offspring in their wills, they assume that those heirs will sell both properties and split the proceeds. What American adult lives in his/her parents' house nowadays, as was proverbially the ideal case in days of yore (*A house built by your father*, one such proverb recommends, *a vineyard planted by your grandfather*)? Who any longer cares a fart about *continuity?* He and Bets less than their parents, their children less than they, their grandchildren no doubt less yet.

Continuity, yes—whereof one aspect, on the family level, is genealogy. Once upon a time, so Ad's impression goes, there would have been one member of the extended clan—some Aunt Jan Gardner or fussy Uncle Bud Bauer—who recorded births, marriages, and deaths on the flyleaves of the family Bible or copied out the family tree for all hands' edification. In his own generation, Ad's younger brother Carl, lately a widower, half-heartedly updated somewhile back their Uncle Bud's *Bauernbaum*, as Ad dubbed it, and distributed copies for amendment and embellishment "if anybody's interested"; for two years now Ad's copy has rested—in peace, he trusts—in his study files, scarcely perused and never annotated despite Carl's mild hope that Ad might see fit to "put it on the computer," whatever *that* might mean. A semi-retired Philadelphia realtor, Carl Bauer assumes that his professorial brother "knows all about" computers, but while in fact Ad and Bets use a desktop PC for family bookkeeping, correspondence, and occasional Internet expeditions, they are neither experts nor enthusiasts in that realm.

Half a thousand mortal respirations since this story's last space-break, however, and back in their "real" house after Labor Day, our man now finds himself inspired by his granddaughter's remark, not to File & Forget the Gardner Family Tree along with the *Bauernbaum*, but instead to retrieve from his files Carl's annotated diagram, lay the two side by side on his big old glass-topped work desk, and re-review them—more accurately, to examine them really closely for the first time. To his mild surprise, he finds himself genuinely interested, and curious. He still agrees with whoever it was who opined that "to have ancestors more distinguished than oneself is surely the least of virtues"; what appeals to him is that all these Freds and Mildreds and Ulrichs and Miriams were *not*, evidently, distinguished: just ordinary women and men like Bets and himself, being born, surviving childhood or not, marrying or not, engendering offspring or not, and soon or late dying. Then there are the mysteries, the unanswered questions: not just the vast though banal one of Lewis Gardner's and Helmut Bauer's Old Country progenitors back to whenever, but such smaller, more intriguing ones as what exactly Lewis and Helmut put behind them (at ages twenty-two and sixteen, respectively) and why exactly they set out—alone, it would appear, or perhaps with a hometown buddy or two—to try their fortunes in the New World. Ad's lively, bumptious Aunt Annabelle (his father's elder sister and everybody's favorite aunt) married Uncle Alfred Murray in 1925, so Carl's diagram indicates; but her only child is listed as having been born in 1923, and his name was Herbert Stolz, not Herbert Murray or Herbert Bauer. An unrecorded first marriage? A never-spoken-of illegitimacy? There's a story there, Ad bets, and another in Betsy's Great-Uncle Frederick Gardner's dates: *b. 1902 (Camden NJ)–d. 1937? (Alaska?)*. What about that aforementioned fussy Uncle Herman "Bud" Bauer's evidently short-lived adventure into exogamy (*b. 1898; m. 1920 Carlotta Petrucci; divorced 1922*)? No children, no subsequent remarriage for Uncle Bud; did he carry to his grave a torch for his perhaps passionate-but-faithless Italiana? Or, having burned his fastidious fingers in her flame, was he simply (or complexly) relieved to be the family's celibate necrologist through his remaining fifty-three years (*d. 1975*)?

Ad bets—even *Bets* bets, when he shares with her some of these musings—that their granddaughter would have pricked up her multiply-ringed ears at these familial mysteries, these closeted stories, if he had noticed them himself in time to point

them out to her that evening in Cape May. He can even imagine her poring over the two family trees in search of more
such tantalizers, perhaps making a high-school project out of
pressing her surviving forebears for details. Was La Petrucci
Philadelphia-Italian or Italy-Italian? What led young Frederick Gardner to the wilds of Alaska in the Great Depression,
and why aren't we certain when and whether he perished
there? Could he imaginably still be alive somewhere, a nonage-
narian who burned his family bridges behind him in the New
Jersey Thirties as his father Lewis had (perhaps) done in the
Liverpudlian 1880s?

Et cetera. "So fax the things out to Denver," Bets recommends. "Draw circles around some of those possible skeletons
in the family closet and add a few leading questions in case
Donna doesn't see the fingerbones in the doorjamb. If she
doesn't take the bait, maybe her mother will." But keep it to the
Bauer side, she advises as an afterthought: "They-all couldn't
care less about *my* family."

Not so, Ad loyally objects, suspecting, however, that it *is*
so among the offspring of his first marriage (with the just-
possible exception of their granddaughter), as for that matter it
is to some extent with Bets herself. One thing for sure: Grandson Mark wouldn't give those charts a second look unless they
came equipped with joystick and audiovisual special effects.

Once he hears himself put the matter like that, it occurs to A. J.
Bauer that some sort of computerized version of the family
trees might be just the thing to interest his grandkids—even
Mark—in their genetic history. He puts "computerized" in
mental quotes, because what he has in mind . . .

Well, he's not sure quite *what* he has in mind until some
mornings later, when, in the course of transferring at last Carl's
Bauernbaum to his PC (in mere outline format, as Ad's uncertain how to duplicate onscreen the branching lines of a genealogical tree), he comes to realize that while the outline version,
with its hierarchical indentations and categories of enumera-
tion (I, II; A, B; 1, 2; a, b; etc.), lacks the graphic appeal of

descending "branches," it has the merit of a sort of hypertextuality: Its program permits the user to display at will only
the roman-numeraled, first-generation ancestors and their
spouses, for example, without their progeny (*I. HELMUT
AARON BAUER, m. Rosa Pohl Fleischer 1883; II. LEWIS
JAMES GARDNER, m. Martha Ewell Stone 1886*), or them
and their offspring (IA–G, IIA–F) without *their* offspring
(IA1, etc.). The ideal computerized genealogical chart, he supposes, would be a bare-bones direct line of descent, whether
patrilineal or matrilineal—a menu-option could instantly reverse those invidiously uppercase males and their lowercase
mates and trace one's descent through one's mother's mother's
mother—hypertexted so that a click of the mouse on IC (Aunt
Annabelle Bauer), say, would display her essential biographical
info, including *m. Alfred H. Murray 1925*, and a click on that
same Uncle Alf would display *his* genealogy, et cetera: just the
sort of "interactivity" that might appeal to Donna and Mark.
The more so if each such name-click displayed a mug shot of
the selected ancestor, perhaps together with a map showing
Liverpool, Boston, Saxony, wherever, and/or views of Ellis Island, the Statue of Liberty, the huddled masses yearning to be
free. . . . Ad knows nothing about computer programming and
software design, and the Bauer PC antedates CD-ROMs; he
bets, though, that if he did and it didn't, he could devise in his
retirement a marketable do-it-yourself hypertexted genealogy
program that the members of an extended family could amplify
to their hearts' content with whatever they knew or discovered
about their ancestors and other relatives—biographical data
("Uncle Alf sold DeSoto automobiles in Green Bay, Wisconsin, after World War II"), wedding videos, voice-over anecdotes and new-baby cries, whatever—such that any particular
family member could download and browse it at his/her will,
following whatever linkages happened to appeal to her/his curiosity . . . et cetera.

   "It might or might not interest Mark," Bets responds
when Ad describes over lunch this hypothetical high-tech
Bauernbaum, "but his grandpa is obviously hooked. Want to

run it by Harold and see what he has to say?" She's half teasing: Her thirty-six-year-old son by her short-lived first marriage is a maverick "networking consultant" out in Silicon Valley with whom Ad has never quite hit it off and who seldom communicates with his mother these days.

"I might just do that." Ad is far from certain what a networking consultant even is, but the whole idea of this open-ended, interactive, hypertextual genealogy program, he reminds his wife, is to bring family members a bit closer together in a shared, ongoing project. "It's a network in itself," he adds, the idea having just occurred to him: "Family members all around the country could e-mail their additions and corrections to the whole Family Net. In fact," for now *this* occurs to him, "it's a network in another sense, too: all those family branches branching off into other families. Maybe Harold *would* be interested."

"You're hooked," his wife declares, "and I've got a tennis date. Keep me posted."

Hooked he is. Back at his workstation that afternoon, Ad imagines clicking on *Rosa Pohl Fleischer* (old Helmut's bride), say, to call up *her* parents and siblings, their names and dates and capsule biographies. He bets he'd see then, among other things, where she got her middle name, and how many male Fleischers had been the butchers that their name implies, as the Bauers must once have been farmers. Click next on any one of those several siblings, or on their spouses, and you're in a whole other exfoliated family tree.

That image intrigues him: the browser swinging from tree to family tree wherever their branches touch, like a monkey in the rain forest, like . . . our earliest, pre-human ancestors. Horizontally, so to speak, on the level of any given generation, if one could track the spouses of all of one's siblings, the spouses of all of *their* siblings and of theirs and theirs et cetera, how many families would be thus interconnected? A hundred? A thousand? A hundred thousand? On a corkboard beside the workstation, he has pinned side by side Carl's version of the

Bauernbaum and Aunt Jan's of the Gardner Tree: twin deltas widening down from Helmut (*m. Rosa*) Bauer and Lewis (*m. Martha*) Gardner, respectively, to the latest generation of their descendants. By switching the positions of these charts and diddling their diagrams just a bit, he finds he can bring their lower corners together at the point where his marriage to Betsy conjoins the family trees. The like applies, potentially, to any of the many marriages there recorded—as would be displayable by a simple mouse-click in Ad's theoretical software program. Can it be imagined, he now wonders, that given enough hypothetical mouse-clicks . . . ?

Although we have established that A. J. Bauer is a retired academic, his erstwhile professional field—vaguely denominated "the humanities"—has not heretofore been mentioned. Sufficient to say that he is acquainted enough with the history of Western thought and literature to have "professed" selected specimens therefrom on the community-college level, and that as a generalist rather than a specialist, he not only subscribes to but actually reads, especially in his retirement, both the *New York Review of Books* and *Scientific American*, cover to cover. He is therefore (or anyhow) acquainted with the Egyptian, Greek, and Hebrew creation-stories, for example, and likewise with the "Eve hypothesis" advanced by some paleontologists: that the DNA of all humans presently inhabiting the planet indicates descent from a single African foremother, presumably not long down from the trees and coupling in the veldt with her male counterpart. Contemplating either of those two pyramidal diagrams on his corkboard, he is now moved to imagine at its peak not Helmut and Rosa Bauer or Lewis and Martha Gardner but the biblical Adam and Eve, or that emergent African Eve and her consort, and to envision a computerized genealogical program so powerful and info-rich that enough clicks of the mouse would lead back even past them, to (depending on the user's "belief system") either the One God who created the two humans who engendered all succeeding ones or the first single-celled earthly life-form that over the eons evolved into multicellular animals, thence into vertebrates, mammals,

primates, hominids, the first *Homo sapiens*, et cetera. At the
pyramid's tip, the aboriginal spark of life; at its base, every human being, if not every thing, currently alive on earth, their in-
terrelationships and line of descent literally at the inquirer's
fingertips.

Among the several courses that "Professor" Bauer (the self-
deprecating quotes are his) once taught at HamCoComCol
was one called The Bible as Literature, in which—he had to
tread carefully here among the largely unsophisticated first-
generation college-goers, many living at home with their unaf-
fluent but stoutly opinioned parents—the familiar "storics" of
Genesis (one did not call them myths) were respectfully compared to their analogues in other cultures. Predictably, when
it was pointed out that Adam and Eve had three children (infamous Cain, doomed Abel, and much-later-born Seth), the first
and third of whom are said to have sired all subsequent earth-
lings, someone would reasonably ask, "Where'd they get their
women?" A discussion would ensue—raucous, indignant, fascinated, depending on the classroom mix—of the problem of
sibling incest in any creation-story wherein a primordial One
creates an original Couple who in turn beget the rest of humankind. If Eve, made from Adam's rib, was "bone of his bone,
flesh of his flesh," was she not, genetically speaking, his sister?
And if somehow not, would not her and Adam's daughters (un-
mentioned by the patriarchal Hebrew scribes, but necessary
to postulate if Cain and Seth are to have mates other than their
mother) have been their husbands' sisters? For that matter
(some sharp-eyed sophomore would here point out), why does
guilty Cain, "marked" by God for the murder of his brother
Abel, complain that whoever sees that mark will kill him, when
according to the scorecard—Abel dead, Seth not yet born—
there *is* no one on earth besides himself and his parents? Professor Bauer would here mention, e.g., an Islamic tradition that
each of those original brothers had a twin sister; that Father
Adam, no doubt to attenuate the consanguinity, proposed that
each son marry the other's twin rather than his own; and that
Cain (Qabil in the Arabic version), desirous of his beautiful

sister Labuda, murders Abel/Habil out of simple sexual rivalry. Did he then take both sisters for himself? Or did one of them subsequently become young Seth's wife, despite her having been old enough, even at her kid brother's birth, to be his mother? Or perhaps Seth's wife was one of his brother Cain's daughters (i.e., Seth's niece) by one of the brothers' sisters?

Et cetera. Reminded of these perennial classroom discussions by his new genealogical pyramid, our Adam now considers the rate of that pyramid's broadening in the light of what began this story: his own family's declining rate of reproduction and his granddaughter's Declaration (it now occurs to him to call it) of Nondependents. One God, says Genesis—with or without the collaboration of the *Shekhinah*, the Female Principle of the Kabbalists—created two humans: "male and female He created them," and they in turn engendered . . . shall we say five (Cain, Abel, Seth, and a couple of nameless daughters?), of whom at least one, Abel, perished without issue. A net doubling of population, then, in each generation thus far. Ad's *World Almanac* informs him that while the base of that human pyramid is expected to number more than six billion souls by the year 2000, from preclassical times until the end of the European Middle Ages the world's population is estimated to have held at a modest and fairly stable two hundred million. Setting aside such freaky imponderables as the longevity of the Patriarchs and the catastrophe of the Flood, and allowing three generations per century, how many such generational doublings would it have taken to attain that "classical" two hundred million?

Not very many: A minute's button-punching on the calculator demonstrates that in only twenty-seven iterations, the series 1, 2, 4, 8, 16, 32 . . . *n* reaches 134,217,728; the twenty-eighth puts it well over the top (268,435,456). Allowing that philoprogenitiveness in some individuals would be offset by infertility, celibacy, homosexuality, or early death in others, in less than one millennium (933.3 years, to be precise, at 33.3 years per generation beginning with Adam and Eve) God's human children could theoretically have exceeded the number es-

timated by demographers to have actually peopled the planet—
all of them cousins at one remove or another.

"Both Lamech and Methuselah lived longer than that," Ad
points out to his wife. "Imagine a family get-together of two
hundred million."

Betsy shakes her head, not simply at that image.

"The birthdays," her husband marvels. "The holiday-card
list."

"The airport logistics," his wife adds, for whom her stepfamily's one-visiting-grandchild-at-a-time policy is a minor
headache. The couple agree that it is sobering to reflect how
different the evolutionary facts must be from Ad's simple arithmetic: the hundreds of thousands of years it will have taken
African Eve's descendants to expand the ecological niche of
Homo sapiens, against all odds, to the two-hundred-million sus-
tainable maximum before . . . what? Before certain advances
in technology and agriculture, Ad surmises, blew the lid off
around the time of the Renaissance, and the Europeans' discovery of the New World afforded them a whole new spawn-
ing-ground. It is heartening to be reminded, they agree further,
that we humans are literally, if not all brothers, at least all blood
kin. But she has another tennis date, has Betsy, or intends to arrange one if she hasn't, with a threesome from that much-ex-
tended family; she'll leave Adam Johnson Bauer to his musings
and reckonings—not before remarking, however, that both she
and, in her opinion, Granddaughter Donna would likely be
more interested in the specifics of their grandmothers' grandmothers' lives than in whether the biblical Seth shacked up
with his niece, his aunt, or his sister. See you later, Calculator.

Yes, well. Such all-but-idle speculations are not the only
thing that AJB does with his time, but in truth he has less to
busy his mind with than formerly, and so when next he returns his attention to what he now calls Donna's Diagram,
he draws a new equilateral delta with the apex labeled GOD and
the base labeled 200,000,000 HUMAN DESCENDANTS. Having pinned one upper corner of it to his corkboard above the
Bauer/Gardner family trees, he accidentally lets the sheet slip

while fetching a second pushpin; the resultant near-inversion of that delta (perhaps together with its dangling now over the *Bauernbaum*) inspires him to a new idea and, anon, a new diagram. At the base of those original charts are DONNA and MARK Putnam (their estranged father's surname), along with the sundry cousins of their generation. Each of those youngsters, it goes without saying, has or anyhow had two biological parents, each of whom ditto, etc. etc. Reversing his previous calculations, Ad imagines and presently draws an inverted delta with DONNA BAUER PUTNAM at its bottom point, her pair of parents at the next level up, her four (biological) grandparents on the level above that, then her eight great-grandparents (most of whom, on the Putnam side, are already unnameable by Adam), her sixteen great-great-grandparents, etc.—until, in only those same two-dozen-plus generations, the girl's direct ancestors equal in number the estimated then population of the earth.

With some excitement, "What am I leaving out?" he asks his wife, who has attended this latest exposition politely but can be of no assistance therewith. "We're not talking aunts and uncles and in-laws and stepparents here, just biological parents and grandparents. There's no getting around the arithmetic, 'cause it takes two to tango, and two hundred million is two hundred million. But the results are impossible."

More obligingly than eagerly, "Run it by me again?"

He does. Twenty-eight doublings of the number one make two-hundred-plus million, Q.E.D. Counting forward from Adam and Eve is obviously an iffy business, since not every couple has four surviving children each of whom in turn et cetera, and so it might very reasonably take hundreds of thousands of years instead of nine hundred thirty-three to get from African Eve and her mate to earth's estimated human population as afore-established. Indeed, the fact that the world's population apparently held steady at that "classical" level for at least a couple of millennia instead of doubling every thirty-three years is proof of the constraints in that direction. But counting *back* is another story: Each one of us necessarily had a mother and father, each of whom et cetera—which seems to mean that around the time of the Norman Conquest every person on the face of Planet Earth must have been the direct ancestor of everybody presently aboard.

"It was our Great-Plus-Grandfather William of Normandy who whupped our Great-Plus-Grandfather Harold at the Battle of Hastings," awed Adam declares. "It was Great-Plus-Grandma Murasaki who wrote *The Tale of Genji* while Great-Plus-Grandpa Leif Erikson discovered Vineland. Everybody who fought and died on both sides in the First Crusade was our great-plus-grandparent!"

"Wait a minute." As if to make sure, Bets consults her watch. "Saint Thomas Aquinas didn't have any kids, so there's one down. Some nuns and popes back then didn't have any, too, if I remember correctly."

He knows, he knows, repeats Ad: There has to be something screwy about his reasoning. For example (it occurs to him even as he speaks), it would appear that our two hundred million great-plus-grandparents in 1066 would have to have had *four* hundred million parents of their own in 1033, when we've already established that for generation after generation there were only two hundred million available candidates for parenthood. So it has to follow (he's thinking fast) that Donna's great-great-grandparents, while indisputably sixteen in number, needn't have been sixteen different people; otherwise we would all be descended from Genghis Khan and Ghazali and the Eskimos, as well as from William the Conqueror and Harold the Conquered. . . .

"Ghazali?"

Eleventh-century father of Sufi mysticism, if not of the Bauers and the Gardners.

His wife pats his arm. "Well, you work on it, honey."

But her husband doesn't (the simple flaw in his geometric reasoning, he soon recognizes, is that while every child must have two parents, not every two need have four, etc.). He's no big-time original thinker, Adam Johnson Bauer, much less any kind of genius: just a middling old-fart ex-academic with a temporary bee in his bonnet from wanting to explain to his grand-daughter, perhaps likewise to himself, that we presently breathing humans are not *de novo*, howevermuch she and her fellow Denver mallsters might blithely feel themselves to be; that she and himself and all of us are indivisibly part of the ever-renewing tissue of life on earth, descended *directly*, through our parents and grandparents, from the primordial blue-green algae, and related to every other living thing.

No: not *explain*. What's to be explained? At age seventeen the girl's convinced that although she "might get married once or twice" (!), she wants no children. Most likely she'll change her mind; quite possibly she won't, given the way young women are nowadays. So bloody what? Retired, he sits in his familiar, once-so-piled-up study and futzes with his charts and calculator while his wife plays tennis with her friends and the world grinds on: atrocious massacres and counter-massacres in central Africa; bitter standoffs in the Balkans and the Middle East; whole species disappearing from the ever-dwindling rain forests before they're even classified; more misery and injustice everywhere than one can catalogue, much less address; and the sky evidently ever on the verge of falling. Not much Ad Bauer can do about all that, beyond acknowledging and bearing in mind the enormous fact of it. He has long since made essential peace with his privileged position: a fortunate life in a fortunate country at a fortunate time. He and Bets vote moderate-liberal, contribute to assorted charitable and cultural causes, and endeavor to lead harmless lives; they eat meat and dairy products only sparingly, limit their intake of table wine, compost their leaves and recycle their trash, try to be good neighbors and to maintain a civil, tolerant attitude toward people with customs and opinions different from their own. Soon enough nevertheless, he knows, catastrophe is bound to befall them in one form or another: cancer, hurricane, fatal accident, crippling stroke. Meanwhile . . .

So one of his children had children and two did not: So what? So all had parents and proliferating foreparents: So bloody bloody what? Just now he feels bearing down upon him, does Adam Johnson Bauer, the weight of that massive inverted pyramid—of which he and his beloved Betsy and each of all the rest of us is individually the vertex—as if it were an enormous hydraulic press, and dear sunny Granddaughter Donna its all-too-human diamond point.

Forget it, Reader.

Brother! Sister! Daughter! Son!

Forget it.

Ninth
Night

So what's he *wearing?*
it may have occurred to Reader to wonder about guy Graybard on this ninth evening of his and Muse Wysiwyg's
Hendecameron, if not before. Its narrative viewpoint being
mainly his, we've had detailed accounts of his companion's
nightly dress and undress; oughtn't we to hear what duds *he*
doffs when dud-doffing time arrives, for the pair's now-ritual
creek-dip between wine and waterbed?

Yes, well, okay—although in the nature of their situation,
their character-functions, and even their names, her appearance is more relevant to this framing-tale than his. Indeed, if it
be noted now that on this partly cloudy and breezy but warm
Wednesday, 9/19/01, the fellow has entered their Imaginarium
wearing khaki shorts, collared tan polo shirt, and brown leather
deck moccasins, that's because this "evening" he has found his
collaborator wearing the same, as if she has become as much an
aspect of him (or he of her) as is he of his Originator.*

Coincidence? Perhaps, notwithstanding her disingenuous
shrug when he remarked it as she served the *vin du soir*—

---

* The case was almost the same on Fifth Night, except that her sweatshirt then had
been ink blue and his (not reported, because irrelevant) a light clay.

Your "marsh-country pinot gris" again? he asked after sniffing, sampling, and inspecting its color by patio-candle light. As on First Night?

"Good guess." She took her seat on the twilit deck, crossed her excellent legs, and raised her glass. "The Mediterranean version this time: *grigio* instead of *gris*."

Ah, so: Spain last night, Italy tonight. And tomorrow?

She looked out over the darkening marsh. "Maybe home?" And before he could ask, "Don't ask: I mean the mythic old muses' home." And then, "Scratch that: She means the mythical abode of the muses, not some nursing home on Mount Helicon."

Understood.

—together with her occasional unsettling prescience, whereof one has seen evidence on earlier nights. "You were wondering," she said now, for example, "what the Hebrew calendar dates Creation from, and according to whom?" Which he had indeed meant to ask last night, but forgot to when Inspiration distracted him. "God knows, excuse the expression, when and how the count-back started. By Jesus's time it was more or less established Judaic tradition, but it wasn't formally codified until the *Seder Olam Rabbah*, second century C.E.? After which it gets reinforced in other more or less authoritative chronologies up through the eighth century. Just rabbinical consensus, you understand: With no pope to lay down the law, 'more or less' is all you get."

Or want. Okay, and thanks, dear Wys.

Her mind evidently on other matters, she stretched and sighed. "Numbers: I love 'em."

Oh?

"Not math itself, particularly; just *numbers*. Measures. *Integers*. Like, are they quote *real*, or quote *only* in our heads, et cet.? That's what I particularly liked about your story last night—"

Our story.

"Yes, well. Despite the fact that that inverted delta toward the end bent our No More Shrinkage rule a bit."

Sorry there.

"No problem." Sigh. "Numbers!"

That figures, Wys: *Sing, O Muse, in mournful numbers,* et cet.? Or Wordsworth's Solitary Reaper: *Will no one tell me what she sings? / Perhaps the plaintive numbers flow / For old, unhappy, far-off things. . . .*

Frowning: "Enough, Geeb, please!" Then, less sharply, "Enough?"

If she says so. Then presently: Creek-time?

"If *he* says so, she guesses."

He says so. And later, with your help, maybe another number-story?

"If you say so."

Was he merely imagining that she rather enjoyed his uncharacteristically (and no doubt briefly) taking charge of their agenda? In any case—while the U.S. stock market temporarily held steady, and American consumer spending showed signs of rising back toward normal, and the administration's ultraconservative attorney general widened the Justice Department's authority to detain suspected terrorists without the usual legal constraints, and Democrats in Congress felt obliged to mute their opposition to the Pentagon's zillion-dollar "Star Wars" missile-defense program, and the nation's airlines, hard hit by people's fear of flying after September 11, were pledged massive federal aid to tide them over—Ms. Wysiwyg set down her wineglass and peeled off shoes, shirt, shorts, and undies *as if obediently* while her Narrative Software did the same. Scarcely to his credit, Graybard must have found her newly deferential air arousing, for when she now turned ladderward he embraced her from behind, an embrace that she responded to with a small sound and turned to reciprocate. By when he then led her down into the silky warm wet, he found himself inspired past the point of waiting for waterbedtime: It being low tide and the water only shoulder-deep, he stood on the creek's soft-silt bottom and gripped her firm one in both hands while she laced her fingers behind his neck, girdled his hips with her thighs, and pressed her forehead to his lips—and they managed together an X-rated Saltyfresh Metaphorical Wet Dream Come True, whose asterisks may not have been *intended* as more than mere tabulation, but in this instance surely were.

* * * * * * * * *

If that was the figurative Appetizer,
Graybard (for one) wondered as the pair sooner or later climbed back on deck—his fine friend leading, he following so closely up the ladder that his face received blissfully the warm creek-droplets dripping from her—what Entrée could imaginably follow? And as if once again reading his thoughts, Ms. Wys (her submissiveness shed already by their third or fourth submarine asterisk) said, "Storytime," took his more than willing hand, and led him straightaway to the narrative bed.

"Something with *numbers*, okay?"

If she says so. . . .

"She has so said." And holding up all but one of her slim fingers, "Preferably *nines*—this being Ninth Night, Nine Nineteen?"

The tease of her smile suggested that she had at least some acquaintance with the two remaining items in their inventory, wherefrom the clear candidate, numberwise, was the one called

9999

❖

THE WORD *ODOMETER* DATES FROM 1791, but mileage indicators didn't appear as standard equipment on automobile instrument panels until after World War I. Frank Parker's memory, therefore, of his parents' bidding him and his older sister, in the rear seat of the family sedan—the big black Buick, it must have been, the family's first postwar conveyance, and most likely during one of their ritual Sunday-afternoon drives down-county—to "watch, now: She's all nines and 'bout to come up zeroes," can be dated no earlier than 1919, Frank's eighth year and sister Janice's eighteenth, nor later than 1922, the year newlywed Jan moved with her husband from Maryland's Eastern Shore to upstate New York, whence thereafter she returned only occasionally, with her own children. And Jan is very much a feature of this memory: More of a mother to Frank through that melancholy period than his disconsolate mother was (still grieving for her war-lost firstborn), it could even have been she who called her kid brother's attention to that gauge on the verge of registering its first thousand or ten thousand miles. In any case, in his eighty-fifth year Frank well recalls a long-ago subtropical Chesapeake afternoon (automotive air conditioning was yet another world war away), his Sunday pants sticky on the gray plush seat, the endless marshes rolling by, and that row of nines turning up not quite simultaneously from right to left—were there tenth-of-a-mile indicators back then?—to what his father called "goose eggs."

For our Frank—who just two hours ago (at a few minutes past 9 P.M. on Sunday, September 7, 1997, to be more if not quite most exact) was prepared to end his life, but has not done so, yet—each of those limit-years has its private significance. Certain sentimental reasons, to be given eventually, incline him to prefer 1919, in particular the third Friday of that year's ninth month: Tidewater Maryland could well have been still sweltering then, and the new Buick might feasibly have been turning up its first thousand. But 1922 (though not its summer) was likewise a milestone year, so to speak, in what passes for this fellow's life-story.

A consideration now occurs to him: Wouldn't the digits 9999, for reasons also presently to be explained, have "freaked out" his mother altogether, as Americans say nowadays? Perhaps she had already taken to the bed whereof she became ever more a fixture, tended first by Janice and their tight-visaged father, subsequently (after Jan's escape to Syracuse) by a succession of "colored" maids, as Americans said back then. In which case it would have been Jan herself in that front passenger seat, "playing Mom" (it was no game), and not impossibly young Frank who, bored with counting muskrat-houses to pass the sweatsy time, leaned over the front seatback, noticed the uprolling odometer, and said, "Hey, look," etc. It doesn't much matter, to this story or generally; Frank just likes to get things straight. 1919 was the second and final year of the great influenza pandemic, which killed perhaps twenty-five million people worldwide (more than the Great War), including some half million Americans—among them young Hubert Parker, who was serving in France with the American Expeditionary Force but was felled in '18 by the deadly myxovirus, not by the Hun or by the stellar "influence" once thought to cause such epidemics. Baseball players in that season's World Series wore cotton mouth-and-nose masks, as did many of their spectators; "open-faced sneezing" in public was in some venues declared a crime, as were handshakes in others. Frank's odometer-mem-

ory includes no facemasks, but then neither does his recollection of the family's home life generally in that glum period.
Perhaps isolated small-towners took fewer precautions than
city folk; perhaps even student-nurse Janice was too discour-
aged by their elder brother's death, their mother's collapse, and
their father's withdrawal into stolidity to give much of a pre-
cautionary damn; or perhaps that mileage-memory dates from
a later year. *1919* is the title of the second novel of John Dos
Passos's *USA* trilogy, a favorite of Mr. and (the late, profoundly
lamented) Mrs. Frank Parker, for not altogether literary reasons. 1919 . . .

In a misanthropic mood, Leonardo da Vinci called the
mass of humankind "mere fillers-up of privies." True enough of
this story's mostly passive protagonist, Frank supposes; likewise even of his (late, still inordinately beloved, *indispensable*)
spouse, their four parents and eight grandparents and sixteen
great-grandparents et cetera ad infinitum as far as Frank
knows; likewise of their middle-aged son (his wife felled by a
heart attack before his mother succumbed to a like misfortune)
and their sole, much-doted-upon grandchild. Prevailingly,
at least, they have all as far as Frank knows led responsible,
morally decent if perhaps less than exemplary lives: no known
spouse- or child-abusers among them; no notable greedheads,
programmatic liars, cheaters, stealers, or exploiters of their fellow citizens. One drunkard bachelor uncle on Frank's mother's
side, but he injured none except himself. Frank and (the un-
assimilably deceased) Pamela Parker, we can assert with fair
confidence, in their lifetimes have done (*did* . . . !) no or little in-
tentional harm to anybody, and some real if not unusual good:
Pam by her own assessment was a reliable though unremarkable junior-high mathematics teacher, Frank by his a competent though seldom more than competent public-school administrator, the pair of them at best B+ at worst B− parents
and citizens, perpetuating the cycle of harmless fillers-up of
privies, all soon enough forgotten after their demise. If anything at all has distinguished this pair from most of their fellow
filler-uppers . . .

There on his nightstand is cabernet sauvignon to dull his senses for the deed. There are the sleeping pills, of more than sufficient quantity and milligrammage; the completed note of explanation To Whom It May Concern (principally his retirement-community neighbors and his granddaughter) and the sealed letter to his Personal Representative (Frank Parker, Jr.). There is the plastic bag recommended by the Hemlock Society to insure quietus, but which our man fears might prompt an involuntary suffocative panic and blow the procedure; he may well opt not to deploy it when the hour arrives.

And what, pray, might be that Estimated Time of Departure?

If anything, we were saying, has distinguished this now-halved pair of Parkers from the general run of harmless, decent folk, it is (*was* . . . !) their reciprocally abiding love—which ought most healthily to extend outward from self and family to friends, community, and humankind, but which in Frank and Pam's case remained for better or worse largely intramural—and a shared fascination with certain *numbers*, especially of the calendric variety: certain patterns of date-notation. If one could tell their story in terms of such patterns—and one could, one can, one will—that is because, as shall be seen, after a series of more or less remarkable coincidences had called the thing to their attention, they saw fit to begin to arrange certain of their life-events to suit it, telling themselves that to do so was no more than their little joke: a romantic game, an innocent tidiness, a kickable habit.

But let's let those dates tell their story. The late Hubert Parker, Frank's flu-felled eldest sib, happened to be born on the ninth day of September, 1899: in American month/day/year notation, 9/9/99; in the more logical "European" day/month/year notation, also 9/9/99, or 9.9.99 (we now understand the possibly painful association of that on-the-verge odometer reading back in the family sedan). Very well, you say: No doubt sundry notables and who knows how many mere privy-fillers shared that close-of-the-century birthdate, as will a much

larger number its presently upcoming centenary.* But did they
have a next-born sib who first saw light on New Year's Day,
1901 (1/1/01 American, ditto European, and a tidy alternating-
binary 01/01/01 by either), birthday of the aforementioned
Janice Parker? The coincidence was a neighborhoodwide How-
'bout-that and a bond between brother and sister, even before
its remarkable compounding by Frank Parker's birth in 1911
on what, beginning with his seventh birthday, would mourn-
fully be dubbed Armistice Day, and another war later, on his
forty-third, be grimly, open-endedly renamed Veterans Day.

By either system, 11/11/11: the century's only six-figure
"isodigital," as a matter of fact. (It will be Pam, the seventh-
grade-math-teacher-to-be, who early on in their connection
offers Frank that Greeky adjective, together with the datum
that his birthday's "precurrence" in the twelfth century—
11/11/1111—was the only *eight*-figure isodigital in their millennium. Work it out, Reader, if such things fascinate you as
they did them; you may note as well that no date in either
the preceding or the succeeding millennium of the Christian
era will exceed seven isodigits.) Not surprisingly, even without
those parenthetical enhancements Frank's birthdate was the
occasion of considerable family and neighborhood comment.
He recalls his parents' joking, before Hubie's death ended most
levity in their household, that they had planned it that way,
and that they were expecting young Hube to supply their first
grandchild on either Groundhog Day (2/2) or George Washington's birthday (2/22) in 1922.

When those dates arrived, Hubert Parker was dead; sister
Jan (nicknamed for her birth-month) was a registered nurse
whose chief patient was her mother and whose impending marriage would soon leave the family "on its own"; and young
Frank was a somewhat introverted fifth-grader in East Dorset
Elementary, his fascination with such calendrics understandably established. It was on one or the other of those two Febru-

---

* The American-style present time of this narrative, remember, is 9/7/97.

ary holidays that he reported to Miss Stoker's class the remarkable coincidence of his and his siblings' birthdate patterns, called their attention to the phenomenon of "all-the-same-digit" dates, projected for them the eleven-year cycle of such dates within any century (2/2/22, 3/3/33, etc.), and pointed out to them what the reader has already been told: that the constraints of a twelve-month year with roughly thirty-day months make 11/11/11 the only six-figure "same-digiter" in any century. Miss Stoker was impressed. Nine months later, on that year's Armistice Day, when like every elementary-school teacher in America his (then sixth-grade) teacher, Miss Scheffenacher, observed to the class that the Great War had officially ended on the *eleventh hour* of the eleventh day of the eleventh month just four years past, they sang a mournful-merry "Happy (eleventh) Birthday" to our protagonist. After everyone had stood with head bowed as the town's fire sirens sounded that eleventh hour, the boy responded with the observation that even those few of his classmates who hadn't turned eleven yet were nevertheless in their eleventh year; additionally, that while the date of his war-lost brother's death in France had not been a Same-Digiter, it had been the next best thing (for which Frank hadn't yet found a name): 8/18/18—when, moreover, luckless Hubie had been eighteen years old.

His comrades regarded him as Special, whether charmed or spooked. Miss Scheffenacher (having provided the term "alternating-digiter," which Frank shortened to Alternator) opined that he would go on to college and Become Somebody someday, and then set the class to listing all the Samers and Alternators in the century, using the American style of date-notation. Not even she had previously remarked the curious patterns that emerged from their blackboard tabulations: that among the Samers, for example, there were none in the century's first decade, four in its second (all in 1911, culminating in Frank's birthday), two in its third (the aforenoted February holidays of their present year), and only one in each of the decades following. She thought Frank should definitely go on to college, and would have declared as much to his parents had the mother not been an invalid and the father a non-attender of parent-teacher meetings and most other things.

Except for the Miss Stokers and the Miss Scheffenachers, however, who "went off" to the nearby state normal school to become teachers, not many young people in small-town tidewater Maryland in those days were inclined or able to pursue their formal education past the county school system; most were proud to have achieved their high-school diplomas instead of dropping out at age sixteen, by choice or otherwise, to begin their full-time working lives. But with his family's blessing Frank did, in fact, complete his first year in that little teachers college and begin his second before the combined setbacks of his mother's death and the Great Depression (his father's car-sales business foundering, the family's savings lost in the general bank failures) obliged him to leave school—on 1/31/ 31, he noted grimly—and work as bookkeeper and assistant manager of Parker Chevrolet-Oldsmobile-Buick.

There he might have remained, and our story be stymied, had not his ever-more-dispirited father committed suicide on the first or second day of May, 1933. Shot himself in the starboard temple with a small-bore pistol, he did, late in the evening of 5/1; lingered unconscious in the county hospital for some hours; expired before the dawn of 5/2, his son at his bedside, his harried daughter en route by train and bus from Syracuse. Although the date was numerically insignificant (so Frank thought), he happened two months earlier to have sighed, in his bookkeeper's office, at the approach, arrival, and passage of 3/3/33, the first Samer since Miss Scheffenacher's fifth-grade February. The fellow had attained age twenty-one, still single and living in his parents' house, now his. The tidy arithmetic of double-entry bookkeeping he found agreeable, but he had neither taste nor knack for selling motor vehicles, which few of his townsfolk could afford anyhow in those hard times. On a determined impulse he sold the automotive franchise that summer, rented out the house, and with the meager proceeds re-enrolled in the normal school to complete his interrupted degree in secondary education.

Three years after his receipt thereof, our calendric love-chronicle proper begins. Twenty-six-year-old Frank, having mustered additional accreditation, is teaching math and "science" to the children of farmers and down-county watermen in a small high school near his alma mater; he looks forward already to "moving up" from the classroom (which has less appeal for him than does the subject-matter) to school administration, for which he feels some vocation. He has dated two or three women from among the limited local supply, but no serious romance has ensued. Is he too choosy? he has begun to wonder. Are they? Is he destined never to know the experience of love? In early March, 1938, he surprises his somewhat diffident self by inviting his principal's new young part-time secretary, barely out of high school herself and working her way through the teachers college, to accompany him to a ham-and-oyster supper at the local Methodist church, the social hub of the community. Despite the eight-year difference in their ages and some good-humored "razzing" by the townsfolk, the pair quite enjoy themselves; indeed, Frank feels more lively and at ease with pert young Pamela Neall than he has ever before felt with a female companion. On her parents' screened front porch later that evening, he finds himself telling her of his calendrical claim to fame: his and his siblings' birthdates, his brother's death-date, the Alternator 1/31/31 that marked his leaving college, and the Samer 3/3/33 that prompted his return. Miss Neall's interest is more than merely polite: Her ready smile widens in the lamplight as he runs through the series; all but bouncing with excitement beside him on the porch glider, she challenges him to guess her own birthdate, and when he cannot, offers him the clue (she's a quick one, this hardworking aspirant to math-teacherhood) that just as he was born on the century's only six-digit Samer, she was born on its only *seven*-digit Alternator.

Frank feels . . . well, beside himself with exhilaration. "Nine Nineteen, Nineteen Nineteen!"

Moved by the same delight, they kiss.

✤ ✤ ✤

Did the course of true love ever run smooth? Now and then, no doubt, but not inevitably. Although the couple were entirely pleased with their "first date" (Frank's joke, which won him another kiss; but it was Pamela who remarked before he that the date of that date was another Alternator, 3/8/38) and no less so with their second and third, Pam's mother and father opposed any sequel on grounds of their daughter's youth and the age differential. Common enough in that time and place for girls of eighteen to marry, but they had hoped she would finish college first. A firm-willed but unrebellious only child who quite returned her parents' love, Pam insisted that the four of them reason it out together, listening with respectful courtesy to all sides' arguments. Her and Frank's (they're a team already): that their connection was not yet Serious and would not necessarily become so, just a mutual pleasure in each other's company and some shared interests; that should it develop into something more (they exchanged a smile), she was determined not to be diverted from the completion of her degree and at least a few years' experience of teaching—a determination that Frank applauded and seconded. Her parents': that they had no objections to Frank as a person, only as a premature potential suitor of a girl who one short year ago could have been his high-school student; that howevermuch their daughter might now vow her determination to finish her education (for which she was largely dependent on their support), love "and its consequences" could very well override that resolve, to her later regret. Better to avoid that risk, all things considered—and no hard feelings, Frank. In the end, the four agreed on a compromise: a one-year moratorium on further "dates" while Pam completed her freshman year at the normal school, spent the summer camp-counseling up in Pennsylvania as planned, and returned for her sophomore year. During that period the pair would not refrain from dating others, and if next spring—at ages nineteen and twenty-seven, respectively—she and Frank inclined to "see" each other further, her parents would withdraw their objections to such dates.

Each repetition of that word evoked the young couple's

smiles, as did such now-voltaged numbers as *nineteen;* without knowing it, Pam's well-meaning parents had undermined their own case and increased the pair's interest in each other. When the girl agreed to have no further dates with Mister Parker before the date 3/9/39, Frank understood that the campaign which he had not till then particularly set out to wage was already half won. As good as their word, for the promised year they refrained from dating each other, though not from exchanging further calendrics and other matters of mutual interest in their frequent letters and telephone conversations; and they dutifully if perfunctorily dated others—Pamela especially—with more or less pleasure but no diminution of either's feelings for her/his predestined soulmate.

Quite the contrary, for so they came ever more to regard each other with each passing month. Had Frank noticed, Pam asked him in one letter from Camp Po-Ko-No, that if his sister Jan had managed to be born on the first of October instead of the first of January, then her birthdate (10/1/01) would be the only "patterned" date, whether Samer or Alternator, in the century's first decade? And would he please *please* believe her that although the senior counselor with whom she had dutifully "gone out" once or twice had proposed the fancy word *isodigitals* to describe what they called Samers, she had found the fellow otherwise a bore? He would indeed, Frank promised, if she would ask him the Greek word for Alternators and not date him a third time, as *he* was not re-dating his history colleague Arlene Makowski. Meanwhile, had Pam noticed that the date of her recentest letter, 8/3/38, was a Palindrome, a numerical analogue to "Madam, I'm Adam"? And that her remarkable birthdate, 9/19/1919, could be regarded as a Palindromic Alternator, as for that matter could sister Jan's? And that he loved her and missed her and was counting the days till 3/9/39?

One weekend shortly thereafter, he drove all the way up into the Pennsylvania mountains in order to see and talk with her for just one surreptitious lunch hour, the most they felt they could allow themselves without their meeting's becoming

a "date." They strolled the little village near Pam's camp, holding hands excitedly, stopping to kiss beside a shaded stream
that ran through the tiny town park with its monuments to the
Union dead and the casualties of the Great War.

"*Sequentials*," he offered, "like straights in a poker hand:
The first in this century was One Two Thirty-four, and there
won't be another till One Twenty-three Forty-five."

She hugged him, pressed her face into his shirtfront, and
reckoned blissfully. "But then the next one comes later that
same year: December Third!"

He touched her breast; she did not move his hand away.

"We give up," her good-natured parents declared that fall.
Their daughter was back at the normal school, their future
son-in-law back in his high-school classroom, and the pair still
not actually dating, but telephoning each other daily and seeing each other casually as often as manageable on the weekends. "You're obviously meant for each other."

But it pleased the couple, perversely, to let their reciprocal desire ripen through that winter without further intima-
cies until the agreed-upon date, meanwhile reinforcing their
bond with the exchange of Reverse Sequentials (3/2/10, 4/3/
21, etc.) and the touching observation—Pamela's, when Frank
happened to recount to her in more detail the story of his father's suicide—that the date of that sad event was not as "meaningless" as he had supposed, for while it might be tempting
to regard 3/3/33 (Frank's "career change" day) as marking the
end of the century's first third, the actual "33 percent date" of
1933—i.e., its 122nd day—would be May 2, when Mr. Parker
died. Indeed, since 365 divided by 3 gives not 122 but 121.666
. . . n, it was eerily appropriate that the poor man shot himself
on the evening of May 1 and died the following morning.

Much moved, "The fraction is so *blunt*," Frank almost whis-
pered: "*One-third*, and that's that. But *point-three-three* et cetera
goes on forever."

"Like our love," Pam declared or vowed, thinking *infinite
isodigitality*—and herself this time placed his hand, her own
atop it, where it longed to go.

On the appointed date, March 9, 1939, they declared their affiancement. In deference to Pam's parents' wishes, however, they postponed their marriage nearly a full two years: not quite to her baccalaureate in May 1941, but to the first day of the month prior, trading off their friends' April Fools' Day teasing for the satisfaction of the American-style Alternator plus European-style Palindrome. Moreover, just as Frank felt his "true" eleventh and twenty-second birthdays to have been not the November Elevenths of those years but 2/22/22 and 3/3/33 respectively, so the newlywed Mr. and Mrs. Parker resolved to celebrate their wedding anniversaries not on the actual dates thereof but on the nearest Alternator thereafter: 4/2/42, 4/3/43, etc.

And so they did, though not always together, for by the arrival of that first "true" anniversary the nation was at war. Not to be conscripted as cannon fodder, thirty-year-old Frank enlisted in the Navy and after basic training found himself assigned to a series of logistical posts, first as a data organizer, later as an instructor, finally as an administrator. Her profession and the couple's decision to put off starting a family "for the duration" made Pam fairly portable; although they missed their first True Anniversary (Frank couldn't get leave from his Bainbridge boot camp) and their fourth (story to come), they celebrated 4/3/43 at his base in San Diego and "the big one," 4/4/44—their third True Anniversary, Frank's thirty-third True Birthday, and their first Congruence of Samers and Alternators, a sort of calendrical syzygy—at his base in Hilo, Hawaii, where Pam happily taught seventh-grade math to the "Navy brats." Whether owing to the tropical ambiance, the poignancy of wartime, the specialness of the date, or the mere maturation of their love, she experienced that night her first serial orgasm; it seemed to her to extend like the decimal equivalent of one-third, to the edge of the cosmos and beyond.

4/5/45 saw them separated again, this time by a special assignment that Frank was dispatched to in the South Pacific. Forbidden to mention to her even the name of his island destination, much less the nature of his duty there (it will turn out to do with logistical support for the atom-bombing of Hiroshima and Nagasaki four months later), all Frank could tell her was that while the first of that year's two Sequentials (1/23/45) saw the war still raging in both the European and the Pacific theaters, he wouldn't be surprised if the show was over by the second. And did his dear Pammy remember first flagging that notable date during their non-date in that little park near Camp Poke-Her-No-No?

How swiftly a good life runs. By their first "irregular" or "corrective" anniversary (4/1/50: The zero in any decade-changing year will spoil their romantic little game, but remind them of their wedding's actual date) they were resettled in Pam's hometown, Frank as assistant superintendent of the county school system, Pam as a teacher in that same system on open-ended leave to deliver—on an otherwise "meaningless" date in May—their first and, it will turn out, only child, Frank Jr. He grew; she returned to teaching; sister Jan's husband deserted her in Syracuse for a younger woman; all hands aged. Some calendar-markers along their way, other than their always-slightly-later True Anniversaries: 7/6/54, a Reverse Sequential on which Frank Jr.'s baby sister miscarried and the Parkers called it a day in the reproduction department; 5/5/55, their Second Syzygy (fourteenth True Anniversary and Frank's forty-fourth True Birthday), when thirty-five-year-old Pam enjoyed by her own account the second best orgasm of her life; November 23, 1958, when Frank came home from the superintendent's office (he had been promoted the year before) to find his wife smiling mysteriously, his third-grade son bouncing with excitement as Pam had once done on her parents' front-porch glider, and on the cocktail table before their living-room fireplace, champagne cooling in a bucket beside a plate of . . . dates. The occasion? "One One Two Three Five Eight," she told him happily when he failed to guess: "the only six-number Fibonacci in the century." "Get it, Dad?" Frank Jr. wanted to know: "One and one makes two, one and two makes three, two and three makes five, and three and five makes eight!" "You can pop *my* cork later," Pam murmured into his ear when he opened the bottle, and they happily fed each other the hors d'oeuvres.

By their Third Syzygy—Frank's fifty-fifth True Birthday, their Silver True Anniversary (a full two months later now than their Actual), and the twenty-second of the bloody D-Day landings of Allied invasion forces in Normandy—Frank Jr. was a high-school sophomore less interested in the Fibonacci series or any other academic subject than in getting his driver's license, his girlfriend's attention, and the Beatles' latest album; Pam was recovering from a hysterectomy; Frank Sr. had taken up golf and looked forward already to retirement in Florida, like Pam's parents. No orgasms that night, but contented toasts to "the Number of the Beast and then some" and the True end of their century's second third (its Actual .6666 . . . *n* point, they would have enjoyed pointing out to young Frank if he ever stayed both home and still long enough to listen, was not 6/6/66 but the year's 243rd day, the last of August).

Life. Time. The Parkers subscribed to both, enjoying the former much more than not while the latter ran in any case. 7/7/77 ought to have been their luckiest day: The expense of their son's lackluster college education was behind them (Business Administration at the state university), as was the suspense of his being drafted for service in Vietnam. Now twenty-seven, the young man was employed as an uncertified accountant at, of all history-repeating places, a large Chevrolet-Buick dealership—across Chesapeake Bay in Baltimore, where he lived with his wife and baby daughter. Frank himself was retired and in good health though somewhat potbellied, eager to move south (Pam's parents, alas, had died) but resigned to waiting four more years for his wife's retirement and Social Security eligibility at sixty-two. They doted on their grandchild, wished that Baltimore weren't so long a drive and that their daughter-in-law weren't so bossy, their son so submissive. In the event, nothing special happened in their house that July Thursday except that Frank Sr. managed a usable morning erection despite his hypertrophic prostate; aided by a dollop of personal lubricant to counteract Pam's increasing vaginal dryness, they made pleasurable love—after which, lying in each other's arms three dozen years into their marriage, they agreed that every day since 3/8/38 had been a lucky day for them.

8/8/88 already! Frank's seventy-seventh T.B., the couple's forty-fourth T.A., Pam's sixty-ninth year! They've settled in a modest golf-oriented retirement community in southwest Florida and would normally be back north at this time of year, escaping the worst of the heat and hurricane season and visiting their granddaughter (now twelve) and her maritally unhappy dad. But Frank Sr. is in the hospital, pre-opping for removal of a cancerous kidney (he'll recover), and so they're toughing out their Fifth Syzygy on location. Pam limps in at Happy Hour (arthritic hip) with a smuggled split of Piper-Heidsieck and a zip-lock plastic bag of dates; they kiss, nibble, sip, sigh, hold hands, and reminisce about that Big One in Hilo back in '44, when she went Infinitely Isodigital.

"I wonder what ever happened to that handsome senior counselor at Po-Ko-No," she teases him, and crosses her heart: "the one that never laid a digit on me."

"Maybe he ran off with my alternative Alternator," Frank counters: "Arlene Whatsername. Did I ever tell you she was born on One Six Sixteen?"

In their latter age, Pam busies herself volunteering at the county library and playing bridge with other women in their retirement-community clubhouse. Frank, as his body weakens, has in his son's words "gone philosophical": He reads more than he ever did since college—nonfiction these days, mostly, of a speculative character, and *Scientific American* rather than *Time* and *Life*—and reflects upon what he reads, and articulates as best he can some of those reflections to his mate. His considered opinion (he endeavors to tell her now, lest he happen not to survive the impending surgery) is that like the actual alignment of planets, these calendrical syzygies and other date-patterns that he and she have taken such playful pleasure in remarking are as inherently insignificant as they are indeed remarkable and attractive to superstition. Human consciousness, Frank Parker has come to understand—indeed, animal consciousness in general—has evolved a penchant for noting patterns, symmetries, order; in the case of *Homo sapiens*, at least, this originally utilitarian penchant (no doubt a great aid to survival) tends to acquire a non-utilitarian, "gee-whiz" value as well: Certain patterns, symmetries, and coincidences become fascinating in themselves, aesthetically satisfying. Even non-superstitious folks like himself and Pam, if they have a bit of the obsessive-compulsive in their makeup, may take satisfaction in noting correspondences between such patterns and their significant life-events, and be tempted to jigger such correspondences themselves into a pattern—which may then become causative, influencing the course of their lives in the same way that superstition would maintain, but for opposite, non-mystical reasons.

"You know what?" said Pam (for so swiftly does time run, this pre-op tête-à-tête is already past tense): "Frank Junior is right."

Operation successful, but along with his left kidney the patient lost much of his appetite for both golf and food. Pam underwent a hip replacement, also reasonably successful. Frank Jr.'s wife's heart without warning infarcted; she died cursing God and her milquetoast husband. The latter within the year remarried (a divorcée five years his senior, with two teenagers of her own) and moved the "blended family" to Santa Fe, New Mexico, where he took a job in his new bride's father's accounting firm. Granddaughter Kimberly pleaded with her paternal grandparents to rescue her from her stepfamily; aside from their increasing frailty, however, they thought it best for the girl to accommodate to her new situation. In just a few short years, they reminded her, she would be off to college with their financial assistance and virtually on her own.

"Are we aware," Pam asked Frank on April Fools' Day, 1990—their "corrective" forty-ninth anniversary—"that our Golden True Anniversary will also be my very first True Birthday?" For so indeed 9/1/91 would be, within the parameters of their game: a syzygy of a different stripe! They would celebrate it, they decided, by taking fifteen-year-old Kimberly to Paris, the first trip abroad for any of them if one discounts a Caribbean cruise the February past. The girl was thrilled, her grandparents if anything more so; the three made plans and shared their anticipatory excitement by telephone and e-mail, crossing their fingers that the Persian Gulf War wouldn't spoil their adventure. More charmed by the date-game than her father had ever been, Kim proudly announced her "discovery" that the Golden Alternator 9/1/91 would in France become a Golden Palindrome: 1.9.91.

"That girl will amount to something," Frank proudly predicted. Amended Pam, "She already does." In mid-August, however, on the virtual eve of Kim's joining them in Florida for their departure from Miami to Paris, Pam suffered the first of what would be a pair of strokes. It left the right side of her body partially paralyzed, impaired her speech, canceled all happy plans, and constrained the "celebration" of her True seventy-second birthday and their Golden T.A. to a grim reversal of 8/8/88: Pam this time the pale and wheelchaired patient; Frank the faux-cheery singer of "Happy Birthday," their granddaughter harmonizing by long-distance telephone.

Through that fall and winter she regained some range of motion, but never substantially recovered and had little interest in continuing so helpless a life solely on the grounds of their surpassing love. Together they discussed, not for the first time, suicide. Neither had religious or, under the circumstances, moral objections; their impasse, which Pam declared unfair to her, was that Frank made clear his resolve to follow suit if she took her life, and she couldn't abide the idea of, in effect, killing him.

"Couldn't you have lied," she complained, "for my benefit?" Her husband kissed her hand. "No."

On the last day of February, her second and fatal stroke resolved the issue for them before it could harden into resentment. The widower postponed his own termination to see the last rites through, for which his son and granddaughter, but not the rest of that family, flew out from Santa Fe (sister Jan was ten years dead of breast cancer; her grown children had never been close to their Aunt Pam and Uncle Frank). Kimberly, tears running, hugged her grandpa goodbye at the airport afterward and pointed out that by European notation, it being a leap year, Nana Pam had died on a five-digit Palindromic Alternator: 29.2.92. Frank wept gratefully into her hair.

Through half a dozen hollow subsequent "anniversaries," mere dumb habit has kept him alive after all, though ever more dispirited and asocial. Frank Jr.'s second marriage has disintegrated. Feeling herself well out of that household, Kim attends a branch of Florida State University, in part to be near her grandfather, and in fact their connection, though mainly electronic, remains the brightest thing in the old man's life. Hefty and sunny, more popular with her girlfriends than with the boys, she discusses with him her infrequent dates and other problems and adventures; she visits him on school holidays, tsks maternally at his bachelor housekeeping, and briskly sets to work amending it. And without fail she has noted and telephoned him on 9/2/92, 9/3/93, 9/4/94, 9/5/95, 9/6/96—not to wish him, grotesquely, a happy anniversary, but merely to let him know that she remembers.

It is the expectation of her sixth such call that has delayed Frank's calm agenda for this evening, his and Pam's fifty-sixth True Anniversary. The man is eighty-five, in pretty fair health but low on energy and no longer interested in the world or his protracted existence therein. His son and namesake, nearing fifty, currently manages a General Motors dealership back in the tidewater Maryland town where he was born and raised; the two exchange occasional cordial messages, but seldom intervisit. Granddaughter Kim, having spent the summer waitressing at a South Carolina beach resort and the Labor Day holiday with her bachelor father ("a worse housekeeper than you, Grandpa!"), should be returning to Orlando about now to begin her junior year in Hotel Management; as a special treat from her grandfather she'll spend part of this year as an

exchange student in France. Usually she telephones in the early
evening, just after the rates go down. Last September, though,
come to think of it, she merely e-mailed him a hurried THINK-
ING OF YOU, GRANDPA!!! KIM :-) XOXOXOX 9/6/96.

He has eaten, appetiteless, his microwaved dinner, cleaned
up after, poured himself a second glass of red wine, made his
preparations as aforenoted, and rechecked the computer (YOU
HAVE NO NEW MAIL). Kim's recent messages have spoken of
a boyfriend, one of her co-workers at the resort, whom she'll
"miss like crazy" when they return to their separate colleges
and has hoped to touch base with between her visit home and
her rematriculation; perhaps in the unaccustomed excitement
of romance she has lost track of the date. She knows that he
goes to bed after the ten o'clock TV news; he'll give her till
then, although his self-scheduled exit-time was 9:19. A touch
muzzy-headed from the wine, as that hour approaches he
changes into pajamas (wondering why), wakes the computer
one last time, then shuts it down for good—a touch worried, a
touch irritated. Call Frank Jr.? No need to worry him; he'll
know nothing that Kim's grandfather doesn't. Call the college?
She has no new phone number there yet. Her summer work-
place, then. But this is silly; she simply though uncharacteristically forgot the date, or remembered but got somehow sidetracked.

Now it's half past nine, and he's annoyed: If he ends his life
per program, the girl may blame herself for not having telephoned. So he'll leave her a message, reassuring her of his love
and her non-responsibility for his final life-decision. All the
same, she'll feel guilty for not having spoken with him one last
time. So what? Life goes on, and on and on.

It's just a senseless pattern, he reminds himself: He doesn't
have to turn himself off on 9/7/97 or any other "special" date.
He can wait to be sure that Kim's okay, tease her for forgetting
her old gramps, then do his business when he's sure she won't
in any way blame herself—on 9/20, 10/2, whenever. *Not* doing
himself in tonight simply for the sake of repudiating the Pattern, he recognizes, would be a backhanded way of acknowl-

edging the thing's ongoing hold on him; but he has these other, perfectly reasonable reasons for delay. . . .

Or is he merely temporizing, rationalizing the Pattern's grip? Mightn't his freedom be better demonstrated (to himself, as no one else will know or care) by going ahead now as planned, following the Pattern precisely in order to prove (to himself) that he's under no compulsion either to follow it or not?

Our Frank is sleepy: the uncustomary wine, the hour, the weight of these considerations. He could get a good night's sleep and kill himself *mañana*, with a clear head. He could do it next May, the sixty-fifth anniversary of his father's suicide. He could put it off till 9/9/99, his and Pam's fifty-eighth True Anniversary, his eighty-eighth True Birthday, and his brother's one hundredth Actual. He could for that matter put it off till the next 11/11/11, the ultimate full cycle, and be the first centenarian ever to autodestruct.

Sitting up in his half-empty bed at ten past eleven, with his left foot he pushes off and lets fall to the hardwood floor his right bedroom slipper, the better to scratch a little itch on his starboard instep. 9/9/99, he wearily supposes, would after all be the aptest date for his final Date: just before life's odometer rolls up straight zeroes, as the calendar's never does.

Or he could do the damned thing right now.

Tenth Night

*Inquired Graybard Storyteller of his enigmatic muse on the "eve-
ning" of Tuesday, September 20, 2001, as fleets of U.S. bombers
and warships moved toward Afghanistan in pursuit of Osama bin
Laden, his Al Qaeda camps and caves, and any more-or-less-innocent
bystanding Afghans mistakable them for,*
Can we talk?

Calm, cloudy, and cooler today in Tidewaterland, with off-
and-on showers, the first rain since Fourth Night in that
drought-stressed venue. On the deck of Ms. Wysiwyg's bright
Imaginarium, our chap, attired as usual, sat under an overhang
to stay warm and dry while his seemingly weather- and water-
proof colleague took her pensive ease in a transparent toga out
in the wet, her legs crossed openly in the masculine style, and
watched raindrops drip from her laurel-wreathed brow into
her wine.

Retsina, tonight's drink is, less resinous than most such but
still too turpentinish for GB's taste, much as he appreciates
its significance: a symbolic progress from the New World's
vineyards to the Old's, from California, Maryland, and upstate
New York through France, Iberia, and Italy to the muses' home
turf and "a beaker full of the warm South," in Keats's phrase
(though the retsina is chilled), "full of the true, the blushful

Hippocrene" (though in hue the stuff more resembles, to Graybard's eyes, a urine specimen).

"Sure." She shook water from her hair and looked up brightly: "Last night's story filled the bill in most respects— plenty of numbers but no ball-busting math; lots of nines for Ninth Night Nine Nineteen, and even a Nine Nineteen in the story: that Pam character's birthdate in Nineteen Nineteen, which means she'd've been, let's see, eighty-two yesterday if she weren't a fictional character and hadn't died in Ninety-two. So okay, that Frank fellow's wine was a *rouge* like Keats's blushful beaker with its quote *purple-stainèd mouth*, instead of a nice crispy-clear *blanc*; that's certainly the guy's last-glass priv-ilege, though even on my deathbed I'd want a wine that I can see through clearly." Twiddling a wreath-leaf: "My only com-plaint is that it was all so bloody *depressing*, Geeb—to which of course your reasonable reply will be What's cheery about Life's Last Act? We agree that autumn hath its splendors— Q.E.D. at asterisk-time last night! But winter? Blah. And while it goes without saying that *anything* may be grist for the muse's mill, this particular Saltyfresh Serviceable Surrogate guesses she's just about had it now with Autumnality, even, not to men-tion Terminality! Hence her sixth and last Ultimatum, to wit: *One more Falling-Leaf tale and she's out of here.* Okay?"

Responded Graybard when her speech was done, Yes, well: We'll just see—to himself reflecting that from his orig-inal ten-tale backlog only one item remained in any case; how they'd manage on Eleventh Night was anybody's guess. But none of that's what I meant, Wys, when I asked Can we talk?

"I think I know what you meant, mate. Drop a couple of those kalamata olives in your retsina, and let's drink up."

It would no longer surprise him, her still-dry visitor al-lowed, if she *did* know in advance what was on his mind, given her track-record in the Prescience way. Inasmuch as Reader most likely doesn't share her foreknowledge, however, and not even Teller himself is 100 percent sure of his present feelings, with her indulgence he'll have a go at articulating same in an Aside.

She shrugged permission, if any was needed, and raised her glass: "To the Patient Gentle Reader?"

Indeed: Here's looking at you, PGR.

Click of wineglasses. Sip of presumably potioned Hellenic paint-thinner, not bad once one's in the spirit of it, and further enhanced now by a light surface film of kalamata oil. Wysiwyg then contemplated by turns the drizzle-misted evening marsh and the tidy navel under her see-through toga while her client unburdened himself of the following

First-person aside to Patient Gentle Reader:

What was on my mind back there, see, Reader—when I asked her Can we talk? and she sidetracked me pronto with all that natter about nines and wines and No more Autumnality, even—was this, as we suspect *she* knows already but you maybe don't and no wonder, as I scarcely know how to put it into words myself even though putting stuff into words is my guy's line of work: That over the nine nights past and now this tenth of this so-called Hendecameron, with its serial *tête-à-têtes* and *cul-à-culs*, Intimate Inspirational Congresses, incremental asterisks and metaphorical whatevers, your Present Teller of these several tales has come to admire, trust, depend upon, eagerly anticipate the company of, relish his association with, and in general, uh, *feel strongly*, shall we say, for the shall-we-say idiosyncratic Ms. Wysiwyg, with not the foggiest notion of who she "really" is and has been, beyond her exotic current-and-doubtless-temporary role as Storyteller's Sexy Helper. That the woman's quirky combination of fetishistic transparency and programmatic opacity he finds both intriguing and frustrating, alluring and annoying, as she no doubt intends. In short—as she likely knew even before Yours Truly realized it himself—that self finds itself on the verge of *falling in love* with this kinky conundrum of a muse-figure, and while that state of affairs poses no moral problems, Q.E.D., it sure makes a chap wonder what he's getting into, so to speak, and where things go from Tenth Night, after which my guy's current inventory is exhausted. Not to mention after the night after that, assuming there'll be one as implied by this project's working title.

Just thought I'd get that said, mate. I mean, *look* at her, would you? Trim and fit, downright edible to behold, tacksharp and bright as this wacko Imaginarium of hers or whomever's; independent-spirited and yet at one's service, provisionally and temporarily at least; laying on the asterisks with one hand, so to speak, and those serial nuisance ultimata with the other. I mean, like, wow! And yet there's something plaintive in this muse's numbers, no?, as in Will Wordsworth's aforecited Reaper's: something dark under all these lights, something hiding under all this transparency, don't you reckon?

Just thought I'd get that said.

"Get it said you did," said she
when the above Aside had gotten itself said, although in the nature of Asides it'd not been said for her to hear, "and I'm much touched, moved, flattered—*honored,* even, Geebs, that you feel what your Aside said you feel."

Though of course (our man put in promptly here, anticipating what she'd say next) it goes without saying that nothing necessarily *follows* from your feelings about my said feelings. . . .

"Correct." She downed her retsina, rose wetly from her chair, and held out her left hand to him. "But that nothing *necessarily* follows doesn't necessarily mean that nothing follows. What follows now, e.g. and s.v.p., is our little creek-dip, okay? Followed by asterisks either in or out of water, your call, followed by Something It's Time I Told You, followed by a story that, whatever its other merits, will happen to meet all six of the wench's damned-nuisance specifications." Which, as Reader may or may not recall, are that it be (1) reasonably recently written, unlike Night One's *Help!* and *Landscape;* (2) 100 percent fiction, unlike Night Two's *Ring* and Three's *Dead Cat, Floating Boy;* (3) having naught to do, at least explicitly, with

Ground Situations, Dramatic Vehicles, and/or Stuck Story-tellers, unlike Night Four's *Detective and Turtle*, among others; (4) free of Sudden Recollection of Repressed-Memory Pecca-dillos in Protagonist's Long-Past Earlier Incarnations, unlike Night Five's *The Rest of Your Life*; indeed, (5) devoid of even Totally Innocent Marital Guilt, unlike Night Six's *Big Shrink*; and, finally, (6) unflavored by Autumnality, not to mention Terminality, unlike several of the above plus Night Seven's *Extension*, Eight's *And Then There's the One*, and Nine's *9999*. A tall order, one might suppose, given Graybard's track record; but he rose unhesitatingly at her beck, tossed off his own retsina, and saluted her empty glass with his.

Clink.

Or, more precisely—the stemware being not glass but clear acrylic for outdoor use—*click*. She then shed her sopping toga and dripping wreath, he his still-dry usuals, and he joined her in the goosebump-raising drizzle and the still-warm saltyfresh creeklet—where, however, they did not consummate their Metaphorical Et Cetera as on the previous night, but at his bid-ding drew deep breath, ducked under, and held on to the lad-der's low steps and each other for as long as they could, face to face and eyes wide open in what light came down from her bright HQ, as if to see who'd have to come up first for air . . . until either want of same or the silliness of the contest fetched them up as one, gasping, coughing, laughing at themselves.

Well, now, said he when he could: *There's* a metaphor for you. For me, anyhow: In over my head?

"For us." She then waited for him to take his asterisked pleasure, whether then and there or elsewhen elsewhere; he her hers ditto, until with chuckle, sigh, and bearded chin-chuck she led the way up-ladder, cross-deck, and onto a double layer of large thick beach-towels spread conveniently under the overhang, out of the wet. Sprawled then thereupon at her elbow-propped and water-beaded ease, knees raised and feet some feet apart, with a level look that belied her faux-hearty barroom tone, "Anybody for a beakful of the Warm South?"

she called as if to the room. "Snort o' the True Blushful?" Then, to him, in a voice that matched that look, "All yours, mate."

* * * * * * * * * *

Somewhile later:
　　Wuff! Whew.
　　"Wuff and whew indeed."
　　Wumpf.

And somewhile later yet,
speaking into the fine space between her shoulderblades: Something it's time you told me, I believe you said?
　　"Mm."
　　Had he entertained the hope that that something might prove to be that she quite reciprocated those feelings that he'd acknowledged Aside to the PGR, as her deportment—particularly in recent Nights and most especially in the course of their Intercourse—quite suggested? If so, *tant pis,* for "Never mind my feelings," she bade him now: "My feelings don't come into it." What it was time he knew, she went on, smiling sidelong at him (and Reader can imagine Present Teller's breath-bated suspense), was that for the several Nights past, never mind how many, there had been no capital-P Potion or -E Elixir in his wine. That whether she had secretly weaned him from it by reducing the dosage as their asterisks incremented, beginning maybe as early as Night Two or Three, or whether indeed there had *ever been* a literal Upgrade Elixir instead of the mere potent idea thereof—a notion-Potion, an inspiring metaphor for Inspiration that did the job and was *ipso facto* as good as real (like herself?), maybe *better* than real because free of side effects, ditto—none of that mattered. "The bottom line—"
　　Dearest daintiest deliciousest bottom line from here to Parnassus!
　　"If you say so. As *I* was saying, the bottom line"—she closed her eyes tight, gave her head a shake—"is the bottom line. Story?"

Story? Yes. Well. Collecting himself, no easy task: Here's one that *has* no bottom line—a circumstance with a whole new voltage on it now.

"Maybe. Title?"

Title. Yes. Well: As our plastic wineglasses said to each other earlier this evening,

CLICK

✣

"CLICK?"

So reads their computer monitor when, in time, "Fred" and "Irma" haul themselves out of bed, wash up a bit, slip back into their undies, and—still nuzzling, patting, chuckling, sighing—go to check their e-mail on Fred's already booted-up machine. Just that single uppercase imperative verb or sound-noun floating mid-screen, where normally the "desktop" would appear with its icons of their several files: HERS, HIS, SYSTEM, APPLICATIONS, FINANCES, HOUSE STUFF, INTERNET, ETC (their catch-all file). Surprised Irma, having pressed a key to disperse the screen-saver program and repeated aloud the word that oddly then appeared, calls Fred over to check it out, but the house cybercoach is as puzzled thereby as she. Since the thing's onscreen, however, and framed moreover in a bordered box, they take it to be a command or an invitation—anyhow an option button, like SAVE or CANCEL, not merely the name of the sound that their computer mouse makes when . . . well, when clicked.

So they click (Irm does) on CLICK, and up comes a familiar title, or in this case maybe subtitle—The Hypertextuality of Everyday Life—followed this time by a parenthesized and italicized instruction: *(Click on any word of the above)*.

"Your turn," declares our Irma. That's not the woman's real

name, any more than the man's is Fred; those are their "online" names, in a manner of speaking, for reasons presently to be made clear. Never mind, just now, their "real" names: They would involve us in too much background, personal history, all the stuff that real names import; we would never get on with the story. Sufficient to say that although these two are unmarried, they're coupled housemates of some years' standing, a pair of Baby-Boomer TINKs (Two Incomes, No Kids) of some ethnicity or other, not necessarily the same, and profession ditto—but never mind those, either. Sufficient to say that what they've just rolled out of the sack from (one of them perhaps more reluctantly than the other) is an extended session of makeup sex after an extended lovers' quarrel, the most serious of their coupleship: a quarrel currently truced but by no means yet resolved and maybe inherently unresolvable, although they're really working on it, fingers crossed.

A bit of background here, perhaps? That's Fred's uncharacteristic suggestion, to which Irma, uncharacteristically, forces herself to reply "Nope: Your turn is your turn. On with the story."

And so her friend—partner, mate, whatever—reaches from behind her to the mouse and, kissing her (glossy auburn) hair, clicks on Hypertextuality. (This parenthesized matter, they agree, is stuff that might be left out of or cut from The Fred and Irma Story—see below—but that they've agreed to put or leave in, at least for the present.) (In the opinion of one of them, there could be much more of it.) (In the opinion of the other, much less—but never mind.)

No surprise, Fred's selection: Hypertextuality is that (sub)title's obvious topic word, modified by the innocuous-seeming article before it and the homely prepositional phrase after (containing its own unexotic substantive [Life] with adjectival modifier [Everyday]). The man of them, one infers correctly, is the sort who gets right down to business, to the meat of the matter. Everybody knows, after all (or believes that he/she knows), what "everyday life" is, different as may be the everyday lives of Kuwaiti oil sheiks and of American felons serving life sentences in maximum-security prisons without possibility of parole (different, for that matter, as may be the everyday lives of FWFs [Friends Who Fornicate] when they're at their separate businesses). The term "hypertextuality" itself may or may not interest our Fred; he's computer-knowledgeable, but not computer-addicted. The phrase "everyday life," however, most certainly doesn't, in itself. The fellow's too busy *leading* (perhaps being led by?) his everyday life to be attracted to it as a subject. With the woman it's another story (possibly to come). But precisely because he hasn't associated something as fancy-sounding as "hypertextuality" with something as ordinary as "everyday life," the juxtaposition of the two piques Fred's curiosity. Not impossibly, for the man's no ignoramus (nor is his companion), he hears in it an echo of Sigmund Freud's provocatively titled 1904 essay *The Psychopathology of Everyday Life.* Everyday life psychopathological? (Try asking Irma, Fred.) (He will—another time.) Everyday life hypertextual? How so? In what sense? To find out, Fred has clicked on the implied proposition's most prominent but least certain term.

There are those (the computer script now declares in effect, along with most of the paragraph above) who out of mere orneriness will select one of the phrase's apparently insignificant elements—the <u>The</u>, for example, or the <u>of</u>—as if to say, "Gotcha! You said 'Click on any word. . . .'" The joke, however, if any, is on them: A good desk dictionary will list at least eight several senses of the homely word "the" in its adjectival function plus a ninth in its adverbial ("the sooner the better," etc.): twenty lines of fine-print definition in all, whereas the comparatively technical term just after it, "theanthropic," is nailed down in a mere three and a half. As for "of": no fewer than nineteen several definitions, in twenty-five lines of text, whereas the fancy word "oeuvre," just before it, is dispatched in a line and a half. Try "as," Fred, as in "As for 'of'"; try "for," Irm, or "or": The "simple" words you'll find hardest to define, while such technoglossy ones as "hypertextuality" . . .

Well. F and friend have just been shown an example of it, no? The further texts that lie behind any presenting text. Look up (that is, click on) the innocent word "of," and you get a couple hundred words of explanation. Click on any one of those or any one of their several phrases and clauses, such as "phrases and clauses," and get hundreds more. Click on any of *those*, etc. etc.—until, given time and clicks enough, you will have "accessed" virtually the sum of language, the entire expressible world. That's hypertext, guys, in the sense meant here (there are other senses; see <u>Hypertext</u>): not the literal menus-of-menus and texts-behind-texts that one finds on CD-ROMs and other computer applications, but rather the all-but-infinite array of potential explanations, illustrations, associations, glosses and exempla, even stories, that may be said to lie not only behind any verbal formulation but behind any real-world <u>image</u>, <u>scene</u>, <u>action</u>, <u>interaction</u>. Enough said?

(If so, click EXIT; otherwise select any one of the four foregoing—<u>image</u>, <u>scene</u>, etc.—for further amplification.)

Restless Fred moves to click on <u>action</u> but defers to Irma (their joint mood is, as mentioned, still tentative just now; he's being more deferential than is his wont), who clicks on <u>scene</u> and sees what the Author/Narrator sees as he pens this: a (white adult male right) hand moving a (black MontBlanc Meisterstück 146 fountain) pen (left to right) across the (blue) lines of (three-ring looseleaf) paper in a (battered old) binder on a (large wooden former grade-school) worktable all but covered with the implements and detritus of the writer's trade. (Parenthesized elements in this case = amplifications that might indeed be cut but might instead well be "hypertexted" behind the bare-bones description, to be accessed on demand, just as yet further amplifications [not given, but perhaps hypertexted] might lie behind "white" "adult male," "MontBlanc" "Meisterstück," etc.) For example, to mention only some of the more conspicuous items: miscellaneous printed and manuscript pages, (thermal) coffee mug (of a certain design) on (cork) coaster, (annotated) desk calendar (displaying MAY), notebooks and notepads, the aforeconsulted (*American Heritage*) desk dictionary open to the "the" page (1333) on its (intricately hand-carved Indian) table-stand, (Panasonic auto-stop electric) pencil sharpener (in need of emptying), (Sunbeam digital) clock (reading 9:47 A.M.), (AT&T 5500 cordless) telephone (in place on base unit), Kleenex box (Scott tissues, actually) half full (half empty?) . . . et cetera. Beyond the table one sees the workroom's farther wall: two (curtained and venetian-blinded double-hung) windows, between them a (three-shelf) bookcase (not quite filled with books, framed photos, and knickknacks and) topped by a wall mirror. The mirror (left of center) gives back a view not of the viewer—fortunately, or we'd never get out of the loop and on with the story—but of the workroom door (presently closed against interruption) in the wall behind. (The two windows are closed, their figured curtains tied back, their blinds raised. Through them one sees first the green tops of foundation shrubbery [from which Irm infers, correctly, that it's a ground-floor room], then assorted trees [L] and a sward of lawn [R] in the middle distance, beyond which lies a substantial body of water, currently gray. Two wooded points of land can be seen extending into this waterway from the right-hand window's right-hand side, the first perhaps half a mile distant, an uncamouflaged gooseblind at its outboard end, the second perhaps a mile distant and all but obscured now by a light drizzle that also blurs the yet-more-distant horizontal where [gray] water meets [gray] sky.)

(Click on any of these items, including those in brackets.)

But "Enough already," says nudgy Fred, and commandeers the mouse to click <u>action</u>, whereupon some of the leaves on some of those trees move slightly in some breeze from some direction, the water-surface ripples, and across it a large waterfowl flaps languidly left to right, just clearing some sort of orange marker-float out there on his/her way . . . upstream, one reasonably supposes, given that the stretch beyond that bird and those two points seems open water.

"That's action?" Fred scoffs, and moves to click again, but determined Irma stays his mouse-hand with her free right

(Irm's a southpaw) while she registers yet a few further details. Atop that bookcase, for example (and therefore doubled in the mirror), are (L to R:) a (ceramic-based) lamp, the carapace of a (medium-size horseshoe) crab, and a (Lucite-box-framed) photograph of three (well-dressed) people (L to R: an elderly man, a middle-aged man, and a younger woman) in (animated) conversation (at some sort of social function).

(Click on any detail, parenthesized or non-, in this scene.)

Irma springs for <u>well-dressed</u>—not nearly specific enough, by her lights, as a description of three people "at some sort of social function" in the photograph on the bookcase in the not-yet-fully-identified scene on their computer's video display terminal. With a really quite commendable effort of will, "Fred" restrains his impulse to utter some exasperated imprecation and snatch the freaking mouse from his freaking partner to freaking click <u>Fast</u> Freaking <u>Forward</u>, <u>On with the Story</u>, EXIT, QUIT, <u>Whatever</u>. Instead, he busses again his lover's (glossy) (auburn) hair, bids her "Have fun; I'll be futzing around outside, okay?," and (having slipped into jeans and T-shirt) clicks with his feet, so to speak, on the scene beyond his own workroom window.

Which twilit scene happens to be a small suburban back yard near the edge of the nation's troubled capital city, where this occasionally dysfunctional pair pursue their separate occupations: Mark the Expediter, as he has lately come to call himself; Valerie the Enhancer, ditto. Those are their "real" given names, if not really the real names of their jobs, and with the reader's permission (because all these digressions, suspensions, parentheses, and brackets are setting this Narrator's teeth on edge as well as Mark's) we'll just follow him out there for a bit while Val explores to her still-bruised heart's content the hypertextuality of everyday life.

Okay. How they got into that "Fred and Irma" business (Mark and I can reconstruct less distractedly now as he waves to a neighbor-lady and idly deadheads a few finished rhododendron blooms along their open side-porch) was as follows: They having pretty well burned out, through this late-May Sunday, their scorching quarrel of the day before—enough anyhow to make and eat together a weary but entirely civil dinner—after clean-up Mark had volunteered to show Valerie, as he had several times previously promised, some things he'd lately learned about accessing the Internet for purposes other than e-mail; more specifically, about navigating the World Wide Web, and in particular (Valerie being Valerie, Mark Mark) about the deployment of "bookmarks" as shortcuts through that electronic labyrinth, the black hole of leisure and very antidote to spare time. Mark is, as aforenoted, no computer freak; the PC in his Expediter's office, their Macintosh at home, are tools, not toys, more versatile than fax machine and phone but more time-expensive, too, and—like dictionaries, encyclopedias, and hardware stores (this last in Mark's case; substitute department stores and supermarkets in Val's)—easier to get into than out of. Tactfully, tactfully (by his lights, anyhow) (the only lights he can finally steer by)—for they really were and are still burned, and their armistice is as fragile as it is heartfelt—he led her through the flashy homepage of their Internet service provider's program, actually encouraging her to sidetrack here and there in the What's New? and What's Cool? departments (she trying just as determinedly to blind her peripheral vision, as it were, and walk straight down the aisles, as it were, of those enticing menus) and then sampling a curious Web site that he had "bookmarked" two days earlier, before their disastrous Saturday excursion to the National Aquarium in Baltimore.

http://www.epiphs.art, it was addressed: the homepage of an anonymous oddball (Net-named "CNG") who offered a shifting menu of what he/she called "electronic epiphanies," or "e-piphs." On the Friday, that menu had comprised three entrées: (1) Infinite Regression v. All-but-Interminable Digression, (2) "Flower in the Crannied Wall," and (3) The Hypertextuality of Everyday Life. Mark had clicked on the curious-sounding second option and downloaded a spiel that at first interested but soon bored him, having to do with the relation between a short poem by Tennyson—

> Flower in the crannied wall,
> I pluck you out of your crannies,
> I hold you here, root and all, in my hand,
> Little flower—but *if* I could understand
> What you are, root and all, and all in all,
> I should know what God and man is.

—and the virtually endless reticulations of the World Wide Web. This time (that is, on this post-meridianal, post-prandial, post-quarrel but ante-makeup-sexual Sunday) the menu read (1) <u>The Coastline Measurement Problem and the Web</u>, (2) "<u>The Marquise went out at five</u>" (CNG seemed to favor quotations as second entries; this one was familiar to neither of our characters), and (3) <u>The Hypertextuality of Everyday Life</u>. That third item being the only carryover, M suggested they see what was what. V clicked on it—the entire title, as no option was then offered to select from among its component terms— and they found themselves involved in a bit of interactive "e-fiction" called "<u>Fred</u> and <u>Irma</u> <u>Go Shopping</u>," of which I'll make the same short work that they did:

Onscreen, the underlined items were "hot": i.e., highlighted as hypertext links to be clicked on as the interacting reader chose. Methodical Mark would have started with <u>Fred</u> and worked his way L to R, but Valerie, left-handing the mouse, went straight for <u>Irma</u>:

> Irma V., 43, <u>art-school</u> graduate, <u>divorced</u>, <u>no children</u>, currently employed as <u>enhancer</u> by small but thriving <u>graphics firm</u> in <u>Annapolis MD</u> while preparing show of her own computer-inspired <u>fractal art</u> for small but well-regarded <u>gallery</u> in <u>Baltimore</u>. Commutes to work from modest but comfortable and <u>well-appointed rowhouse</u> in latter city's <u>Bolton Hill</u> neighborhood, 2 doors up from her <u>latest</u> lover, <u>Fred M.</u>

(more on Irma) (on with story)

"My turn?" Mark had asked at this point, and clicked on <u>Fred M.</u> before Valerie could choose from among <u>divorced</u>, <u>no children</u>, <u>enhancer</u>, <u>latest</u>, <u>well-appointed rowhouse</u>, and <u>more</u>.

Fred M., <u>software expediter</u> and <u>current</u> lover of <u>Irma V.</u>

(more on Fred) (on with story)

"That's the ticket," in Mark's opinion: "Who cares how old the stud is or where he majored in what? On with their story already."

"My friend the Expediter," Val had murmured warningly, having raised her free hand at his "Who cares?" Whereat her friend the Expediter (it was from here that they borrowed those job-titles for themselves: Valerie in fact does interior design and decoration for a suburban D.C. housing developer; Mark, a not-yet-successful novelist, does capsule texts on everything under the sun for a CD-ROM operation in College Park, distilling masses of info into style-free paragraphs of a couple hundred words), duly warned, had replied, "Sorry there: Enhance, enhance."

But she had humored him by clicking on <u>on</u>, whereupon the title reappeared with only its last term now highlighted: "Fred and Irma <u>Go Shopping</u>."

"Off we go," had invited M. But when the clicked link called up a three-option menu—<u>Department Store</u>, <u>Supermarket</u>, <u>Other</u>—V said "Uh-oh," and even Mark had recognized the too-perilous analogy to their debacle of the day before. Expediter and Enhancer in <u>Supermarket</u>, he with grocery list in one hand, pencil in other, and eye on watch, she already examining the (unlisted) radicchio and improvising new menu plans down the line. . . .

"Unh-unh," he had agreed, and kissed her mouse-hand, then her mouth, then her throat. By unspoken agreement, bedward they'd headed, leaving the Mac to its screen-saver program (tropical fish, with bubbly sound effects). Somewhile later

Valerie/Irma, re-undied, had returned to check for e-mail; the marine fauna dispersed into cyberspace; there floated CLICK in place of CNG's unpursued interactive e-tale—and here we all are.

Rather, here's Valerie at Mark's workstation in their (detached suburban) house (V's studio is across the hall; unlike those FWFs Irma and Fred, our couple are committed [though unsanctified and unlegalized] life-partners, each with half equity in their jointly owned [commodious, well-appointed, 1960s-vintage] split-level in Silver Spring [MD]), and here are Mark and I out on the dusky porch, deadheading the rhodos while thinking hard and more or less in synch about certain similarities among (1) the sore subject of their Saturday set-to, (2) a certain aspect of their recent makeup sex, (3) the so-called Coastline Measurement Problem afore-optioned by CNG, (4) an analogous problem or aspect of storytelling, and (5) how it is, after all, to be a Self, not on the World Wide Web but in the wide web of the world. Can M think hard about five things at once? He can, more or less expeditiously, when his attention's engaged, plus (6) Zeno's famous paradox of Achilles and the Tortoise, plus (7) the difference between Socrates's trances and the Buddha's. Our chap is nothing if not efficient— a phrase worth pondering—and I'm enhancing his efficiency as worst I can, by impeding it. Valerie, meanwhile (at my off-screen prodding), has reluctantly torn her attention away from that photograph on that bookshelf in that creekside workroom in that onscreen scene hypertexted behind the word "scene" in the definition hypertexted behind Hypertextuality in CNG's menu-option (3) The Hypertextuality of Everyday Life, itself hypertexted the second time up behind the word CLICK. Twenty-year-old wedding-reception photo, she has learned it is, of (present) Narrator with (present) wife and (late) father at (post-)wedding do for (now-divorced) daughter and (then-) new son-in-law—and nothing accessible therebeyond. Inter-activity is one thing, restless Reader; prying's another. Having lingered briefly on the shrub outside the RH window (*Vibur-*

num burkwoodii: grows to 6 ft [but here cropped to 4 for the sake of view and ventilation], clusters 3 in. wide, blooms in spring, zone 4, and it's a lucky wonder her professional eye didn't fix on those figured curtains, or we'd never have gotten her outside) and then on that waterfowl (great blue heron [*Ardea herodias,* not *coerulea*]) flapping languidly up-creek (off Chesapeake Bay, on Maryland's Eastern Shore, where Narrator pens these words as he has penned many others), she's "progressing" unhurriedly toward those two intriguing points of land in the farther distance but can't resist clicking en route on that orange marker-float out yonder near the creek channel:

> Marks an eel pot, 1 of 50 deployed in this particular tidal creek at this particular season by waterman Travis Pritchett of nearby Rock Hall MD in pursuit, so to speak, of "elvers": young eels born thousands of miles hence in the Sargasso Sea and now thronging instinctively back to the very same freshwater tributaries of the Chesapeake from which their parents migrated several years earlier to spawn them in mid-ocean: one of nature's most mysterious and powerful reproductive phenomena. Pritchett's catch will be processed locally for marketing either as seafood in Europe and Japan or as crab bait for Chesapeake watermen later in the season.

Travel-loving Val goes for Sargasso Sea, and there we'll leave her to circulate indefinitely with the spawning eels and other denizens of the sargassum while we click on item (1) some distance above: the sore subject of their Saturday set-to:

They love and cherish each other, this pair. Although neither is a physical knockout, each regards the other and her- or himself as satisfactorily attractive in face and form. Although neither can be called outstanding in his or her profession, both are entirely competent, and neither is particularly career-ambitious in her or his salaried job. Both enjoy their work and take an interest in their partner's. Most important, perhaps, although neither has a history of successful long-term relations with significant others, both have enough experience, insight, and un-arrogance to have smoothed their rougher edges, tempered their temperaments, developed their reciprocal forbearance, and in general recognized that at their ages and stages neither is likely to do better than they've currently done in the mate-finding way; indeed, that despite their <u>sundry differences</u> (at least some of which they've learned to regard as compensations for each other's shortcomings: See below), they are fortunately well matched in disposition, taste, and values. Neither drinks more than an occasional glass of wine at dinner, or smokes tobacco, or sleeps around, or fancies house-pets; both are borderline vegetarian, environmentally concerned, morally se-rious but unsanctimonious secular unenthusiastic Democrats. Mark has perhaps the quicker intelligence, the duller sensibil-ity, the more various knowledge; Valerie perhaps the deeper understanding, the readier human insight, the sounder educa-tion. They've never quarreled over sex or money. Both wish they had children, but neither finally wants them. (<u>Etc.</u>— though that's really enough <u>background</u> for <u>their Saturday set-to</u>, no?)

They do have differences, of course: M enjoys socializing with others more than V does; she enjoys traveling more than he. He's the more liberal (or less frugal) with money; she's the more generous in the good-works way. He's less ready to take offense but also slower to put their occasional tiffs behind him. She leaves closet and cabinet doors ajar and will not learn how to load their dishwasher properly (by *his* standards) (and the user's manual's); he wears his socks and underwear for two days before changing (turning his briefs inside out the second day!) and often makes no effort to stifle his burps and farts when it's just the two of them. (Etc., although [etc.]) These lapses or anyhow disharmonies they've learned to live with, by and large. The difference that really drives each up her or his wall is the one herein amply hinted at already, if scarcely yet demonstrated: at its mildest, a tease- or sigh-provoker, a prompter of rolled eyes and of fingertips drummed on dash-board, chair arm, desk- or thigh-top; at its sorest . . .

<u>Saturday</u>. Their week's official work done and essential house-chores attended to, they had planned a drive up to nearby Baltimore to tour that city's Inner Harbor development, which they hadn't done in a while, and in particular the National Aquarium, which they'd never. After a not unreasonable detour to an upscale dry-goods emporium in the vast shopping complex at Four Corners, a quick shot from their house—where Val really did need to check patterns and prices of a certain sort of figured drapery material for a job-in-the-works (and, having done so, pointed out to Mark that there across the mall was a Radio Shack outlet where he could conveniently pick up the whatchacallit-adapter that he, not she, insisted they needed for their sound system's FM antenna [while she popped into the next-door Hallmark place for just a sec to replenish their supply of oddball greeting cards, which was running low])—they zipped from the D.C. Beltway up I-95 to Baltimore and reached Harbor Place in time for a pickup lunch about an hour past noon (no matter, as they'd had a latish breakfast)—hour and a half past noon, more like, since the main parking lots were full by that time, as Mark had fretsomely predicted, and so they had to park (quite) a few blocks away, and it wouldn't've made sense not to take a quick looksee at the new Oriole Park at Camden Yards that was such a hit with baseball fans and civic-architecture buffs alike, inasmuch as there it stood between their parking garage and the harbor and since their objective, after all (she reminded him when he put on his Fidget Face), wasn't to grab a sandwich, see a fish, and bolt for home, but to *tour* Harbor Place, right? Which really meant the city's harbor area, which surely included the erstwhile haunts of Babe Ruth and Edgar Allan Poe. They were on no timetable, for pity's sake!

Agreed, agreed—but he *was* a touch hungry, was Mr. Mark, and therefore maybe a touch off his feed, as it were, especially after that unscheduled and extended stop at Four Corners; and it was to be expected that the ticket line at the Aquarium might well be considerable, the day being both so fine and so advanced. . . .

"So we'll catch the flight-flick at the IMAX theater in the Science Center instead," Val verbally shrugged; "or I'll stand in the Aquarium line while you fetch us something from the food pavilion, and then you stand while I do The Nature Company. What's the problem?"

The problem, in Mark's ever-warmer opinion, was—rather, the problems were—that (a) this constant sidetracking, this what's-the-rush digression, can take the edge off the main event by the time one gets to it, the way some restaurants lay on so many introductory courses and side dishes that one has no appetite for the entrée, or the way foreplay can sometimes be so protracted that (etc.). Having no timetable or deadlines doesn't mean having no agenda or priorities, wouldn't she agree? And (b) it wasn't as if this were just something that happened to happen today, or he'd have no grounds to grouse; it was the way certain people went at *everything*, from leaving for work in the morning to telling an anecdote. How often had he waited in their Volvo wagon to get going in time to drop her off at her Metro stop on the way to his office and finally gone back into the house and found her with one earring and one shoe on, making an impulsive last-minute phone call while simultaneously revising her DO list with one hand and rummaging in her purse with the other? (Valerie is a whiz at cradling the phone between ear and shoulder, a trick Mark can't manage even with one of those gizmos designed for the purpose.) How often had he been obliged to remind her, or to fight the urge to remind her, in mid-narrative in mid–dinner party, that the point of her story-in-regress was their little niece's *response* to what Val's sister's husband's mother had said when the tot had walked in on her in the guest-bath shower stall, not what that widow-lady's new Cuban-American boyfriend (whom she hadn't even met yet at the time of the incident) apparently does for a living? And (c) . . .

But he never reached (c) *(click on it if you're curious)*, because by this time V was giving as good as she got, right there on the promenade under the old USS *Constellation*'s bowsprit, where their progress toward the distant tail of the National Aquarium ticket line caesura'd for this exchange. As for (a), damn it to hell, if in his (wrongheaded) opinion she was a Gemini who preferred appetizers to entrées both at table and (as he had more than once intimated) in bed, then *he* was a bullheaded whambamthankyouma'amer of a Taurus whose idea of foreplay was three minutes of heavyweight humping to ejaculation instead of two; and (b) who, because he himself had his hands full thinking and breathing simultaneously, couldn't imagine anyone's doing five things at once better than he could manage one; for the reason that (c) . . .

But she never reached (c), for the reason that (b) (now [b1]) reminded her that (b2) *his* idea of a joke was the punchline, his idea of a whodunit the last page, revealing who done it (no wonder he couldn't place his Middle-less novels even with an agent, much less with a publisher); and (a2) if she might presume to back up a bit, now that it occurred to her, his idea of a full agenda was a single item, his top priority always and only the bottom line, his eternal (and infernal) *Let's get on with the story* in fact a *Let's get* done *with the story*, for the reason that— (b3), she guessed, or maybe (a3), who gave a damn?—his idea of living life was the same, *Let's get done with it,* and every time she saw him ready and fidgeting in the car a full ten minutes earlier than he knew as well as she they needed to leave for work, she was tempted to suggest that they drive straight to the funeral parlor instead and *get done with it* (etc., okay? On to the freaking fish already!).

But they never reached the FF ticket line, far less the marine exhibits themselves, and that's a pity, inasmuch as in the 2.5 million recirculating gallons of scrupulously monitored exhibit-water in the National Aquarium's 130-odd tanks and pools are to be found some 10,000 specimens (eels included), concerning every one of which much of natural-historical interest might be said. Under the volatile circumstances, however, it is no doubt as well they didn't, for how could they imaginably have moved and paused harmoniously through the exhibits (Valerie tranced at the very first of them, Mark glancing already to see what's next, and next after that) without reopening their quarrel? Which quarrel, mind, was still in noisy progress, if that's the right word, there under the *Constellation's* mighty bowsprit—which bowsprit, at the time I tell of, extended halfway across the promenade from the vessel's prow toward the second-floor Indian restaurant above the first-floor Greek one in Harbor Place's Pratt Street pavilion, but which at the time of this telling is alas no longer there, nor are those restaurants, nor is the formidable frigate-of-war (sister ship of Boston's legendary Old Ironsides) whose bow that bowsprit sprits, or spritted, said vessel having been removed indefinitely for much-needed, long-overdue, and staggeringly expensive major overhaul— to the glancing amusement of passersby (the lovers' spectacular, hang-it-all-out quarrel, I mean, of course, not the *Constellation's* shifting to some marine-repair Limbo) including Yours Truly, who happened just then to be passing by and sympathetically so saw and heard them, or a couple not unlike them, toe-to-toeing it, and who then or subsequently was inspired to imagine (etc.).

Embarrassed, wasted, desperate, and sore, tearfaced Valerie anon turned her back on the dear, congenitally blinkered bastard whom she so loves and just then despised and stomped off back toward the Light Street food pavilion and their parking garage, no objective in mind except breathing space and weeping room. Mark was damned if he'd go chasing after the beloved, indispensable, impossible, darling bitch, but he did so after all, sort of; anyhow trudged off in the same general direction, but made himself pause—Valerie-like, though in part to spite her—to half attend a juggling act in progress at the promenade's central plaza. Although he was as aware as was V (and no less alarmed) that the heavy artillery just fired could never be unfired and that it had perilously, perhaps mortally, wounded their connection, he nonetheless registered with glum admiration the jugglers' so-skillful routine: their incremental accumulation of difficulties and complications at a pace adroitly timed to maximize dramatic effect without straining audience attention past the point of diminishing returns, a business as tricky in its way as the juggling itself—and now he couldn't refind Valerie among the promenaders. Well, there was The Nature Company yonder; she had mentioned that. And beyond it were the food concessions; she must have been as hungry by then as he, but probably as appetiteless, too, from their wring-out. And somewhere beyond or among those concessions were the public restrooms, whereto she might have retreated to collect herself (V's better than M at self-collection), and beyond them the parking ramp. Did she have her car keys? Probably, in her purse; anyhow there were spares in a magnetic holder under the rear bumper-brace. Would she drive off without him, for spite? He doubted it, although she seemed more hurt and angry than he'd ever known her to be; anyhow the ramp-ticket was in his wallet—not that she mightn't pay the hefty lost-ticket fee just to strand him or, more likely, just to get out of there, with no thought of him either way. Most probably, however, she would just collapse in furious tears in the Volvo's passenger seat, poor sweetheart, and then lay into him with more of her inexcusable even if not wholly off-the-mark insults when he tried to make peace with her, the bitch.

Well, she wasn't in The Nature Company, where among the coruscating geodes and "Save the Rain Forest" stuff his attention was caught by one of those illuminated flat-projection earth-map clocks that show which parts of the planet are currently daylit and which in darkness (the East Coast of North America was just then correctly mid-afternoonish; darkness was racing already across Asia Minor, dawn approaching Kamchatka and Polynesia). What (momentarily) arrested him in this instance was not that vertiginous reminder of on-streaming time and the world's all-at-onceness, but rather the profusion of continental coastlines, necessarily much stylized in so small-scale a rendering, but considerably articulated all the same. Chesapeake Bay, for example—180-some miles in straight-line length, but with upward of 9,600 miles of tidal shoreline in its forty major rivers and their all-but-innumerable creeks and coves—was a simple nick up there between Washington and Philadelphia, yet quite distinguishable in shape and position from Delaware Bay, just above it; even the Delmarva

Peninsula between them, no bigger here than a grain of rice, had overall its characteristic sand-flea shape. Framed nearby, as if to invite speculation on the contrast, was a large-scale, fine-grained aerial-photo map of Baltimore's Inner Harbor, every pier and building sharply resolved, including the no-longer-present-as-I-write-this *Constellation:* One could distinguish not only individual small watercraft paddling about or moored at the harbor bulkheads but their occupants as well, and strollers like varicolored sand-grains on the promenade.

One could not, however (Mark duly reflected, looking now for the exit to the food courts and/or for a glimpse of Valerie's . . . yellow blouse, was it? Yes, he was almost certain: her yellow whatchacallit blouse with those thingamajigs on it and either a white skirt or white culottes; he couldn't recall which and saw no sign of either), even with so fine a resolution, distinguish male from female, for example, or black from white from Asian; much less identify himself and Valerie having it out under the frigate's bowsprit if they'd happened to be there doing that at that moment; much less yet see the thingumabobs on her whatchacallits and much less yet the individual whatsits on each thingumabob (etc.)—any more than the most finely drawn map of the Chesapeake could show every barnacle on every pile of every pier on every creeklet (etc.): the famous Coastline Measurement Problem afore-referred-to, in terms whereof the estuary's shore-length could as well be put at 96,000,000 miles as 9,600 (etc.). Which-all led him to, but not yet across, the verge of recognizing . . .

Yellow blouse? Yes, out there by the Polish-sausage stand, but minus thingumajiggies and blousing a red-faced matron whose steatopygous buttocks were hugely sheathed in pink cotton warm-up pants (though there might, to be sure, he reminded himself, be a truly saintly spirit under all that [maybe helplessly genetic] grossness). *No Middles to his novels,* V had told him! His eye ever on the destination, not the getting there! Already figuring the server's tip while she lingered over the appetizer! No greater evidence of the degree of Pal Val's present pissed-offness than that she had been sidetracked neither in

The Nature Company, as even he had briefly been, nor in the food court (where she would normally have been provisioning the pair of them, bless her, with goodies both for present consumption and for future relishment at home), nor on the pedestrian overpass to the parking ramp, where in other circumstances she was entirely capable of dawdling to contemplate at length the vehicular traffic below, the cumulus formations overhead, the observation elevators up-and-downing the Hyatt Regency façade nearby. Unless she had indeed withdrawn into a women's room (he had forgotten to locate the WCs; couldn't've done anything in that precinct anyhow except dumbly stand by), she must have beelined for the car, as did he now finally too.

No Valerie. Well, she was more liable than he to forgetting the level- and pillar-number of their parking slot. Not impossibly, in her present turbled state, she was wandering the ramps in a weepy rage. Plenty turbled himself, he walked up one level and down one, gave up the search as counterproductive, leaned against the Volvo's tailgate for some minutes, arms crossed, then trudged back, *faute de mieux*, toward the walkway/footbridge/overpass/whatever. Halfway across it he stopped, disconsolate, and simply stood—facing uptown, as it happened, but really seeing nothing beyond his distress.

Which let's consider himwith for just a paragraph. A physically healthy, mentally sound, well-educated, (usually) well-fed, comfortably housed and clothed, gainfully employed, not-unattractive early-fortyish middle-class male WASP American is at least temporarily on the outs with his housemate/girlfriend, a comparably advantaged and not-unattractive professional who has declared her opinion that he hasn't the talent to achieve his heart-of-hearts career aim and that this deficit is of a piece with one general characteristic of his that she finds objectionable. So Mr. Mark's pride is bruised, his self-respect ruffled, the future of his closest and most valued personal relationship uncertain indeed. *So what?* he has asked himself before any of us can ask him. The world comprises approximately 4.7 zillion more mattersome matters, from saving the tropical rain forests to finding money enough in the chaotic post-Soviet Russian economy to bring their fiscally stranded cosmonauts back to earth. Not that love and loss, or commitment and (potential) estrangement, aren't serious even among Volvo-driving yuppies, but really, what of real consequence is at stake here? If this were fiction (the wannabe writer asked himself), a made-up story, why should anyone give a damn?

Well, it *wasn't* fiction, from Mark's perspective, although out of aspirant-professional habit he couldn't help considering (as he resumed his troubled path-retracement back to and through the Light Street pavilion in search of his dear damned Valerie) how, if it were, it ought properly to end. Reconciliation? On what terms? Uneasy armistice? Virtual divorce? In each case, signifying what of interest to a reader who presumes the characters and situation to be imaginary?

From *our* point of view, of course, they *are* imaginary, and so these questions immediately apply (in a proper story they would never have come up; bear in mind that it was heart-hurt Mark who raised them) and shall be duly though not immediately addressed. Even their allegedly Middle-challenged poser understood, however—as he rescanned in vain the food concessions and monitored for a fruitless while the traffic to and from the women's room after availing himself of the men's—that more's at stake here than the ups and downs of early-middle-aged Baby-Boomer love. Not until "tomorrow" (the Sun. following this sore Sat.) will CNG's interactive e-fiction serendipitously supply them the terms "Expediter" and "Enhancer" to shorthand the characterological differences that erupted under the *Constellation*'s awesome bowsprit; but already back there on the footbridge Mark sensed that the conflict here is larger than any temperamental incompatibility between "Fred" and "Irma" or himself and Val: It's between fundamentally opposite views of and modes of dealing with the infinitely complex nature of reality.

Valerie sensed that, too; she was, indeed, already deep into the pondering thereof when, almost simultaneously, she espied him approaching from the second-level fooderies and he her at a railing-side table on the open deck out there overlooking the promenade. So far from roaming the ramps in a weepy blind rage or storming off alone in the Volvo (Val's better than Mark, we remember, at shrugging off their infrequent blowups; he himself tends to forget that and to project from his own distress), our yellow-bloused Enhancer, her chair tipped back and feet propped on balcony rail, was finishing off a chocolate-chocolate-chip frozen-yogurt waffle cone while simultaneously (a) teaching her sumbitch lover a lesson by neither fleeing nor chasing after him; (b) facilitating their reunion by staying put, as her mother had taught her to do in little-girlhood if "lost" in, say, a department store or supermarket; and (c) calming her still-roused adrenaline with a spot of yogurt while keeping an eye out for friend M and at the same time considering, in a preliminary way, his criticisms of her and the differences, as she saw them, between Socrates's famous occasional "trances," the Buddha's, and her own. They had in common, those trances, a self-forgetfulness, a putting of circumambient busyness on hold in favor of extraordinary concentration. But Buddha under the bo tree was transcendently *meditating*, thinking *about* nothing in particular while subsuming his ego-self into the cosmic "Buddha self"; Socrates, tranced in the agora or come upon by his protégés stock-still in some Athenian side street, was strenuously *contemplating*, presumably in finely honed logical terms, such uppercase concepts as Knowledge, Reality, Justice, and Virtue. Herself, however—beguiled indefinitely by . . . by the hypertextuality of everyday life, we might as well say, as encountered in the very first fish tank in the National Aquarium, or in the book beside the book up-shelf from the book that she had gone to fetch from the library stacks, or on the counter across from the counter in the department en route to the department that she had been vectored toward in the Wal-Mart next door to the supermarket that she was finally aiming for—was not so much meditating or contemplating as *fascinating:* being bemused and fascinated by the contiguities, complexities, interscalar resonances, and virtually endless multifariousness of the world, while at the same time often doing pretty damned efficiently several things at once.

"*Damn*," said Mark, hands on hips on deck beside her. "Damn and damn."

"The same," came back his unfazed friend. "That said, is it on with our day or on with our spat?"

"Spat!" had all but spat more-than-ever-now-pissed-off M.

"Pity." Val gave her (glossy auburn) hair a toss and licked a drip from her (waffle) cone. "I thought *you* were the big mover-onner and I was the overdweller-on-things. Lick?"

"No, thank you. There's a difference between moving on and hit-and-run driving, Val."

"Shall we discuss that difference?" More a challenge than a cordial invitation.

"No, thank you. Because what happened back there was no accident."

"So let's discuss *that:* its non-accidentality."

"No, thank you very much," the fire gone out of him. "Because there'd be no bloody end to it. Let's go the hell home."

But "Not so fast, buster," had countered Ms. Valerie, and although they did in fact then go the hell home after all, they ventilated reciprocally all the way, each charging the other now with spoiling the day. Through that evening, too, they had kept scarifyingly at it, heartsick Mark from time to time declaring, "What it all comes down to . . . ," and tearful Valerie being damned if she'd let him shortcut to that bottom line before he'd had his nose thoroughly rubbed en route in this, that, and the other. Exhausted half-sleep, as far apart as manageable in their king-size bed; then a grumpy, burned-out Sunday, both parties by that time more saddened and alarmed than angry, each therapeutically pursuing her or his separate business till Happy Hour—which wasn't, but which at least brought them civilly together as was their custom for their (single) glass of wine with a bit of an hors d'oeuvre, over which they exchanged tentative, strained apologies, then apologies less strained and tentative. Through dinner prep, each guardedly conceded a measure of truth in the other's bill of complaints; through dinner itself (with, uncharacteristically, a second glass of wine, much diluted with club soda), a measure less guarded and more generous. Thereafter, by way of goodwill respite from the subject, M had offered to show V that business he'd mentioned sometime earlier about navigating the World Wide Web. She had welcomed the diversion; they had booted up Mark's Macintosh, shortcut to CNG's e-piphanies homepage with its e-tale of Expediter Fred and Enhancer Irma; had aborted it early in favor of makeup sex (etc.)—and here they are.

Mm-hm. And where is that, exactly?

That exactly is in separate rooms of their (jointly owned, jointly tenanted) Silver Spring house and likewise in their extraordinarily strained but by no means severed connection. More exactly yet, it is (a) in Mark's case, on their pleasant, now-dark side porch, where—having thought hard and efficiently about those five or seven interrelated matters aforelisted (Saturday set-to, makeup sex, Coastline Measurement Problem, analogous aspect of storytelling, selfhood in the world's wide web, etc.)—in a sudden access of loving appreciation of his companion and their indispensable differences he turns from his idle rhododendron-tending to hurry herward with the aim of embracing her and ardently reaffirming that she is not only to him indispensable but by him treasured, and that he is determined to temper his maddening get-on-with-itness with as much of her wait-let's-explore-the-associationsness as his nature permits. And (b) in Valerie's case, in Mark's workroom, where—having floated a fascinated while in the Sargasso Sea of everyday life's virtual hypertextuality (but at no time so bemused thereby as to lose sight of the subject of their Saturday set-to)—in a sudden access of loving etc. she bolts up from Mark's Mac to hurry himward with corresponding intent. The physical halfway point thembetween happens to be the fourth-from-bottom step of the staircase connecting their house's ground floor (living room, dining room, kitchen/breakfast room, lavatory, front and rear entry halls, side porch, attached garage) and its second (main bedroom and bath, V's and M's separate workrooms with hallway and #2 bath between, library-loft [accessible from main BR] over garage) (additionally, in basement and thus irrelevant to their projectable rendezvous: TV/guestroom, workshop, utility room). Where they'll actually meet is another matter, perhaps suspendable while Narrator tidies a few loose ends. To wit:

- Any reasonable reader's suspicions to the contrary notwithstanding, "CNG" stands in this context not for Compressed Natural Gas, but rather for Center of Narrative Gravity: in a made-up story, the author's narrative viewpoint; in real life-in-the-world, however, <u>the self itself</u>, of which more presently, unless it's clicked on now. . . .
- Presently, then. Meanwhile, as to the aforedemonstrated essential difference between Ms. Valerie's sensibility and Mr. Mark's, it is nowhere more manifest than in the way each, in the other's opinion, tells a story. "Anna train squish" is how Val claims Mark would render Leo Tolstoy's *Anna Karenina*; indeed, given the man's Middle-challengedness, she suspects he might skip the train. She, on the other hand (claims he, whether teasingly or in their Saturday Set-To mode), would never get beyond Count Tolstoy's famous opening sentence—"Happy families are all alike," etc.—indeed, would never get through, much less past it, inasmuch as she would need to pause to explore such counter-evidence as that her family and Mark's, for example, while both prevailingly quite "happy," are as different in nearly every other respect as aardvarks and zebras; and once having clicked on <u>Mark's family</u>, or equally on <u>hers</u> (or, for that matter, on <u>aardvarks</u> or <u>zebras</u>), she would most likely never get *back* to <u>Tolstoy's proposition</u>, not to mention on to its second half and the eight-part novel therebeyond.
- Myself, I'm on both their sides in this matter, not only because M and V seem equally reasonable, decent, harmless souls, but also because their tendencies represent contrary narrative impulses of equal validity and importance. A sat-

isfyingly told story requires enough "Valerie"—that is, enough detail, amplification, and analysis—to give it clarity, texture, solidity, verisimilitude, and empathetic effect. It requires equally enough "Mark"—i.e., efficiently directed forward motion, "profluence," on-with-the-storyness—for coherence, anti-tedium, and dramatic effect. In successful instances, a right balance is found for the purpose (and adjusted for alternative purposes). In unsuccessful instances . . .

Friend of Valerie and Mark's: So, how'd your vacation go, guys?

M: Cool: Spain in ten days.

V: Really terrific, what little we got to see. The very first morning, for example, in Ávila—Do you know Ávila? Saint Teresa and all that?—we were in a Parador Nacional, just outside the old city wall. You've stayed in the Spanish *paradores,* right? So, anyhow, the one in Ávila's this fifteenth-century palace called Piedras Albas ('cause that's what it's made of, white stones from [etc., *never getting past the breakfast* churros, *inasmuch as "hypertexted" behind them, for Valerie, lies all of Spanish history, culture, geography, and the rest, inseparable from the rest of Europe's and the world's. Mark had had practically to drag the rapt, protesting woman out of that stern and splendid place, to get on with their itinerary*]) . . .

- So what? you ask, unless one happens to take some professional interest in storytelling, which you, for one, do not? Thanks for clicking on that Frequently Asked Question, reply CNG and I: The "so what" is that that same right-balance-for-the-purpose finding applies to the measurement of coastlines, the appropriate scaling of maps, and— hold that clicker—not only interpersonal relations, Q.E.D., but *intra*personal ones as well.

Intrapersonal relations?
Thanks again, and yes indeed. For what is Valerie, finally,

what is Mark, what are you and what am I—in short, what is <u>the self itself</u>, if not what has been aptly called a "posited center of narrative gravity" that, in order to function in and not be overwhelmed by the chaotically instreaming flood of sense-data, continuously notices, ignores, associates, distinguishes, categorizes, prioritizes, hypothesizes, and selectively remembers and forgets; that continuously spins trial scenarios, telling itself stories about who it is and what it's up to, who others are and what they're up to; that finally *is*, if it is anything, those continuously revised, continuously edited stories. In sum, what we're dealing with here is no trifling or merely academic matter, friends: Finding, maintaining, and forever adjusting from occasion to occasion an appropriate balance between the "Mark" in each of us and the "Valerie" ditto is of the very essence of our selfhood, our being in the world. We warmly therefore hope, do CNG & I (click on that <u>&</u> and see it turn into an =, + much <u>more</u> on intrapersonal relations), that that couple work things out, <u>when</u>ever and <u>where</u>ver they recouple.

<u>When</u>. One short paragraph from now, it will turn out, although given the infinite subdivisibility of time, space, and narrative (not to mention <u>The Hypertextuality of Everyday Life</u>), it could as readily be ten novels hence or never. See <u>Zeno's paradoxes</u> of time and motion; see swift <u>Achilles</u> close forever upon the tortoise; <u>see Spot run</u>. . . .

<u>Where</u>. Not on that fourth-step-from-the-bottom *Mittelpunkt*, it turns out, but back where this story of them started. Mark (inescapably himself even when determined to be more Val-ish) is off the porch and through the dining room and up the staircase and into the upstairs hallway by the time Valerie (who, decidedly herself even after deciding to be more Mark-like, has stepped from M's workroom first into the #2 bathroom to do a thing to her hair or face before hurrying porchward, then into their bedroom to slip a thigh-length T-shirt over her undies in case the neighbor-lady's out there gardening by streetlight, then back into M's workroom to exit the Internet so that their access-meter won't run on while they finish mak-

ing up, which could take a happy while), hearing him hurrying herward, re-rises from Mark's Macintosh to meet its open-armed owner with open arms.

To her (glossy) (auburn) hair he groans, "I love you so damned much!"

To his (right) collarbone she murmurs, "I love you more."

They then vow (etc.), and one thing sweetly segues to another right there on the workroom's (Berber) wall-to-wall, while the screen saver's tropical fish and seahorses burble soothingly per program themabove.

- *The Marquise Went Out at Five* (*La Marquise Sortit à Cinq Heures*) is the title of a 1961 novel by the French writer Claude Mauriac and a refrain in the Chilean novelist José Donoso's 1984 opus *Casa de Campo* (*A House in the Country*). The line comes from the French poet and critic Paul Valéry, who remarked in effect that he could never write a novel because of the *arbitrariness*, the vertiginous *contingency*, of such a "prosaic" but inescapable opening line as, say, "The Marquise went out at five"—for the rigorous M. Valéry, a paralyzing toe-dip into what might be called the hyper-textuality of everyday life.

Not too fast there, Mark. Not too slow there, Val. That's got it, guys; that's got it . . . (so "CNG" [= I/you/eachandallofus] encourages them from the hyperspatial wings, until agile Valerie lifts one [long] [lithe] [cinnamon-tan] leg up and with her [left] [great] toe gives the Mac's master switch a

Eleventh
Night

"Endings,"
the male character here called Graybard imagines the female
character here called Wysiwyg saying, with distaste, when that
pair re-rendezvouses in her see-through dwelling-space at 9:11
"P.M." on Friday, September 21, 2001—the eleventh and presumably final "night" of their Hendecameron: "Blah."

Mm?

Toss of elaborately blond-wigged head. Frown at dark breeze-
less night-marsh. "Dénouements, wind-ups, finales—blah. That
was my favorite thing about last night's *Click* story: no proper
ending, just a mid-sentence click-off. Amen!"

Yes, well. But not just *any* old mid-sentence, right? The sentence that would've been the closing sentence anyhow, as we
daresay you noticed. He salutes her with his bubbled champagne-flute. Much obliged for your assistance, Miz Muse, as always. Click?

Passive. Distracted. "I guess. Yeah, sure: click. To eleven
nights without chardonnay?"

Better yet, how about *to us?*

Regarding him across their tipped glasses as they sip: "And
who might *that* be, Geeb?"

Aha: the Big Question. Stalling for time (he says aloud, as if
reading from text while stalling for time), he compliments his

inspirer on her smashing Eleventh Night costume, with the frills whereof she has been fidgeting through this dialogue: Art Nouveau gauze draperies and Gibson Girl hair-thing with tastefully scattered red leaves, like the "Autumn" panel of an Alphonse Mucha *Seasons* series, circa 1910.

"She begs his pardon?"

Turn-of-last-century poster-artist, Prague and London, as she doubtless knows, having quite possibly inspired and maybe even modeled for him in one of her earlier luscious incarnations. Or are you strictly a lit-lady?

Unlipsticked lips compressed; fine unplucked eyebrows shrugged. "You tell me."

"You understand what a fix we're in, yes?" his dispatcher had asked him, in effect, that cloudywarm "morning" (i.e., less than half an hour past, at 9:00 A.M. by the clock on Original Author's writing-table. "What a narrative corner we've painted ourselves into, with a little help from your peekaboo pal?"

Without replying, Graybard stood by: his job-description.

"All I wanted, all we needed, was a bit of a frame-tale to connect those eleven miscellaneous items and make them into a *book* instead of a mere collection, right? So we come up with this wacko Wysiwyg/Muse/Imaginarium idea and decide to give it a spin, see whether it'll fly, never mind the mixed metaphor—but then *wham!*, along comes Nine Eleven, and suddenly it's a whole nasty new world out there, and how're we supposed to float a butcher's dozen irrelevant stories about Autumnality and Innocent Marital Guilt and Stuck Storytellers et cet., now that big-time shit has hit the national fan and Apocalypse has moved in just around the corner?"

Butcher's dozen?

"Baker adds one for good measure; butcher lops off excess lard. So Miss Wys comes to our rescue by defending the relevance of Irrelevance and proposing an eleven-night Hendecameron, but then with her other hand she ups the ante by disqualifying *Help!* as a story, which left us with ten tales for

eleven nights; but la-dee-da, we figured we'd cross that narrative bridge when we came to it, so along you guys go with the
Come-and-Get-It costumes and serial No-Nos and saltyfresh
skinnydips and incremental asterisks and occasional teasers like
those Fourth Night *Shabbos* candles, and never mind who the
chick Really Is and where she came from and what she's up to in
that flaky *pied-à-mer* of hers with its see-through everythings
and whether she grocery-shops and cooks and cleans and does
laundry in there or just pours white wine and spreads her Metaphorical legs at story-time: Let's go along for the ride, so to
speak, we figure, and see where it takes us. So the nights go by
and the wines get sipped and the muse gets shagged and the
tales get told, and next thing we know it's Eleventh Night!
Summer's over and so's the party; the Empire's at war again,
with no well-defined enemy and a clutch of ever-uneasier allies;
orgies of flag-waving and budget-busting, but not a clue to
when where and how the next terrorist mega-shoe will drop on
the US of A—any more than you and I have a clue how to wind
this gig up and get offstage without egg on our faces. Ayiyi!
End of uncharacteristic Authorial Outburst."

Mm-hm. Ten Nights and Good Night, maybe?

"Very funny. Getcherass out of here now, s.v.p., and go save
ours—and a good *Shabbos* to Miz Whoeversheis."

Shabbat, I'm told one says nowadays: Sephardic instead of
Ashkenazi?

"*Shabbat* shmabbat: Pen's filled, mate; computer's booted
up; *hasta la vista* and may the Force be with you. Go fetch us a
finale, okay?"

Tall order, but one does what one can, and so—while an un-
comfortable alliance is forged between outraged America, volatile Pakistan, and our former enemies in the Afghan Northern
Alliance; and bombs are readied for dropping on the noxious
Taliban (our once-upon-a-time Afghan allies) and on Osama
bin Laden's cave-dwelling Al Qaeda terrorists; and prospects
for any sort of Israeli-Palestinian accord go up in smoke and
down the drain; and life in the USA becomes less convenient,
more constrained and anxious, for what bids to be a *very* long

time to come, now that its vulnerability has been so painfully exposed—our Graybard treks once more (and finally?) next door, in a manner of speaking, to his muse's sanctum, reflecting gravely as he treks that it is, after all, perhaps not the worst of times to have most of one's life behind one; to be on one's actuarial Home Stretch; to be, in a word, *Autumnal.* . . .

As if privy to all the above,
his odd collaborator awaits him in the aforedescribed Art Nouveau get-up on her storied and once again Sabbath-candled deck, an inverted champagne-flute beside each candlestick and an unopened bottle of Mumm's *brut* ice-bucketed beside—the whole scene garnished, like her gown and hair, with red and yellow leaves.

Sweetgum, he'd guess.

"My favorite leaf." She twirls one idly between thumb and forefinger, gestures with it at the champagne: "Why can't they put this stuff in clear glass bottles? Anyhow, pop my cork whenever you're ready, Geeb—over the railing, please."

Her mirthless tone and expression belie the feeble double-entendres. Aiming marshward, our man obligingly works the mushroom-shaped cork with his thumbtips until the bottle fires like a sunset gun and arcs its stopper out into the dusk. Biodegradable, he supposes as it plicks into the creek.

"Like the rest of us." She holds out her glass for filling. "I notice we've switched to narrative present tenses."

I noticed that, too. My guess would be that that's because past-time narration implies a present from which Narrator can retrospect, and *that* implies that he's aware of what happened next back then and how the story ended. It's all history already except the telling. Whereas in *our* case . . . but hey, I just work here: What do I know?

"Same here, and thanks for the lecture." Frowning at her glass, at the nightscene, "*Endings,*" she then complains as afore-narrated, and goes on to declare her dissatisfaction with the wind-ups of, e.g., those three first-magnitude narrative navigation stars invoked in this Hendecameron's Invocation: Homer's

Odyssey, "Scheherazade's" *Thousand Nights and a Night,* and Boccaccio's *Decameron:* "So okay: The big Wandering Hero gets back to his faithful missus and grown-up son after a decade of whacking Trojans and burning their city and another decade trying to get home—thousands dead and the world turned upside down, just because his neighbor-king's wife dropped her drawers for visiting royalty! So much for the yarn's beginning, and no wonder the word *Trojans* makes most folks think of a brand of condoms. But never mind all that, and never mind that most of the guy's ten-year trek consists of wandering from the marital straight and narrow: one whole year in the sack with Circe and seven with Calypso, so only two of actually sailing from Troy to Ithaca and losing all his shipmates along the way, while Faithful Wifey keeps her legs together and stalls her lamebrain suitors with that weaving-unweaving trick, which they'd've caught on to in three days instead of three years if they hadn't been drinking up the winecellar and humping the housemaids. No: What bugs me is that after Mister Trickydick gets his free ride home from Phaeacia to Ithaca—about which I could say plenty, but never mind—and strings his big macho bow that those wussy suitors couldn't even bend, it's not enough for him to slaughter them all for partying hard at his expense: He has to hang the poor serving-pussies as well—a round dozen of them, just on old Rat-Fink Eurycleia's say-so: no Due Process, not even any questions asked! Strings 'em up like thrushes in a net, Homer says, and I quote: *They held their heads in a row, and about them all / There were nooses, that they might die most piteously. / A little while they struggled with their feet, but not for long*—the cruelest lines in the whole bloody epic, for my money—all so Big O can give his long-time-no-see bedmate the first big O she's had in twenty years. I swear! I swear!"

Well . . .

"And some say the *Odyssey* was composed by a woman? Not bloody likely!"

Yes, well . . .

"And okay, so your pal Scheherazade puts her life on the line and fucks the Sultan to keep him from raping and butchering a virgin per night as he's been doing for three years already, and she spins her thousand nightsworth of stories and bears him three sons no daughters and finally pleads for her life on their behalf—"

I believe we've covered this ground already, Wys: no particular sign that she *loves* the guy, et cet. (although it's pretty clear that Shahryar has come to love *her*), and not a hint of remorse for his having popped her thousand predecessors. . . .

"Worse! They marry off her kid sister to his kid brother, the Butcher of Samarkand, who'd been matching Shahryar virgin for virgin before Scheherazade came onstage and has gone on popping 'em right through the Thousand and One Nights because Big Bro hasn't bothered to spread the news of his own moratorium; so poor Dunyazade gets to be the blushing bride of an even more monstrous serial rapist-murderer than her big sister's bridegroom! And we're supposed to applaud their double wedding as a happy ending? It makes me want to puke!"

Refill?

"Fuck Homer! Fuck Scheherazade! Fuck Boccaccio and his fucking rich lords and ladies who don't give a flying fuck about the Black Death that's killing half of Florence, as long as they can play their flirty little games and tell their naughty little stories and be waited on hand and foot by their lucky servants, and then la-dee-da, wasn't that *fun*, guys; let's do it again next time the world ends! Jee-*sus*, excuse the expression!"

Yes, well, Wys . . .

Glass extended: "Hit me again, Sam. Yes well what?"

He has never seen her so *agitato*—and that not only, as it seems to him, from her exception to those literary monuments, which he suspects of being more the occasion than the cause of her distress. Refilling her glass (he has not yet half finished his own), Well, he protests in those old taletellers' defense, *autres temps, autres moeurs*, for one thing; it's to be expected that texts from a patriarchal time and place will have their patriarchal aspects—or, in Boccaccio's case, their aristocratic aspects.

She slugs her champagne. "Do tell."

What's quite wonderful, I needn't remind you, is that gallery of formidable women, especially in Homer: Penelope obviously, but also spunky Princess Nausicaa and her mom, Queen Arete, not to mention Circe and Calypso, right on up to the goddess Athene.

"Always subservient to Boss-Man Zeus."

Well, yes, but on a *very* long leash. And Scheherazade of course takes on the bloody patriarch with the only weapons in her arsenal, sex and storytelling, and while she can't turn the place into a feminist utopia or even bring the beastly brothers to justice, at least she and Dunyazade defang them.

"For the time being. How long will sex and storytelling keep them distracted?"

A lot longer than ten nights and a night, we bet. As for Boccaccio, those ladies of his are no wussies either, as I remember: The whole gig is Pampinea's idea, and as the make-pretend crown passes from head to head, the queens- and kings-for-a-day rule with equal authority and match each other story for story. Granted that the servants are servants and the gentry gentry, you'll admit that genderwise it's an egalitarian aristocracy, making the best of a horror show that they can do absolutely nothing about.

"Well: They could at least *acknowledge* it from time to time, for pity's sake, the way we've acknowledged what's been going on Out There while we futz around here." More calmly, "But I know what you mean, Geeb."

Of course you do; and I know what *you* mean, Wys. But it's you who taught *me* about the relevance of Irrelevance in these situations. If we're going to fuck Homer and Scheherazade and company, I say let's do it gratefully, not dismissively. You take the two gents and I'll take the lady—if she's so inclined?

To his most agreeable surprise,
"She's so inclined," replies the female entity here called Wysiwyg. She sets down her flute, holds out her hand to him, and for the first time this evening smiles. "Help me out of

this silly rig, if *you're* inclined, and let's rack up the asterisks—after which, you and I have serious narrative business to take care of."

Indeed: serious enough, one would think, that its anticipation might, if not unman our man, at least prove materially distracting from Intimate Metaphorical Congress. Be it once again remembered, however, that their incremental asterisks are not performance ratings; at the same time, be it remarked that the spectacle of Ms. Wys stepping out of her leaf-strewn autumn finery like a rebirth of tenderluscious spring may go far toward dispelling all thought of 9/11 *et sequitur ad nauseam*, not to mention all thought of the story—*her* story, surely?—yet to be somehow dreamed up and told at last.

* * * * * * * * * * *!

Whereafter,
intertwined and pleasurably spent on the marsh-nymph's storied (and internally lighted) waterbed—

"Scratch that." Her lips against his portside ear: "She's not a marsh-nymph."

Just a manner of speaking, Wys, but have it your way: . . . *on his muse's* et cetera?

"She's not his muse, either."

Up on one elbow: I deny that! Not *merely* his muse, for sure. Not *his muse exclusively*, no doubt. But His Muse she has most certainly been being, for which he's most grateful indeed.

"Have it your way, for the time being. But there's no quote *storied and internally lighted waterbed.*"

There isn't?

"Nope. You guys just dreamed that up."

We did? Then what . . . ?

But suddenly there isn't, in fact, any Storied Et Cetera—and don't ask Narrator what, in that case, the couple are coupled upon in post-metaphoricoital lassitude. I just work here.

"Nor no see-through bed-work-playroom *pied-à-mer,* as you charmingly called it, with all that transparent furniture and stuff. No deck. No ladder. No creek. No saltyfresh tidemarsh."

Hey, come *on*, now! But just as suddenly there are no longer those now-so-familiar surroundings: only two intertwined bare bodies suspended as if in lightless space.

"No *intertwined bare bodies as if* et cet.," and the entity here called Graybard feels himself reduced to an incorporeal consciousness attending a disembodied, female-timbred voice.

" . . . whose presumably final words to him, he hears that voice say now," he hears that voice say now, "are that *none of the above-mentioned items ever existed* outside a certain party's imagination. Bye-bye, dear Geeb; thanks for the ride."

And with that she's gone, as indeed is he, and their narrative page is blank

. . . until something or someone inspires our chap to exclaim *Only in a certain party's imagination?* All *right!* Whereupon there they all are, as before: buck-naked Wysiwyg and ditto Graybard; the internally lighted waterbed on which the pair now sit chastely side by side, their backs to the see-through wall; the bright Imaginarium round about and above and below them; the laddered deck; the dark marsh out there with its moon-tugged brackish tides; and beyond all those a "real" world wherein Muslim militants plot sundry horrors against a less-than-blame-free United States of America.

"*That* was a close one. . . ."

Says the muse-nymph, her bedmate adds, *with just a hint of smile in her voice?*

"Likewise in his."

To which he responds . . . ?

Taking his hand in hers, "On with the story, friend."

Story, dot dot dot question mark?

"Yup. *Her* story, s.v.p.: *Wysiwyg.*"

WYSIWYG?

❖

SO WHAT'S A NICE GIRL like her doing in a place like this?
her story's teller might well begin by asking. Whence her
obsession with transparencies literal and figurative, and with
narrowing as far as possible the unclosable gap between Appearance and Reality—an obsession extending even to her
acronymic *nom de guerre, de plume, de sport,* whatever?

"A *nom,* be it remembered, not of her own choosing. You
had to explain it to me, back in our Invocation. But go on: She's
all ears."

By no means, but never mind. This marsh, Reader, this
night, this moon, these tides, are real; likewise humankind's
black plagues of religious zealotries, intolerant orthodoxics,
and tyrannies of every sort, not to mention that catastrophic
final gift of the Terrible Twentieth to the Terrifying Twenty-
first, the literal global plague of AIDS. All real. But this glassy
Imaginarium is, well, *imaginary*—Q.E.D. a few pages past.
Is its presiding spirit likewise? A spirit pure and total, is she,
dreamed up out of airy Nothing to do the narrative job now
ten-elevenths done?

Hip to hip beside him, her hand on his upraised knee:
"Nothing pure about her, Geeb. But on with her effing story."

Her effing story indeed. Not every nymph is *ipso facto*
nymphomanic; whence then this full-bloom-summer one's readi-

ness for Intimate Congress with (among who knows how many other interlopers) a decidedly autumnal and soon-to-be wintry Graybard? Granted, their asterisked couplings are Metaphorical—but no less so are the couplers, and so within the metaphor their guilt-free intercourse is *as if* literal, no?

"Excuse me? *As if* literal? Figuratively literal? *As good as* literal?"

He considers: *As if* as good as literal, okay? To get right down to it—

"By all means do, the *as-if*-nymphomanic nymph encourages the would-be teller of her story. It's around here somewhere, that *it:* Stop mincing metaphors and get right down to it."

To get right down to it (he presses on), is his frisky friend *merely* a metaphor or *also* a metaphor? If Merely, then why such anomalous specifics as those sundry see-throughs, the Friday-night candles, and her occasionally dark and/or distant moods? "Can no one tell me what she sings?" And if Also, then who is she and has she been, before and beyond her current casting?

"You tell *me*, friend," she challenges with a smile her grateful but cornered Narrator, his back both literally and figuratively against the wall.

"A *glass* wall, mind you," she reminds him: "a *see-through* wall. You can't step through it to the other side, but you can take a shot at telling us what you see back there."

Yes. Well: What I see . . .

Let's see, now: What I see—"as through a glass, darkly," mind, and more or less reversed, inasmuch as the images beyond the wall that my narrative back is backed up to are reflections in the see-through mirror directly before us, at the foot of this storied waterbed—what I see, let's say, might be, um, e.g. . . . a Nice (part-)Jewish Girl unaware of that ethnic datum until her thirteenth year? Raised as the much-loved only child of a mild-mannered secular-WASP couple in, um, Bloomington, Indiana, shall we say? Or Madison, Wisconsin?

Iowa City? Dad a professor at the university there—Psychology, maybe?

"Close: Cognitive Science."

Cog Sci it is: still a subset of Psychology back then, but nudging toward separate-discipline status. Mom a something-or-other in the university's . . . Development office, maybe? Like a younger version of Whatsername in our Fifth Night story, *The Rest of Your Life*?

"Julia Fischer. Information Services."

Thankee. Back in the, let's see, Nineteen late Sixties early Seventies, this would've been, our Miz Saltyfresh being presently on or just over the age-thirty threshhold—

"Over."

And we'll skip the period detail, okay? No Johnson/Nixon/Ford/Carter-era stuff; no South Vietnam and Cambodia down history's bloody pipes; no Yom Kippur War and Arab oil embargo: just life as a preschooler, kindergartner, and elementary-school university brat in pleasant Bloomington/Madison/Wherever.

"Sigh: Pleasant it was, Geeb, even in those turbled times, and they the dearest of parents. *Except*, dot dot dot."

Except for their deciding early on to withhold from her, Until She's Old Enough to Understand, the reason for a dark-haired dark-eyed Mediterranean-featured youngster's being the spawn of two stereotypical upper-midwestern Scandinavian Americans named, let's see . . . Lars and Helga Lindstrom?

"A bit over the top, but you're in the ballpark."

Gus and Kristina-with-a-K Ullmann, then: Emphasis on the *Krist-*, inasmuch as while the family was programmatically agnostic, both Mom and Dad were long-lapsed Lutherans who respected their former faith as they respected the current or former faiths of their sundry Protestant, Catholic, Jewish, Muslim, Hindu, and Buddhist colleagues, friends, and students. Kristina being alas infertile and the couple desirous of child, they adopted the newborn daughter of one of Doctor Gustav's graduate students by one of her other thesis advisors, a married man who'd sworn to his illicit young lover that no contraceptive precautions need be taken themby, inasmuch as he'd been bilaterally vasectomized years since, and who then disavowed paternity on those grounds, implying that she'd been unfaithful to his unfaithful self with some other stud.

"Heartless, unprincipled shit! But sexy and gentle-mannered, I've been told, until the chips were down."

These being the days before DNA testing, there was no way to resolve the issue, had it been pressed—which it was not, nor ever even made public, Ms. Grad Student preferring to carry the child openly to term as a nine-month reproach to her faithless lover (who indeed left wife, family, and university not long before the infant's birth). She confided her angry secret to none save her dissertation director, Professor Ullmann, who in a second-trimester office conference discreetly broached to her the subject of adoption versus single-parenting and was given the whole tearful tale to believe or not. Ms. Feldman happened to be secular Jewish, her professorial ex-paramour Italian-American *goyishe;* whether or not she'd been impregnated by someone else, therefore (the Ullmanns accepted her indignant denials on the grounds of her general honorableness: She would not reveal the adultery to her ex-lover's wife, for example, much less ask her for corroboration of that alleged vasectomy), and, if so, whether that impregnator was Jew or Gentile, her daughter was by Jewish law Jewish—as she let the Ullmanns know upon surrendering the infant to them for adoption. How they elected to handle that fact was strictly their business: She herself meant to emigrate to Tel Aviv upon receipt of her doctorate and would not attempt to communicate with the child or otherwise make her existence and relationship known to her unless both the girl herself and her adoptive parents came to desire such communication—in which case it would be up to them to track down the biological mother, who intended neither to conceal nor to advertise her whereabouts.

And so the tot was raised as Trudy Ullmann—Tru for short, Gertrud for long, the name chosen for its sounding, to Gus and Kristina anyhow, sufficiently North European on the one hand

and potentially Jewish on the other to serve its bearer whichever way she might choose to go, if and when: Add an *e* to Gertrud, like the celebrated Ms. Stein, subtract the terminal *n* from Ullmann, maybe one of the *l*'s for good measure, and she's got a passably Jewish name if she wants one, when the time comes.

That time, they decided (against the prevailing wisdom among their Child Psych colleagues, who held it best to apprise adoptees of their status as early as possible, certainly before preschool, cushioning the news with some such bubble-wrap as "Other parents have to take what they get; we *chose* you, because you're special"), would be upon the girl's pubescence, more or less, depending on How Things Went. Unless fiercely principled young Dr. Beth Feldman or her scruple-free ex-lover had a change of heart and unbagged the cat, or some family friend or colleague thoughtlessly did likewise, they would raise young Trudy as their own flesh and blood, attributing the differences in their coloration and physiognomies to the vagaries of genes: "You're the image of your Nana Ullmann's [conveniently deceased] sister Greta!" etc., or perhaps the lucky inheritor of said Greta's splendid pecan-or-maybe-nutmeg hair plus Kristina's Uncle Benjamin's mahogany eyes, which every girl in East Lansing used to swoon over back in the 1930s? Professor Ullmann's switching campuses in Trudy's second year — from Indiana to Michigan or Wisconsin, or vice versa — afforded them some insulation against disclosure by indiscreet old friends and neighbors who knew that Kristina had never been pregnant. Every Trudy-birthday thereafter, the parents agreed, they would review their delayed-disclosure policy in the light of their daughter's development, their own feelings, and the experiences of other adoptive parents whom they might come to know while flying their own false colors, and would change or drop that policy if either came to feel it misguided. If not, they would feed the truth to her in gently calibrated increments as she approached and entered adolescence, even offering her instruction in Judaism, a proper bat mitzvah, and reunion with her biological mother, should she so incline.

Meanwhile she was theirs, theirs, theirs; their as-if flesh and blood, and her identity their literal creation.

Such are the follies, here and there, of the highly intelligent and educated, firmly principled, entirely well-meaning, and otherwise sensible—and there's no disputing that the three Ullmanns richly enjoyed Trudy's childhood years.

"*This* Ullmann did, for sure. *Bliss was it in those days to be alive*, et cet. Piano and dance lessons and recitals! Homework-help galore, and class honors ditto! Summer camping trips to Montana, winter ski trips to Colorado, and once all over Europe in a camping trailer!"

Plus team sports and household responsibilities, minor illnesses and accidents, passing spats with best-girlfriends, first crushes on boys—

"*To be young was very heaven*, back there back then."

She loved her parents unreservedly, did our Trudy, and they her; she loved her friends, her schools, her teachers, neighbors, neighborhood, and town. High-percentile bright, though less than highest; accomplished in half a dozen arts, though called unequivocally to none; uncommonly lovely of face and form—

"Though no raving beauty. We get the picture, Geeb."

In every way a delightsome child—until just a month or so before her thirteenth birthday, when in quick succession she experienced her first menstruation, was told by the seventh-grade Bad Boy (following a class discussion of major world religions, in course whereof young Trudy had proudly declared her parents' agnosticism and her own) that she should haul ass to the nearest synagogue with the kikes she so resembled, and by her closest girlfriend (to whom she had triumphantly confided the onset of her menses, thus winning the bet between them which would reach puberty first) that they two were lucky *not* to be Jewish, inasmuch as Jewish mothers slapped their daughters' faces for good luck at first menstruation! Duly reporting all this to her mom, our girl was by her tearfully hugged and kissed, informed that that face-slapping business was a good-luck custom of the superstitious or otherwise tradition-bound in sundry cultures, including the Jewish, and surely most often delivered as a lovingly ceremonious pseudo-slap rather than an actual wallop. That, as Trudy well knew, the word *kike* is as offensive an ethnic slur as *nigger, wop, dago, heeb, spic, sheeny, mick,* and *gringo,* never to be used except perhaps in self-deprecating camaraderie within the respective eths. And— considering that her thirteenth birthday party would soon be a happy memory like its dozen predecessors—that the birthday-girlwoman and her parents were going to have a Quiet Talk About This & That just as soon as Dad got home from lab: half an hour or so hence, she'd guess. In that brief meanwhile, Mom suggested (herself just home from her own university office and looking forward to dinner prep with her daughter, a family cus-tom long enjoyed by both and by Dad as well when he extri-cated himself from classroom and laboratory and rejoined the family, no one of whom could have imagined that that pleasant ritual was now History), Trudy might want to review a certain written statement that her parents had prepared well in ad-vance of the day they knew must sooner or later arrive, in the interests of the full, accurate, and fair accounting that their daughter most certainly deserved of—well, let Mom just fish the thing out of Dad's home-office files, here it is, and let Trudy just thumb through it up in her room while she herself just changes out of office-clothes, and then just as soon as Dad ar-rives and fixes their pre-dinner Sip and Nibble, they'll just go over the whole thing together, answer whatever questions, and just take things from there. And not to worry: The whole com-plicated business couldn't've worked out better for the three of them!

"And some folks thought the world ended on the morning of Nine Eleven O One! Mine went to hell at five-thirty P.M. on a fine April Tuesday eighteen years before that. Get me the fuck out of there!"

The fuck out of there she'll get, our pubescent Ms.-Wysi-wyg-to-be, but not before Narrator wonders, with her, how two by-no-means-insensitive adults, having concealed The Truth from their daughter for so perilously long, could see fit to break it to her at last in a *written statement*, for pity's sake! What must Kristina Ullmann have been thinking as she exchanged pantsuit for dinner-prep jeans and sweatshirt? What must Gus have felt when he whistled in from campus to find his house in an uproar? Okay, so it was a *lovingly* written statement, the joint effort of loving and articulate parents to get things said Just Right for the record, and no doubt originally meant to follow rather than precede a gentle face-to-face, heart-to-heart disclosure; of course Kristina phoned her husband's office to alert him the minute her fearfully baffled daughter took to her room that manila envelope marked FOR OUR TRUDY, WITH OUR LOVE—but found he'd left for home already; and of course she began to question the wisdom of having moved so promptly instead of first discussing with him Trudy's anti-Semitic news from school and reviewing for the thousand-and-first time their longstanding plan of action for When The Day Came But In Any Case No Later Than Her Thirteenth Birthday, so that at least he'd have been there with her when the first hysterics sounded from the other side of the poor girl's door. . . . But whatever happened to their earlier plan of revealing to her *incrementally*, as she *approached* thirteen, her status as beloved adoptee and, discreetly, the circumstances of her birth and adoption? The case has to have been that by a combination of unspoken denial and comfortable procrastination they had painted themselves into an ever-tighter corner (not unlike Narrator's approach to Eleventh Night): They would cross that bridge when they came to it, they must have gotten the habit of telling themselves—and then found themselves over the edge of a chasm both bridgeless and unbridgeable.

"Something like that. They'd tell me later that they never understood it themselves—and him a psychologist, sort of! They'd gotten so used to living in a fiction, they said, they were afraid to face the facts."

A fiction, yes.

"A fucking *lie*, Geeb. But on with it."

Yes. So the girl's in hysterics—in clinical shock, virtually, smashing up her room, cursing and flailing at her Quote Par-

ents (as she'll call them for a long while after), who, scared wit-
less, simply plead guilty as charged and go literally to their
knees to beg a forgiveness that will be years in coming, to the
extent that it comes at all.

"Oh, it came, it came—by maybe halfway through college?
The poor sweet shmucks meant well, and never forgave themselves. But the years till then are best passed over."

Anyhow summarized: Model daughter becomes delin-
quent hellion; everything from drugs and sexual promiscuity
to shoplifting, indulged and excused by penitent Quote Parents. Is saved from utter self-ruin only by high-school junior-
year flirtation with Orthodox Judaism; changes name to Beth
Elman after tracking down (with Gus and Kristina's dedicated
help) her birthmom and discovering that the luckless Dr. Beth
Feldman had succumbed to metastasized uterine cancer not
long after immigration to Israel, where she'd worked as a counselor to other Jewish immigrants on a kibbutz in the Negev's
Beersheba Basin. Her newly pious daughter and Quote Parents
dutifully visit that kibbutz and environs in summer '87 to pay
their respects to Gus's late former advisee's grave, upon the
starkly simple stone marker whereof Trudy/Beth reverently
places a desert pebble, per custom. Back home, does her catch-
up Hebrew homework at the local university's Hillel House,
where she meets and dates but does not bed a Nice Jewish
Freshman. Sustains her Jewhood, as she self-mockingly calls
it (though not her Orthodoxy, which softens, semester by semester, from Conservative through Reform to all-but-Non-
Observing), into her senior year, when also, to the QPs' vast
relief, she repairs her damaged academic standing sufficiently
to be admitted the following fall as a freshman pre-med—not
at Johns Hopkins, to which she aspired, but as geographically
close thereto as she can manage: the University of Maryland's
main campus, down near D.C. Her declared ambition is to become a Hopkins M.D. and carry on her birthmother's work by
practicing either on a kibbutz or with the selfless Médecins
Sans Frontières.

"All an act. *Beth Elman*, for pity's sake!"

Not an act, Narrator protesteth: just desperate-but-honest self-invention. One notes, by the way, that there's been no mention in all this of our young pre-meddie's putative sire. . . .

"Oy: Doctor Shithead. We tracked *him* down, too, and found he'd left teaching, or it him, after marrying one of his last students—a girl half his age, upon whom he managed to spawn a son despite his alleged vasectomy—and had gone into private practice in a Milwaukee suburb as guess what? A counselor of at-risk adolescents! Protagonist much inclined to confrontation and exposure of the bastard to wife and child, but asked herself What Would Doctor Mom Do? and wound up giving the prick a free pass for their innocent sake. So never met Half-Brother. . . ."

Amen. But she can't help wondering, down there in College Park, Maryland, whether she hasn't inherited some of her birthdad's inclination to flying false colors—an unfair self-doubt, in Narrator's opinion, inasmuch as *he* deceived others, whereas *she* was only and earnestly . . . not even deceiving herself, really, but *searching* for herself.

"And misleading herself and others by the way, just as Gus and Kris misled her with their self-deceptions or whatever."

Yes, well, maybe—but she's surely more sinned against than sinning, in that department. Commutes often up the turnpike to Baltimore, does our Miz Beth, to breathe the aggressively competitive atmosphere of pre-meds at Hopkins's Homewood campus. *Throats*, I believe they're called?

"Short for Cutthroats, and not my style."

. . . as she confided to one of their number: a Nice Jewish Boy who took her to a rowhouse party of fellow Throats and turned out to be neither Nice nor Jewish, belying the former by lacing her drinks with whatever was the date-rape pharmaceutical of choice back in the Reagan/Bush late Eighties—

"Mere alcohol in quantity, would be my guess."

—before Throating her indeed, and then some, with what despite her liquored stupefaction she perceived to be a fully foreskinned phallus.

"Oyoyoy. But at least I threw up on the sumbitch."

In retaliation wherefor he roughly took her anal virginity, the vaginal having long since been broadcast to the studs of Bloomington High. This latter violation she inferred only after the fact—upon waking with a three-star hangover on a battered couch in the club basement of a Hopkins Jewish frathouse whereto she'd been gently transported by two bona fide NJB Throats who'd belatedly rescued her from her soused assailant—on evidence of rectal hemorrhaging, which her rescuers (doctors' sons both, carrying on family tradition) had considerately treated with Bacitracin™ and Osco Pantiliners™ borrowed from a sympathetic girlfriend. Who also gave the victim a lift back to College Park, urging en route that criminal charges be brought against the party-crashing date-rapist.

"She being a pre-law at the state U's Baltimore campus."

But our Wys, when recovered at both ends and reasonably sure that the assault had left her neither pregnant, infected, nor hemorrhoidal, found herself less concerned with seeing justice done than with shucking what she now saw to be her desperately improvised identities. She was not Beth Feldman's and Professor Lothario's daughter, except DNAwise; she was Kristina and Gustav Ullmann's, whose grievous but single lapse she presently forgave at least to the extent of removing the quotes from *parents*. She was not "Beth Elman," but Gertrud Ullmann. She didn't really want to be a doctor; maybe she'd go back to painting, for which she'd once been told she had a promising gift. Or if not painting, perhaps art history. Or theater.

"Not theater: No more pretending to be somebody she isn't."

Music, then, maybe; she'd always enjoyed her piano lessons. . . .

"Maybe she'd just have herself a nice nervous collapse."

But she didn't. Dropped out of university, yes, and shifted up to the old Maryland Institute of Art in Baltimore on the basis of a hastily cobbled portfolio from junior-high and early high-school days plus a handful of not-bad drawings she'd done in Israel. Quickly realized, among those young seriosos, that hers was at best an amateur flair, not a pre-professional gift—but okay, as long as she pretended to no more than that either to others or to herself. And she found, quite unexpectedly, that what she truly had a gift for, if that's the right word, was modeling for others.

"And here we go."

Especially in the drawing, painting, and sculpture Life Classes. . . .

"Here we go: *Au naturel* was second nature to her."

Not even nudity, but *nakedness* in the presence of others: an offhanded nakedness, free of exhibitionism. Even fully dressed, mind, she found that her art-school classmates—male and female, gay and straight, even Representational and Non-—were drawn to her as a subject, for reasons not invariably clear to themselves. It was as if her way of holding a pencil or a coffee-cup, or brushing her hair, or stepping out of or into her clothes, not only spoke to them as subject-matter (even if the result was an unrecognizable abstraction), but inspired their rendition. And *un*dressed . . .

"What You See Is et cetera."

The Life Class modeling helped defray her tuition, and when word got around that she grooved on nakedhood there were feelers, so to speak, from lap-dance joints and porn-flick producers, among other entrepreneurs, to all of whom she said

"Fuck off, Charlie."

Or words to that effect—not on account of the nudity and naughtity of those pursuits, but because they involved both exhibitionism and imposture of one sort or another, and even in those Life Drawing classes our Wys never *posed*, in the sense of striking an attitude. She simply sat or stood, being quote *herself*, and even her teachers couldn't resist fetching out their sketch-pads. Speaking of words, by the way—"words to that effect," awhile back?—we should note that not only her graphic- and plastic-arts comrades were drawn to her as subject and inspiration for reasons beyond her and often their understanding, but occasionally musician-friends of theirs from the nearby Peabody Conservatory as well, and even the odd poet or aspiring fictionist from up at the Hopkins Writing Seminars, of whom more presently. By the time she abandoned any artistic ambitions of her own and went to work full-time, modeling nude for the Institute and clothed for sundry women's-wear photoads—

"Nothing phony-sexy or faux-glamorous, mind: just Here It Is, on sale for thirty-nine ninety-five if you're interested."

—her naked face and form had inspired a cello sonata, a quote Meditation for two pianos, a scalp-to-sole sonnet sequence, and—

"Here it comes."

—from her student-architect current lover and first real boyfriend in years, chosen after what one imagines to have been as thorough a vetting as Ms. Ullmann could subject a chap to, and to whom she had confided her only half-humorous growing obsession with Transparency—a sheaf of scale drawings and construction plans for a see-through studio/retreat/love-nest for the pair of them, to be built ASAP on a certain Eastern Shore waterfront property whereof, the fellow declared, he sort of owned a share. Glass walls, floors, and ceilings! Clear Lucite and Plexiglas furniture!

"And maybe call it our Transparium! That really spoke to me, Geeb, when I'd come to fool myself that I could never be fooled again. I mean, the guy didn't *fuck* like a sixty-percent-gay bisexual, and his drag-queen boyfriend, who actually owned the marshfront acreage, didn't know his stud was cheating with me any more than I knew et cetera. He thought the place was to be for *them!* I give up."

She gave up: quit modeling; quit quote *dating;* almost quit trusting people altogether. Found work with the Maryland attorney general's Consumer Protection office, pursuing complaints of false advertising and suchlike scams. Put off potential friends and Significant Others with her insistence on reciprocal up-front Full Disclosure. Took evening courses here and there toward her uncompleted baccalaureate—including one in Introductory Creative Writing, taught by that young poet-admirer aforementioned: he of the scalp-to-sole Shakespearean sonnet sequence. . . .

"Three quatrains and a couplet on the tushie alone."

Two hundred to adore each breast, / But thirty thousand to the rest. No Andrew Marvell, this one, but an apparently principled fellow who encouraged her, after a couple of extracurricular full-disclosure sessions, to try writing a story about her serial hoodwinkings—better yet, a memoir, all the rage in the trade these days. Declared he'd be tempted to an extended poem thereabout, if his vows to the muse didn't prohibit poaching his students' material; he felt much obliged to her already for inspiring those sonnets, and hoped that when the course was done and they were no longer Teacher and Student, he might have the privilege of viewing her undraped person again, inasmuch as even the memory of her navel was enough to inspire a sestina. No need to wait, she replied, and would've peeled off her top then and there, but he demurred on pedagogical principle, and she was so impressed thereat that she actually gave his memoir-suggestion a try.

"Fucking case history was all it was. Tossed it before she even got to her thirteenth birthday. To play the Muse of Inspiration is not *ipso facto* to be inspired."

Toss it she did—but then retrieved it from her Macintosh's Trash icon, copied it to diskette, and urged her instructor to make whatever use of it he would, with her blessing—and of her Undraped Person as well, inasmuch as she was dropping the course forthwith and thereby releasing him from his admirable scruples. Should they start with the aforepraised bellybutton and proceed wherever Inspiration might lead?

Well, maybe, *sure*, her now-former instructor allowed, if she was really thus inclined. . . .

"Which she really was: her one inarguable talent."

And although they were lovers for only one ode and two villanellesworth of nights before he shamefacedly confessed that, contrary to his earlier declaration, while he truly never cribbed from his students, he did in fact shag attractive and willing female ones from time to time—but only if the course was Pass/Fail instead of letter-graded, mind, and the shaggee completed all her writing assignments on schedule. He ought to've told her that up front, he supposed. . . .

"As did she, once again deceived and disappointed despite its having been she, in their case, who took the sexual initiative. Anyhow, no more horizontal tutorials thereafter."

But the good chap conscientiously reviewed that shall-we-say uninspired memoir-draft—

"That's putting it tactfully: just a synopsis, really, of her Misadventures Thus Far."

—and gave it as his professional opinion that the material was more suited to prose fiction than to narrative verse, neither of which was his long suit, he being strictly a lyricist; also that its prolixity deserved, if not a memoir, then a full-fledged novel, or at least some sort of story-series. Since she herself had abandoned the thing, and it was alas not for him, with her permission he would pass it along to an acquaintance and sometime colleague of his: a bona fide publishing fictioneer whose project-in-the-works, deponent happened to know—a framed story-collection called *The Book of Ten Nights and a Night*—had been sidetracked by the Nine Eleven terrorist attacks on New York and Washington at least until the author's imagination could come to some sort of terms with that enormous event. Given her consent, he would relay to that fellow her Story Thus Far, or at least the story of that story, together with her *carte blanche* to make what use of it he might, if only as a diversion until his stalled opus got back on track. Permission granted?

"She'd think about it, she said."

And briefly did, and presently with a shrug said, Sure—on one condition. No Horizontal Interviews, her poet-friend supposed, and assured her she needn't worry, as the chap was happily married, disinclined to infidelity, and elderly to boot:

Together or separately, those three constraints ought to keep things vertical.

"To which Let's-Call-Her-Trudy responded, *Tant pis:* Verticality wasn't the condition she had in mind."

Forget about manuscript review and approval, her advisor advised: No self-respecting fictionist would likely allow that. Due credit given on acknowledgments page? Some share of no-doubt-modest royalties?

"*None of the above,* she declared," she declared. Her condition was simply that her poet-pal tell his novelist-pal that he'd *invented the whole story himself:* just an odd incidental inspiration about a woman so often and consequentially deceived by appearances that et cetera. He'd thought there might be a poignant lyric somewhere in there: *Can no one tell me what she sings?,* or some such. So far, however, no one had, and so if Pal Novelist had any use for it, there it was. As for Ms. Anonymous: She and her hang-ups seem to have inspired a clutch of apprentice painters and sculptors, a couple of wannabe composers, one gifted though unprincipled architect, and a well-meaning if less than utterly up-front poet. If they happen to inspire a storyteller too, so be it: Maybe she'd check the Help Wanteds for Muses. . . .

So, then: Did he do it?

The poet-chap, we mean? Pass her story along to his alleged novelist-acquaintance, we mean? Or was that fictionist in fact the poet's fiction, a rather elaborate diplomatic device for disengaging himself from his comely but kinky sometime inspirer? Whatever the case, Abracadabra and Allakazam! Next thing we know of her is that she finds herself here on the tale-spinning page, installed in a weirdo see-through pad not unlike the one suggested by that earlier, not-quite-straight inspiree of hers and being there visited eveningly, in the role of Saltyfresh Serviceable Surrogate Muse, by the Graybard embodiment of some scrivener's Narrative Imagination. Sipping wine himwith by mid-September sunset; peeling out of her peekaboos or whatever to dunk in the murky-but-noctilucent tidewater prior to Metaphorical Intimate Congress; prompting and sometimes critiquing his recycled tales. . . .

"And, as she understands it, no harm done to anyone."

Not only no harm!, Graybard here vigorously protests. Granted that nothing we've done since Nine Eleven has any relevance whatsoever to that disaster and whatever may follow it—

"Only the relevance of Irrelevance, as I believe we established. . . ."

Establish it we did, thanks, and lo and behold: Ten nights and a nightsworth of tales now framed and told! Our Hendecameron done!

"He wishes." She picks herself up, fetches from her deck their empty champagne-flutes, tips into them the last of the Mumm's (just a splash apiece, no doubt at world temperature by now), and returns to sit cross-legged before him on the waterbed. Having handed him his, however, she does not yet raise hers either in salute or to sip.

Problem?

But of course he knows what the problem is, and knows that she knows that he knows: Tale Eleven—*Wysiwyg?*—remains incomplete. So Ms. Let's-Call-Her-Trudy, serially misled by appearances, comes to devote herself quixotically to narrowing, in her fashion, the onerous gap between What One Sees (in others and so, by extension, in herself) and What One Gets—in the course whereof she is interloped upon by Present Company, assists in a musely way his Dispatcher's narrative project, and here they are. So now what? Where's the dénouement? How does Wys's story end, and theirs?

"That's Problem One," his grave colleague affirms, and considers her wine-flute. "Problem Two is that the more he gives her a quote *real* identity and case history, like this Gertrud Ullmann story-in-progress, the less she can really be Wysiwyg the Accommodating Muse. Your Trudy is just another Four-Tees fuck-up: one more more-or-less-pitiful real-life loser. You forgot, by the way, to give her the grandma from Minsk that somebody mentioned back in our Invocation."

So I did. Four Tees?

Gesturing toward the relevant areas with her glass, "Two Tits, a Tush, and a Twat. Screw her."

Yes, well: *Been there, done that,* a chap could say, but doesn't. Says instead, As to Problem One, dear Wys, you're jumping the gun: We're *in* the story's ending, right here right now, sentence by sentence; its dénouement is whatever you and I do from this page forward. As for Problem Two: Forget about Gertrud Ullmann, cobbled up by Yours Truly (minus the grandma; sorry about that) for the purpose of getting Wysiwyg to where she and Graybard are now. Here. Together. About to wind up this story, this Hendecameron, and the last of this wine.

"Maybe."

Poor Blinkered Four-Tees Trudy, in this taleteller's estimation, comes to be the *inverse* of Wysiwyg: What she gets, after a certain point, is pretty much what she's come to *see,* including the way she's come to see herself.

"With a little tutoring in the School of Hard Knocks."

Granted. But we here declare her to be a Fictional Character: one possibility among many. My Wysiwyg is no Trudy Ullmann; she's you. *You're* you.

"Me, dot dot dot."

You. The woman who discoursed so relevantly on the relevance of Irrelevance, with glosses both pertinent and eloquent on Homer, Scheherazade, and Boccaccio. The woman whose No-Nos and Yes-Yeses navigated this Hendecameron from *Help!* through *Click* to Here and Now. Whose nightly potions re-leaded her Graybard's narrative pencil. *That's* you, Wys: Here's looking at you!

"Not yet. I mean, *look* all you want to, of course. But no toasts just yet."

And why not? he asks, he asks—taking private hope from that Not *Just* Yet.

"Because . . ." Fiddling with flute: "Because. *Your* Wys, you say. And *her* Graybard. . . ."

And *our* dénouement. Since the ontological order of things

precludes your going back with me to my guy's Scriptorium and its circumambient Real Life, I'm staying here with you, Wys, in this Imaginarium of ours, till this book's last period and beyond. Here's to Us.

Considers. Shakes head. "Not yet."

I, uh, *love* you? As they say?

"Yeah, right. They do say that."

GRAYBARD LOVES WYSIWYG, Reader: TRUE LOVE.

"Mm-hm. And suppose you *were* to stay here—"

Yes! But only with your Yes, of course.

"—if *we* stayed here—a notion that she acknowledges to be not without its appeal—where does that leave Whatsisname?"

The bloke who sent me? No problem: It leaves him cuddling with *his* one and only, back in Literalville. Here's to 'em.

"Not just yet. What I mean is, without you, what does he do for an encore after this all-but-done Hendecameron?"

That's *his* problem, mate. We half suspect he's just something you and I dreamed up anyhow. Like Trudy Ullmann?

"And me."

And me—to the end of encountering you. To us?

This time she actually half raises her glass, and her extraordinary eyes as well—though only to said glass, not yet to him. As if turning his words into a counter-toast, "*To the end*," she says in italics—and now at last, grave still but smiling, she lifts those eyes to him. "Are you sure you know what you're getting into here, Geeb?"

Of course I'm not sure, any more than you are. But I know what I've seen and what I see. Enough said?

" . . ."

Correction, Love: * * *, yes?

"Yesyesyes: * * * * * * * * * *!"

Et cetera, *ad in*—

"*Finis.*"

AFTERWORDS

9:11 9:21,
that odd clock-calendar flashes: *9:11 9:21,* until one or the other of our imagined couple uncouples to pull its plug. Whereupon, by some odd circuitry, not only that digital distraction goes dark, but the whole Imaginarium: no moon or stars, even, to be seen through tonight's cloud cover; no will-o'-the-wisps flickering in the marsh round about; not even (when at some point they rinse their love-sweat in the warm tidewater) those phosphorescing algae that on nights past had made their bodies sparkle. Whatever from here on out these lovers may Get, neither they nor we can See, except with the mind's eye.

Embracing the darkness and each other, "Right and proper," they agree: Transparency hath its merits—especially in the Forthrightness way, Q.E.D.—but readerly voyeurism is another story.

"Another what?" one half teases.

Responds the other, We'll just see. Meanwhile, a recess from Time and Narrative alike, in the full understanding that although stories end (or, sometimes, merely cease), the Big T famously does not. Its passage, however, may perhaps be ignored—at least for a time?

"So to speak."

And *in* time, so to speak, one or the other of them will remark this night's recentest conjunction to have been their twelfth. Further, that while by their reckoning it's still Eleventh Night, enough They-Know-What has surely passed to put the hour past midnight (*her* time, which is their time now—not that they're attending its passage, mind): by their agreed-upon calendar, the early hours of "Saturday," "September 22," "2001."

Autumnal Equinox, yes? Unless that was yesterday.

"Yesterday, today, tomorrow—in any case, even shorter days ahead from here on out."

The shorter our days, Love, the longer our nights. On to the Twelfth?

"When and if it comes." For we do not imagine the orchestrators of 9/11 to be resting on their bloody laurels. "Meanwhile, if it must be On with anything, let's on with Eleventh Night, and Our Story."

In which,
limbs twined still in metaphoric post-Congressional lassitude, the pair speak quietly of that *other* Twelfth Night—Twelfth Day Eve, to be precise, in the Christian calendar: the merry-making night before the Feast of Epiphany, dozenth day after Christmas, when tradition has it that the infant Jesus was shown forth to the Magi for certification of His Messiahhood.

"Four days after the kid's *bris*, presumably."

Which ritual circumcision gets passing mention in Luke Two Twenty-one, as we recall, though not the identity of the *mohel* who on His eighth day did Him snip. In any case (back to Twelfth Night), a time of whoopee-making borrowed from the Roman Saturnalia; occasion of Will Shakespeare's play on opposite-sex twins and cross-dressing doubles, wherein Viola's disguising herself as a man will have been vertiginously compounded by the Elizabethan custom of assigning female roles to male actors: a man playing the part of a woman disguising herself as a man.

"And beloved by another quote *woman*, Olivia, who marries Viola's look-alike brother thinking he's quote *she*, whom she takes for a him . . ."

All which reminds one that in Shakespeare, as in most art and no small measure of life, what you see, at first glance at least, is *not* what you get. But this present Twelfth Night eve, we were saying: Sept Twenty-two O One, the Neverlasting Now. . . .

"Hardly a time for antic revelry, while smoke still rises from the innocent dead at Ground Zero. Irrelevant stories, yes. Partying, no."

Anyhow, the buck-naked can't cross-dress like Will's Olivia/ Viola/Voilà: What they *feel* is what they get.

"You Graybard male, on the tactile evidence; me Wysiwyg feem. There's revelry enough."

But we *have* had an epiphany or two, you and I, have we not? For which thankee, Wys.

"We have. For which thank*ee*, Geeb. Yom Kippur, our Day of Repentance, is just a few nights down the road, and whatever I have to repent, it isn't Us."

Amen to that. Tomorrow, next week, next month, who knows what? Nerve gas in the subways, smallpox in the reservoirs—

"Anthrax in the mail. Bull market gelded. . . ."

All painfully possible. One of us recalls wondering four decades ago, in the wake of JFK's assassination, whether one would ever laugh again, and being told—

"*Oh yes, we'll laugh again—but we'll never be young again.* Something like that?"

Mirabile dictu, her very words. Nor middle-aged again, for that matter, this time around. Nor innocently secure-feeling again, one supposes, to the extent that we-all seem to have been, more or less, till Nine Eleven.

"So . . ."

So our question is, Will there be a story henceforward to go on with?

Some moments' pause. Then:
"A story . . ."

And presently: "We'll just see, Love. In the dark. Together." We'll see.